PRAISE FOR REPUBLIC OF EQUALITY

"The characters are real ... descriptive prose and scenes are focused and vividly written; the political and historical points are compelling and manifold ... will resonate powerfully in the minds of contemporary readers." ROMUALD DZEMO, READERS' FAVORITE

"You'll want to keep reading this book from chapter to chapter all the way through, and you'll enjoy the thought-provoking writing and humor along the way." CHRIS HOWSE, TURNING POINT USA

"What is even more remarkable about this social commentary is how completely satisfyingly it explores a blooming romantic relationship ... brims with a non-intimidating intelligence ... quite an interesting storyteller." VINCENT DUBLADO, READERS' FAVORITE

"Hejna's novel is adept at tackling touchy subjects like race relations head-on...An often blunt satirical tale that's genuinely edgy." KIRKUS REVIEWS

"Readers will find themselves completely immersed in the book because of great story-building and characterization ... details are given in just the right amount at the right timing ... a good thoughtful read." RISAH SALAZAR, READERS' FAVORITE

Republic of Equality - 2033

A Romantic Comedy and Political Thriller

Previously published: as "Republic of Equality – 2033: A Romantic Dystopian Satire," and under the author's prior pen name, Sam Adams.

Author: David Hejna is a retired lawyer. During his last ten years of legal practice, David served as the General Counsel, Vice President and Corporate Secretary for a high growth technology company. His 30+ year legal career included positions with a prominent law firm and a large corporate law department. He has a law degree from the University of Michigan Law School and bachelor's degree in philosophy from the University of Michigan.

Copyright © 2021 David Hejna, as the original trustee and beneficiary of, and as the successor-in-interest to, Equal Opportunity Trust-1000. All rights reserved. In accordance with the U.S Copyright Act and the Paris Treaty, no part of this book may be reproduced in any form or by any electronic or mechanical means, including information scanning, uploading, electronic sharing, storage, retrieval and distribution systems, whether on the internet of any other form of electronic or hard media, without permission in writing from the publisher, except by reviewers, who may quote brief passages in a review. Violations constitute unlawful piracy and theft of intellectual property and are subject to serious copyright legal claims and penalties.

For permission to reprint material from this book, please email FreeThinker1000@outlook.com

ISBN: 9798714461699 (replacing prior edition 9798569064038)
Imprint: Shady Lane Books, an imprint of Free Thinker Publishing LLC
Printed: in the United States of America
Last Update: August 6, 2021

Disclaimer: This book contains opinions and humor, including political and cultural satire. This book is a work of fiction set in the future. Names, organizations, characters, places, locales, incidents, events, political and legal documents and treaties, discussions of and references to history and science, the environment, global warming, and climate change, in this book are the product of the author's imagination or are used fictitiously or for satirical humor. Any similarity or resemblance to actual places, locales, incidents, events, political and legal documents and treaties, understandings of history or science, the environment, global warming, and climate change, or to actual persons existing or dead, or organizations existing or defunct, is coincidental and not intended by the author or publisher. The author and publisher are not responsible for any websites, books or other materials mentioned in this book, including any content, sites or materials referenced or linked therein.

Dedication and Acknowledgment

To my wife, Barbara, with many thanks for your help and extraordinary patience

"Power tends to corrupt and absolute power tends to corrupt absolutely."

Lord Acton

Republic of Equality - 2033

A Romantic Comedy and Political Thriller

By David Hejna

Chapter One

Life looked good in 2033. Tom was twenty-two and a member of the Equality Party. He was near the end of final exams in his senior year of college, having excelled in Equality Studies. He had a job lined up in the Chicago office of the Bureau of Truth. Tom figured he'd take the train downtown while continuing to live in the rent-controlled high rise near the Evanston campus where he'd been for the last few years. He felt at home in Evanston, a progressive college town with an eclectic urban feel. Just across the northern boundary of Chicago along Lake Michigan, Evanston felt more like an extension of the city than a suburb.

Tom was more than just a member of the Party. He was a rising star. It seemed so easy. You just volunteered for everything. Tom had spending money through a scholarship stipend and high social credit score. He had spent his middle and high school years in the Party's prestigious Boarding School System. He had been in the Cadet Corps during those years and the Youth Brigades while in college. Tom had medals, ribbons and badges for social media posts, recruiting activities, litter patrol, wetlands restoration, karate, marksmanship, composing patriotic socialist songs and leading patriotic socialist marches.

In the Party's Boarding School System, Tom had learned about the Party's early achievements. Free national health care and day care. Free public colleges and universities. Free smart phones and laptops. The Big Blue Deal and Paris Strange Accord. The Republic paid for some costs by cutting the defense budget by seventy-five percent and the country felt safer than before. The Republic had also received worldwide acclaim, from friends and foes alike, when our leaders announced that we'd support and fund all programs of the United

Nations and every existing and new form of global treaty, but we'd no longer try to run the show or bother about the details. There was an out-pouring of national pride and worldwide acclaim, from friends and foes alike, when the leaders changed the country's name, which had taken on some negative associations, to the new "Republic of Equality." There were some mixed reactions when they changed the flag to a blue fist on a red background.

Tom was now sitting in his usual place in the front row of Modern European History for the final exam, his last college exam ever. He figured he'd ace it. The class had no particular relation to Equality Studies, but Tom had developed an interest in the subject. He finished early but waited until the end of the allotted time and kept checking his work. He didn't want to be over-confident and blow his perfect A grade point average.

Tom was euphoric when the exam session ended. He wandered toward the long line for free coffee at one of the ubiquitous Equality Cafés near campus. The drizzle had stopped and he felt okay with the chilly air in his light windbreaker.

While standing in line, Tom was thinking about what he'd do during the break before starting his new job. He eventually looked around and noticed the girl behind him.

"Did you know these coffee shops were privately owned by capitalists a generation ago and they charged really high prices?" Tom asked casually with a friendly smile, though he cringed inside at the dumb opening line.

"Yeah, we learned that in first grade when we began drinking coffee," she said, while smiling just slightly at his awkward attempt to make small talk.

"So, do you come here often?" Tom asked, feeling embarrassed again about his banter skills.

"Not really. These lines are crazy," she said.

"Where do you like to go for coffee then?" Tom asked.

"I often just make it myself. It's not hard. You should try it," she said.

"There's no other coffee place you like around here?" Tom asked.

"When I hear about a good coffee place, it ends up closing. Maybe I'm bad luck."

"I know a place that's still open and has great coffee. Mojo's. They have some connection to New Zealand," Tom said.

"New Zealanders have good taste in coffee. I used to go out with a guy in London who spent time in New Zealand. He drank coffee all day long and couldn't sleep."

"Is that why you left him? He drank too much coffee?" Tom was smiling and flirting.

"One of the reasons," she said with a smile. "But how did you know I left him instead of him leaving me?" She was flirting back.

"I just met you, so I can't say for sure, but I doubt if anyone would leave you." Tom wasn't sure how she'd react but hoped for the best.

She was smiling calmly and making eye contact but didn't say anything. She was attracted, amused, and wanted to see what he'd come up with next.

"Okay, sorry, that probably seemed like a pick-up line. But, uh, I like your smile."

Tom had been rejected by pretty girls who viewed situations like this as a pick-up, so he had tried to develop a sense for when a girl was interested. The girl standing next to him seemed interested, but it didn't make sense for her not to be attached. Maybe she had high standards.

Maybe she was spoiled or hard to get along with. Tom wanted to find out.

"Did you notice the coffee here is getting even weaker?" she whispered.

"Maybe," Tom said quietly.

"The workers are gradually making it weaker," she said, this time close to Tom's ear. Her warm breath felt good.

"Why would they do that and how would you know?" Tom whispered close to her ear as he picked up the scent of her shampoo. This whispering was fun, he thought.

"The workers are mad that management took away the tip jars. You know, for equality, since office workers don't have tip jars. It's another new rule. I heard someone say this in the back of class."

"How does making weaker coffee get back at management?"

"It doesn't. They couldn't figure out how to get back at management. So they decided that weaker coffee would make their own jobs easier. They won't have to open and grind as many bags, and they'll have fewer customers to handle because fewer people will want the weaker coffee. They think that's fair since they don't get tips anymore," she replied.

They reached the free coffee take-out window and asked for coffee without anything special added and stood together quietly for a moment.

"Would you, uh, like to meet at Mojo's for some really good coffee sometime?" Tom asked.

"Sure."

"By the way, my name is Tom."

"I'm Izzy."

They smiled and shook hands and made plans to meet the next morning. They headed off in different directions holding their cups of free coffee.

Tom thought about Izzy as he walked over to the lake. She reminded him of an actress named Hedy Lamarr in a 1941 movie called "Come Live with Me," a romantic comedy with Jimmy Stewart. Tom had been taken with Hedy and learned that she worked on scientific inventions as a hobby. It wasn't that Izzy looked exactly like Hedy Lamarr. The resemblance to Hedy involved something else about Izzy's personality, her calm poise and quiet playfulness.

A chilly wind whipped in gusts around Tom. He wondered if he was projecting onto Izzy some qualities that didn't exist. He'd done that before. He doubted that Izzy worked on scientific inventions as a hobby like Hedy Lamarr. He doubted that Hedy Lamarr was the same in real life as her characters in movies. He took the last sip which was now bitter with coffee grounds that had slipped through the cheap filters. He thought about how the Equality Cafés were going downhill as he tossed the cup in a trash barrel and headed toward his apartment building.

When Tom got back to his place, he turned on his laptop to spend time on an anonymized search of the internet, including dark web sites, for any new clues to the location and condition of his parents. He knew they were in the last major round up of unrepentant capitalist deplorables who were taken to the Alaskan Reserve nine years ago. When Tom took a break for lunch, he turned on the Equality News channel. The newscaster was repeating a story about someone who got the most social credits last week. Tom knew the report would segue into the person who got the most demerits. He turned off the news and continued his internet search.

After listening to some music and going to bed early, Tom lay awake thinking back to his early years. He was ten years old when the Soft Coup began. The term "Soft Coup" was adopted to celebrate the political activities and events that fundamentally transformed the country into a totalitarian socialist one-party system emphasizing collective welfare and equal outcomes across race groups (also called equity) rather than equal opportunities for individuals.

The Party set up the Boarding School System to select and train the smartest kids for future leadership roles and give their parents a break from child-rearing duties that trained professionals could handle better. Tom had felt honored to be selected and picked up with other kids and transported in a yellow school bus to a middle school facility about 200 miles away in Ann Arbor. Tom and the other kids were too young to question why they had to go so far, and they also sort of liked the idea. Their parents had mixed reactions to the departures, hugging and crying and saying they'd miss them, while also saying the kids would benefit in the long run with better credentials and career opportunities under the socialist regime.

The political instructors in the Boarding School System had taught the kids about the left wing movement's beginnings long ago - many decades before the Soft Coup - among forward-thinking grad students and faculty members. Tom's instructors had taught how each college graduating class, year after year, had then brought the movement's ideas and values to other universities as grad students, or to educational publishers, non-profits and think tanks, teachers' unions and government workers' unions, kindergartens and grammar schools, every manner of old and new media, government leaders and staffers for the old liberal party, and eventually all levels of the business world during decades of growth and progress.

By sixth grade, Tom and his friends had become pretty militant and were disappointed to learn that the Soft Coup was "soft" because there were elections, rather than an armed take over, leading to the transformative events. From the perspective of thirteen year old militants, an armed takeover would have been way cooler. But the election itself was a heroic coup, nonetheless. The movement had worked tirelessly in the year leading up to the Soft Coup to influence voters through all manner of strategies, technologies, and a massive network of inspired supporters embedded nearly everywhere. The old conservative party had been an easy target because the leader was not a well-oiled politician. He had the brash manner of a tough business leader and made off-the-cuff tweets and unrehearsed speeches that were perfect for highly curated soundbites and edited snippets, without context, to create a phony narrative and turn off a lot of people. Eventually most people who watched the mainstream media believed that the old conservative party, its leaders and supporters, and the few cable news channels they watched, were racists, fascists, selfish capitalists, climate-change deniers, and other deplorables.

As a natural result, in the final year leading up to the last two-party elections and the beginning of the Soft Coup, the old liberal party raised enormous contributions from well-meaning movie and sports stars, celebrities and influencers, university leaders and business leaders, millionaires and billionaires. The old conservative party only managed to recruit a few supporters to put up yard signs, and the movement activists quickly took them down. Few conservatives wore campaign caps in public for fear of being beat up.

If it weren't for the secret ballot system, the old conservative party probably would have received far fewer votes. It didn't really matter, though, because the movement's strategists and operatives were prepared to win by all means necessary. There were claims of election irregularities and fraud, but thankfully the news media, social media tech controllers and aligned thinkers in the judicial system felt it would be a waste of time to hear witnesses or review any evidence, and many people naturally concluded there was no evidence at all.

An important nail in the coffin of the old conservative party came after a rally of hundreds of thousands of die-hards in DC to express their beliefs about election irregularities and fraud in a few battleground state elections. The brash conservative President spoke at the rally and encouraged them to march to the Capital Building where Congress would be reviewing and counting the Electoral College votes and engaging in permitted challenges and debates. A few hundred people invaded the Capital Building in a chaotic riotous protest after the marchers heard that the Vice President would deny a five day postponement requested by four battleground state legislatures so they could finish reviewing claims of election irregularities.

For Tom and other young students learning about the Soft Coup several years later, the riot in the Capital Building seemed pathetically weak. Few, if any, of the protestors even had guns. Thousands just stood around outside on the Capital steps holding placards like a peaceful protest. They obviously lacked any plan for an actual take-over of the government. They didn't organize sympathizers in the military to join like you'd expect in a real coup. There didn't even seem to be any real leaders. In any event, the end result was beautiful for the left. The riotous trespassing protestors were widely condemned by all sides, and the efforts to review and debate the Electoral College certification that night collapsed. And the movement seized the opportunity to create a compelling narrative about a right-wing fascist domestic terrorism plan to destroy democracy through a full-blown insurrection and government coup take-over.

The "Righteous Purge" stage of the Soft Coup then began as a long relentless grinding campaign of strategic and opportunistic suppression of conservatives in positions of power or influence or anyone else who could be a threat to a socialist take-over. Of course, there was no need to purge the universities or school systems nor the mainstream media nor most celebrities. And most big companies and many government institutions were already committed to left-wing views. So the initial purge focused on the military, where special task forces ran software analytics programs on social media sites and conducted innumerable interviews and in-depth investigations, all designed to root out every member of the military who might be a white nationalist or overly patriotic. Anyone who had ever been a member of the old conservative party was automatically suspect.

As the military purge progressed, influential conservative leaders and politicians were gradually singled out and attacked and smeared with phony accusations supported by phony dossiers and fake evidence and coerced false testimony by loose acquaintances who were themselves in trouble. The charges could involve anything but often focused on collusion with groups that had been added to the massive list of suspected domestic terrorist organizations. As the targeted conservatives spent their time and resources trying to defend themselves, they were systematically shamed and ostracized as "enemies of the people," doxed and harassed, and kicked off social media. They lost their jobs, were blacklisted and became unemployable, and lost their college and advanced degrees through mass degree rescission actions.

Their families and known friends were automatically suspect and often presumed guilty, unless they could prove their innocence, though that was a pickle because no one knew any details of the claims beyond being called a racist, fascist, domestic terrorist, or a supporter of the brash leader of the old conservative party. It became a form of McCarthyism on digital steroids but from the left instead of the right, even audaciously targeting lawyers and anyone else who spoke up to defend anyone else. But it was totally justified because the goal was so beneficial in ferreting out and destroying all the hateful racist fascist conservatives who were around every corner, in every nook and cranny, even under your bed at night.

The Righteous Purge was only one step toward the real goal of creating a one-party system and socialist state. It was a critically important step, nonetheless, because true one-party totalitarian socialism had never been chosen voluntarily in a constitutional process after free speech, open public debates, and free and fair elections. Accordingly, the Righteous Purge eventually expanded to target even moderate liberals who still held old-fashioned views about freedom. They had naively believed the goal was a moderate welfare-oriented system with plenty of free enterprise, free speech, and free voting with multiple parties, as in Scandinavia where its system worked well enough given its size and demographics.

But the current Scandinavian system wasn't anything close to true socialism. Some moderate liberals were doxed and ended up in hospitals after brutal beatings by far left militia groups. Some fled the country or joined the underground. Bodies of moderate liberals kept showing up for several months as an on-going warning to anyone who might resist the goal of a true socialist totalitarian state and one-party system.

Meantime, with the old liberal party in control of the executive and legislative branches of government, the movement weakened the filibuster and reconciliation rules and pushed through new voting laws prohibiting voter identification or signature requirements; requiring all voting machines and software to be procured and administered exclusively by a special Commission appointed by the President; requiring universal mail-in ballots, ballot drop boxes, and collection processes established by the new Commission; and prohibiting election monitoring and ballot chains of custody.

With those voting law changes in place, most people expected the old liberal party would retain control of the federal government forever and would also gain control of at least two thirds of the states. That would give the old liberal party the ability to pass and ratify Constitutional amendments, and the party was quick to announce its intention to do so. Among other things, the initial proposed Constitutional amendment would restrict the right to bear arms in order to protect people from gun violence; restrict freedom of speech and assembly in order to protect against Hate Speech, Disinformation and Domestic Terrorism; and remove whites from guaranties against racial discrimination since that could never have been the original intent.

The conservative chat rooms went crazy again all across the dark web. But this time there was serious chatter about organizing a massive peaceful protest. The FBI monitored all chat activity and put together a new report sometimes called the Steal Dossier which concluded that there was a plan for a heavily armed rally and march of 10,000,000 conservatives in DC and large groups in many state capitals. The report also concluded that there was on-going involvement by the old conservative party leaders and the other defendants who had been indicted for the capital riot. The actual evidence could not be revealed because that would expose sources and methods as well as improper wire-taps.

Yet with the Steal Dossier in hand and the support of the DOJ, the President issued an executive order banning the proposed rally as a planned insurrection, invoking martial law, suspending the Bill of Rights, classifying the old conservative party as a domestic terror organization, and prohibiting any of the former members of that party from forming any new political organization. The executive order also provided that past membership in the old conservative party was probable cause for a wire-tap warrant and sedition investigation.

Faced with the prospect of mass arrests and trials supported by the full might of the armed forces under martial law and a suspended Bill of Rights, conservatives across the country generally recognized they didn't stand a chance. A few die-hards in remote areas tried to resist and were crushed. Many signed loyalty oaths to get off with probation and re-education. Some fled to other countries and some joined the underground.

In due course, when the time seemed right, the President surprised nearly everyone by calling for new special elections for all elected federal, state and local officials. He explained that, in fairness, the country needed new elections now that the old conservative party was banned and all of the conservative and moderate liberal politicians had vacated their offices in the Righteous Purge.

Even more surprisingly, the President and Vice President announced that they would both resign and not stand for reelection. In explaining their decisions to step down, they said they were exhausted from working on so many executive orders. Speculation about other reasons for the abdications, arising from a private meeting with influential Chinese officials, was dismissed and suppressed as disinformation.

The very next day, the leaders of the old liberal party rebranded it as the Equality Party with great fanfare and announced its dedication to true socialism, social justice and equity, an end to institutional racism, environmental and climate justice, equality of outcomes across the races, and a related long platform of worthy left wing idealistic utopian policies and causes. On a more practical level, the Equality Party's Central Committee immediately emerged as the only real power in the country because they could decide who could be in the Party and who could be kicked out.

Every existing and aspiring politician was therefore under the thumb of the Central Committee and had to sign a loyalty oath, under penalty of perjury, unconditionally supporting the Central Committee and the Party's goals. To ensure collective social justice and equity in the upcoming special elections, the Central Committee decreed that all candidates would be members of the Equality Party hand-picked by the Central Committee. The Equality Party naturally won a clean sweep in the elections. The people who were elected, or reelected, as the case may be, knew they would be figureheads and administrators and could be removed and replaced easily under the new system of Central Committee control.

The super-rich naively believed they could continue to survive and prosper by merely increasing their already huge support for the left wing movement and re-directing their massive contributions to the renamed Equality Party. The tech companies were especially naïve in believing their actions in kicking conservatives off their platforms would curry favor forever. The Equality Party fundamentally hated capitalism and the huge disparity in wealth between the super-rich and the rest of the people, or at least the new political elite. Moreover, the Equality Party knew it held complete power over the super-rich and their companies through the ability to impose confiscatory taxes, repressive legislative and regulatory mandates, and potential government acquisition and nationalization for the collective good.

And the Party didn't hesitate to demonstrate its power in the business world by acquiring and merging the last remaining conservative news companies, rebranding the new entity as Equality News LLC, and replacing all the personnel with young Party members. The Party paid an extraordinarily low acquisition price after threatening the majority owners and board members with criminal charges in a military tribunal for violating the new Crimes Against Disinformation. The Party's longer-term corporate take-over targets included grocery store chains, housing developers and apartment companies, automobile and energy companies.

By the time Tom and his school friends had completed their core seventh grade course, Advanced History of the Soft Coup, they appreciated the full beneficial impact of the massive victory over racist-capitalist oppression and the outdated concepts about free speech and free voting in an age of pervasive right wing disinformation and sedition. They loved how quickly the Equality Party had grabbed even more control by abolishing the Electoral College, and by expanding the Supreme Court with young activists who didn't think the Constitution or Bill of Rights should stand in the way of collective progress. Tom and his friends knew those changes didn't matter much since martial law was still in effect and the Bill of Rights was therefore still suspended, but they loved the symbolism and sense that the Soft Coup and total Party control would withstand the test of time even after martial law might eventually be lifted.

Tom and his friends also loved learning that the Equality Party honored a legacy movement goal by defunding and dismantling all state and local police forces. The Party concurrently created a new federal police force which then occupied the original state and local police facilities. Most personnel were the same, but the leaders were replaced by Party members, and there was centralized command and control from DC. The new federal police force was quickly expanded to become even larger than the original state and local forces combined.

To bolster social justice by suppressing subversion, Director Stalinsky created a separate Political Police force a few months later. The Political Police worked partly through Cyber Command's computer programs to monitor and control social media posts, and partly through a huge network of volunteer Block Minders who earned rewards by informing on neighborhood subversives. The Political Police and Block Minders also enforced the Hate Speech Laws, the

Crimes of Disinformation, and the Crimes of Domestic Terrorism. These crimes were defined so broadly they could cover anything you said or did that the Party didn't like. The differences were in the penalties, which gave the prosecutors greater flexibility.

But Alex Stalinsky's original monumental goal for the Political Police turned out to be overly ambitious in seeking to suppress both subversive speech or actions and private cynicism. It became evident over time that private cynicism could never be suppressed, and that allowing private cynicism actually had a benefit of releasing frustrations as long as it didn't cross the line into subversion.

By 2033 a few leaders still used the full term "Equality Party" in speeches, but most people just called it the Party as no other political parties were ever allowed. An opposition party would serve no purpose and slow down progress with a lot of bickering over egos and nonsense. The Party and its small elite group of ideologues and intelligentsia could figure things out. People often referred to the Party and the Republic interchangeably now. The word "Republic" wasn't accurate, but the Party liked the way it sounded. For historians it was reminiscent of the old "Union of Soviet Socialist Republics (USSR)."

Another gradual change was the switch from "white" to "European American" and then to "Euro" for short. The term "white" had taken on so many negative associations that it had become a racial slur. Meantime, the term "African American" had mostly shifted back to "Black," and "Hispanic American" or "Latino" had mostly shifted to "Brown." "Native American" was shortened to "Native," and "Asian American" was shortened to "Asian."

Correct use of the term "Mixed" was determined by rules involving the race classes of the parents and grandparents. The Party had to draw the line somewhere. You couldn't be classified as Mixed by going all the way back to a great grandparent in an oppressed race class. There were proposals to compute your race class based on a percentage of DNA from the oppressed groups, but no one had been able to get a consensus on what the percentage should be.

Though few knew the extent, a surprising number of people formed a subversive underground organization which still stubbornly idealized the country's suspended founding documents - those hateful ancient relics which failed to recognize the benevolence of totalitarian socialist control with the best self-appointed masterminds making decisions for the silly ignorant masses. Even without a quota system, the underground was well diversified among races, classes and backgrounds, and included former moderate liberals along with many libertarians and conservatives. The Party hated the underground's subversive goals and hated the underground's ability to achieve diversity without quota mandates even more.

The underground became a prime target of the Political Police and Block Minders.

Chapter Two

Tom was an early riser so he got up around 7:00 am, threw on some workout clothes and his light jacket and baseball cap, and headed over to the campus gym. He went straight to the weight training area, hoping not to run into his former girlfriend, Ashley Bennington. She was probably on her way to DC for her new job at the headquarters of the Ministry of Truth & Justice. Tom and Ashley broke up a year ago partly because she wanted to go to DC for her career and Tom wanted to stay in the Chicago area.

Tom's desire to stay in the Chicago area was rooted in the fact that he had never lived anywhere else. Tom's parents had also gone to Northwestern University. They majored in Business Administration and interned for Chicago companies, but surprised everyone by not pursuing corporate careers. Instead, Tom's dad worked at a Starbucks while his mom worked at a Peet's Coffee. They became managers quickly and saved as much as possible while living frugally.

Within a few years, Tom's parents had decided to open their own coffee place and call it Paradise Coffee Cafe. They found a good location with plenty of foot traffic close to campus and downtown Evanston. They worked out a deal with an equipment supplier to take installment payments, lined up a supplier for the best coffee beans on the planet, got local plumbing and electrical vendors to lower their fees in exchange for free coffee credits, and got sore backs doing their own painting and flooring work.

Tom's parents didn't want Paradise Coffee Cafe to look like a national chain, so they designed and decorated everything themselves with a mix of warmth and eclectic charm, funky tables and chairs – nice but not so comfortable that people would sit forever - posters of famous paintings, international travel posters displaying classics like the Eiffel Tower and Greek Isles, creamy painted shelves with nicely displayed bags of coffee beans, mugs and other coffee things, bookshelves with real books for atmosphere or if anyone actually wanted to read something.

Their concept for Paradise Coffee Cafe also involved music. Tom's dad had played the saxophone and clarinet and his mom had played the piano when they were growing up in Evanston. They programmed special playlists with folk, country, jazz, blues, big band, and classical. Some people came for the music as much as the coffee. Before long, the café featured live performances by local talent who'd play for tips. After a few years, they added several more Paradise Coffee Cafes in the Chicago area.

Tom rarely thought about his parents for several years after cutting off contact when he was thirteen in the Boarding School System. But he had been thinking more about them during the past two years. He felt sad about them, and disappointed in himself, especially when he considered that he was their only child. He was thinking about them as he walked back from the gym, wondering if they had ever been on the same campus sidewalk. He guessed they would not be happy about his membership in the Party, but they'd probably understand his reasons.

After Tom got back to his place, he showered, put on clean clothes, and headed out to Mojo's. It was still chilly compared to typical May days in Evanston, so he wore his light jacket again.

Tom suspected that he was being followed. He'd learned a little about tradecraft by reading spy novels. After stopping to look in a store window, Tom had glanced back and saw a guy looking in a different store window while sneaking glances over toward Tom.

A block later, Tom had stopped, turned somewhat and bent over to tie his shoe. He had glanced back and saw the same guy pull the same act by another store window. Tom expected to see the guy again but wasn't concerned because he figured it was his annual security check.

Tom waited for Izzy in a booth in the back with a view out the window. He stood up when he saw her enter. She walked over casually.

"Hey," Tom said.

"Hey," Izzy said.

Izzy smiled and said, "So here we are. I hope the coffee is as good as you said."

"I think you'll like it. If not, we can go back to Equality Café," Tom said with a smile.

Izzy smiled and rolled her eyes.

"So what can I get you?" Tom asked.

"I'd like to try whatever you have."

When Tom got back to the table and sat down with the coffee mugs, he said, "I hope you like dark roast with nothing added."

"Perfect. Thanks."

They relaxed and smiled at each other for a moment.

Tom said, "Don't freak out, but I'm being followed by the short dude with the blonde buzz cut walking by on the sidewalk. I think it's just my Party security check."

As Izzy looked out the window, the guy glanced at Mojo's nonchalantly while apparently whistling a tune. He also seemed to be checking out an apartment building across the street.

"That's Iggy, my neighborhood Block Minder. He must be doing some security checks for extra social credits."

"How'd he get a name like Iggy?" Tom asked.

"He said his parents named him after an early punk rocker, Iggy Pop."

"People can be so weird," Tom said.

"Yeah. I think he has a crush on me," Izzy said.

After a pause, Tom said, "I wonder if we were in any classes together. I always sit in front."

Izzy was looking down at her steaming coffee as she replied, "We were in Modern European History together. I always sit in the back."

"My favorite topic and favorite professor," Tom said.

Izzy lowered her voice and asked, "You don't think Professor Laska is too far out there with those cynical quips?"

"Confidentially, I think he's funny," Tom said quietly.

"What about his vague references to banned books and websites?"

"Most kids find the banned stuff anyway," Tom replied.

"So is Modern European History your major?" Izzy asked in an innocent yet slightly amused way.

"No. I was in Equality Studies and just graduated. I'm also in the Party and was in the Youth Brigades. A safe path to a safe job and good social credit score," Tom explained.

"Okay, I'm teasing you. I already knew that. Someone pointed you out in class and said you're a rising star in the Party who maybe has hidden depths."

Tom thought that was odd, but Izzy added, "I've never known a rising star in the Party with hidden depths. I never even heard of that."

"I don't know why they call me a rising star anyway. I just volunteer a lot. I have a lot of medals and badges," Tom said.

Tom paused and then said, "I'm so glad we ran into each other at that Equality Cafe."

"Tom, do you think that was a coincidence?"

Tom liked hearing Izzy say his name, but didn't know what to think. "Are you talking about fate?" he asked.

"Of course not. After the final exam, I just walked a bit behind you and got in the coffee line," Izzy said.

Tom smiled and blushed slightly but didn't say anything because he couldn't think of anything to say.

"Maybe we could go to the gym together? Do you go there?" Izzy asked.

"Yeah, I mostly run and use weight machines. The Party likes us to know martial arts, so I'm also working on a black-belt," Tom said.

"I like to run and use stair climbers. I learned judo and boxing. Kick-boxing too."

Izzy lowered her voice. "You said you like Professor Laska's cynical humor. Can someone be a rising star in the Party and also be cynical?"

Tom whispered, "I guess anything's possible."

They smiled at each other comfortably for a few moments.

"It must feel good to graduate. Do you have a job lined up?" Izzy asked.

"Yeah, I'm glad to be done. I have a job at the Bureau of Truth in downtown Chicago. I start next Monday.

"What kind of job?" Izzy asked.

"Entry level. I don't know what I'll work on. Whatever they tell me, I guess."

"Will you move down to Chicago?" Izzy asked. Tom wondered if she seemed disappointed that he might be living farther from Evanston. He couldn't really tell.

"I thought about that but decided to stay here and take the train down. I've lived my whole life in Evanston. My parents lived here too," Tom said.

"You say that in the past tense. Where do they live now?" Izzy asked.

"They were taken to the Alaskan Reserve about nine years ago," Tom said quietly. He began to choke up but mostly shook it off while looking at the ceiling in the far corner. His eyes were moist.

"I'm so sorry. Do you want to talk more about that?" Izzy asked with a look of concern.

"No, not now. I don't act like this very often," Tom said.

Tom recovered his composure after a few moments. Their coffee had cooled enough and they were taking sips. "How do you like your coffee?" Tom asked.

"Everything I dreamed about it. Seriously, excellent."

After taking another sip, Izzy asked, "So what else do you like to do in your free time besides the gym?"

"I like watching old movies from the 1930s through the 1950s. In high school, I'd wake up in the middle of the night and sneak off to watch TV and saw a lot of them," Tom said.

"I watched some of those movies last summer with my grandparents in London. I liked the old-fashioned values. You know, good wins over evil, crime doesn't pay. There's a sense of simpler times," Izzy said.

"Some of those movies are dated or corny, but there are a lot of great ones. I also like the music, the full orchestrations and rich moody harmonies," Tom said.

"But some old movies had racism or racial stereotypes. I don't like that," Izzy said.

"Me neither."

"Last week I saw a good romantic comedy called "Too Young To Be Kissed," probably from the early 1950s," Tom said.

"I don't think I saw that," Izzy said.

"I don't remember the actor or actress. It's about a woman in her 20s who has worked hard to become a professional pianist. But she can't get anywhere until she pretends to be her own fictitious younger sister and they think she's a phenomenal teen prodigy. The male lead is a good looking concert promoter who takes her under wing only because he thinks she's about fourteen. I won't tell you how it works out, but it's funny and cute," Tom said.

"I'd like to see that sometime. On the serious side, did you ever see a drama from around 1940 called "The Mortal Storm" with Jimmy Stewart?" Izzy asked.

"I don't think so," Tom said.

Izzy said in a lower voice, "It's set in Nazi Germany after Hitler becomes Chancellor. It shows the horrible impact on Germany's people in general and one Jewish family in particular. Some of their non-Jewish friends turn against them but Jimmy Stewart tries to help. I was very moved."

"I can get really emotional watching movies or documentaries about the Holocaust," Tom replied.

Tom paused, lowered his voice, and added, "Did you hear about the round-up of some underground people last night?"

"Yeah, the Political Police got three high school seniors. I'm not sure they were really in the underground," Izzy whispered.

"I wouldn't know. They were apparently putting up subversive posters," Tom whispered.

"You know what the posters said?" Izzy asked.

"No, what?" Tom asked.

"There was a cartoon. A Native with a full headdress and his young son with one feather in his head band are looking up at a poster of Director Stalinsky. The caption said, "Dad, is he really one of us?"" Izzy whispered.

"I didn't know you could still get in trouble for something like that. Most people probably figure Stalinsky has phony Native credentials," Tom whispered.

"They say Stalinsky is more sensitive than the others," Izzy whispered.

Tom and Izzy relaxed and smiled at each other. A young student couple came in and began to study the menu board intently. The barista was patient but eventually asked if they'd like some help. The guy asked questions about different beans from different countries but didn't seem to understand the answers. Tom thought he saw the barista roll his eyes. The female student suggested they celebrate the end of finals with mocha lattes. The guy quickly agreed and exhaled a sigh of relief.

Tom and Izzy waited for the noise of the expresso machine to stop. "So, Izzy, what's your major and what year are you in?" Tom asked the ubiquitous campus questions.

"I switched from Art School to Modern European History after my second year. I'll be a senior in the Fall. I might keep going with history into grad school."

"Is the idea that you can enjoy art even if you don't finish Art School?" Tom asked.

"Yeah. I'll always enjoy art. I'll keep drawing and painting, and I'll sign all my work. Maybe someone will discover my art and decide I was ahead of my time after I'm dead."

"That's so grim. Or do all artists talk like that?" Tom asked.

They relaxed and smiled at each other and took another sip of coffee.

"So, Izzy, we do have something sort of in common. I don't know a lot about art, but I started in Music School and switched after two years."

"Why did you switch?"

"I love classical music and respect the people who become professionals. But I just wanted to do something different and figured I can still listen to music," Tom said.

"What instrument did you play?" Izzy asked.

"Clarinet." Tom felt embarrassed and looked down.

"I like all kinds of music, including classical. Some people think only nerdy guys are into playing classical music. But here you are. Not nerdy at all," Izzy said.

"Thanks. I guess," Tom said.

"Do you still play your clarinet?" Izzy asked.

"I lost interest. Maybe that's why I'm not nerdy now. But I still listen to classical music and music in general," Tom said.

"Tom, maybe we can go to a concert sometime. The free faculty concerts at the Music School. You can point out your former Music School girlfriends in the audience."

Tom wondered if Izzy was the jealous type, but that seemed unlikely based on her attractive looks. He decided she was being playful.

"There might be a lot of nerds at a Music School concert," Tom said.

"I can handle that if you can," Izzy said.

They sat for a few moments. Tom thought of another topic. He had aced his Equality Art & Logic course, where his instructor, Professor Dilettant, had an impressive background as a social justice warrior, though his art credentials were obscure.

"Izzy, since you were in Art School, what do you think about the role of art in promoting equality?"

"You want to talk about that?" Izzy asked with a puzzled look.

"I'd like your views. Do you think good art lifts the spirits? And the best way of lifting the spirits is by showing people as equals so no one feels oppressed?"

Izzy hoped Tom was joking and decided to play along. Instead of answering, Izzy asked, "Does good art need to include people at all? What about animals? Don't they lift our spirits up?"

"Animals are fine if the scene is politically correct. But, not if one animal is eating another one. Or dominating another animal," Tom said.

Izzy was pretty sure Tom was trying to be amusing. "Is it bad for art to show reality? Isn't reality the same as truth? Isn't the Party for truth?" Izzy asked.

"Wow. We didn't cover those questions in class. I'd have to ask Professor Dilettant."

"And how about art without people or animals?" Izzy asked.

"Paintings of flowers or fruit could be good. You don't mean degenerate art from the 20th century like cubism?" Tom asked.

"Why not? Have you seen much cubism?" Izzy asked.

"Not much since it was banned. We saw examples in our course and learned that most people didn't like it," Tom said.

"I'm not a fan of cubism, but I like earlier abstract artists. I love Kandinsky in particular. How could the Ministry of Culture denigrate Kandinsky's colorful and expressionistic paintings as too individualistic and bourgeois?" Izzy asked rhetorically.

Getting sharper in tone while keeping her voice low, Izzy continued, "Do you really think most people like the art that's being produced now? The endless portrayals of heroic protestors tearing down statues of George Washington and Columbus or throwing bricks at police and burning down buildings? All those paintings of an upraised fist? That is tiresome crap!"

Izzy quickly looked to see if anyone was around. She was sitting across from Tom in the booth with her back to the wall. She had a good view of the empty customer seating area and the far end of the cafe with the counter and entrance. Then Izzy smiled and said in a low voice, "Forget I said that. You must think I'm a dangerous subversive."

Tom doubted that Izzy was an active subversive. He figured she might be a harmless cynic and safe enough if she used discretion not to cross the vague line into subversion.

Tom stuck his head out of the booth to look around and then said in a whisper, "I was teasing you with this stupid discussion. I love Kandinsky. Just don't spread it around because I have my reputation to think about."

Izzy laughed briefly and whispered back, "Tom, I'm so glad you love Kandinsky."

They smiled at each other for a few moments. Tom had been waiting to ask a question that was on his mind. "Did you say something about London yesterday?"

"I was there last summer staying with my grandparents. I went to museums and libraries … hung out with friends," Izzy said.

"Did you have any really close friends in London?" Tom asked.

"You want to know about my last boyfriend? The coffee addict?" Izzy asked.

"Yeah, I'd sort of like to know. That is, if you don't mind."

"It was over before the summer ended," Izzy said, looking down.

Tom was thinking about her former boyfriend, and wondering if he might end up the same way, in the past tense.

Izzy continued, "He was too tall anyway. My boyfriends have always been very tall or about my height. I'm five six." She was smiling playfully.

"I wanted to be six feet tall. I've gotten used to being five ten," Tom said, smiling back.

"So, you're four inches taller than me, which makes you just right."

"What is just right about being four inches taller?" Tom asked.

Izzy replied, "Maybe aesthetics of how a couple looks? Maybe when they stand and kiss, they don't get stiff necks? Or maybe it's…you know."

Tom smiled but didn't say anything.

"Dancing, of course," Izzy said.

They broke out laughing.

They heard a loud police whistle and then a gun shot and looked out the window. They saw two Political Police officers chase and grab a middle aged man who had been running down the sidewalk. The officers wore the standard black uniforms and helmets. As they cuffed the man, a large Political Police van pulled up. One of the officers slapped the man hard across the face a few times and then shoved him into the back of the van.

Suddenly two women and another middle aged man raced out of a building entrance across the street and down the sidewalk, and four more Political Police officers ran out the same entrance and caught the group a half block away. The officers cuffed the three people, slapped them around, and pushed them into the back of the same van. One officer went to sit in the passenger seat by the driver. The other officers climbed in back with the prisoners and slammed the back door shut, and the van took off fast.

Tom and Izzy exchanged a brief look of concern but didn't say anything. Arrests had become so common during the huge round-ups after the Soft Coup that the country got used to them. People developed a way of not showing concern, or even much interest, when they saw arrests for fear of being viewed as sympathizers and getting dragged in. There were fewer arrests now because most people were careful not to do or say anything wrong. They still refrained from expressing much concern or interest when they saw arrests.

After several moments of silence while Tom and Izzy looked down at their almost empty coffee mugs, Tom went for refills.

When he came back with new mugs, Izzy said, "Your right arm would be good for a charcoal drawing." She didn't say this flirtatiously. More like a physician with a patient.

"How come?" Tom asked.

"The muscle definition. We did figure drawing in Art School. Have you seen the Statue of David in Florence? The human body can be so beautiful as an art form."

"Maybe it depends on the person, though?" Tom asked.

"Yeah, that's true," she said and they laughed.

Izzy had to leave, but they wanted to get together again that same evening. Izzy had volunteered to help at a faculty awards event, but she could get away by about 8:00 pm. Tom was buzzed by the caffeine and Izzy's interest in making plans for that same evening. He wasn't listening well or focusing on details, and forgot that he had to attend a separate Party awards event that same evening.

As they were saying goodbye, Tom said, "Izzy, I don't know your last name."

"I'm Isabella Fanella."

"I'm Tom Hardy."

They exchanged contact information, smiled and lightly kissed and briefly embraced, and headed in different directions.

When Izzy got to her place, she freshened up, located an encrypted thumb drive in a small hidden drawer in her antique cabinet in her bedroom, and put the thumb drive in her purse under her Smith & Wesson pocket gun.

She floated quickly down the three flights of stairs thinking about Tom, looked around, walked quickly to her fifteen year old silver Mazda Miata and drove down through Evanston and then down to Lake Shore Drive, the curvy wide ribbon of pavement that runs north and south by the long east side of Chicago, the "City by the Lake."

She noticed the clouds had mostly cleared and managed to get her sunglasses from her purse and opened the sunroof. Izzy loved this drive, especially with fewer cars on the roads each year, even though she had to drive slower to avoid the increasingly serious potholes. She glanced to her left periodically at the lake and park with sailboats, joggers, bikers and walkers. She put on the Carpenters' greatest hits, beginning with "Close To You," thought about some childhood memories, and began to sing along as she thought about Tom.

Izzy glanced the other way at the residential buildings of different vintages and styles. Some buildings had balconies and most of the balconies had laundry hanging on lines to dry. She wondered if the people liked hanging their laundry in nice weather or couldn't afford costly dryer repairs since so many people kept sinking into poverty in the socialist utopia. Maybe they removed their laundry machines to make space to cram in another roommate to share expenses or another homeless person on orders of the local Block Minder.

Izzy was glad her parents had so much money in overseas investments. She could have ordered a brand new luxury car instead of the old Mazda, but her dad had cautioned her not to draw unnecessary attention to herself.

Her dad's name was Rocco, but he was called Rocky by everyone on the faculty of the University of Chicago Law School. He looked distinguished but sufficiently left wing with his silver hair pulled back in a pony tail. He had a friendly manner and charming Italian accent.

Izzy passed by the Chicago downtown area after about ten miles on Lake Shore Drive. She went another nine miles and got off at East 57th Street and took her normal route into the Hyde Park neighborhood and over to her parent's place on a residential street.

With mixed memories and feelings about her parents' place, Izzy was glad to see the security yard signs and decals on the door and windows. She parked, closed the sunroof and locked the car, and walked briskly to the entrance while casually looking around.

As a member of the underground, Izzy tried to remain extra alert. But most people had developed a habit of glancing around and looking over their shoulders for fear of being watched or followed, harassed or bullied, whether by the Political Police or the far left vigilante groups.

Izzy hugged her parents when she arrived, and then gave her dad the thumb drive. He said grazia and took the thumb drive to the basement and returned a few minutes later with a new thumb drive that she put in her purse under her gun.

"Did you hear that the Political Police picked up one of our guys?" Izzy's dad asked. "A young guy, new recruit. His alias is Charlie."

"What happened?" Izzy asked.

"Our nurse contact in the hospital got in to see him. The officers caught Charlie moving weapons. There were rifles under a false floor in his van. Charlie thinks a girl he was dating snitched, but he blames himself. They'd only been going out a week and he tried to impress her by saying he was in the underground. He thinks she decided to get the snitch credits. We gotta do a better job training new recruits, especially from small towns," her dad said.

"I don't mean to be unkind, but men are so dumb about women. What's going to happen to him?" Izzy's mother, Audrey, asked.

"Charlie will probably be sent to Camp III. It's especially sad because he didn't even know about the guns. Charlie only knew he was supposed to drive the van. He picked it up in the parking space and found the key, bought the groceries, and was in the parking lot waiting for instructions with the address of the safe house. Suddenly he sees Political Police outside the van. When they found the rifles under the false floor, they figured they caught a serious underground guy. They interrogated Charlie for three days and nights. They tortured him in ways I don't want to mention. He's barely alive, with broken teeth and broken bones. He gave his real name, but thankfully his relatives had already fled the country last year. He gave some alias names but didn't know our real names or what anyone looks like. He also gave his credentials to our dark web site. But our cyber team's program detected an unknown IP address seeking access and redirected the investigators to our fake dark web site which identifies about two dozen people who actually work for Stalinsky. But they'll probably figure that out."

"Daddy, that's so awful." Izzy began to cry and her mother gave her a tissue.

Rocky continued, "We know this happens. People in the underground take risks because we agreed that someone has to do this. Some day we'll have enough trained freedom fighters and resources that we can rise up and restore freedom. But Izzy you can go to London if you want. Do you feel safe? Are you concerned that you are being followed?"

Izzy collected her thoughts, drew and exhaled a deep breath, and said, "I feel safe enough and I'm not being followed. I feel okay about staying in for now."

They were silent for a few minutes while some Italian opera music played quietly in the background.

"I met a guy who I'm going to try to recruit," Izzy said.

"So how did you meet?" Audrey asked.

"We met in a line. He turned to look around and we talked. By the time we got through the line, he asked if I'd like to meet for coffee. So we met at a place the next day and talked a lot more. He's interesting and fun. Cute too."

"You want to recruit him and also go out with him? Is he a nice boy?" Audrey asked.

"Yeah, I like him."

"But you only met him once in line and once for coffee?" Audrey asked.

"Yeah, but we talked a lot and made plans to meet again tonight after I finish my volunteer service at a faculty awards event."

Audrey asked, "I hope I don't sound too old-fashioned, but you haven't said what he is studying or what he wants to do in life."

"Mama, I don't know him very well yet." Izzy paused and looked down. "Okay, he just graduated in Equality Studies and has a government job lined up."

Audrey looked down and didn't say anything.

"Mamma, I know what you're thinking, but there's more to him. He started in Music School and knows about art too. He also likes vintage movies like I watched with Grandma and Grandad last summer."

"Is he in the Party?" Rocky asked.

"Yeah. His full name is Tom Hardy in case you want to check him out. I think he may have hidden depths," Izzy said.

The underground had coined "hidden depths" as a code term for a potential recruit, someone with sympathies for freedom and representative government.

Rocky said, "The name Tom Hardy has come up in small talk with Chairman Lemmon when I handle the legal work for his overseas investments. Tom Hardy is a rising young star in the Party. He was in the Boarding School System and Youth Brigades, and Lemmon might appoint him as a special assistant. Izzy, I'd be concerned that you are getting involved with a true Party believer who may feel a duty to report you when he learns you're in the underground."

Izzy looked at her dad, puzzled and deflated, and the room was silent. Audrey was looking down and stealing glances at Izzy with concern and curiosity.

After several moments, Izzy said, "Daddy, when Tom talks to me, he's totally not like other Party people. He's more fun and interesting. He never said good stuff about the Party like you'd expect. And he's said things that make me think he's cynical. He says he's in the Party for the extra social credits and a safe job. I think he's a Euro."

Rocky thought for several moments and replied, "Izzy, just be smart and careful. Don't mention your underground work unless you reach a point when you are really serious about each other. It would be good if you can get him to disclose some Party secrets. If you reach that point, you can tell him about yourself, but don't say anything about me or anyone else. If he's really on the level, he'd be in a great position to help us."

They switched to other topics and switched between English and Italian from time to time to keep in practice. When Izzy left, she took the same route in reverse, but drove without glancing at buildings or the lake. She was thinking more about Tom.

Chapter Three

After saying goodbye to Izzy at Mojo's, Tom had gone back to his place, turned on his laptop and accessed a video call with Buddy Lemmon. As Chairman of the Party, Buddy Lemmon was probably the most powerful person in the country.

Buddy opened the call by giving Tom the Party's fist salute and saying, "Hey Tom, how are you?"

"Fine Buddy, and you?" Tom gave the same salute back.

"Tom, this is a quick follow-up on your proposed role as my special assistant. Everything looks good on the normal background checks so we'll just do some final security clearances. You'll still have your new job at Stalinksy's Bureau of Truth in the other building. But your manager will reduce you to part-time after your orientation. That way, you can spend part of your time on my projects. Like I said before, don't ever tell anyone at BOT that you know me or are working for me. I'll explain more later."

"Got it. Thanks Buddy." Tom wondered if he was supposed to be a mole for Chairman Lemmon into Director Stalinsky's Bureau of Truth.

Chairman Buddy Lemmon had taken a special interest in Tom's development since Buddy visited Tom's Youth Brigade to hand out awards four years ago. Tom got the most awards and Buddy spent extra time with him. They had met a dozen times over the years at Youth Brigades and other Party events. Buddy had also made a point of initiating dozens of video calls to check in and catch up with Tom.

Buddy's personal interest in Tom had become stronger when he learned that Tom had discontinued contact with his parents at age thirteen. Buddy nurtured a hope that he could become a father figure to Tom and that Tom could develop into the type of son Buddy had always wanted. Buddy only had one child, Buddy Junior, who was about five years older than Tom.

Buddy and Beatriz had spoiled Buddy Junior rotten. He was their only child and they felt guilty for spending so little time with him based on their Party schedules and events. They overcompensated by giving him every expensive toy, but he quickly broke them. They got expensive nannies and replaced them whenever Junior complained enough. It became a game for Junior to see how fast he could get rid of them. Many nannies left on their own.

The Boarding School System didn't exist when Junior was going to high school, but Buddy had pulled strings to get Junior a position as a quarterback on the private high school football team. Then it turned out that Junior sucked at football. Buddy called in favors to get Junior into Northwestern, but Junior would have flunked if Buddy hadn't continued to intervene. Junior did some bad things and Buddy used his clout to keep Junior out of trouble with the law. Junior wasn't stupid and eventually developed a way of putting on some charm and became friends with some other well-connected spoiled rich guys like him.

Buddy now mainly confined Junior to living on the Party's private island. But the island wasn't a hardship. Fine food and drinks, live music and other entertainment, beautiful accommodations with maid service daily, soft white sand beaches and salt water pools with cabanas and chaise lounge chairs, celebrities and Party big shots. Buddy Junior especially liked all the pretty young women and teenage girls, all trying hard to cooperate for extra social credits or at least to avoid demerits, knowing they could get cushy government jobs on the mainland in due time so long as they didn't blab. A few tried to blab anyway and were relentlessly smeared with negative posts, then kicked off social media and sent to the Alaskan Reserve.

After the call with Buddy Lemmon ended, Tom spent some time thinking about the history of the Party, its two factions and their respective leaders. Alex Stalinsky had been the initial Chairman of the Party after the Soft Coup. Back then, Stalinsky's most senior advisor and closest confidant was Buddy Lemmon. Back then they got along.

Now at age 70, Stalinsky's face was lined from age and worry. He was a man of average height with narrow shoulders and a narrow face, dark plastic glasses, and a pseudo-intellectual look. He wore tweedy sport coats that academics used to buy with patches on the elbows even though they were new. He sometimes held a pipe in his hand or chewed on the stem. The top of his pointy head was smooth and bald, so he compensated by keeping the curly white hair on the sides long. His smile was crooked. His eyes were cold light gray.

Stalinsky had worked his way up from local community organizer and agitator during college to become a thought leader of the old liberal party, though he was more behind the scenes. He had lived wherever it would help him, beginning with college and grad school at the University of California at Berkley, then a series of Social Justice faculty posts in Portland, Minneapolis, Seattle, NYU and Yale. He had worked hard for the old liberal party during all those years and felt a sense of delayed entitlement when he finally moved to DC as Chairman of the new Equality Party.

Yet, part of the delay was Stalinsky's own fault. He was only a Euro and was unsuccessful in courting a series of oppressed race females to marry. Success in that endeavor would have significantly enhanced his street creds. If Stalinsky had pulled that off before the Soft Coup, he would have automatically qualified for the spouse "M" Mixed race class. But he remained unmarried and had to use his influence to obtain phony DNA records. He eventually viewed the setbacks as a blessing in disguise because he got the lab to go all out and issue phony Native credentials. He was known for making lofty idealistic speeches but not for anything concrete or practical, and many people were annoyed by his speaking style the more they heard him, generally patronizing and didactic, often condescending and arrogant if you paid enough attention.

After the Soft Coup, Stalinsky, as a dedicated Soviet-style socialist, obtained Central Committee approval of a Living Wage System. Everyone got paid the same Standard Living Wage and would also get 2% annual increases for the rest of their working lives. In addition to advancing social justice by equalizing compensation outcomes, a goal of the Stalinsky Living Wage System was to reduce the stress that many people had suffered when they were working so hard in the past striving to succeed and prosper.

Ideally, under the Living Wage System, everyone would focus on whatever job they wanted and were qualified for, and society would become happier and less materialistic. Like utopia. Naturally, there were exemptions for Party leaders because they were running the whole frigging country for the benefit of everyone else. The exemptions were confidential, but the masses were able to draw some conclusions based on the high lifestyles.

Unfortunately, far too many people applied for easy jobs for which they were over-qualified. And far too many people applied for interesting jobs for which they were not qualified at all. No one wanted hard jobs. So Stalinsky made periodic adjustments to lower the Standard Living Wage for jobs with too many applicants and to increase the Standard Living Wage for jobs that had too few applicants. But he was always about a year behind. As a result, many people took jobs they didn't want because the jobs they wanted were already filled.

Many people stopped working altogether because they could move in together and get by on a lower Subsistence Wage that everyone received, whether or not they worked. But twenty-five percent of the workforce quit their jobs the day after the program was launched. So Stalinsky decided you'd only get the Subsistence Wage if you couldn't work due to a physical or mental disability. The disability system was generous and there were many legitimate cases of people with disabilities. Far more people milked the massive bureaucratic system with phony certificates from shady doctors.

Some naysayers predicted a shortage of qualified Chief Executive Officers on the theory that few people would want those jobs for the same compensation as clerical workers. But the naysayers were wrong. Just as many qualified people wanted to be CEOs, sometimes for the satisfaction and challenge of solving problems and growing a successful organization, sometimes for self-esteem and prestige, sometimes for the power to make decisions and tell everyone else what to do.

In contrast, there was always a shortage of qualified doctors, even with Stalinsky's efforts to increase the Standard Living Wage for them. The rather few people who were smart enough to become doctors weren't thrilled about spending so much time studying and working long hard hours through rigorous pre-med college, medical school, residencies and internships for comparatively little money. Many existing doctors fled the country or switched to easier jobs.

After major shortages of qualified applicants for harder jobs in all sectors of the economy, Stalinsky directed his Ministry to force qualified people to take vacant jobs in the interest of greater social justice and the general welfare of the country. Everyone had to keep an up-to-date resume on file with the Ministry. Any organization with an opening could petition the Ministry for a worker. The Ministry's Cyber Command developed special software programs to match open jobs with qualified workers. It didn't matter if a worker already had a job, if the software program found that the worker would be better qualified for another job.

If a worker didn't want a mandated job assignment or transfer, there was an online appeal process which no one eventually bothered to pursue because it was never fully implemented. If you turned down a mandated job assignment or transfer, you'd lose your current job if you had one, and would not even get the Subsistence Wage amount. In that case, you'd need to sponge off friends or relatives or else join the risky black market economy of secret trading and bartering. You might also risk smuggling products from other countries. You could reduce the smuggling risk by trying to bribe the inspectors who weren't happy with their Living Wage amount. But bribery also had risks if the inspector turned you in for snitch credits.

The productivity of the workforce plummeted as a result of the systemic mismatch between jobs and people. Also, no one saw any reason to work harder or better than anyone else, and coasting on a job became a national pastime. If a young person joined the workforce with a positive attitude about working hard, the other workers would give the young person grief for making them look bad. Or they'd pick on the young person for being ambitious, which was a code word for saying a person was a racist, even if the person was a member of an oppressed racial group. The young person would catch on quickly and get into gaming the system, which was more fun than working hard anyway.

The Living Wage System also governed what people could pay themselves as business owners. After paying the Standard Living Wage to themselves and their employees, the rest of the profits, if any, went to the government as taxes. As you might expect, businesses kept shutting down and terminating their employees across the country. The former private business owners, who were curiously viewed as highly desirable and effective managers, got decent jobs in the exploding public service sector, often managing large departments of other bureaucrats. They made much less money than before the Soft Coup, but they weren't particularly unhappy since it was easier work, they had more time for their families, and there wasn't much nice stuff left to spend money on anyway.

After three years under the Living Wage System, the economy had mostly collapsed, unemployment and homelessness had skyrocketed, taxes had soared along with the massive national debt, lines of people waiting outside food pantries and soup kitchens were a mile long by 4:00 am every day, and private cynicism had grown substantially. The Central Committee directed Stalinsky to abandon the Living Wage System and return to a limited free job market and generous minimum wage amount, subject to a maximum of 700,000 pages of rules and regulations. Stalinsky was mortified and felt impelled to develop a brand new program, but the new program led to his final fall from grace.

Stalinsky's new program involved a Wealth Tax to help pay for all the free stuff and half-baked pie-in-the-sky meretricious programs like the Big Blue Deal. That ruinous program was somewhat derived from an older proposal with green in the name. Stalinsky changed the name to Blue after scientists brought out satellite images showing that reductions in CO_2 emissions actually reduced the greening of the planet because trees and plants thrive on more CO_2 rather than less. It turned out the politicians and policy makers didn't get the difference between carbon, a pollutant particle like coal soot, and carbon dioxide or CO_2, a colorless odorless gas molecule which is a critically important natural component of the air. Also the green version had a lot of programs that didn't involve the climate or environment anyway.

The Central Committee initially approved of Stalinsky's Wealth Tax because it only confiscated personal wealth in excess of a reasonable $500,000 "Wealth Ceiling." Wealth included 401(k)s, bank accounts and investments. Stalinsky naturally included a secret exemption for Party leaders since the Party leaders were running the whole frigging country. But Stalinsky's computer math statistical data modeling programs vastly over-stated the projected tax revenues. He had grossly underestimated the number of people who grabbed their assets and fled before new emigration restrictions could be enforced. Stalinsky had to reduce the Wealth Ceiling down to $25,000, subject to the secret exemption, which became less secret as the masses observed the ever fancier lifestyles of the Party elite. The Central Committee was furious about the math modelling mistake and even more furious when they learned that the episode created even more cynicism among the masses. Stalinsky proposed to increase the Wealth Ceiling to a more generous sounding $100,000, by also including in the computation the value of home equity, furniture, cars, clothes, and other property. The Committee rejected that solution based on a concern that there'd be too much fudging of values.

In connection with Stalinsky's fall from grace and ouster as Chairman, and in recognition that he had a lot of support among the far left vigilante militias and his Political Police, the Central Committee appeased Stalinsky with a lifetime appointment as Director of the Ministry of Truth & Justice and as Chairman of that Ministry's new Committee on Social Control. The new Committee on Social Control would advance social justice by focusing on social controls, including controls to censor, ban, edit, and curate the news, social media, television, movies, theatre and books. The big tech and social media companies were already doing a heroic job with censorship and self-censorship, but Stalinsky felt he and his associates could make improvements through formal government control. The separate Ministry of Culture would retain its authority over art and music, which Stalinsky didn't know much about.

To Stalinsky's deep chagrin, the Central Committee then appointed Buddy Lemmon, Stalinsky's former senior advisor, as the new Chairman of the Party and of the Central Committee, and as Chairman of a new Committee on Equal Outcomes with a broad mandate to advance the equality of outcomes among the race classes. Chairman Buddy Lemmon looked good at age 64. He was a big man with broad shoulders and wore motorcycle boots that made him even taller than his six feet three inch height. He usually wore a black or navy blue tee shirt and black or dark blue jeans. In cool weather he added a black leather jacket, and in cold weather he switched to a long black leather belted coat and a black leather cap like those worn by Polish partisan fighters during World War II.

Buddy Lemmon didn't have memorable facial features, yet he exuded power with his size, the way he carried himself and the way he spoke. He had cool blue eyes that became warm when he was with people he loved or liked. For other people, he could make his eyes warmer without much effort when called for. He had grown a full beard and mustache when he was young and wanted to be taken more seriously. Now he was clean shaven. For several years, he shaved his whole head which looked good and powerful on his thick neck. But he let his gray hair grow back a few years ago and kept it clipped to a modest length. Some young zealots quipped privately that Buddy's current haircut made him look like a reactionary conservative. But his overall look remained rebellious with jeans and tee shirts, motorcycle boots and leather jackets.

Lemmon was a street-smart self-made man who did well at the University of Wisconsin in Madison on a combined academic and football scholarship. Except for Madison, he had lived in the Chicago area his whole life and had no desire to move to DC. Buddy had worked hard for the movement and rose in its ranks all the way up to the old liberal party's Committee for Strategy and Tactics, where he excelled with his analytic skills and persuasive talents. Earlier in his movement activities, Buddy became known for idealistic speeches that were actually interesting and inspiring with his baritone radio announcer voice.

Buddy's Committee on Equal Outcomes, and Stalinsky's Committee on Social Control, would both ideally view their broad mandates as complementary in advancing equal outcomes and social justice. And in practice the two committees operated in similar ways. Buddy and Stalinsky appointed smart highly educated loyal Party members to their respective committees, with precise racial quota diversity, but chose sycophants because only sycophants applied. But the two Committees eventually began to bicker and compete and issued conflicting and overlapping reports, studies, and policies. The Central Committee tried to resolve the conflicts, often in favor of Buddy Lemmon, sometimes in favor of Stalinsky.

During the last few years, Chairman Buddy Lemmon's speeches had become more pragmatic and substantive and therefore reflected increasing tension with Director Stalinsky. Few people realized that the changes in Buddy reflected the steady and growing influence of his wife, Beatriz. She was a Latina whose parents were among the people who fled on risky rafts from socialism in Cuba. Marrying a Latina long before the Soft Coup gave Buddy extra street creds in the movement and automatically qualified him for the spouse "M" Mixed race class after the Soft Coup took place.

Sometimes Stalinsky and Buddy went rogue and the Central Committee didn't get involved. Stalinsky went rogue first by developing the Political Jails and huge Alaskan Reserve gulag prison system. He didn't initially create his own private militia because he already had support from the far left vigilante militia groups, and his Ministry already included the FBI, Cyber Command, the Political Police and its related system of Block Minders. Most of his Political Police were already volunteers in the far left militias anyway.

Buddy went rogue by creating the Boarding School System, Cadet Corps and Youth Brigades. He also had the foresight to form his own private militia to defend against the Stalinsky forces and allies. He was aware that the regular federal police, regular military, national guard, and coast guard were professionals who had an aversion to taking sides in domestic politics, though there were some questions about how the top brass might act in case of major civil unrest. In any event, the regular military and coast guard were busy guarding the boarders, not so much to protect against people getting into the country, but to keep people from getting out with money or other assets.

The Central Committee also directed Buddy Lemmon and his new Committee on Equal Outcomes to create a major new program to motivate good social conduct and help equalize outcomes across races. They envisioned a program of social credits loosely based on a system that had been in effect in China for many years. Director Stalinsky was furious because the social credit program was originally his idea back during the Soft Coup. He thought he should run the new program or at least be lauded for his early vision with another statue of himself.

Under the new Social Credit Point System, you could earn social credits for activities that benefited society and lose social credits (also called demerits) for activities that harmed society. As classic examples, you earned credits if you volunteered at a food pantry, but you got demerits if you were caught speeding or driving drunk. You earned credits by volunteering to clean up litter and got demerits for littering. There was a full online list of beneficial and harmful activities, with a keyword search function and a related fuzzy logic analytics feature, so anyone could figure out what to do. The program grew over time as more good ideas came up.

A higher social credit score initially covered a range of modest benefits, such as expedited passport and drivers' license services, discounts at museums and national parks, discounts on internet service charges, minor tax credits and public recognition for top achievers with cash awards and ribbons, medals or badges. You couldn't lose if you did the right thing all the time, and you could get extra benefits if you went above and beyond.

Buddy Lemmon's Committee on Equal Outcomes soon added companies to the Social Credit Point System because it seemed like an oversight to have left companies out. At the same time, the Committee logically expanded the program so you got more credits working for a company with a higher social credit score than a company with a lower social credit score. It also seemed sensible a year later when the Committee provided even more social credits if you worked for the government or a non-profit rather than working for a capitalist enterprise.

Since the Party had done so much good, it also seemed natural when the Committee on Equal Outcomes began awarding extra social credits for being an active Party member, and even more credits on a confidential basis if you were a rising star or had a higher leadership role. It also seemed sensible that you could earn credits for social media posts supporting the Party or its public positions. And you'd get demerits for criticizing the Party or its public positions. After all, didn't the Party represent the best interests of everyone? If you weren't for the Party, you were against the people, and it made sense to discourage anti-social behavior.

Some skeptics questioned the financial burden of the Social Credit Point System. But the cost of administration and benefits were rather modest initially. Everyone's information was kept current in a convenient data base, and the system generated credits and demerits through automated programs. Even greater efficiencies came within a few years through the mass proliferation of Party cameras with facial recognition software tied into automated social media monitoring programs with analytics functionality and artificial intelligence. You could walk down a street, pick up some litter, smile at the camera, check your account and see 10 extra credits.

For fairness, there was an appeal process in case you thought the Party had shorted you on credits. But no one eventually bothered to appeal since the results were rarely favorable and you lost credits if you lost the appeal. That seemed fair in relation to the other people who did not burden the system with useless appeals. The Committee eventually added substantial cash values for social credits that could be used like a debit card.

The Committee also established a program to promote better equality outcomes across races by awarding social credits every January 1 to everyone over the age of 13, which had become the age at which you could vote. The annual credits varied based on racial classification. Blacks got 30,000 credits, Browns got 20,000 credits, Asians and Mixed race got 10,000 credits, and Euros got 1,000 credits. No one outside the Committee understood how they came up with the disparities in annual credits between the races. Eventually even the Committee members forgot.

The annual credits based on race were only supposed to be a temporary way of helping equalize outcomes across racial lines. There was supposed to be an annual review process to determine whether the amounts for any given race could be reduced. But no one wanted to reduce the race credits for fear of being viewed as a racist so the annual race credits became a permanent institution. It made some sense for Euros to continue getting so few annual credits because they were still categorized as the oppressor class. In reality, Euros now suffered from systemic institutional racism on many levels, including strict quota limits for Euro employees, boards of directors, and elected officials.

Any town with a higher percentage of Euros on its town council than the Euro percentage of the town's population faced high fines and criminal investigations, and would show up on newsletter lists of racist organizations. The elected Euros would be doxed and harassed, and far left violent vigilantes would soon arrive.

One time the Committee on Equal Outcomes went too fast in rolling out a program for social credits and demerits based on social "attitudes" rather than "activities." For efficiency, the attitudes were to be determined by computer algorithms applied to social media postings to analyze and classify the content and compute an appropriate number of credits or demerits. Though active Party members were not concerned, there were reports that the masses felt the concept was too vague and subject to interpretation. The controversy calmed down when the Committee brought out several data scientists and statisticians claiming that data science and statistical models fully supported the program's accuracy. They also pointed out that anyone was free to use the appeal process that was still on the books.

Tom had grown cynical about the Party like most people. But Tom had refrained from revealing his cynicism to anyone, even in private, before getting involved with Izzy. The Party had no tolerance for cynicism among its own Party members.

Chapter Four

After drifting back to the present, Tom opened his laptop and searched for Izzy on the internet and social media and didn't find anything, which seemed odd. He then spent most of the day searching for information about his grandparents. He vaguely remembered a family driving trip to visit them in Montreal. He spent time on genealogy and public records sites and figured out all four of his grandparents' full names and middle initials, but couldn't find current contact information. His parents were apparently both only children so he had no aunts, uncles or cousins.

In the late afternoon, Tom had a sandwich with stale bread from Equality Foods. He wondered if other people had mixed feelings when they were getting into a relationship just when they were beginning life as adults. Just about to start his first job in downtown Chicago, Tom wondered if he might be happier remaining independent. He then guessed he was afraid of getting serious with Izzy and eventually being dumped. Deep inside he wasn't sure he deserved someone like her.

Tom decided to go to a bar and order a drink like a single grown-up. He had walked past a local bar near his building many times but had never gone inside. When he entered, he felt the local patrons were sizing him up. He took a stool at the counter and, after being carded, ordered a vodka martini, shaken but not stirred. He'd never had a martini but had heard a spy order one in an old movie. Then he added, "And make that a double." He'd heard someone say that too. The bartender smiled and asked Tom if he watched a lot of old movies.

When the bartender came back with the double drink in a tall glass, he said "Here you go kid." Tom thought the drink was too strong but drank it anyway and decided he would never order a martini again. He had been trying to avoid looking at himself in the mirror behind the bar, but glanced up and stared for a moment at his young face compared to the other patrons, all in their 30s and 40s. He thought for a moment about growing a mustache.

Tom got up unsteadily and walked over to the park along the lake and headed north. He turned and walked over to busy Sheridan Road where he went down to a crosswalk. He was having difficulty focusing with the double martini in his system. He crossed the street and walked into the shady residential neighborhood. He was in front of Izzy's building debating whether to call or just ring her bell. He couldn't remember if they had plans for this evening or the next evening, whether there was a set time or whether she was going to call him. Calling her would be safest but showing up and ringing her bell could be more personal. He really wanted to see her. He rang her bell.

Izzy was surprised and upset. She let Tom in, asked him to wait a moment, hurried off to her bathroom, then hurried back but paused and placed her hands on her hips. She said he should always call before dropping in and reminded him about her faculty awards event. She said she was running late and had to go. She grabbed her raincoat and rushed past Tom. While closing the door, she said he could help himself to a glass of water if he wanted to stay.

Izzy's reference to an awards event caused Tom to remember suddenly that he was supposed to be at a Party Youth Brigade awards ceremony to hand out medals. He panicked and rushed out and jogged to the Party ceremony where he arrived a few minutes late. He was able to go through the motions even though he was tipsy and preoccupied. Maybe Izzy was really upset about him showing up at the wrong time and not calling first. He wondered if she had little tolerance for human errors.

Izzy was ten seconds late for the faculty awards event, no doubt due to Tom's untimely arrival at her place, and lost 100 of the promised 500 social credits. She thought about telling Tom to see how he'd react and whether he'd offer to make up by paying for coffee the next morning. She wasn't sure she wanted to say much and wondered if the incident was an honest isolated mistake. But maybe he had another side that was irresponsible or inconsiderate. She was more concerned that he had seemed tipsy and smelled like booze.

When the dining at the event ended, several young faculty guys swarmed Izzy pleading to dance. She hoped Tom was waiting at her place, but didn't want to seem too eager, and decided it would be best if he had to wait awhile as penance for messing up. Besides, she was all fixed up for dancing and sort of liked the attention. And maybe it was a mistake to get serious with Tom. Maybe he was a lush or might turn into one later.

The DJ dimmed the lights and announced that he would play Sam Cooke songs followed by Nat King Cole classics. Izzy danced with a few of the nice looking young faculty guys. Most people were moving their feet a bit and swaying around, not touching during faster songs, and politely holding each other during slower songs. That worked well for the Sam Cooke music and Izzy was having fun.

When the DJ switched to the Nat King Cole romantic songs, Izzy was dancing with a faculty guy who knew more about dance steps. He was talking while dancing but she couldn't hear very much over the music or maybe just didn't care and wasn't paying attention. The guy danced Izzy into a dark alcove. He stopped and held her tight and began moving his hands down her back. Izzy said he was getting fresh and should knock it off, while wondering if he had enough influence to affect her grades. He kept holding her tightly, kissed her neck, and moved a hand to her butt. Izzy didn't want to use judo, unless necessary, due to the potential impact on her grades. She used all her strength and tenacity to twist and struggle and pry herself away and then slapped the guy hard across his face. He looked shocked and silly.

Izzy turned toward the main room, stood up straight, and walked swiftly through to the coat room where she grabbed her raincoat. As she left the building, she pulled her phone from her purse and looked around to make sure the guy wasn't following her. She paused on the steps and took a few deep breaths of the night air. She walked briskly up the busy street and then into her quiet neighborhood. When she got to her place, she was surprised and saddened to find that Tom wasn't waiting.

Meanwhile, the Party's Youth Brigade awards ceremony had just wrapped up and Tom was walking toward the door to leave.

"Hey Tom, do you have a few minutes? Come back this way and we'll go in the small conference room." Tom turned around, said "sure," and followed Chairman Buddy Lemmon.

After Buddy closed the door and they sat down, Buddy said, "Tom, I'm sure you'll pass your final security check and I'm looking forward to having you work as my special assistant. I want to let you know a little more about my broader vision. First, though, remember that everything we talk about is strictly confidential. Okay, all my current advisors are sycophants. I need new ideas and viewpoints and more energy. I'm starting with you on a trial basis, but I'd like to build a new brain trust of young smart precocious free thinkers. Now, when I say free thinkers, I need to emphasize confidentiality again. You're free to think for yourself and tell me whatever you want, but you must keep everything absolutely confidential."

"I signed the NDA and you have my word that I'll honor it."

"Okay, so I'll eventually have a major falling out with Director Stalinsky. We don't agree on much anymore and it's just a matter of time. Stalinsky was effective in the Soft Coup, but he's not pragmatic and his strategic policy ideas lack long-term vision. I'm going to outline some things that you presumably learned in college, but I want to be sure we're on the same page. Frankly, I also just gotta vent about some stuff.

"So the realignment toward China was classic Stalinsky. Stalinsky always felt the Party's principles aligned with the Chinese Communist Party's principles. He liked China's social credit–demerit system and one-party political system. He saw China becoming strong and figured "If you can't beat them, join them." None of us knew back then that Stalinsky was also getting payments from China through his family members' phony business deals and kickbacks from his family members to him.

"So Stalinsky was the driving force behind abrogating the old treaties with the remaining western-style democracies and accepting new treaties with China. But look at the results now. We have a lot of free stuff but we're paying by mortgaging our country with debts we can't afford. So many factories are closed, we have high inflation and massive debts, and we just had to transfer the Port of Los Angeles to China to help pay the interest on our loans. You'll recall we had to turn over Hawaii to China last year.

"If we don't pay our loans, China can keep taking over our ports, rail lines, airports and highways. They started this in Africa with the "Belt and Road Initiative" many years ago. China could end up owning another piece of our country, maybe the whole West Coast. Stalinsky thought China would be satisfied to dominate the Far East and would treat us like a valued and respected partner with equal rights. I thought it was crap but Stalinsky had seniority and more power back then."

Tom said, "Yeah, you were obviously right."

Buddy continued, "Some naïve people thought we could just keep printing money forever. But no country has been able to pull that off. We got away with it while the dollar was the global reserve currency, but we had no control over keeping that. So when the global community switched to the yuan, the dollar lost half its value overnight, and our costs of products and services keep soaring with hyperinflation as the dollar keeps sinking. A frigging loaf of stale bread costs three times more than a year ago.

"Most of our Party leaders are now getting indirect Chinese payments like the Stalinsky family, but China plans to cut them off next year. China only pays people off while they are weakening a target country. They don't respect or trust local corrupt ass-kissers after weakening a country enough. Next year most of our Party leaders will be replaced by Chinese nationals with dual citizenship and total allegiance to the Chinese Communist Party. They'll leave me and a few others in place as figureheads and administrators, but China will make the policies and control everything. Most people in this country would need to learn how to speak Chinese.

"Tom, I could just go along with that. I personally believe the Chinese people, and for that matter Asians in general, are really good nice people, and may be smarter than us in a lot of ways. But I've been disappointed with some Chinese leaders' policies. So I've been working on a last minute secret plan to realign away from China and toward Russia. I thought about realigning with the remaining western-style democracies, but they're too weak now. Russia is stronger and I can make a deal with Boris. He has an increasing fear of China, as well as Turkey and Iran since they both have nukes now. Of course, it's crucial that Boris is actually different from some of his predecessors, but I'm feeling comfortable. We'll need to "trust but verify."

"Anyway, I'm thinking about selling Alaska to Russia in exchange for paying off some of our debts to China, including all debts secured by mortgages or deeds of trust on our assets. Once we announce the realignment and abrogate our China treaties, the Port of Los Angeles will only be worth a fraction of what China paid for it. So, Boris will use one of his Russian companies to buy the Port of Los Angeles from China for peanuts and then transfer it to our Party. He'll only add 20% for his profit and overhead.

"Tom, what I'd like you to do is give this strategy a lot of fresh thought and put together a matrix of pros and cons. You'll probably come up with the same things I came up with and my sycophants endorsed, but that's okay if that's the way you really see it. But if you think of other things, that's good too. You can use your credentials to log into your Party account where you'll find a complete dossier with all of the details and analysis by me and my sycophants. Now don't freak out about this. I know you're young, but you are way smarter than anyone on my staff and they lack the courage to tell me anything different than what I come up with anyway. So this is sort of a trial deal to see what you come up with."

"Buddy, I'm glad to work on this. I'm flattered that you chose me." They gave the fist salute and said goodbye.

As Tom walked to his apartment, he was thinking somewhat about his new project for Buddy, but his mind kept returning to Izzy and his feeling that he'd messed up by ringing her bell instead of calling. He was tired and didn't recall any definite plans with Izzy following her awards event, and he didn't want to bother her again so soon and maybe mess up again. He reminded himself never to have another double martini.

Chapter Five

After Tom got up the next morning, he exchanged texts with Izzy about meeting at Mojo's again. When they met about an hour later, Tom treated and they sat in the back booth.

Tom said he was sorry for messing up the prior evening and that he'd always call first instead of just dropping by. Izzy said she appreciated that, but gently asked if Tom had a drinking problem. Tom explained that he went to a bar for a grown-up drink as a rite of passage, but didn't like the way it made him feel and wouldn't do it again.

Izzy asked if Tom would like to know about her best friend Gina Rossi. He said "okay," but wondered if Izzy wanted to fix him up. He looked down and felt sad for a moment. He decided he was probably over-analyzing as he looked up and saw Izzy's friendly smile.

Izzy explained that she and Gina had known each other since they were fourteen, and had started at Northwestern's Art School together four years later. Gina stayed in Art School when Izzy switched to Modern European History, but they were still best friends forever. During Gina's first year, an Art School professor had taken an interest and invited her to his place one evening to show his art work. He became sexually aggressive, but Gina pretended to cry and said she was pregnant and also had several sexually transmitted diseases. The guy lost interest and promised a good grade if she'd keep quiet. She only told Izzy.

Gina had spent her second year abroad studying art in Florence and loved the Uffizi Gallery, but her favorite artwork in Florence was the Statue of David. In Evanston and Florence, Gina had gone out with a variety of guys. Gina's current boyfriend was Izzy's first boyfriend in Art School, but Izzy didn't want to mention that to Tom yet.

Tom asked Izzy if she'd like to know about his best friend, Noah Greene, and she said sure. Tom explained that he had met Noah in the Boarding School System's middle school facility in Ann Arbor, and they were both taken to high school at Petosky Academy in the northwest part of the lower peninsula. Noah had introduced Tom to a group of Jewish kids and they all became close. Tom told Izzy about his warm feelings for his friends and his sadness that he had gradually lost contact with them over the past two years. Izzy listened intently.

They left Mojo's and walked toward the campus. Izzy had a politically incorrect idea and wanted to see how Tom would react, but hesitated and wondered if he might think she was immature. After several moments Izzy leaned close and said quietly with a conspiratorial tone, "My parents named me after Isabella, Queen of Spain, who sponsored Christopher Columbus. My parents thought he was an Italian hero."

Tom replied with a tone of concern, "How can I be associated with someone associated with Queen Isabella? I could be kicked out of the Party and lose all my social credits! I'm sorry, but we can't go on."

"You're breaking up with me over this?" Izzy asked with a pout.

Playfully, Izzy assured Tom that, if he wanted to break up over losing social credits, she wouldn't bother him again, turned her back, and walked off at a leisurely pace, her raincoat unbelted, the belt hanging down and swinging slightly.

Tom ran and caught up, got in front of Izzy and gently held her shoulders, looked into her stunning blue green eyes, said he was willing to take the risks to continue seeing her, and asked if she would forgive him. Izzy gave Tom a long somewhat inquisitive look before smiling, nodding slightly, and saying okay.

As they walked toward the lake, Izzy said, "Columbus did seriously bad things like the slave trade and oppressing natives. By the

Middle Ages, I think slavery was mainly in Africa, especially North African. I hate that slavery was taken to this country. Europe had a pretty bad feudal farming system, but at least it wasn't based on race and didn't involve buying people."

Izzy continued, "There was already some slavery among some Native tribes in this country and on the islands when Columbus arrived. Did you know that, in North African at that time, there were a lot of white slaves, Europeans, and they were treated poorly? Yeah, pirates captured them in raids on European coastal towns and ships and sold them in the North African slave markets. There are some interesting history books. I have them in my booklist in my notes app so I can send the names." She forwarded her booklist: "Christian Slaves, Muslim Masters: White Slavery in the Mediterranean, The Barbary Coast, and Italy, 1500-1800 (Early Modern History: Society and Culture)" by Robert C. Davis; and "White Gold: The Extraordinary Story of Thomas Pellow and North Africa's One Million European Slaves," by Giles Milton.

"But Izzy, looking back and saying that other people were doing bad stuff in other places doesn't excuse Columbus for doing bad stuff, right?"

"I totally agree," Izzy said. "I don't mind that they took down the Columbus statues. His motivations weren't so great. I think he mainly wanted to be rich and famous."

Izzy added, "But Tom, they went way too far in tearing down statues of the founders like George Washington, Jefferson, Adams, Madison and Hamilton. The founders were already wealthy and well-established. They could have just sat back and enjoyed life. But they risked their lives, liberty, and property to rebel against England for high ideas about political liberty, self-determination, representative government, free speech and other basic human freedoms and rights. They weren't perfect of course, and the country took way too long to stop slavery and address racism, and there's no excuse except to put it in the context of the times. But the founders had a lot of good aspects."

After several moments, Izzy asked, "So Tom, did you actually want to go into the Party's Boarding School System, and how did your parents feel about it?"

"My parents said it was best and I sort of wanted to go. I guess I felt neglected and didn't like capitalism because my parents spent so much time on their coffee café business."

"So that's how you know about good coffee?" Izzy asked.

"Yeah, my parents were good at the coffee business." Tom paused and then asked, "What about you? Were you in the Boarding School System?"

"They tried to get me and Gina, but my dad got exemptions," Izzy said.

"You know why they eventually closed the Boarding School System?" Tom asked.

"No."

Tom lowered his voice. "They had created a Frankenstein. A lot of the kids were really precocious and found ways to get around the security and do anonymized internet research. The kids talked privately and developed independent views. I'd guess some are now in the underground or the Alaskan Reserve, but most are probably going along to get along like me."

Izzy seemed pensive. Tom thought of something else. "I heard that berets went out of fashion even in France. Yet here you are - with a beret and looking stylish. It goes with your long raincoat." Izzy wore her beret the way she learned with the fabric pulled from the left brim over the right brim, slanted forward, and tilted down toward her right eyebrow.

"I don't wear it very often. I love this beret. It belonged to my Nonna and it's the real deal. She bought it when she was in high school in Paris in the 1970s."

"Nonna? So, you are of Italian derivation? How does that work if your grandma was in high school in Paris? Wouldn't she be French?"

"So, my dad's dad was from Naples. But he fell in love with a Parisian girl who came over to study in Italy. We call her Nonna and my Italian grandpa Nonno."

"I love the sound of the Italian language. More lyrical than English or German. But I don't hear an accent. Maybe something in your style of phrasing."

"We came over when I was fourteen, but I can still speak Italian pretty well. My brother was eighteen when we came over and he has a charming accent."

When Tom and Izzy reached the lake shore area, they walked down a paved path looking for a park bench. A guy jogged by and said "G'day" in an Australian accent. Some Aussies had arrived since Australia became part of China, but they usually went to England. Canada was no longer a good choice since it was now on China's takeover list. China wanted the huge deposits of coal, oil and gas that Canada had left dormant based on climate concerns, and China still had its fossil fuel exemption under the Paris Strange Accord.

China had lobbied to substitute "Strange" for "Climate" in the name of the Paris Accord when it was renewed. It was a private way of poking fun at the rest of the world after China got to keep its exemption from complying with the Accord, even though China was the biggest emitter of both CO2 and carbon particulate matter and continued to build new coal fired power plants which emitted both. To celebrate its odd exemption from the Paris Accord as an inside joke, China claimed that a man named Lester Strange had first sounded the climate crisis panic alarm many decades ago. China operatives dummied up a Wikipedia page about a fictitious Lester Strange as a self-taught climate genius. No one wanted to admit they had never heard of him.

Tom and Izzy found a bench and sat to look out at Lake Michigan. No sailboats were out but a few ringtail gulls floated and glided in the breeze.

"So, why did your family leave a beautiful place like Italy?" Tom asked.

Izzy looked sad for a moment. "We loved Italy, but you can probably guess if you think about your Modern European History class."

Tom paused. "Okay, after NATO was dissolved, Turkey became expansionist and took over areas in Europe that had been in the Islamic Ottoman Empire, including Greece and the former Yugoslavia, which shares a border with Italy. There was a concern that Turkey might keep expanding west. A Turkish news commentator urged that they take over the Vatican and behead the Pope. I can see how an Italian family might leave Italy, no matter how beautiful it is."

"Tom, excellent answer! Have you thought about being a professor? I know a lot about professors and you'd fit right in."

"Is that a dig?" Tom asked while smiling at Izzy.

There was a pause for a few moments before Izzy said, "A lot of people wanted to leave Italy but lacked money or had ties to jobs or family. My parents were professors by then and were associated with old-fashioned liberal causes like freedom of speech, which helped them get jobs at the University of Chicago, at that time anyway. You know, in Hyde Park where I go to visit them."

"Both of your parents are professors? What was that like?" Tom asked with a small smirk which he quickly suppressed.

Izzy caught the smirk but wasn't sure what it meant. "My parents are smart kind people who love my brother and me as the apples of their eyes. We've always been very close."

She paused. "What was that smirk about?"

"There are some great professors like Laska, but a lot of professors annoy me," Tom said.

Izzy lowered her voice to a whisper. "You mean the ones who go above and beyond just towing the Party line? The autocratic, self-righteous, fuzzy-minded, cutting edge woke ones? My parents are like Laska."

Tom smiled but didn't say anything.

Izzy added, "My mom's parents are both professors too. They're also like Professor Laska."

"That's a lot of professors for one family. If you say your dad's parents are also both professors, I might think you're teasing," Tom said.

"Okay, my grandparents in Italy are definitely not professors. My Nonno – my dad's dad - was from a working class family in Naples but he went to Music School in Milan. He met my Nonna – my dad's mom – when she came from Paris to study music in Milan. They worked their way through school, bussing tables and singing in restaurants and for weddings. They got married and got jobs singing with the Naples opera."

"So that's how you know about classical music?" Tom asked.

"We visited them every Sunday when we lived in Italy. They had music playing in the background. My Mamma studied the piano when she was growing up in England."

"This is so confusing. Your mom was from England?" Tom asked.

Ever since the Soft Coup, with the increased emphasis on racial identity combined with the lack of reliable news to discuss, people talked a lot more about their heritage and racial backgrounds, especially when getting to know someone. Genealogy had become a bigger national pastime than baseball. The conversations could go on forever and were often interesting.

"Yeah, Mamma was English but came to Italy for a college year abroad. She met my dad in Turin and they fell in love. Sort of like how my dad's mom came from Paris for music school in Italy and married my grandpa."

"So your mom's side was from England," Tom said.

"Mamma was born and raised in England, but her mom was from India. My grandma, Deepika – she goes by Dee - from India was actually half Indian and half Portuguese. She was from the west coast of India, which was a Portuguese colony instead of a British colony. The Portuguese part eventually joined the rest of India."

"So how did your maternal grandma from India end up in London?"

"Dee did well in college in India and moved to London for grad school. She met my granddad in the school library. He had immigrated from Germany."

"Let's see. The Party's race system doesn't look beyond grandparents. So, if I got this right, you're ¼ Italian, ¼ French, ¼ Indian and ¼ German."

"Yeah, that's how I got my Mixed race "M" classification with my extra social credits. The ¼ East Indian makes me part Asian. They didn't factor in Dee's Portuguese part."

"Okay, but what's the story about the German part?"

"You paid attention! My mom's dad, Hans, was from Germany. He emigrated to London after college. That's where he met Dee when they were in grad school."

"Your heritage has been very good to you. You know, uh, how you look." Tom was smiling.

He didn't say what he really thought - that she was the best looking girl he'd ever seen. Maybe that would seem effusive or make her feel self-conscious. Maybe she'd think he was using flattery for other purposes.

"Thanks. You look nice too." Izzy was smiling.

No one was around but Tom lowered his voice and looked down. "I have the Euro "E" but I make up for it by being in the Party. They like having Euros who show enthusiasm."

Izzy lowered her voice. "Tom, you're smart to make up for your "E" with Party activities. You get extra social credits, right?"

"Yeah, some. So, being an "M", you can vote and even take an airplane within the Republic if you have enough social credits. I'd love to fly on a plane," Tom said.

"No one cares about voting anymore. The Party candidates say the same things and who knows what happens to those electronic ballots. By the way, I'll never fly just within the Republic because I'd rather save the planet. So I only fly between New York and Europe, usually England or Italy." The intensity with which Izzy said that caused Tom to wonder if she was being serious or facetious.

People with access to foreign news were aware of recent English studies showing climate change was driven by long solar activity cycles which affected major wind and sea current patterns, changes in the tilt of earth, cooling of the earth's core and other factors, and that the climate had entered a cooling period which was more typical of entropic trends over hundreds of millions of years. In expressing concerns about a new minor ice age, the new English studies echoed the concerns of scientists back in the early 1970s.

"So Izzy, tell me more about your grandad who was originally from Germany. What's he like and does he ever talk about Hitler and the Nazis?" Tom asked.

After taking a moment to collect her thoughts, Izzy replied, "My grandad's name is Hans Huber. He was born in East Berlin in 1957 and still has a mild Berliner accent. Although he seems very serious, Hans has an inner warmth once you get to know him. He rarely makes a joke, but his jokes are funny if you like dry humor. And Hans hates everything about the Nazis and Stalinist socialism."

Izzy went on to explain how Hans got out of East Germany in 1977. He was with a group of about a dozen students at Humboldt University that dug a tunnel under the Berlin Wall. Like so many others behind the Iron Curtain, they wanted to get out of the socialist police state. The group planned the route and length of the tunnel by making surreptitious observations and calculations from various rooftops and high windows, and from old maps that showed the area before the wall went up. They began by digging into the basement of a safe apartment building nearly two blocks away and, out of fear of informers, limited the group to trusted friends. The work was done at night and on weekends, and the tunnel dirt was removed in sacks hung under their clothes and scattered in parks. The tunnel took nearly two years to complete.

The group had no money or valuables when they emerged on the West Berlin side of the famous wall, but the authorities and some charity groups helped. West Berlin was prosperous and Hans got jobs waiting tables. While living frugally, he saved and applied for admission as a grad student at the London School of Economics. Based on his excellent grades from Humbolt University and his application essay, Hans was accepted and reached London in 1979.

Izzy paused to ask Tom if he was getting bored, but he wanted to hear more. Izzy explained that Hans' brother, Ernst, stayed in East Germany because he had a family and a job with a research institute in Potsdam where they were living. Ernst traveled to Leningrad sometimes for his job. On one of those trips, he got mixed up with some Russian dissidents and was rounded up and sent to Siberia where he perished. Izzy told Tom about a book Hans let her read about the Soviet political prison camps, "The Gulag Archipelago" by Aleksandr Solzhenitsyn. She recommended his one volume condensed version.

Tom wanted to know how Hans' family felt about Nazis. Izzy explained what Hans had told her. Hans' family was in a circle of cultured Berliners who privately despised Hitler and his hateful ranting speeches about having a pure master race. They thought he was a joke and wouldn't last long. They were disgusted when he transformed the government into a totalitarian fascist socialist system and removed all opposition figures through secret assassination campaigns or by sending them to Dachau or Sachsenhausen. They were further disgusted when the Nazis imposed increasingly oppressive laws and brutal actions against Jews and other so-called undesirables. Many cultured Berliners were too naïve to imagine that Hitler's actions would lead to mass murder. Many ended their relationships with Jewish friends after the Nuremberg race laws were passed.

Hans' dad was friends with a Jewish guy in Berlin who feared for his life and his family. Hans' dad's family hid the Jewish family - two parents and two kids - in a secret room they built with a false wall in the 3rd floor finished attic of their large home. Instead of making a door and concealing it behind a cabinet or bookcase, they made a square opening midway up the wall – more like a smallish window – and hung a framed painting over the opening. They could remove the painting so the Jewish family could go through the opening and then Hans' dad or another family member could place the painting back over the opening. They practiced many times and became proficient. The secret room had two mattresses, a bucket of water and a bucket for human waste. Hans' dad or grandad dumped the waste bucket at night under a pine tree with low branches in the back yard.

Hans' dad and grandad obtained extra ration cards through a student underground movement and sometimes on the risky black market to buy food for the Jewish family. The Jewish family usually spent the daytime in the larger regular part of the attic which had some furniture, but they kept quiet and couldn't look out the windows. The Jewish parents had brought school books and other books and spent time teaching and reading to their kids. Hans' dad's family and the Jewish family grew close as the years went by and the kids grew older. The families spent time visiting together in the attic, talking about war news or playing cards, or listening to an illegal radio that could pick up the BBC.

The SS conducted a search of the home one time. The Jewish family heard barked military commands and pounding of heavy boots. They scrambled and tossed themselves through the opening to the secret room and Hans' grandad got to the attic just in time to hang the painting, take a seat on a sofa, open a book, and take out his pipe. The SS looked all over for a hidden door. They never looked behind the painting because they didn't think about an opening midway up the wall.

Hans' dad's brother, Dieter, had been drafted into the Wehrmacht regular army and ended up in a Russia POW camp in Poland until a year after the war ended. Hans' grandad and dad were exempt from active military service because they owned and operated a factory that made shoes and boots for the Wehrmacht, and Hans' grandad had connections in the Wehrmacht's regular army from his military service in World War I. In a final effort to defend Berlin from the Russian forces, Hans' grandad and dad were forced to dig antitank trenches and erect street barricades and were given Molotov cocktails. Between work details they managed to obtain and provide food for the Jewish family and stayed with them at the end of the battle for Berlin. After the war, Hans' dad and grandad had to spend several months in a Russian POW camp, even though the Jewish family tried vigorously to explain how they had saved them. Years later, Hans' dad and grandad were named Righteous Among the Nations, an award bestowed by the State of Israel on non-Jews who took an active role to rescue Jews during the Holocaust.

Tom was intensely interested in Izzy's account. He had learned about the Holocaust from his Jewish friends in the Boarding School System and his own research. But he had not heard about any Jewish people who survived in Berlin. He was deeply moved and saddened thinking about the horrors of the Holocaust, how it occurred in a so-called civilized society and in a systematic way, and in thinking about all the innocent people who perished, the pain and heartache for those few family members who survived, and the loss of talent and creativity of so many dear people who could have benefited the rest of humanity with scientific, medical, artistic, musical, literary or other contributions.

Izzy continued her account by explaining that, while Hans' dad and grandad were POWs, Hans' mom and grandma were raped by gangs of Russian soldiers who had taken over East Berlin. They viewed it as payback for what the Germans had done in Russia. Hans' mom sought protection by latching onto a brutish junior officer who kept the other Russian soldiers away and provided extra food which was in short supply. For survival, she let him have his way with her like a sex slave. She faked being nice and he began to look on her as a sort of girlfriend. She saw no end in sight as the Russians planned to occupy East Germany indefinitely, the city seemed doomed to remain in a state of devastation, there was no word from Dieter and no sign that Hans' dad and grandad would be released, and Hans' mom believed most Germans would be sent to Siberia for life sentences of hard labor. She got cyanide pills, which she and her mother took to end their hopeless miserable lives.

They stood and walked slowly back up the paved path for several minutes in silence. Tom was deeply moved by Izzy's accounts of real people. Tom explained that he had really enjoyed his Jewish friends, and that he'd like to think he'd be as brave as Hans' family. He was also saddened by the brutal treatment of the East German women by the Russian forces.

Tom thought it was important to learn about history under the maxim, *"those who don't know history are condemned to repeat it."* Tom was concerned about the Party's current oppression of Euros and wondered how far it would go. Every time it seemed like the Party was done, there'd be a new restriction. The latest one banned Euros from public beaches and swimming pools based on a dubious infectious disease risk analysis.

They walked in silence for a few minutes.

"Tom, did you hear gun shots last night? Gina lives near you and said there was gunfire about midnight."

"Yeah, it didn't last long," Tom said.

"Gina thinks it was another assassination of a Political Police leader."

"Do you think there will be reprisals?" Tom asked.

"You mean like last time? When they picked up fifty random people and said they'd shoot one per day until the assassin gave himself up?" Izzy asked.

"Yeah, that shooter never gave himself up so they executed fifty innocent people. Some people blame Stalinsky for reprisals against innocent people, and some blame the underground for assassinations that triggered reprisals. I wonder if the shooters are rogue actors instead of the underground. Or maybe there are different factions in the underground," Tom said.

After several moments, Izzy asked Tom if he'd like to talk about his family. Tom said his dad's side was English and French. His mom's side was mostly English and Dutch, plus something called Black Irish that he didn't know much about.

As they continued to walk back, they stuck to light topics, what Izzy's friends were doing for the summer, how Tom's fellow graduate friends were set with new jobs or interviews, who had stopped dating someone and who was dating someone new. They still hadn't met each other's friends but were becoming familiar with them anyway.

"So tell me something you do as a rising star in the Party," Izzy said quietly.

"As they say in old spy movies, I could tell you, but then I'd have to kill you."

"So you really can't tell me stuff?"

"The loyalty oath and non-disclosure agreement is over 100 pages long, single spaced. You can get in serious trouble if you violate it." Tom glanced at Izzy and whispered close to her ear, "If you get caught, that is." He also winked.

Izzy whispered back, "I can't decide if you're a secret subversive yourself or a Party informer who will turn me in if I say the wrong thing."

When they got to Izzy's building, they made plans to go to a faculty concert at the Music School that same evening. They kissed and hugged.

Chapter Six

After Tom got back to his place, his phone vibrated and he saw a message from Buddy Lemmon's assistant scheduling a video call for a half hour later.

Buddy was in a good mood. "Tom, I accelerated your final security clearance. Your last full check was a year ago. I got a report that said nothing has changed except you are now dating Isabella Fanella. I know her dad so I waived her interviews after he vouched for her. Congratulations on your new position as my special assistant."

"Great Buddy, thanks." Tom's mind raced with questions about Buddy Lemmon knowing Izzy's dad.

"Can you be at Party headquarters at 3:00 pm this afternoon for a meeting of the Committee on Equal Outcomes? It will last less than an hour."

"Sure," Tom said. The screen went blank.

By the time Tom finished his call, Izzy was meeting Gina Rossi for lunch at Vinney's in downtown Evanston. The regular lunch crowd was emptying out and Izzy was sitting in a booth when Gina arrived. They smiled and hugged and sat next to each other on one side of the booth facing out toward the room as planned.

Izzy asked for two glasses of prosecco.

"I want to drink a toast to my new boyfriend," Izzy said as she held up her glass.

"To your new boyfriend. Tell me all about him," Gina replied as she clicked Izzy's glass.

Izzy didn't want to seem like a teenager with a crush, even if that was basically the way she felt. After taking a sip of the sparkling wine, Izzy told Gina a few things about Tom.

After listening politely, Gina said, "So can't you tell me more about what he looks like or do you have a picture?"

"I don't have a picture yet, but go to Facebook and look for Tom Hardy in Evanston. But don't friend him."

Gina eagerly pulled out her phone and found Tom's profile.

"You did good!"

"Thanks. And the thing is, I don't think Tom knows how attractive he is!" Izzy said.

"Excellent!" Gina exclaimed. They clicked their glasses in another toast.

"That reminds me of you. So modest about the way you look," Gina said.

There was a comfortable silence for a few moments.

While sitting next to each other on the same side of the booth, Izzy discreetly opened her purse which she had placed on the seat between them. Gina slipped an encrypted thumb drive into Izzy's purse and removed an encrypted thumb drive that was already in the purse under Izzy's gun. They continued to talk and look at each other during the exchange.

"Tom only messed up one thing. He stopped by without calling first and then he was really sorry about it. It was a misunderstanding or something. He'd gone out for a drink in a local bar as a rite of passage. I was concerned at first, but he said it was a bad experience and he'd never do it again. It's crazy soon, but I think we are really into each other," Izzy said.

Gina was delighted for Izzy. She loved her like a sister.

"So how's Angelo doing?" Izzy asked.

"He's working on another self-portrait."

"I'm not surprised." Izzy rolled her eyes.

"I still think you're too hard on him. It's sort of endearing the way he over-compensates for being insecure about stuff," Gina said.

For the past few months, Gina had been dating Angelo Manetti, Izzy's first college boyfriend from Art School. Angelo's family had immigrated a few years ago from Florence, where his Italian ancestors had lived for generations. Like many people in Florence, members of the Manetti family learned a lot about art, took art classes, and tried various forms of artistic expression. But not a single Manetti had become a professional artist of any kind, not even an art teacher.

Angelo was on a mission to fix that flaw in his family history. He had some artistic talent and was happy that his family moved from Florence to Evanston. He believed he could shine by comparison with fewer artistic people around. He also liked being fawned over at the Art School based on his Florentine origins. Unfortunately, Angelo had a somewhat self-absorbed side which had bothered Izzy increasingly over time. Gina had somewhat more patience for guys like that.

After they finished their meals and were saying goodbye, Izzy said she was meeting Tom for a faculty Music School concert that evening. Gina grimaced. Then she smiled and said it would be a good chance for Izzy to dress up. Izzy thought about some ideas as she walked back north, casually glancing around and behind her.

As Izzy was saying goodbye to Gina at Vinney's, Tom was on his way to the meeting of the Committee on Equal Outcomes. He had grabbed his laptop and walked over to take the "L" to downtown Chicago.

The "L" stood for "Elevated" and was an old light rail transit system that spread in various directions from downtown Chicago. Part of the "L" system remained elevated above ground and also looped around the central downtown area which came to be called the "Loop." Other parts were underground like a typical subway and rose to elevated tracks as they spread into neighborhoods.

After reaching the Party headquarters reception area on the top floor of a high rise on Michigan Avenue, Tom admired the view of Equality Park and Lake Michigan to the east. As Tom looked at the patriotic socialist art on the walls, he thought about the comments Izzy might make. He wondered why the art community kept producing the same stuff. Then he realized it was the same reason he was in the Party, mainly for a safe job and social credits. A fringe benefit was staying out of trouble with the Political Police, at least in theory.

An administrative assistant escorted Tom into the meeting room. Buddy was sitting at one end of a granite conference table and Tom sat in the vacant chair to the right. Buddy pounded his gavel once to begin the meeting even though no one was talking. Buddy introduced Tom and said Tom would be his special assistant. The other Committee members wondered if Tom would be a glorified note-taker and gofer, but were pleasant in welcoming him.

Buddy went around the room asking the other members to provide updates. After each presentation, Buddy led the Committee in discussions, conclusions, and decisions about next steps. Tom was impressed that Buddy was highly focused and effective and wasn't surprised that Buddy was used to getting his way. Though rough around the edges, he was probably the smartest person in most meetings. The admin was typing furiously on his laptop. Tom was making notes on his own laptop, though he wasn't sure what he was supposed to do with them.

Buddy asked Tom to stay for a few minutes after the meeting ended. The others left and the last one closed the door.

"Tom, the Party is going to take over Mojo's Coffee Company and turn the stores into Equality Cafes. Between us, this is a Stalinsky plan."

"Oh, like the grocery store take-overs and rebranding as Equality Foods?" Tom asked.

"Yeah. The truth is, most people can't afford Mojo's and the business has been declining. When we take over, people will still be able to buy the beans at our Equality Foods stores if they want to brew at home, but they'll have to pay a lot or use a lot of their social credits. We'll keep using the beans at Party headquarters and we'll have free bags in the reception area that you'll be able to take anytime."

"That's a nice perk," Tom noted.

"I'm telling you this so you don't go to Mojo's anymore beginning two weeks from now. Your security clearance had a note about being a frequent customer and I don't want you to get hurt. We're using the movement's basic tactics. Stalinsky operatives will launch a social media and news campaign to smear Mojo's as degenerate fascist capitalists and whatever else they throw in. Stalinsky's team will organize boycotts and large noisy protests outside each Mojo's and the homes of the officers, directors and managers. They'll have operatives among the protestors throw bricks through the windows and set fire to cars in the parking lots. We don't want any significant damage to the buildings or the equipment and we don't want looting. We just want to drive down the acquisition price to almost nothing and then also get Mojo's to include the buildings, equipment and all the beans."

"Do you want me to work on this?" Tom asked while trying to remain calm. He had noticed that Buddy's eyes had cooled as he spoke.

"No. This is baby stuff. Marxist Socialism 101. I want you to work at a higher strategic level. We'll talk more about that in the near future. I just want you to stay clear of Mojo's beginning in two weeks because there's always a risk of collateral damage."

Buddy reached down toward the floor next to his chair and brought up a box and gave it to Tom while explaining that it was a personal gift to celebrate his new position. Tom opened the box and saw a Smith and Wesson subcompact 9 mm pistol like the one he used in the Youth Brigade weapons and militia training segments.

Buddy was beaming so Tom beamed back and said thanks. Buddy made a move to stand up so Tom joined him. Buddy put his large hands on Tom's shoulders and looked down at Tom with a smile.

"Tom, I've enjoyed getting to know you since that first time we met at your Youth Brigade about four years ago. I've watched you grow and develop. This gun is a special expression of my trust and confidence in you. Now I'm going to say something I say to everyone who works for me. Beatriz says I shouldn't say it anymore, but old habits die hard. If you ever betray me, you will spend the rest of your life in Camp III at the Alaskan Reserve." Buddy's eyes were cool.

"Buddy, that will never happen." Tom just meant he'd never spend the rest of his life at the Alaskan Reserve but figured Buddy could draw his own conclusions.

They rode the elevator down in silence. Tom was relieved to see that Buddy's eyes were warm again as they said goodbye and gave the fist salute. He could see why everyone said Buddy had charisma. It was accurate if his eyes were warm or you were too far to notice when they were cooler.

As Tom got on the "L" heading back to Evanston, he placed his laptop and the gun box on the seat, checked social media on his phone, and saw that a subtle campaign against Mojo's had already begun – something about a heavy fine for letting the cafes put their tip jars back.

A text arrived from Izzy saying she was back at her place in Evanston and looked forward to seeing him at the Music School concert that evening. Tom put a finger to his lips and gently placed his finger on Izzy's text as a way of kissing it. Like most people, they didn't text much anymore as the data fees kept rising. He figured Izzy could probably afford to send more texts and appreciated her sensitivity to his situation. He was glad for the social credits from his Party work and looked forward to the possibility of getting more through working for Buddy Lemmon.

When Tom got off in Evanston, he stopped by his apartment to drop off his laptop and new gun, wash up and change clothes.

Izzy had agreed to meet Tom outside the Music School before the evening concert began and Tom got there early. His heart skipped a beat as he saw Izzy approaching. She was wearing a pretty summer dress and sunglasses as she walked casually toward Tom and the setting sun. She took off the sunglasses as she reached him.

"Izzy, you look nice," Tom said quietly with a smile.

"You too," Izzy replied softly.

Tom was glad she noticed that he had dressed up. He was wearing dark slacks and a Madras sport shirt. Tom and Izzy kissed and went inside to find good seats. They ended up in the front row because of Tom's thing about front rows and Izzy didn't seem to care.

They didn't know what to expect since you basically got whatever the Music School faculty wanted to do and no one complained since the music was enjoyable and admission was free. That evening was dedicated to a mostly forgotten minor jazz artist named Blossom Dearie. The ensemble was going to play straight through the collection of popular songs on her 1964 album, "May I Come In?"

The regular ensemble had been expanded to include several senior music students and recent graduates. In fact, the program listed a recent graduate named Jenny Dale as the featured vocalist. Tom was surprised to see her listed and wondered how she would sound singing jazz with her operatic training.

The ensemble was basically a small orchestra and a concert grand piano. The performers and conductor were dressed in 1950s style dark suits and cocktail dresses on loan from the Theatre Department. As the overhead lights dimmed in the intimate concert hall, a spotlight lit up a circle in center stage, and Jenny walked out to scattered applause by a mostly student audience that had been thinned by departures after final exams.

They began with "Something Happens to Me", followed by "(I'M) In Love Again" and then "When I Get Blue." Jenny was doing a decent job and didn't sound operatic at all. For the first few songs, she emulated the precocious teenage voice that Blossom Dearie had perfected and continued to use even when she was much older. Jenny seemed slightly uncomfortable, probably not used to performing outside her normal repertoire or with a teenage voice.

Jenny was more relaxed when she began singing in her own voice while using stylings she had apparently worked hard to perfect. She was jazzy, melodious, playful or moody, as the songs required. Tom couldn't help looking up at Jenny from time to time. All fixed up with theatrical makeup and the vintage cocktail dress, and from fifteen feet away in the theatrical lighting, she was looking good and singing like a pro. But Tom mostly looked down and read the comprehensive program guide with information about Blossom Dearie and the music that was flowing out through the concert hall.

By the time Jenny was singing "Quiet Nights," she was glancing down at Tom from time to time. During "Don't Wait Too Long," and "I wish You Love," she looked right at Tom for a few moments and seemed to accentuate the relevant lyrics when she looked in his direction. One time Jenny seemed to blow Tom a kiss, though it might have been a broader gesture to the audience in general. Tom didn't notice because he was reading the program guide, but Izzy noticed.

When the intermission finally arrived, Izzy turned in her seat to look at Tom and asked if he knew the girl who was singing.

Tom paused before turning to look at Izzy and then said, "Okay, she was my girlfriend during my second year of college, back when I was in Music School. We don't need to stay for the rest of the show. Let's get out of here," Tom said.

"Oh no, we don't need to leave. I was really enjoying the music. Let's stay and then you can introduce me to Jenny. I'd like to meet her," Izzy said.

"Okay. Would you like anything to drink?" Tom asked.

"A sparkling water with lime would be nice. Thanks."

Tom got two plastic cups of Perrier with lime wedges and made his way back to Izzy. The intermission ended, the lights dimmed, the spotlight came on and Jenny came back to center stage. The rest of the show was even better as Jenny sang the jazzy songs with even more flair, sometimes adding a few dance steps or swaying rhythmically on the stage. Tom continued to take a great interest in the program guide.

Tom knew how to get to the large room in the basement where the performers packed their instruments in their cases and compared notes about the performance, what they did well and what they wished they had done better, hoping for compliments and often getting them.

Jenny came over with outstretched arms and a theatrical smile. Tom managed to keep it friendly rather than romantic by making the hug brief and moving so the kiss landed on his cheek. He was pleased with his quick moves but looked funny with the red lipstick smudge.

Tom introduced Izzy and they chatted about the performance. Tom wasn't surprised that Jenny dominated the conversation and talked about her career. She had developed a way of boosting her ego to compensate for her sad lonely childhood spent mostly working on her vocal talent after being teased by kids about some flaws in her appearance. The braces had helped and the remaining minor overbite was appealing.

"So I'll be leaving soon to perform at the Spoleto Festival," Jenny said.

"I'm so impressed!" Izzy said. "The summer music festival in Spoleto Italy? I love that festival. My grandparents used to sing there decades ago."

Jenny seemed mildly chagrinned. "No, I'll perform at the Spoleto Festival USA in Charleston, South Carolina. It's based on the one in Italy and is really about the same thing, but easier to get to, at least for people in this country."

There was an awkward pause. Jenny then talked about her interest in working in New York City until she excused herself after she saw the ensemble's conductor at the far end of the room.

Tom and Izzy made their way back to the plaza in front of the concert hall. The moon was out and nearly full. No one was around. They kissed and embraced before heading over to Izzy's building. After reaching the entrance, they kissed and embraced again and made plans for Tom to come over to Izzy's place to hang out the next morning.

Tom heard a siren as he walked south on Sherman. In the darkness between street lights, he turned and saw a Political Police car speed past with flashing lights. He instinctively stepped off the sidewalk toward some bushes by an apartment building. He was full of adrenaline and shaking but considered his response normal. He waited for another siren but didn't hear one. He walked to his apartment building while trying to keep in shadows and darker places.

Chapter Seven

While Tom was sleeping that night in Evanston, his parents were busy cleaning the coffee service facility for Camp I of the Alaskan Reserve.

They had worked their way up from Camp II where they were originally assigned nine years ago after arriving on one of the last long crowded trains a few years after the Soft Coup. The train windows had been covered with plywood to protect the prisoners from the mostly peaceful protests of left wing mobs at various places along the way. The prisoners got bread and water twice a day on the long ride to Alaska.

Their first year at Camp II had been tough, with hard forestry service in frigid weather, stinky latrines, bad food and coffee, and large rooms full of snoring people in creaking bunkbeds huddled under thin blankets in the 50 degree temperature of the barracks in winter. But Tom's parents worked hard, learned the unwritten Camp II systems and protocols, and developed a network of connections with seasoned inmates who had insights and influence.

By the end of that first tough year, Tom's parents had used their network to get jobs in the Camp II coffee facility. Over the next several months, they developed a friendly relationship with the coffee facility manager, a well-regarded senior inmate. He appreciated their hard work, dedication, and useful suggestions based on their experience in private coffee shops, especially their special techniques for cleaning the pots and urns, cleaning and changing the filters and water lines, tinkering with the temperatures and force of the water, grinding and blending the beans in special ways and at certain temperatures, and making the coffee stronger with more beans. The manager liked them as workers and for enhancing his reputation with better coffee. The Reserve headquarters administration heard about the coffee and began ordering large quantities which had to be delivered in large urns using a push cart over a long distance with stops for security checks. Eventually, headquarters reassigned Tom's parents to manage the Camp I coffee facility, a short walk from headquarters. They were assigned to a special barrack with their own private room and a double bed and even a small wood chair.

After a year of learning the Camp I systems and protocols and developing a new network, Tom's parents began to pilfer coffee beans to use in the camp's black market barter system. Unlike administrators and guards, the inmates only got coffee in the morning. There was a demand for beans from inmates with lighter work assignments who wanted to brew coffee discreetly in unauthorized afternoon breaks, and from inmates with heavier work details who wanted to brew coffee in their barracks after dinner. Tom's parents had to be careful because the administration assigned some inmates to serve literally as bean counters around the time when the administration agreed to switch to Mojo's beans. Tom's parents formed a trusted relationship with several bean counters and rewarded them with some of the pilfered beans.

Tom's parents had not been politically active and their arrival at the Alaskan Reserve was not the result of the mass political trials of the most active political conservatives and their families and friends, those who were on the Party's long "enemies of the state" list. The political trials were called Truth & Reconciliation Proceedings. They were not actual trials, but rather mass electronically generated indictments and convictions with evidence generated through automated software programs that trolled and scraped the internet and gathered and analyzed data from social media and all manner of other electronically stored records. No one was required, nor permitted, to show up for any sort of hearing since there were no hearings. The computers and software programs did all the work and performed complex analytic computations to produce scores on a scale of 1 to 100 based on data science. If you scored higher than 50, you were convicted.

Fortunately, and especially while the Alaskan Reserve was still being constructed, most of the people convicted in the political trials were given light penalties, such as fines, probation, community service and reeducation while wearing ankle bracelets. Probation meant that good or bad behavior could lead to a soft government job or incarceration as the case may be. But there was no real understanding of where to draw the line between good or bad behavior. Director Stalinsky, who was developing the Alaskan Reserve, liked the vagueness about acceptable behaviors. The vagueness motivated people to err on the side of good behavior in case of doubt.

At the Party's direction, the government also pursued a relentless campaign of compliance actions against capitalists – anyone who owned a business with more than five employees – for any violations of the massive business and employment regulations. Capitalists had to fill out voluminous online forms and submit extensive documentation, under penalty of perjury. Cyber Command's analytic software programs combed through the forms to find problems, and capitalists were also subjected to random surprise onsite compliance audits. As with the political trials, there were no hearings or appeals for capitalist crimes, and the penalties were similar, especially before the Alaskan Reserve was completed. Most capitalist offenders in that early period avoided incarceration for a first offense.

Tom's parents were caught up in the first round of capitalist compliance audits. They didn't tell Tom the details, but they were forced to sell their coffee business to the Party to pay a high fine for violating new recycling regulations they had never heard about. The Party paid a low price for the business, which Tom's parents then paid to the government for taxes. The Party rebranded their coffee shops as more Equality Cafes. Tom's parents got in more trouble before long. They tried to post social media messages complaining about having to sell their coffee business to the Party. They thought they were posting on a safe dark web site, but it was a trick. Cyber Command shut them down and they were sentenced to probation and community service and reeducation for three years. Unfortunately, they were still on probation when they were denounced for expressing the seditious view that the Party sucked and socialism sucked compared to free enterprise. With that violation, they were rounded up and forced onto the last trains of other stubborn capitalists to the Alaskan Reserve.

When Tom's parents became the de facto coffee king and queen of Camp I, they were accepted into a group of other resourceful inmates with leadership roles known as the royalty. The royalty initially had some hope of getting out or at least being able to bribe a guard to smuggle accurate messages. But they kept hesitating about the message idea because it could be a major risk to the recipients as well as to themselves. No one wanted to end up in Camp III.

Tom's parents thought about Tom often and talked about him in their room. They liked to imagine what he looked like and what sort of personality he had, whether he had a steady girlfriend and what she was like. They wondered whether he remembered much about his early childhood, or ever thought about them, and if so what he thought. They wondered if he remembered anything they had tried to teach him, whether he had taken an interest in learning about political and economic systems, and what his current views might be. They wondered if the Party's Boarding School System had been the right path for Tom. They knew he was smart and hoped he had been able to get into a good college even though he was a Euro. They hoped there was an exception for someone like Tom whose ancestors had immigrated in the 20th century, and considering that he had been a good kid who was nice to everyone regardless of race, creed, color or anything else.

When Director Stalinsky had worked as the originator, chief proponent and designer for the mass trials and the Alaskan Reserve, he didn't trust the large technology companies to develop the software programs. So he created his own Cyber Command of loyal software experts and data scientists. His ego-driven self-satisfaction reached new highs when he rounded up some technology billionaires. Stalinsky hated the idea that they had so much wealth even if they had made it lawfully. He hated their hypocrisy in expressing support for oppressed people groups instead of donating 99% of their money for redistribution to those groups. He loved his wealth tax system after the Soft Coup which took most of their wealth, whether the billionaires liked it or not, unless they had an exemption. Except for those who had exemptions or fled the country, former high flying billionaire capitalists were now in Camp III doing the hardest time anyone could imagine. Stalinsky was in charge of exemptions and used them strategically.

The Alaskan Reserve had three enormous main camps, each with its own satellite system of hundreds of subcamps. Camp I was the most desirable camp with farming operations and the best and most plentiful food. Camp II had huge forestry operations, which was harder work, and obtained food from Camp I, though it was older and picked over, less varied and less plentiful. Camp III had a huge coal mining operation which was even harder work and nobody knew what they ate or how much they got.

Each camp had administrative buildings, kitchens, laundries, showers, latrines, vehicle repair shops, huge warehouses with all manner of tools, trucks and vehicles, cottages for wardens, officers and senior staffs, comfortable barracks for guards, and many thousands of barracks for inmates with triple high bunk beds, closer together in Camp II, and crammed tightly in Camp III. Some inmate crews were assigned to build more barracks, and they formed teams of diggers, concrete workers, carpenters, drywallers, plumbers, electricians and roofers. Some inmates were rewarded with lighter crew assignments for cooking, cleaning, laundry and other duties. Camp maintenance was light if you got groundskeeping, but road construction and roof replacements were tougher.

The main original purpose of the Alaskan Reserve was to round up and detain everyone who was a serious threat to social justice control, and then sort out those who were totally irredeemable from those who might potentially return to society in the future. In theory, most would have opportunities to redeem themselves by participating in comprehensive reeducation programs, performing farming, forestry or mining labor service, following camp rules, and engaging in other requirements, such as confessing and renouncing racism and capitalist oppression, and signing a loyalty oath.

In the early years, another beneficial purpose of the Alaskan Reserve was to provide protective resettlement for moderate conservative politicians, those who had disagreed with the Party in the past but were generally considered redeemable. They had often suffered from vicious attacks by far left militia groups who had engaged in a terror campaign of vigilante social justice and control, including self-help reparations. Though the protective resettlements were originally announced as temporary, they became permanent over time for reasons that were never provided.

Camp I had some family subcamps with parents and children in the same barracks. There were many more subcamps with barracks only for children and nearby barracks for their parents with various levels of visiting privileges. There were many adjacent subcamps for single males and single females, separated only by a barbed wire fence so they could talk to each other when they had time and weren't too tired. There were even mixed gender subcamps with adjacent barracks for single males and single females. Some males naturally self-identified as females or vice versa.

The more fortunate inmates in Camps I and II were those classed as moderate political conservatives - called CONs for short because CON was stitched above their left shirt pockets. Subject to oversight, CONs could obtain certain administrative positions, such as barracks leaders and work crew managers. They could easily get kitchen duty or vehicle repair work instead of latrines or forest work. In exchange, CONs were expected to inform the guards about any subversive activities. Tom's parents, like other capitalist inmates, tried to be reclassed as CONs. But that never happened because capitalist business owners were considered more creative and entrepreneurial, and therefore more dangerous, than moderate political conservatives.

Resourceful veteran CONs sought jobs in the huge warehouses for all the personal stuff that inmates brought to the camps in suitcases and backpacks. Inmates had to turn over electronic devices because they were not allowed, street clothes because they got shabby prison uniforms, money because they wouldn't need it, and jewelry because it could interfere with work assignments. The warehouse administrators and guards began taking some of the possessions as it became clear that no one would ever be released. With the same rationale, CONs assigned to warehouse work could take stuff if they were careful, though some were caught and reassigned to Camp III.

For their loyalty and diligence, CONs obtained many special benefits and privileges, including better and more ample food with more variety, candy bars and ice cream, alcoholic beverages and weed, weekly access to the library and brothel. The library provided access to restricted internet surfing and a curated set of books, music and movies.

CONs could also earn privileges to communicate with a few family members and friends, but only in writing, and only with delays and censorship to protect the system and the Party from seditious smears and propaganda. No one heard anything negative. Friends and family of those CONs could send modest care packages and they received warm notes of thanks. The Ministry did a good job to create a sense that inmates who did not return either liked the Reserve and wanted to stay or were stubbornly and pridefully resisting their re-education opportunities or were unrepentant lazy slackers on labor service projects. The Ministry was also good in explaining that any inmate communication with family and friends was an earned privilege, and that lack of communication meant the inmate chose to violate the rules.

In the first few months after the Alaskan Reserve began operations, some CONs returned to society from Camp I if they did everything right and passed a lie detector test to ferret out any hidden cynicism. Once released, the theory was that they would never say anything beyond what the public knew or preferred to believe. Those former CONs desperately wanted to avoid being sent back, so it was reasonable to believe they would remain in good standing by praising the Party and the camps for turning them away from their racist and capitalist beliefs. But most of those former CONs eventually disappeared, either by fleeing the country or joining the underground. So further releases were not allowed.

Camp III was the polar opposite of Camp I. Life at Camp III was hardly life at all. Camp III had huddled masses of individuals who were proven, or presumed, to be deplorable and irredeemable, and were therefore classified as Deported Depraved Deplorables, or 3Ds for short. These individuals were so unfit for human society that they were viewed as sub-humans. Racists wore a red "R", capitalists wore a black "C", and political subversives wore a blue "P". Many had all 3 letters. Little was known about Camp III except that no one ever got out, not even for a transfer to Camp II. Inmates of Camps I and II did anything necessary to avoid reassignment to Camp III.

The Camp III inmates barely survived, if they survived at all, in dim light or darkness, in ragged uniforms, on stale bread and thin soup with occasional old vegetables or small pieces or rotten horsemeat, with scurvy and other diseases, mostly doing heavy forced labor or trying to sleep with bed bugs and lice, with three snoring individuals in each bunk, meaning nine in each triple bunk bed, under thin shared blankets in icy cold barracks. They were packed so tight in each bunk that when one wanted to turn over they all had to turn.

The luckiest ones in Camp III worked in the administration and guard kitchens where they took great risks to pilfer some decent food. The next luckiest inmates worked in the inmate kitchens where they made the thin soup and baked the bread, but were not allowed serve it fresh or even slice it. In the early days, the guards made bets on whether inmates would fight over the bread or agree on ways to divide it fairly without fighting. But the inmates cooperated on fair systems of dividing the bread, and developed friendships and helped and supported each other in many ways, and the guards hated them for that, especially as they saw the friendships and support crossing all racial lines. The guards couldn't reconcile the views they were indoctrinated to believe – that Camp III inmates were irredeemable sub-human deplorables – with the evidence that they cared about other people.

The Camp III coal mine operation was massive and also super-secret because it violated the Big Blue Deal and Paris Strange Accord. But the country's grid was out-of-whack due to the unpredictable variations and unreliability of wind and solar. The last thing anyone wanted was to hook up the camp security systems to unreliable power, so they had a massive coal-fired power plant in a central location. Some leaders thought Alaskan oil would have been a better choice, but it was too risky to have a bunch of engineers and redneck types drilling oil. It might get out to the public. Plenty of 3Ds could be trained to work in mines and operate a coal-fired power plant.

Director Stalinsky didn't release public information about the Alaskan Reserve, except to the extent required to generate constant fear of being locked up indefinitely, and a sense that Camp I was best and Camp III was worst in case you had to go there. The camps were blanketed with a sophisticated thicket of electronic jamming systems that even blocked satellite or drone photos of the camps.

As a way of providing some controlled information, once a year, the Alaskan Reserve allowed Amnesty International to access the Trieste Family Subcamp and publish documentaries of the visits. Trieste looked like a back-to-nature style resort. Nice big wood cabins with curtains and regular beds. Pleasant cafeterias and swimming pools. Trails to hike, ponds to fish, and a small zoo with a few animals. School rooms, playgrounds and soccer for kids. An Equality Café and camp band of talented CONs. Amnesty International issued nice reports. Director Stalinsky reviewed and approved the reports first and required a large disclaimer about Trieste Family Subcamp not being representative of other camps. He figured that would keep the masses fearful, and keep the inmates' families hoping for the best and believing what they wanted to believe rather than becoming subversive.

Trieste Family Subcamp was the only place without an electrified barbed wire fence and watch towers with armed guards. Trieste had electronic monitoring of GPS ankle bracelets on the inmates and an invisible electronic fence like regular people with suburban homes have for their dogs. Everyone wanted to get into Trieste and it was a major incentive for good behavior. The Trieste inmates knew they were in the best camp and that they'd end up in Camp III if they tried to escape.

On a larger scale, the whole massive camp system operated with rewards for good conduct and punishments for bad conduct. Everybody in Camp I hoped they might be released some day and wanted to avoid reassignment to Camp II or Camp III. Everybody in Camp II wanted to earn admission to Camp I and avoid reassignment to Camp III. Everyone in any camp or subcamp wanted to get lighter camp work instead of farming or forest work or coal mining and ideally wanted to be reclassed as a CON.

Everyone wanted to avoid being beaten or whipped by guards or attacked by guard dogs. That was less common in Camp I which had professional guards. The guards at Camp II and Camp III were violent career criminals, generally large and brutish, with only basic training, men and women whom Stalinsky's teams actively recruited from federal prisons under work-release programs. Those nasty guards lorded their power over the inmates. Camp III guards treated their 3Ds as infectious pond scum, a view they learned under the continual education programs that Stalinsky's administrators provided.

As Camps I and II relied more on inmate CONs to run their operations over time, a system of unauthorized trading and bribes developed. Inmates who worked in the officers' kitchens started to hide and remove good food, liquor and candy bars in their underwear or in hidden inner pockets or pouches hanging beneath their oversized clothes. There was a risk of searches in the beginning but they were able to bribe low level guards with some of the stuff. They would trade these bounties for anything that someone else had filched somewhere else, fingernail clippers, writing paper, a pencil, a book, a length of rope for suicide. Interestingly, these CON inmates often gave the stolen food away to help inmates who were suffering from malnutrition, diseases or depression.

No one in the public knew how to find out who was in the Alaskan Reserve or how to contact anyone, other than a CON with censored communication privileges. People were afraid to press very hard or ask probing questions because they might be sent next. That had happened a lot in the early days. Sometimes women without young children, having communicated with husbands who were privileged CONs in Camp I, and having obtained advice from broad-minded lawyers, walked into federal police stations with suitcases and confessed to the right level of subversive impulses to provide reasonable hope of joining their loved ones as CONs in Camp I. Once in Camp I, they hoped to obtain assignments to mixed gender barracks with their husbands, whether through luck or for faithful service while following all the rules or after several months of networking and bribes.

Of course, Tom knew very little about the Alaskan Reserve, except that it was probably where he might be able to find his parents.

Chapter Eight

When Tom got up the next morning and walked north toward Izzy's place, he guessed it might be an artist's garret with paintings stacked and strewn about. Two evenings ago, when he'd stopped by at the wrong time without calling first, was a blur. Izzy buzzed him in and he climbed up three flights of wide stairs. She opened her door and they kissed and embraced.

They went through the foyer into a large living room. Tom saw a brick fireplace painted a cream color, a sofa and arm chairs in floral prints, a cherry wood coffee table and end tables, and lighter cherry wood floors. Two large book cases painted a cream color were crammed with books, old music and movie discs, and a serious music system. He saw Izzy's laptop near a banker's lamp on an antique burled walnut desk.

"Izzy, I really like your place. It has a warm feeling. The opposite of my place. How come you don't have any art on the walls?" Tom asked.

"I had some framed prints but took them down as a protest against my experience in Art School. I'll put them back up some day."

Izzy showed Tom a framed photo of her family on her desk. He recognized Izzy, about three years younger, pretty with a friendly smile, in a simple sundress and sandals, holding a straw sun hat down at her side. Her parents were smiling and attractive. Her brother was darker like her dad and wasn't smiling. Tom wondered who took the photo.

Tom asked Izzy how Buddy Lemmon knew her dad. She explained that her dad did legal work for some of the Party leaders' overseas investments. Tom wondered if her dad actually liked the Party but decided not to ask.

Izzy offered water with lemon juice and they walked down a hallway to the kitchen. It was sunny like the living room. The whole unit faced south with views of the park across the street. The kitchen's sage green cabinets had a distressed glaze finish to make them look older and add character.

Izzy opened a cabinet to show products from Equality Foods, which she explained had been a private capitalist company before the Party took it over. Tom sensed she was teasing about his awkward effort to make conversation about the capitalist origins of the Equality Cafes when they met. He couldn't think of anything to say so he was glad when she handed him a glass of lemon water.

"This is refreshing. Thanks," Tom said.

"I'm glad. I want you refreshed for a game I'd like to play."

"What game?" Tom asked.

"You'll find out soon enough."

After they finished the water, Izzy took Tom farther down the hall to show her art studio in the second bedroom. It looked professional, with a large easel, table and chair, and all manner of paints, brushes, rags and other professional art supplies. The easel was turned toward the window and he couldn't see what was on it.

"So can I see some of your own artwork?" Tom asked.

"I never show anything that isn't finished. Unfortunately, I've only finished a few pieces to my satisfaction. I gave those to my parents and my brother Joey. I keep my unfinished stuff in the closet or my storage space and just take out what I want to work on."

Izzy added, "Tom, go back to the living room, and just give me a minute," as she walked further down the hallway in the other direction. Tom guessed the hall led to the bathroom and Izzy's bedroom.

As Izzy returned, she was struggling to carry a narrow wood box with a handle. Tom saw "Horseshoe Game Set" printed on the top.

"It might be fun. Do you mind carrying this to the park across the street?" Izzy asked.

When Tom and Izzy got down to the park and tried throwing horseshoes, they were both bad and got bored quickly. They sat on a bench to watch some kids play on a jungle gym.

"Izzy, can I know some more personal or deeper stuff? Maybe what you were like growing up. Your thoughts and feelings then and now. Stuff like that?" Tom asked.

"I did my homework, brushed my teeth, and did well in school. I never got a traffic ticket or even a parking ticket or a ticket for jaywalking or littering. I don't know how I'd react if I were pulled over. I might be really nervous," Izzy said.

A teenager was slouched in another bench in a corner of the small park under a large maple. He had a baseball cap on backwards, large sunglasses, black tee shirt, long cut-off jeans and sandals. He was smoking a cigarette and projecting an attitude of rebellion as he bobbed his head, apparently in time with music in ear buds, while looking mostly down at his phone. He held a large apple up by his mouth and occasionally took a bite.

Izzy glanced around and continued in a quiet voice, "I think about things I learned from my grandad, Hans, in London and research I did there last summer. This may not be what you wanted to talk about, but I took an interest in learning about the countries that imposed socialism and a one-party political system. They all tried the same idealistic path that has never worked anywhere. Smash the democratic capitalist system and build a utopian paradise controlled by a few masterminds. The Party controls the government which in turn controls everything. You end up with poverty for everyone, except the political class. Free college, but they don't let very many kids in. Yet political class kids always get in. Free health care, but there aren't enough qualified doctors or facilities, so health care is rationed and people die waiting for cancer treatments, except for the political class. I felt like I was reading about this country since the Soft Coup. I can give you some banned audio books on an encrypted thumb drive if you want. Some of them also cover the facts and myths about so-called Scandinavian socialism."

Izzy's list included "Socialism Sucks" by Robert Lawson and Benjamin Powell; "United States of Socialism: Who's Behind It. Why It's Evil. How to Stop It" by Dinesh D'Souza; "American Marxism" by Mark Levin; "The Problem with Socialism" by Thomas DiLorenzo; "You Say You Want a Revolution?: Radical Idealism and Its Tragic Consequences" by Daniel Chirot; "Sweden's Dark Soul: The Unravelling of a Utopia" by Kajsa Norman. She also included, as somewhat relevant, "Debunking Howard Zinn: Exposing the Fake History That Turned a Generation against America" by Mary Grabar.

Tom was concerned about Izzy's risky public statements, even in her quiet voice.

"So Tom, what about you? Can you tell me some deeper stuff?"

"I like working for the Party and I owe loyalty and confidentiality. I won't reply to your views on socialism because I assume you were having fun with facetious college humor."

Izzy looked surprised and hurt, then puzzled and concerned. "Tom, of course I was joking around." She glanced over at the teenager on the other bench.

They walked back to Izzy's place without talking. They were both thinking about what happened. Izzy made more lemon water.

After a few gulps, Tom asked, "So was that your Block Minder on the other bench pretending to be a teenager?"

"Probably."

"You aren't worried that he may have had a high tech listening device to zoom in when you talked about socialism?"

"Crap! I'm always thinking he'll just come over and ask annoying questions. He doesn't seem sophisticated, you know, about listening devices. But now you're making me nervous."

Tom paused for a few moments. "Well, if he has a crush on you like you said, he probably won't turn you in. Anyway, you talked about joking at the end. You'd just spend some time in re-education class this summer. Has he ever caught people for serious stuff?" Tom asked.

"According to Iggy, he caught a lot of subversives for several years after the Soft Coup. People who had to go to Political Jail or even Alaska. He's pretty senior so his Block Minder role doesn't limit him to our neighborhood. He told me that he gets all over Evanston and even picks up some assignments outside Evanston for extra credits. He bragged about scoring huge social credits back in the day and must still be living off them. Now everyone is so careful to stay out of trouble most of the time, I doubt he catches many. He might get some credits now for hanging around and being a deterrent."

They talked more about socialism versus regular welfare systems. Tom said he felt there should always be a government safety net of programs for people who needed help, well-run programs serving underprivileged people in effective ways instead of squandering most of the resources on bureaucrats and crony vendors and the wasteful proliferation of redundant programs. Tom especially favored programs to train people for jobs because he believed most people would feel happier by being part of the workforce.

They heard someone outside yelling through an amplified outdoor speaker. They went over and opened the window and saw that an open back truck had pulled into the park across the street. About a dozen elderly Euros, males and females, were standing up crammed into the open back of the truck. There was a public address speaker on top of the truck's cab.

The speaker blared, "People of the Republic! We are celebrating Euro Confession Day! The Euros standing in this truck have voluntarily signed the collective guilt confession! They have confessed that they can never redeem their racist selves or change their unconscious racist bias or embedded Euro privilege in their genetic DNA code! Under the Republic's benevolence, they will not be harmed or imprisoned! These Euros will be granted ten social credits for their voluntary confessions! They have chosen a spokesperson who will read their collective confession so we may celebrate victory over Euro privilege and systemic institutional racism against oppressed people groups!"

"I just can't watch this. Let's go back to the sofa," Izzy said.

After they closed the window and sat down, Izzy added, "I don't get why they keep doing the shows every month. No one goes down to watch anymore."

"I was standing around after class last year with some Black and Brown friends. They whispered that most Blacks and Browns feel sorry for Euros now. But they don't feel safe speaking up and don't know what they can do about it," Tom noted.

After a long moment, Izzy said, "Gina and her boyfriend want to get together with you and me. Is that okay, and do you want to put together a music playlist?"

"Sounds good. What kind of music?" Tom asked.

"Anything except classical music or hard rock. I should mention that Gina's boyfriend, Angelo Manetti, is my first college boyfriend from when I was in Art School."

"I assume you left him rather than the other way around?" Tom asked.

"Yeah. You are so sweet to say that, Tom."

"By the way, why can't I find you on social media?" Tom asked.

"Oh, I did social media when I was younger, but deleted myself after a bad experience. I still check social media but I don't post stuff."

"I'm sorry to hear about the bad experience. Do you want to talk about it?"

"It's in the past and I'd rather keep it there," Izzy said.

They were silent for several moments.

"Tom, I want to draw you," Izzy said. "I was thinking about your right arm. But I first want to see your torso with both arms in case that would be better."

"Okay. But you won't use a degenerate cubist style, right?" Tom asked with a smirk.

"I could do a very interesting cubist drawing of you."

"All weird and mixed up without much sense of reality? I used to feel like that after my Equality Logic classes. The instructor was a grad student who asked if $2 + 2$ could equal 5. Just theoretically, if the Party decided 5 was needed for equality. Can he really write a PhD dissertation on that?"

"Tom, I know you're joking, but you're getting so cynical. Am I a bad influence?"

"Probably. But it's worth the risk."

"I wouldn't use cubism, but I won't just draw you like a still life bowl of fruit. My style is impressionistic. I go for the essence. Everything else supports the essence."

"Okay," Tom said, wondering what she meant.

Now, take off your shirt." Izzy said.

"You first," Tom replied, smiling.

"No, Tom, I mean it. This is not about whatever you are thinking it's about. This is about artistic expression. Now take off your shirt."

Tom took off his shirt and Izzy said, "The torso is excellent. Well defined pecs. Even six pack abs. Now stand with your arms just hanging down."

"You don't want me to hold up the Party's fist salute?"

"More cynical humor? I may have to turn you in. And then turn in myself since I corrupted you," Izzy said.

"No doubt about it. We are becoming dangerous cynics."

"I just decided something. Sit down on that chair," Izzy said.

Tom sat on the chair and Izzy said, "Now, bend over maybe halfway so you can rest your right elbow on your right knee. Okay, now with your right elbow resting on our right knee, bend your right elbow up so your right forearm goes up and your right hand is under your chin. That's good, now rest your chin on the top of your right hand with your fingers sort of curled back and pointing down toward your chest."

"You think this shows off my arm muscles? Maybe if I flex my bicep like this?" Tom asked in a serious tone while flexing.

"No, no. I changed the whole concept. Now, let your left arm fall down so the left wrist rests on your left knee. I want your left arm sort of resting across your left knee and hanging down a bit in a natural relaxed way." She was smiling.

"This is a famous pose, right? The Thinker?"

"Yes, by Rodin. You have nice muscles and a knowledge of sculpture too? Where did you learn about The Thinker?" Izzy asked.

"I have hidden depths you have no idea about."

"The Thinker never has clothes on. It has to do with getting to the human essence. So take off everything else," Izzy said.

"Do you have an ulterior motive?"

"Tom, this is only about art. If you think anything else, you'll be disappointed. But I changed my mind again. Since you're an amateur model, you can keep your undershorts on. Your left arm and hand will cover that area anyway and I can use my imagination for your butt."

Izzy explained that her Art School classes had used nude figure models, males and females, and it was no big deal. Tom asked if Izzy ever modeled for the class and she said there was no way she'd do that. She said she was too private and modest. Tom was glad to hear that. He didn't like the idea of a whole classroom looking at Izzy in the nude, no matter how aesthetically artistic that would probably be.

Izzy said the models were usually college kids in liberal arts who needed extra money or social credits, though some exhibitionist art students modelled for free. Izzy's teacher had pressed her hard to volunteer and said he'd give her an A+. He apparently had a thing for Izzy and even said he could fly her to an exotic private island for a weekend party. But Izzy didn't want to model nude in the class or go to an island with a creep. She left Art School after he gave her a bad grade.

Izzy put on a smock which had evidently been used a lot based on the assorted smudges and smears. The smock itself could have passed for abstract art.

She came back closer to Tom and said, "I'm sorry but this just isn't working for me so I changed my mind again. I want to draw "The Thinker" wearing jeans. It will be one of a kind. Do you mind putting your jeans back on?"

Tom put his jeans back on and sat and posed while Izzy worked for hours with only a few breaks to stretch and drink water. She was fast but also a perfectionist, changing quickly between a variety of professional-looking charcoal pencils and compressed charcoal sticks, various erasers, paper cones and rags and other smudging and blending devices and materials. She used her fingers or thumbs from time to time.

After a couple of hours, Izzy took a deep breath and exhaled. She put a sheet over the drawing and they carried the easel to the living room. Tom was eager to see the drawing, but it wasn't about seeing himself in a picture. It was about seeing how Izzy saw him and whether Tom liked her art.

After Tom sat on the sofa, Izzy walked calmly to the easel, stood still for a moment, then removed the sheet with a flourish. Tom saw right away that she had a lot of talent for an impressionistic style. Tom couldn't recognize himself in any specific way. But he saw his essence. Not surface happiness. His deeper essence. Tom saw himself pensive and concerned about his parents.

Then Tom saw what Izzy had drawn in small block letters beneath the drawing. "WHAT WILL THE PARTY DO NEXT?"

Tom couldn't help laughing and Izzy joined.

"Would you like to have the drawing?" Izzy asked.

"Sure, if you don't mind giving it up. Could you sign it and also change the wording to "I" instead of "THE PARTY?""

"Okay. I'll do that tomorrow and roll it up in something you can carry it in."

After a pause, Izzy asked, "So, why did you become so cynical?"

"Do I seem very cynical?" Tom asked.

"I've picked up things. You say stuff and then wink. You never say anything good about the Party. You were funny when you talked about art and equality. When you were posing for the drawing, you made a joke about the fist salute. And you laughed at what I wrote under my drawing."

"Okay, but you'll keep this between us, right?" Tom asked.

"Sure."

"So, I began to have cynical views when I got to be close friends with a group of smart kids at Petosky. Then it was a lot of things over time. During my first year at college, I did anonymized research in overseas libraries. I read a lot about different political - economic systems. You know, socialism vs free enterprise. I read about Marxist theories and the Russian revolution. Lenin, Trotsky and Stalin. I found books, podcasts and streaming video interviews by conservatives from before the Soft Coup or from later after they fled to the remaining democracies. Mark Levin comes to mind, a show called "Life, Liberty and Levin." There were other commentators like Tucker Carlson, Maria Bartiromo, Sean Hannity and Steve Hilton on something called Fox. Also Charlie Kirk with Turning Point USA (tpusa.com). And Rob Schmitt and others on something called Newsmax. Sometimes they talked fast and came across as overly passionate or even angry, but they seemed very smart, knowledgeable and credible. I also found an interesting site called #WalkAway Campaign founded by a gay man named Brandon Straka who used to be on the left. There were other old banned sites with a lot of information or resources, Prager University (PragerU.com); Foundation for Economic Education (fee.org); The Leadership Institute (leadershipinstitute.org); Young Americans for Freedom (yaf.org); Foundation for Individual Rights in Education (thefire.org); Blaze Media (theblaze.com); Young Americans for Liberty (yaliberty.org); Legal Insurrection (legalinsurrection.com); Foundation Against Intolerance and Racism (FAIR) (fairforall.org); and Campus Reform (campusreform.org)."

Tom paused for a few moments to collect his thoughts. "At last summer's Youth Brigades, the political speeches and patriotic campfire songs were starting to annoy me. I had learned that the top 1% of income earners already paid 33% of federal taxes before the Soft Coup. The top 10% was already paying about 70%. After the Soft Coup when it became clear there would be far higher taxes, the economy tanked quickly because most of the top 1% and a lot of the top 10% left the country. People lost jobs as companies closed, and most people who had jobs became poorer as their employers struggled with less successful businesses. Meantime, tying in with what you said earlier, the Party officials and their cronies have big fancy homes in gated enclaves with private security forces. They drive big new luxury cars and SUVs. They belong to fancy private clubs, fly in airplanes, and go on fancy vacations."

"I always felt that sucked," said Izzy. She thought for a moment and then said, "But, there's so much conflicting stuff online. How do you know you aren't reading rumors and conspiracy theories?"

"I don't automatically believe anything I see online. Or on the news or social media either of course. I look for sources that seem objective and reliable. I've looked at so many sources over time that I have a pretty good sense for honest journalist and fair commentary vs agenda-driven curated narratives. It's best when you see video along with audio so you can assess credibility with visual metadata the way a jury evaluates witnesses, taking into account shifty eyes, a crooked smile, a nervous twitch or wringing hands, body language that expresses openness or hiding something, a defensive or arrogant expression in response to an innocent question, a tendency to speak in vacuous platitudes or to demagogue points, to attack and demean people with other views rather than debate the merits of their views. None of that stuff is conclusive but it helps an overall assessment of credibility. If you listen carefully and analyze the statements along with the video, some speakers seem consistent, honest and objective, while others seem full of crap. It also helps to know history so you can put things in perspective and better gauge whether someone is spinning or lacks knowledge or insights."

Izzy said quietly, "Since you don't seem to like the Party very much, I don't get why you try so hard to be a rising star."

"I have my reasons."

"Such as?" Izzy asked.

"Partly what I said about social credits and a safe job. Partly based on a personal thing. Remember, I said I'd tell you more when I got to know you better."

"Don't you know me well enough so far?" Izzy asked.

"Probably. But I want to think about it," Tom said.

"Have you ever thought about joining the underground?" Izzy asked.

"I guess a lot of people have those thoughts in private moments."

Tom had to take off so they confirmed their plans for the evening. They kissed and hugged before they said goodbye.

Tom went back to his apartment to prepare for another video call with Party Chairman Buddy Lemmon. Tom had spent all his free time on the analysis of realigning away from China and toward Russia. He had read the complete dossier and done some research, but now he tried to think at a strategic level. He took a break for a PB&J sandwich and then spent a few hours reviewing his list of pros and cons and analysis that he had already submitted online.

After Tom was connected, Buddy said they could skip the Party's fist salute in calls that were just between them. Tom smiled as he realized that Buddy was viewing him as an insider.

Buddy said, "Tom, I really liked your pros and cons and analysis. It was refreshing to see how you thought it all through independently and reached good conclusions. I don't know how you developed such a good grounding in international politics, economics and trade, but I don't mind if you read banned materials, assuming I can rely on your loyalty."

"I would never support Stalinsky in case that's what you're thinking."

"Bingo. Now in your analysis, you said you have one point that you prefer to discuss in real time. Okay, let's have it."

"Buddy, this is way out of the box. What about adding India to the new alignment with Russia? India has nukes and a decent military and has done well with technology and industry so adding India would make the new alliance stronger. India has had good relations with Russia at various times. India might like to join the alliance to balance China's dominance. Also, by adding India, we won't seem like anti-Asian racists when we abrogate the China treaties."

There was silence for nearly thirty seconds. Tom would have thought the call was interrupted if he hadn't heard Buddy's heavy breathing.

Buddy said, "It's an interesting idea, but I need to tell you about a separate initiative that has some relevance. Director Stalinsky has always wanted to shift Asians from the oppressed to the oppressor category because Asians are successful in general and it messes up equality statistics. The results look like the oppressed groups are doing better than they are. I've always resisted any re-class of our Asian community that would reduce their social credits, but only because of our relationship with China. Now with our proposed realignment away from China and toward Russia, I was planning to go along with Stalinsky to shift our Asian community out of the oppressed groups. But we have a lot of East Indians in our Asian community. So how can we add India to the new alliance and still re-class our Asian community so they get fewer social credits? Won't India take that as a slap in the face and mess up the new alliance?"

Tom thought for several moments. "I see two ways to go. You could do the Asian re-classification and exempt East Indians. But you'd need a reason for the exemption, and that might come across as an insult to East Indians - as though they still need more social credits because they are not as successful as other Asians, which obviously isn't even true. So, the other way is to keep India with the Asian community and make the whole Asian shift into a positive thing. Like, "congratulations to our Asian community for your excellent focus on education, close families, hard work, and success in rising out of the oppressed classes." You could also make the re-class less controversial by updating the term "oppressor" to something like "advantaged" and the term "oppressed" to something like "disadvantaged." I mean, any remaining unconscious bias isn't the same as intentional oppression, right?"

Buddy was silent for several moments and Tom heard his heavy breathing. "Tom, I appreciate your input. Stalinsky hates any messaging that suggests an oppressed class can succeed by working hard and lifting itself up because he says it's a denial of systemic institutional racism. But we've already set the stage for the Asian re-class to happen, and I can win over the Central Committee on messaging and changing the terminology. I like your ideas. You'll find 10,000 extra social credits in your account."

After a long moment, Buddy said, "You know, I'm getting tired of running this frigging country and dealing with Stalinsky. I've been having a series of video calls with Boris about the new alliance, and I think he's getting tired of running Russia. We don't say it directly, but we commiserate about the challenges of running a country with so much centralized control from the top down. You know, not enough food and too many shoes in one year and the opposite the next year. Or twice as many left shoes as right shoes. I've done a lot of my own research recently. History shows you can't run an economy with centralized planning and controls, subsidizing and picking winners and losers with taxes and nationalization schemes. You can't succeed without individual and business incentives as a way to be productive and efficient or without the freedom to innovate and compete to satisfy market demands."

After a pause, Buddy added, "That's all confidential, obviously. Tom, I'd like you to come over for dinner sometime. Buddy Junior is almost always on the island. I think you'd enjoy meeting my wife, Beatriz. This is short notice, but do you have plans for this evening?"

"Buddy, I'd really enjoy that sometime. But I have plans with my girlfriend tonight."

"Okay, Tom, I understand. Have a good time."

Tom was jazzed up after the call and wondered what he could do with the extra social credits. He thought about getting something nice for Izzy. The problem was that there was less and less nice stuff to buy unless you were willing to risk getting caught up in a smuggling charge. He hoped Buddy might provide access to one of the restricted stores or sites with high end stuff for the Party elite.

Tom saw that Izzy had sent a text asking what he was going to wear that evening for the visit with Gina and Angelo. Instead of a direct answer, he replied as a question, asking if clean indigo jeans, a beige oxford button shirt and brown slip-on shoes would be okay. She said that sounded perfect with an exclamation point. He figured he scored a few points with the question-dialogue idea. But he was actually happier that he was improving his gender relationship skills. Tom thought of an old phrase, "Vive la différence." He guessed you could be fired and kicked off social media for using that phrase now.

Tom felt weary and put his elbows on the table with his forearms raised up, and brought his forehead down to rest against the palms of his hands. His mind brought up an image of his parents doing hard labor in Alaska, and then the image switched to "The Scream," the iconic expressionist painting by Edvard Munch symbolizing the anxiety of the human condition. He went to his bedroom, kicked his shoes off, lay down and slept for about an hour.

Chapter Nine

After Tom woke from his nap, he hastily changed clothes and freshened up. He drove north to pick up Izzy and then they drove back south to Gina's building. Gina buzzed them in and they found her apartment easily since the door was open and she was standing in the hallway. Tom laughed as a realized that Izzy and Gina, as a joke about socialist groupthink, had dressed and fixed themselves up exactly the same way from head to toe.

Gina introduced Tom to Angelo Manetti and explained that Angelo had come from Florence Italy a few years ago and was Izzy's boyfriend back in Art School. Angelo was short but his head was larger and resembled the head on the Statue of David in the Florence museum, including thick curly hair, broad face and prominent brow, large sad eyes and strong nose, rosebud mouth and narrower chin above a thick strong neck.

Gina and Tom talked enthusiastically. They both felt like they already knew each other from everything Izzy had said about them. Tom gave Gina his phone with a music playlist that she connected with her music system. The first album was "Lady Sings the Blues" with Diana Ross from the 1970s. When Gina said she liked the music, Tom said a little about Diana Ross and Billy Holiday, and how Diana Ross had portrayed Billy Holiday in a movie.

Gina wanted to know more about blues music and Tom got into a long monologue and began to vent. Tom explained how some Euro musicians used to play blues music but stopped after a prominent Euro band was beat up in Portland by a group of far left militants with baseball bats who accused them of cultural appropriation of Black people's music. All of the militants happened to be Euros themselves, mostly with four year college degrees. A group of Blacks was sitting at the front of the audience enjoying the music and came to the defense of the band. The far left militia guys said the Euro band was a minstrel show and called the Black guys Uncle Toms. The Blacks rushed the far left militia guys who then ran away. By stepping in when they did, the Black guys probably saved the drummer's life.

Tom saw Angelo and Gina smile when James Taylor's "Sweet Baby James" album began playing. Tom smiled as he remembered that the next albums were Linda Ronstadt, Paul Simon, and then the album "Carolina In My Mind" by Allison Krauss with Jerry Douglas.

After the first James Taylor track ended, Gina asked Izzy to help in the kitchen. But when they got to the kitchen, Gina asked quietly, "Do you want to test Tom like we did in high school? You know, I flirt and see if he stays true to you? If he passes, that's good. If he fails, you don't want him anyhow."

Izzy thought for several moments. "Aren't we supposed to be more mature now that we're twenty-one?"

"It just seems like a good idea to me," Gina said.

"With Angelo here?" Izzy asked.

"I can show Tom my drawings in the other room. You and Angelo already saw them," Gina said.

"Gina, is there something else going on? You never suggested the love test when I was seeing Angelo. Now all of a sudden you want a love test with Tom. Do you have an ego thing going on? Like maybe you want a challenge of getting such a nice looking guy to go for you?"

"Izzy, I'm so hurt. I'm only thinking about you. A lot of pretty women will go after him when he starts working in downtown Chicago. You gotta know if he's a player."

"Maybe we should wait a week so he knows me better," Izzy said.

"It's up to you, but I don't think guys change. Better find out if he's a dog now before you fall farther for this guy," Gina said.

"You'd only flirt, right? You can't make the first move for a kiss or a touch," Izzy said.

"Yeah, that's our rule. Do you want to make it more interesting like for a hundred bucks?"

"No, Gina, I don't want to take your money. I'm 99% sure he'll pass the test," Izzy said.

"How 'bout a thousand? That's still not much for you or me."

"Gina, we're talking about my life and you want to bet money? Is this another Sicilian thing? I can't believe you sometimes."

"Izzy, no one's forcing you. Either you want to find out or you don't."

Izzy nodded and said, "Okay, I'm sure he'll pass, but if not, then I'm done."

"If he goes for me, can I keep him?" Gina asked.

"No way! If Tom blows it, we throw him back to the sea. You got Angelo now anyway. Gina, you are a real piece of work, you know that?"

They both broke out laughing. Izzy felt a bit nervous about the test but didn't show it.

Gina and Izzy came back and Gina asked Tom if he'd like to see some of her drawings that Izzy and Angelo had already seen. He wasn't very interested but said okay after Izzy urged him to take a look. Gina led Tom down a hall to her bedroom.

Gina's bedroom was dimmed somewhat by the soft light of a small table lamp. On one wall were two original charcoal drawings of male nudes in a realism style. The drawings were good and showed talent. Tom was looking at the drawings overall but then the faces caught his eye. He realized it was the same model from two different views - front and side. Then Tom realized the model was Angelo and felt embarrassed and looked away.

Gina asked Tom to come closer so he could see her signature. Tom leaned over her shoulder. He liked her fragrance but couldn't tell what it was. Maybe jasmine.

Gina turned and tilted her head back toward Tom and said, "Tom, you're a really good looking guy. Does Izzy ever tell you that?"

"No she doesn't say that sort of thing," Tom said.

Gina turned around so she was fully facing Tom and said, "You're also such a nice guy. Does Izzy really appreciate you?"

"Yeah, I guess so ... I hope so," Tom said.

"But do you think tonight was a fix-up for us to meet?"

"I wondered. I messed up a date with Izzy the other night after I had a hard drink. Did she say anything?" Tom asked.

Gina moved even closer and said, "No, but she sometimes lets things develop naturally. Did you notice how she encouraged you to come here to my bedroom with me?"

Tom remained silent. He didn't want to be dumped and left alone. He thought of an old song lyric, "if you can't be with the one you love, then love the one you're with."

"Tom, I'm really attracted to you. Do you feel anything about me?" Even in the dimmed light, he could see that Gina's eyes were sympathetic and encouraging.

"You seem nice and fun. You're attractive, Gina."

"Izzy said you aren't sleeping together yet. What does that mean? I would have already been sleeping with you. Is she not really into you?" Gina had moved even closer.

Tom replied quietly, "I, uh, think she probably just wanted to go slower."

Gina moved even closer, nearly touching, her fragrance stronger. She parted her lips somewhat while looking softly into Tom's eyes. She tilted her face up and closed her eyes. Tom noticed her long lashes and then saw that they were store-bought. He gently placed his hands on her shoulders to hold her still while he took a short step back and said quietly, "Gina, I'm really flattered that you seem to like me and everything, and if I were unattached who knows, but I'm really into Izzy. I really don't want to blow it."

Gina started to laugh and Tom looked confused. She explained the love test and said congratulations. He said thanks but didn't join in her laughter. She said he should lighten up because Izzy would be happy about the results.

Tom recovered his composure as they went back to the living room but remained standing and put his hands in the pockets of his jeans. Gina went over and whispered in Izzy's ear. Izzy came over and gave Tom a warm kiss and tight hug but Tom wasn't very responsive. Tom slumped down in a corner of the sofa and didn't say much. When the pizzas arrived and Gina was paying, Izzy sat next to Tom and quietly asked if anything was wrong. He smiled briefly and said he was fine but remained quiet.

As they were eating the pizza, they heard heavy pounding on the door and a barked command, "This is the Political Police. You must open the door immediately or we will shoot the lock off."

Gina rushed over and opened the door. Two males and two females stood in black uniforms and helmets with large guns drawn.

"Line up against that wall and show us your IDs. If females need to get IDs from purses, we will allow that," the younger male officer barked.

The two female officers monitored Gina and Izzy as they opened their purses and came back to stand by the wall with their IDs. Tom and Angelo stood by the wall and fished their IDs from their wallets. The officers checked the IDs, ran the information through a data base, examined the group with a facial recognition program tied to a data base, and patted them down.

"Turn around facing the wall with hands behind backs," the younger male officer barked. The two female officers cuffed the group and then went to search the apartment.

The young male officer barked, "Now you will turn around to face us and inform us of what you have to confess and what you have to report. It is your duty to the Republic!"

The group turned around to face the officers but remained silent.

The tall senior male officer said in a stern tone, "It will go better if you come clean now. We have methods to find out sooner or later."

"I didn't watch the Equality News channel today," Gina said.

"Me too, I forgot to watch that news channel," Angelo said.

"Wise guys. You will be laughing all of your way to interrogation rooms," the senior officer shouted.

"Officer, they're harmless college kids," Tom said. "As a member of the Party, would I hang out with subversives? Buddy Lemmon will vouch for me if you call him."

The younger male officer, thick and brutish, apparently an enforcer, slapped Tom hard across his face, then made a hard back hand slap across the other side of Tom's face. Tom staggered but kept his balance.

The officer screamed at Tom from inches away, "You are a lying pig! You don't know Lemmon! We are not going to look foolish by making your prank call!"

The officer then punched Tom hard in the gut and Tom doubled over, the wind knocked out of him, gasping for breath. The officer screamed, "And it would go worse for you if you did know Lemmon! We work for Director Stalinsky, you stupid college punk!"

Tom's face was stinging as he tried to stand back up straight. He was unsteady but managed to say, "Officer, I have a job lined up at Director Stalinsky's Bureau of Truth. I am scheduled to start on Monday. The BOT vetted me."

The room was silent while the enforcer checked his device for Tom's job data and then said, "Okay, sorry for being rough. It's my job and my orders. You are not to play childish games about knowing Comrade Lemmon. We will now finish the searching of this unit."

The senior male officer shouted to the two female officers searching the kitchen that they should reduce the search to Light Level One.

"Is it okay if we continue our harmless conversations?" Tom asked.

"Okay, since you're in the Party," the senior officer said. "You may talk among yourselves, but you will be wise to remember that we are listening."

While the two male officers stood guard and the two female officers continued their light search, Angelo began talking about growing up in Florence. Tom figured that Angelo was the type of person who talked more when he was nervous. He had a classic Italian accent and good sense of humor, including self-deprecating jokes about his short stature and large head.

Tom understood most of what Angelo said, and enjoyed his humor, but found it harder to stay interested in the details. The history of art in Florence. His parents and brothers, his aunts and uncles, his cousins, nephews and nieces. He obviously cared a great deal about his relatives. By the time Angelo worked his way up to Art School, he became aware that he had talked too much and said he was very sorry in his Italian accent with sad brown eyes.

The two female cops came back and said the unit was clean and then uncuffed the group.

"So was there any particular reason for this search? Maybe a false report?" Tom asked the senior officer.

"I will now inform you this was a random routine search. You are free to carry on here," the senior officer replied.

The officers gave the Party's fist salute, so Tom and others reluctantly gave the same salute. The last officer slammed the door.

Izzy rushed over to Tom to check his face and ask if he was okay. His face was still raw but she didn't see blood. He said he'd been through worse. They held each other for a while.

Angelo was now visibly upset and shaking. "What the hell was that?" he asked.

"Those random checks don't necessarily expect to find stuff. It's intimidation and deterrence," Tom said.

"But we didn't have this in Italy. This is like the old USSR or East Germany. I mean what the hell? I might go back to Florence," Angelo said.

"I am so tired of the fricken fist salute. I almost gave them the finger," Gina said.

Tom and Izzy slumped down on the sofa, while Gina and Angelo slumped in the chairs. They began sipping their wine while listening to the last Paul Simon song.

"They'll leave this apartment alone for years now, unless they have probable cause. They've had major budget cuts," Tom said.

"Why do they talk like cheap knock-offs of Nazi officers from old movies?" Izzy asked.

"Stalinsky has a training program. For intimidation," Tom said.

"But the regular police are so professional. I heard about the Political Police but didn't think it would happen to me," Angelo said.

Gina went to her bedroom and came back with an unmarked box and asked if anyone wanted to play an illegal game that the cops' search had missed. Gina explained that her family had saved an old Monopoly Game. Most people threw empty Monopoly boxes into the anti-capitalism bonfires and kept the boards and pieces in other boxes. Monopoly had been banned for over ten years and there were probably as many games as ever.

For the most part, the group did not pay much attention to Tom's music playlist. They were concentrating on Monopoly and Gina was concentrating even harder than the others. But even Gina noticed when the music changed to an album called "Unforgettable" in which Natalie Cole added her voice to sing duets with earlier recordings by her dad, Nat King Cole. Tom saw Gina smiling with her eyes closed between her turns at the game. She was swaying to the music slightly and seemed sensual. He felt attracted and alienated at the same time. He wondered for a moment what it might have been like to be with her.

"Does it seem surreal that people hang out, get into relationships, and carry on their daily lives, all under the boot of the police state?" Izzy asked.

"Surreal is a good word," Tom replied.

"It's a crappy way to live," Gina added.

"Do you think the underground will ever change things?" Izzy asked. She wondered how Tom might respond.

"Maybe in fifty years," Angelo said.

"Maybe sooner," Gina replied.

They were silent for several minutes while they took turns at Monopoly.

"Did you hear about the Black family that was caught hiding a Euro family in the Hyde Park area?" Tom asked.

"Yeah," Angelo said. "The families had lived in the same neighborhood and were close friends for thirty years. But the Euro parents were on a list of racist deplorables scheduled for transport to Alaska. The Black family and other long-time friends who were Black, Brown, Mixed and Asian went to bat for the Euro family. But the Political Police were pissed off that anyone of color stood up for the Euros, so they just changed the charge from racists to fascists.

"Yeah, the Euro parents had made a campaign contribution to the old conservative party before the Soft Coup. Their Block Minder found out somehow," Tom said.

"The Black family knew the Euro family really well and thought the fascist charge was crap, so they hid them in a secret room behind a fake wall in the attic. But their Block Minder heard the Black family was buying extra food rations on the underground market, which suggested that they were hiding people. So there was a raid and they were all caught," Angelo said.

"That's only what the news said. I heard both families got away in the nick of time after the underground got a tip about the raid. They got them to a safe house and then out to one of the underground family camps in the forest in another state," Gina said.

Over 1,500,000 innocent people, rather than surrender for transport to the Alaskan Reserve, were living in a variety of secret camps in forests. They had been smeared in the Righteous Purge as fascist racist conservative deplorables. They actually included people of all races and merely supported the old Constitutional freedoms like free speech, religion and peaceful assembly, the right to own property, the right to bear arms, representative government with meaningful voting integrity systems, judicially approved search warrants, and the right to be tried by a jury of peers and with a qualified defense lawyer. The camps were self-governed and selected their own leaders. They generally had underground bunkers and camouflaged entrances. The refugees frequently moved and rebuilt the camps to avoid detection. They cooked only at night when campfire smoke would be less visible. Some large family camps had up to 1,500 men, women and children, as well as horses, cows and other farm animals. In large camps, the adults set up shops and services based on their skills and backgrounds. All camps with children emphasized their education with banned books the parents brought along. Each camp had underground fighters to serve as warning sentries and help protect the refugees from raids by the Political Police and marauding far left vigilante militias. The underground fighters also helped procure food from sympathetic farmers and raided local police stations to obtain guns and ammunition.

"You don't hear much about hidden Euros these days. I wonder how many there are," Tom said.

"More than you'd think. But it's not much of a life, and they get so little food and are always in fear. Some turn themselves in for transport to Alaska, either because they can't take it anymore, or they feel bad about the risks they create for the people who help them, especially in urban areas," Gina said.

Gina eventually won Monopoly after buying more and more properties and putting up numerous apartment buildings and hotels. Angelo poured more wine and they listened to the last three tunes on Tom's playlist featuring Miles Davis on trumpet with his jazz group, including George Coleman on tenor sax, playing "I Thought of You," "All Blues," and "Stella by Starlight."

Tom was quiet as he drove Izzy back to her place. Izzy said she was really sorry if the Gina love test upset him. Tom said he felt embarrassed like the subject of a practical joke. He added that he was glad he passed, but then remained quiet.

He pulled the car into a space near Izzy's building and said he was tired. Izzy asked if there was still something wrong. Tom said he understood the idea of the test to see if he'd be faithful, but confided that he was actually upset because, for a moment, he felt tempted and came close to kissing Gina and losing Izzy. He explained that Gina was very good at doing the test.

"Tom, part of being good means a person is tempted but resists. Anyway, Gina said you might be a player or a dog and that I might get hurt," Izzy said. "I was 99% sure you'd pass and now the 1% doubt is gone. I was taking a chance too, since I would have been really upset if you went for Gina. Tom, I really want to keep seeing you."

They were sitting in the car and Tom was facing forward while Izzy was facing him. Tom glanced at Izzy and smiled briefly but didn't say anything. He got out of the car and came around to Izzy's side and opened her door. She got out slowly and stood up facing Tom. After an awkward moment, they embraced as tightly as two people can embrace and then began to kiss.

But they were still tired from the visit with Gina and Angelo and raid by the Political Police. Tom walked Izzy to the door of her building and they kissed again and agreed to meet at the gym the next morning.

When Tom went to bed, he wondered how similar the Political Police and Block Minders were to the Nazi SS and Gestapo or the Soviet KBG. He thought about his parents in the Alaskan Reserve but didn't believe it could be like the Nazi death camps with gas chambers. Yet he worried that the Alaskan Reserve could be like the brutal Nazi forced labor camps where so many people perished over longer periods or like Stalin's Soviet Russian gulag camps in Siberia which were apparently somewhat similar.

Tom couldn't fall asleep and his mind drifted back to his time in the Party's Boarding School System, in particular his high school years at Petosky Academy. Tom had been in puppy love with a girl named

Leah. She taught Israeli folk dances when the group had an illicit internet music device. Late on clear nights with light from the moon or stars, the group would dress in dark clothes and slip out the same window that Tom's best friend Noah Greene used when he snuck out to meet his parents. The group would leave at the rate of one kid every minute and gather in a clearing in a wooded area.

Tom had learned about the Holocaust from Noah, but he learned more from Leah, whose ancestors were Jews in Poland and Hungary. Most of her Polish ancestors were murdered in Operation Reinhard but others perished from untreated diseases and starvation food allotments in Nazi slave labor camps. Some of her Polish ancestors were murdered earlier during the Nazi occupation. They were marched out of the towns and into fields where they were shot while kneeling or standing naked next to open trenches and pits that would serve as mass graves. They were forced to undress first so the Nazis could confiscate their clothes and jewelry. In Hungary, Leah's ancestors were transported to their deaths in the last year of the war when German defeat was easy to foresee but true believers in the master race theory kept pressing for a judenrein post-war continent. A few of Leah's ancestors survived by fleeing to the forests where they managed to join Jewish partisans.

Leah had also told Tom her family accounts of a great uncle who fought in the Warsaw Ghetto Uprising. The Jews who still remained in the Ghetto at that point, after all the prior mass deportations to Nazi death camps, had little hope of survival but wanted to make a statement for Jewish honor. They dug and built hidden bunkers and smuggled weapons and explosives into the Ghetto. They ambushed German patrols with riffles and destroyed their vehicles with Molotov cocktails. The Germans were shocked and afraid. The livid Nazi commander ordered a mission to burn the ghetto, block by block and kill anyone who didn't immediately surrender for transport to Treblinka where most would be gassed to death. About 13,000 Jews died in the ghetto, about half of them burned alive or suffocated, but it took the Germans almost a month. Near the end, some starving Jews made their way out of the walled ghetto in rags through the complex system of smelly infectious sewage pipes. Many were caught as they emerged and taken to Treblinka to be gassed but some got away and passed as gentiles as they tried to reach the forest to find partisans. Leah's great uncle was sent to the Treblinka Death Camp where he was among the lucky few selected for slave labor in the camp operations. He participated in the 1943 Treblinka revolt and escaped to the forest.

Leah's Hungarian ancestors had been rounded up in Budapest and were told they would be resettled in Poland for their own protection from anti-Semitism. Each person was restricted to two pieces of luggage, so they wore as many layers of clothes as they could fit on. Their luggage went in one freight train car while the people were crammed into cattle train cars so tightly that most had to stand while a few took turns sitting. There were no bathrooms so they had to use a bucket when they needed to relieve themselves. There was one small window covered with barbed wire and many people fainted from the stuffy smelly air. They were not given any food and they only got water once on the five day trip to Auschwitz. Many on the train arrived at Auschwitz already dead. Except for one sixteen year old girl, all of Leah's Hungarian ancestors perished in Auschwitz or the later Death Marches toward camps further west as the Russians moved closer. The sixteen year old was Leah's great aunt who had written a personal memoire in 1947 and gave a recorded video of her experiences for the USC Shoah Foundation. She had also told Leah what happened a few months before passing away following Leah's Bat Mitzvah.

Tom had wept when he heard Leah's accounts of her ancestors in the Holocaust. He was still deeply moved whenever he thought about Leah's accounts or his own readings or what he had learned earlier from Noah Greene. Tom had read over 50 survivor accounts beginning with "If This Is a Man," by Primo Levi.

Chapter Ten

Tom and Izzy met at the gym the next morning as planned. When Izzy was doing her second turn around the track, she noticed a young woman running beside her. Each time Izzy tried to burst ahead, the woman kept up. When Izzy finished her third turn, she slowed down and got off and the woman followed her.

The young woman smiled and introduced herself as Ashley Bennington, gave her personal pronoun preferences, and said she was a Euro but was in the Equality Party. Ashley had a serious manner and plain yet unobjectionable features. Izzy introduced herself and said she was Mixed. She didn't like to burden people with her personal pronoun preferences and nobody had made a mistake so far.

"I saw you come in with Tom Hardy. Are you going out with Tommy?" Ashley asked.

"Yeah, we're going out. Why do you ask?"

"Tommy and I went out for a while. We haven't been in touch and I hoped he met someone," Ashley said.

"Yeah, he met me."

Izzy wondered how Ashley would look with makeup, but then decided she probably never bothered.

"It was just one of those things. I wanted to go to DC, and Tommy just wanted to hang around Chicago. Can I give you a word of advice?" Ashley asked.

"Okay."

Ashley lowered her voice and said, "Despite his reputation as a rising star in the Party, I never felt that Tommy was very deeply committed."

"Wow. I'm so glad you told me! I've been wondering myself," Izzy said in a serious tone with a serious look.

Ashley said it was nice to run into each other, and then laughed about her pun. As they said goodbye, Ashley said to give her best to Tommy.

Izzy walked over to Tom, who was resting by the weights and said, "Hi Tommy, guess who I just met?"

"My old girlfriend. I saw you talking."

"She doesn't seem like your type," Izzy said.

"You got that right," Tom replied.

As they left the gym, Izzy and Tom kissed and said they looked forward to getting together that evening. During the day, Izzy had to drive down to Hyde Park for another visit with her parents.

After Izzy got back from her visit to Hyde Park, where she had made a thumb drive exchange with her dad, she went to the basement of her building to do her laundry.

Iggy the Block Minder caught up with her in the laundry room. He tossed his dirties in a machine, added soap, and watched intently as the machine started up.

Izzy was always careful to get along with Iggy and even flatter him sometimes. You always wanted to be nice to Block Minders.

Iggy glanced at Izzy, said "Hey," and took a seat next to her, even though there were several other choices because no one else was there.

In his whiney nasal voice, Iggy said, "So, I noticed you're going out with a good looking guy. I'd never use the term myself, but some people might call him a "pretty boy." Sometimes they turn out to be Gay. Sometimes they don't come out until later after they're married and have children."

"Oh, I'm not sure that happens anymore. Have you been watching those movies from the 1970s and 1980s again?"

"So you feel good about this guy not being Gay? I mean, nothing against Gays, but it wouldn't work for you, right?" Iggy asked.

"Well, so far he seems to be hetero in my opinion, but how could I say for sure if we might not find out until later?"

"That's my point. He seems like a pretty boy to me. You might be better off with a guy like me, for example," Iggy said.

"Iggy, I'm sure you could be a good guy, but it would never work because I'm taller. It's just a personal hang-up."

"But we're like soulmates because our names are so similar. Izzy and Iggy. Izzy and Iggy. Izzy and Iggy. So, does he treat you nice? Because if not, you know, I might be able to do something," Iggy said.

"Iggy, he's nice. There's nothing to worry about."

"So what's his name if you don't mind saying?" Iggy asked.

"Tom Hardy. He just graduated in Equality Studies and he's a member of the Party – just like you."

"Oh wow, I was assuming he isn't even in the Party. Well, that's great. That's just great. Totally awesome. And Equality Studies won't hurt either. Does he have a job lined up?" Iggy asked.

"Yeah, at the Bureau of Truth in the Ministry of Truth & Justice."

"That's awesome. So what kind of job is it anyway?" Iggy asked.

"Some entry level job. They'll tell him more when he starts."

"That's too bad he can't start higher than entry level. A college graduate can sometimes start with a better job than entry level, you know. I wonder why that happened," Iggy said.

Izzy didn't respond since there didn't seem to be a question. They watched the washing machines flopping the clothes around through the glass windows.

"So Izzy, you got anything to report?" Iggy asked.

"No. I'll let you know if hear anything, of course," Izzy said.

"Yeah 'cuz there's only so much I can do if you withhold info, unless you were my girlfriend. You wanna go to the movies sometime? I get discounts," Iggy said.

Izzy gently declined the offer. She put her clothes in a dryer and told Iggy she was going upstairs to do a few things. She waited an extra half hour before going back down, but Iggy was still there, looking at his phone. As she hurried out with her clothes basket, she heard Iggy say, "Catch you later." That was his cute way of reminding everyone of his important role.

Later that same afternoon, there was a special meeting of Director Stalinsky's Committee on Social Control in Washington DC. Stalinsky now hated Buddy Lemmon even more than before. The Central Committee had recently given Buddy's Committee on Equal Outcomes full approval rights over any new programs of Stalinsky's Committee on Social Control. Buddy's Committee got the approval rights after Stalinsky's Committee released a half-baked proposal to develop composite profiles of each race with sizes and shapes of heads, ears, noses and other scientific data points using facial recognition software and advanced analytics algorithms.

Stalinsky thought his Committee's composite race profiling proposal was a logical step to fight against all the forged race IDs and phony DNA test results that Euros were getting so they could be re-classed as Mixed or Native. He secretly planned to dummy up his own composite profile with a photo of a long-forgotten Native which would align with his phony DNA certificate.

Despite the fallout from the flawed composite race profiling proposal, an appointment to Stalinsky's Committee was a prestigious position with a lot of social credits, even though nearly all members were still sycophants. Stalinsky had taken a chance in adding Professor Robert Miller, who was more out-spoken and worked remotely from Chicago but flew to DC for monthly meetings. Stalinsky had put up with Miller because of his extra scientific prestige. But they didn't agree on much and Stalinsky was losing patience.

Stalinsky pounded his gavel several times to begin the meeting even though no one was talking. The members were all looking at the young woman sitting to Stalinsky's right.

"I'd like you to meet Ms. Ashley Bennington, who will work as my special assistant. Her main priority is organizing the far left vigilante militia groups into a cohesive armed force under my central command and control. The far left militias will join us because we'll be stronger in resisting the dangerous fascism of Buddy Lemmon."

The sycophants applauded. Stalinsky pounded his gavel a few times after the applause had already ended.

Stalinsky was beaming as he continued to the next topic. "This afternoon, my Ministry's data scientists in the Bureau of Truth will publish a comprehensive Equality Report showing there has been no improvement since the Soft Coup. The report will acknowledge that a lot of people have advanced and others had declined in their incomes and wealth stats, but only through individualistic efforts or lack thereof, while the overall aggregate statistics have remained about the same across all racial groups. Obviously, systemic institutional racism is still deeply ingrained in the fabric of society."

"That is profoundly disturbing," said one of the sycophants, while beaming back at Stalinsky.

"I agree," said another sycophant, also beaming.

"Me too," said the remaining sycophant, beaming too.

Despite being sycophants, they were smart and understood right away that the new Equality Report would caste a bad light on Buddy Lemmon and his Committee on Equal Outcomes and all their work tinkering with the Social Credit Point System.

Stalinsky said, "I want to build on the momentum of this new disturbing report by rolling out a fresh action to promote equality of outcomes through social justice control. Any suggestions?"

No one said anything. They had no idea what he wanted.

Stalinsky said, "Chairman Lemmon has no talent for racial politics. I almost feel sorry for the big jerk. It's so obvious that we need a new group to blame for the lack of equality. That will energize our faction and intimidate everyone else. I want our data scientists to develop models establishing that the direct descendants from Christopher Columbus living in this country have so much accumulated Euro privilege and racist DNA that they are a key roadblock to equality of outcomes. Let's include all of the usual buzzwords. What the hell, throw in environmental justice since there has to be a correlation."

"Our data scientists can do that?" asked a sycophant in an effort to contribute. She was a new member of the Committee.

Stalinsky looked sharply at Professor Miller. "Robert, you're a Professor Emeritus of Computer Science, so tell us if I'm on target with data science."

"Of course, statistical analysis and modelling can be manipulated to produce any results you want and our data scientists have ample incentives. We already have everyone's DNA records. You just need Columbus tissue samples or DNA records. You can definitely get a scientific DNA study to focus on descendants from Columbus. But why Columbus descendants?" Professor Miller asked.

"The answer is so obvious, Professor. Everyone already hates Columbus, plus his descendants are probably a small group that can't defend themselves. We can control the size of the group by specifying the percentage of Columbus DNA that's considered racist. We'll put them in a new super-oppressor category and cut their social credits to zero to enhance equality of outcomes and social justice or whatever. Maybe we'll go further and make Columbus DNA racists begin each year with a lot of demerits. Frankly, I'd like to add restrictions on how many can get into college as students or faculty, and restrictions on how many can get professional jobs like lawyers and accountants. Let them dig the frigging ditches for a change!"

"Dig ditches!" screamed a sycophant.

"Yes, dig ditches!" screamed another sycophant.

"Yes, ditches! The deeper the better!" screamed the remaining sycophant.

The Committee apparently didn't know about modern ditch digging vehicles and equipment that creative entrepreneurs had developed and risk-taking capitalists had funded and which made ditch digging much easier than in the olden days.

"Why not ask the scientists to focus on your remaining billionaire crony capitalist supporters and eliminate their huge tax exemptions and cut their annual social credits?" Robert asked.

Stalinsky stood up with a red face and yelled at Miller, "This Committee will never go after our few remaining friends and long-time supporters among the patriotic technology geniuses, wall street hedge fund managers, movie stars and sports stars who have chosen to stay in the country and support us on social media. More importantly, I am really tired of your attempts to be amusing with your annoying cynical questions especially when you already know my answer."

Stalinsky remained standing but calmed down enough to speak in a normal tone. "Professor Miller, this is a good time to get to a sensitive point. We all appreciate that you were appointed partly based on Diversity, Equity & Inclusion for Gays. But Gays have succeeded at least as well as any other group and will soon be removed from the oppressed categories if I have anything to say about it. That means you're just another white guy and I can't justify keeping you on this Committee. I'm also removing you from Cyber Command."

Professor Robert Miller slowly rose from the table and gathered his thoughts while he put his phone in his pocket, pulled his Committee membership ID and building keycard from his wallet and tossed them on the table. He said, "Please call me a Euro instead of white."

Stalinsky replied, "Robert, I'm sorry for using the old term. Some habits die hard. Your resignation is accepted and you are excused."

After the door slammed closed, Stalinsky said, "That was sad to see. A complete melt-down, just because I used the word "white.""

"Complete melt-down," said all three sycophants in unison.

Stalinsky continued, "So, when I said Columbus descendants, I just meant at least a certain percentage of Columbus DNA. Anyone else in his lineage with less than that percentage would be exempt. We'll have the scientists start out with 50% of Columbus DNA and see the size of the group that comes up. I'm hoping to get between 5,000 and 10,000 scientifically determined racist DNA Columbus descendants. Of course, we also need the data to show that the group has a lot more money, status, and success than average, since that will prove they had too much Euro privilege. We need the scientists to run programs to check and clear our own DNA and the DNA of the Party leadership. We need unofficial data before we launch and we'll adjust the results as needed. But we are going to do this by all means necessary. I'm giving a bonus if Buddy Lemmon is in the Columbus racist DNA results."

Stalinsky banged his gavel and ended the meeting. The sycophants stood, gave the fist salute without even thinking about it, walked quietly out the door, rode down the elevator without speaking and scurried off in different directions. Stalinsky sat down, leaned back in his chair, put his shoes up on the marble table, and smiled about his prescience in having already checked his DNA against the Christopher Columbus gene sequence.

When Tom arrived back at Izzy's place, it was a mild May evening. Izzy suggested they go to a retro dance club called "Stardust" she had heard about where instructors teach old styles of holding each other and gliding around to music from the 1930s through the 1950s.

Izzy brought out some old style formal clothes that she had found for them at a vintage store. She went to her bedroom and changed into a sharp cocktail dress. Tom went in the bathroom and put on a white shirt and navy blue summer weight suit. When he came out, he found a YouTube video on what to do with the dark blue necktie.

Tom and Izzy took the "L" down to Stardust on Lawrence in Chicago. Many decades ago, it was called the Aragon Ballroom and had big band orchestras and crowds of people who knew stylish dances. Stardust didn't have a website. Part of the fun was that it was "off the grid."

A large cut glass ball hung from the ceiling and rotated slowly, creating light and shadow effects through the semi-darkened room. Decorative wall sconces added to the effect. Tables around the perimeter with small lamps offered a place to take a break for cocktails. Stardust was not a place for trendy people. It was a respite for an eclectic mix with a shared interest in good music and dancing and simpler times. Tom guessed he was the only Party member there.

The instructors were a mixed bunch of talented enthusiasts of various ages. They all wore vintage evening clothes. Some of them were making graceful moves around the floor to Ella Fitzgerald singing "I Get a Kick Out of You" with a big band from her Dream Dancing album. A couple of 20-something instructors literally danced their way over to Tom and Izzy, introduced themselves as Fred and Ginger, and offered to teach "big band era dancing."

The DJ made an announcement in a baritone voice. "Good evening and welcome to Stardust. I'm going to run a playlist I mixed from Rod Stewart's 5 CD set of Great American Songbook albums. Now, if you're thinking Rod Stewart was just a raucous rock singer, this will be a real treat. You'll be amazed by his smooth vocal stylings on popular songs from the 1930s to 1950s. I'll begin with "Isn't It Romantic."

Fred and Ginger began teaching a basic box step and demonstrated how Tom and Izzy could hold each other, how Tom could lead and Izzy could follow, how partners could dance farther apart or closer together. They demonstrated a way of holding and dancing to slower songs, like a close embrace, gracefully or sensually or both, depending on the song and mood. They had a good sense for when to add turns, twirls and dips to the lesson.

The box step was fairly easy and Tom and Izzy were having fun. Tom was holding Izzy's right hand in his left hand, up and slightly out to the side, and Izzy placed the back of her left wrist behind Tom's neck. Tom held Izzy closely with his right hand behind her back, and Izzy sometimes rested her head on his shoulder. He focused on giving cues to his next moves with touches of his hand and gentle body language.

They began to relax and meld together as they moved around the dance floor like they had been dancing for months. After the Rod Stewart mix, the DJ played Jean Frye Sidwell singing "My Foolish Heart" by Ned Washington and Victor Young Washington. Izzy looked up at Tom sometimes and they smiled at each other as they glided to the music.

When the DJ began playing Glenn Miller's "In The Mood," Fred and Ginger came back and offered lessons on the Fox Trot, a smooth, progressive dance with long continuous flowing movements across the dance floor. Inspired by the big band era tunes, Tom and Izzy picked up the Fox Trot quickly, including corner step turns, sway side step moves, and short promenades with lady underarm turns. But when the DJ played "Moonlight Serenade," Tom and Izzy switched back to a slower box step and held each other more closely.

When that popular tune ended, the DJ announced a fifteen minute break to be followed by a set of Latin music for advanced dancers only. There was scattered applause.

Tom said in a low tone, "I know who that older guy is at the corner table. Professor Robert Miller is the only person on Stalinsky's Committee who isn't a sycophant. We learned about him in Equality Studies. He must be in his late 60s or early 70s."

Izzy had a blank look on her face.

"He was the top Professor of Computer Science at MIT for decades before moving to the University of Chicago. He's a multi-talented genius and was also influential in climate change science and related social justice policies. But he marched to the beat of a different drummer. When he retired from academia, Stalinsky recruited him to add prestige to the Committee on Social Control," Tom said.

"Why don't you go over and introduce yourself. You can talk about equality stuff."

"Okay, but only if you come too," Tom said.

"You lead and I'll follow."

"You mean we dance our way over?"

Tom and Izzy smiled and walked over to Professor Miller. Tom wasn't sure if he should give the fist salute. They introduced themselves and Miller reached out to shake hands. The Professor was alone with a cocktail and seemed to have been in a funky mood. He appreciated their friendliness and invited them to join him.

After they sat down, Professor Miller said, "You'll see this in the news. I'm no longer on Stalinsky's Committee or Cyber Command." Miller didn't say that like it was good or bad, his idea or somebody else's. Tom didn't know if he should say congratulations or that he was sorry, so he didn't say anything. Izzy also remained silent.

The Professor leaned closer and continued in a lower voice and somewhat slurred words, "Stalinsky wants to shift Gays to a new super-oppressor or super-advantaged classification. They seem to be changing terms from oppressor to advantaged but that's beside the point. The point is that we'll be even worse off than Euros because we'll be in this new "super" class. Stalinsky says Gays have succeeded better than Euros as a group. We'll probably start each year with a bunch of demerits instead of any credits. He says he loves Gay people and just wants to be fair and logical on equality of outcomes. But we aren't even a race. And some of us do fine while others struggle, and the successful outcomes may have nothing to do with being Gay at all. By the way, when he says Gay he means the full acronym."

The Professor took a slug from his drink, kept his voice low, and added with increasingly slurred words, "Stalinsky also wants to pick on Christopher Columbus' descendants. Where do you draw the line? I'm also Jewish. What if he decides Jews are too successful? What group will he target next? What if he targets light skinned Blacks as oppressors or advantaged over darker Blacks? Or Blacks who immigrated later versus Black descendants of slaves, regardless of whether some slave descendants might be doing better. Stalinsky could keep targeting small groups that no one will defend out of fear they'll be next. He'd use bogus data and make flowery speeches about equality and social justice. He doesn't care about any of that. He just likes boosting his ego by having power over people."

After a long pause, Izzy changed the subject. "Professor, I like to read about the history of science, especially when something was considered settled science and then the consensus eventually changed.

Can you recommend any reading materials about the past concerns over human-caused global warming and climate change?"

"Sure, I'll give you a list when I see you with your parents in Hyde Park next week," Miller said.

"Hey I don't get it," Tom said. "Do you already know each other?"

"I didn't want to rain on your excitement about recognizing Professor Miller, but he's a friend of our family. He lives near my parents in Hyde Park," Izzy explained.

"My reading list won't cover the newer English studies but you'll find it interesting. Let me just say that I have a lot of respect for the younger generation of scientists in England who have taken a close look at prior work and reached very different conclusions. It seems that we're headed toward global cooling again. The younger scientists and policy makers have interesting views. They concluded that renewable energy sources are too variable and dependent on the changes in sun and wind so the power companies would never be able to stabilize their electrical grid currents without most of the power coming from steady reliable fossil fuels. At the same time, the younger environmentalists became concerned that electric vehicle batteries, solar panels and wind turbines had to be replaced periodically and were made with toxic rare earth metals and minerals from massive nasty mining operations, some of which are in limited deposits mainly in China. Given the need to mine the materials continually, the term "renewable" didn't seem accurate anyway. The younger group is also concerned that solar and wind farms take huge land areas and disrupt natural habitats, kill birds and wildlife, and create visual pollution. So, they're drawing a distinction between coal power plants, which are the real problematic polluters if they don't have modern carbon capture technology, and cleaner energy sources like natural gas and oil which also don't have the same problems as wind and solar. The younger group advocates a balanced approach, including nuclear plants with new safety systems."

The Professor explained further, "I try to stay up by reading about climate change and global warming on a banned website called CFACT.org, but I don't know for sure if it's accurate. Anyway, I'll give you a list of books. You'd need to be careful because the books are banned and the books and authors were attacked on many levels. I'm not saying that site or these books are necessarily right, and you could read mainstream climate science writings for comparison."

The Professor's counter-culture climate change reading list included, "Unsettled: What Climate Science Tells Us, What It Doesn't, and Why It Matters" by Steven E. Koonin; "Apocalypse Never: Why Environmental Alarmism Hurts Us All" by Michael Shellenberger; "False Alarm: How Climate Change Panic Costs Us Trillions, Hurts the Poor, and Fails to Fix the Planet" by Bjorn Lomborg; "The Real Inconvenient Truth: It's Warming but it's Not CO2; The case for human-caused global warming and climate change is based on lies, deceit, and manipulation" by M J Sangster PhD; "The Mythology of Global Warming: Climate Change Fiction VS. Scientific Facts" by Ph.D. Bruce Bunker; "The Great Global Warming Blunder: How Mother Nature Fooled the World's Top Climate Scientists" by Roy W Spencer, a former senior NASA climatologist; "Inevitable Disaster: Why Hurricanes Can't Be Blamed On Global Warming" by Roy Spencer; "The Deliberate Corruption of Climate Science" by Tim Ball PhD; "Inconvenient Facts: The science that Al Gore doesn't want you to know" by Gregory Wrightstone; and "The Weaponization of Weather in the Phony Climate War" by Joe Bastardi.

As they worked on their next round of drinks, Tom was starting to get tight from the booze and whispered in a joking conspiratorial way, "So Professor, what's next now that you're off Stalinsky's Committee and talking like a free thinker – join the underground?"

The Professor took a gulp and whispered back slowly with a quirky smile and slurred words, "What makes you think I'm not already in the underground?" Tom thought he saw the Professor wink at Izzy. They were all silent and motionless for a few moments. Then they broke out laughing and ordered another round.

The DJ was getting ready to start the new Latin music set. Tom and Izzy saw Fred and Ginger on the dance floor. Fred had removed his suit coat and tie and unbuttoned his shirt all the way down, though he left the tails tucked in. Ginger had apparently slipped out of her dress and was wearing a leotard with tights. The DJ played a series of rumbas and mambos, dances originally from Cuba in which dancers move their hips a lot among other things. Then the DJ added tangos and boleros. The dancing was energetic, exciting, and sensual.

Near the end of the Latin set, the DJ asked the dancers to clear the floor, except for Fred and Ginger who had agreed to perform the "Samba de Gafieria." Fred and Ginger's performance was amazing, tightly choreographed and synchronized, with fast footwork, spinning and swaying, swirls and twirls, rhythmic hip gyrations, body rotations back and forth and other sensual moves as they came close after dancing apart, and as they paused mid-beat in a hot embrace and then broke out to dance even faster. They'd dance holding hands with out-stretched arms and some distance between them for a moment, then come in close to dance tightly together face to face, then Ginger would flip around so Fred was dancing behind her and they were both making hip moves with no distance between them at all. Fred flipped Ginger upside down and around and over his back a few times, she did a back flip all on her own a few times, and at the end she ran and jumped to land with her legs wrapped around Fred's waist in a sensual embrace. They got a lot of enthusiastic applause and took some deep bows combined with quick dance moves and flourishes of their arms and hands.

As the applause died down, the DJ dimmed the lights more and began playing a vintage big band recording of "Isn't It Romantic" by Rodgers and Hart. Tom and Izzy remembered the Rod Stewart version from earlier. The music was perfect for a box step so Tom and Izzy excused themselves from the Professor and walked over to the dance floor. They got into a close position and began moving slowly with the music, which got even better when a vocalist known as Hildegarde began singing the lyrics on the old recording. After a minute, Izzy moved her left hand behind Tom's neck and pulled gently down as she raised her lips and they kissed as they continued to dance, though they danced even more slowly. Izzy closed her eyes for a few moments as they drifted along.

Tom and Izzy kissed and held each other for a long moment after the music stopped. They agreed it was getting late so they went over and said goodbye to Professor Miller. As they were leaving, they heard Rod Stewart singing "Stardust."

When they got on the "L," they sat close together on the seat and Izzy rested her head on Tom's shoulder. Tom noticed a guy sitting several seats down in a double seat arrangement for four people. But the guy was alone, slouched down, facing back toward Tom and Izzy. He had a Frank Sinatra style stingy brim hat and was holding a Party propaganda sheet in front of his face and appeared to be watching Tom and Izzy through a narrow scissor cut opening. The guy moved his hat up a bit to scratch above his ear, and they saw the blonde buzz cut.

"It seems odd that Iggy keeps showing up, especially this far from Evanston," Tom whispered.

"He's concerned about my future. He thinks you're a latent Gay who will come out later in life," Izzy whispered back.

"Why would he think that?" Tom asked.

"He says you're too pretty. A pretty boy."

"Maybe he's a latent Gay dude," Tom said.

"I wondered about that, but I don't think so."

Iggy put away the propaganda sheet and came over to stand by Tom and Izzy.

"Hey Izzy."

"Hey Iggy. This is my boyfriend, Tom."

"Hey Tom. So I saw you guys come out of Stardust."

"Oh? Do you go there to dance?" Izzy asked while suppressing an urge to smile at the image. She sensed that Tom was suppressing an urge to laugh.

"It's an underground hang-out. You kids need to be more careful where you go."

"Oh man! We just thought it was a fun place!" Izzy said.

"I was following Professor Miller. Then I see you guys go sit with him. That's not good. Really not good. You need to watch out who you associate with."

"It's nothing, Iggy. Tom just recognized Professor Miller from learning about him in Equality Studies and wanted to introduce himself. Then Miller asked us to join him," Izzy said.

"So did he tell you he was kicked off Stalinsky's Committee and Cyber Command?"

"He said that would be on the news or something," Tom said.

"So did he say anything subversive? Anything about the underground perhaps?"

"No. We were dancing part of the time," Tom said.

"Okay, but you gotta stay away from Stardust. It's got a bad element. Yeah, a really bad element. My shift replacement is in there now, but he doesn't blend as good as me."

"Thanks Iggy, I'm so glad you're watching out for us!" Izzy said as Iggy went back to his original seat.

When they got off at their Evanston stop, Iggy stayed on the train. They glanced around as usual for Political Police or far left vigilantes as Tom walked Izzy to her place. They heard helicopters and saw searchlights shining down in the distance.

When they reached Izzy's building, she asked Tom to come up and hang out. Izzy poured some wine and they settled on the sofa to listen to Van Cliburn's recording of the "Rachmaninoff Second Piano Concerto," perhaps the most romantically moody music ever composed.

By the slow second movement, they finished their wine and began to kiss, and then made out like teenagers until the music ended. They said they were really into each other, but Izzy said she wasn't quite ready to take it to the next level. They both figured that meant they'd get there tomorrow.

Chapter Eleven

After Tom got up the next morning, he took a breakfast bar and mug of coffee over to his desk and turned on his laptop. He had to review a lengthy Equality Report that Stalinsky's team had published, and had to prepare for a video call with Buddy Lemmon. When they were connected in the afternoon, Buddy asked what Tom thought.

"Stalinsky's report is significant if the data is accurate. No overall improvement in equality of outcomes between race classes since the Soft Coup," Tom said.

"I have moles in his Ministry so I expected this. Stalinsky wants to oust me and become Chairman again. He's starting with this report using bogus data science to make me look bad. He'll start a smear campaign against me using Saul Alinsky tactics. He also hired a special assistant to consolidate the far left vigilante militias and integrate his Political Police. Stalinsky is telling his faction that he needs his own militia to save the Republic from me and my militia. If it comes to an armed conflict between our militias, the regular military brass will probably stand down until they see who's winning."

"Wow, Buddy, an armed conflict? Is that going to happen?"

"Probably. I want you to contact my Youth Brigades and the alumni as an urgent priority. Work with my militia leader, Laura Zena, to attach the Brigade personnel to my militia units. I want them all on standby, armed, organized and ready to go on three hours' notice in case Stalinsky starts something. I'll send you the contact information and our militia org chart.

"Stalinsky's new special assistant is Ashley Bennington. She was in my Youth Brigades but crossed to the dark side when she went to DC. I recall you went out with her, so I need to ask if that creates a conflict of interest."

"Oh man, Buddy. This is so weird. Yeah, we went out during part of our junior year. We haven't had contact since we broke up, and I don't have any conflict of interest. She was radically idealistic and not very smart."

"Good fit for Stalinsky," Buddy said.

Buddy paused. "Tom, I want to bounce something off you. I've been working on an idea to take the news cycle away from Stalinsky's Equality Report. His report points out problems but doesn't offer solutions. What if we could show that the disappointing equality results were caused by Stalinsky's own "open borders policy." I'd like to get our data scientists to look at this. I mean a legitimate scientific study without any predetermined outcome."

Buddy continued, "Maybe the study will show benefits from the 250,000,000 immigrants in the last thirteen years. But, if the open borders policy did more harm than good, for example, by reducing the opportunities and outcomes of the Blacks, Browns, Asians and Natives who were already here, shouldn't we have a legitimate study to figure that out?"

Tom was silent for several moments. "I'd like to understand more about your goal. Hasn't the ship already sailed? I mean, more people want to get out of the country now instead of in."

"Yeah, Tom, but I want to know the past impact. If it's bad, I can use it against Stalinsky. But either way, I really want to know the frigging truth for a change. I don't want fake data or phony conclusions. I want a real study with high credibility that will get a lot of serious attention and take the news cycle away from Stalinsky's Equality Report. I also want to sponsor a high credibility study in order to maximize my own credibility compared to Stalinsky's credibility."

"Okay, what about bringing a broad cross section of scientists and prominent old thought leaders back from retirement like a Blue Ribbon Commission. Maybe they could include recommendations for immigration policy changes. Maybe the policy can be modified to have some reasonable limits, some background checks, maybe some standards and qualifications like other countries have. You know, for the future, in case you turn the country around and people want to start immigrating again. It might send a positive message, like you're going to make the country great again," Tom said.

"I like the idea of a Blue Ribbon Commission. I'll talk to Beatriz."

Buddy ended the call by saying, "So your top priority is contacting the people from the Youth Brigades and coordinating with Commander Zena to prepare for trouble from Stalinsky. I need solid results in twenty-four hours. I told Zena the same thing."

Izzy spent most of the day working on a special underground planning and organizational assignment for her dad. The underground had seen indications of a major conflict brewing between Chairman Lemmon and Director Stalinsky.

She finished the first part of her dad's project by the time Tom arrived for dinner. Izzy had ordered Domino's pizza, one of Tom's favorite meals. Later, while Tom handled the clean-up, Izzy dimmed the lights and put on one of Tom's classical music favorites, the "Faure Piano Quartet No. 1 in C Minor."

Tom joined Izzy on the sofa. They both held half-finished glasses of wine.

"Tom, can we talk about us?" Izzy asked.

Tom never liked that question, but it was different with Izzy. He knew the answer.

"Izzy, I'm falling in love with you."

"Me too, Tom. With you. Are we going to be exclusive?"

"I already am."

"Me too. Do we have a long term future?" Izzy asked.

"I hope so."

"Me too," Izzy said.

They kissed and embraced.

"Would you like to make love?" Izzy smiled while looking into Tom's eyes.

"I was hoping you'd ask."

Tom figured they'd head to Izzy's bedroom so he was unprepared for what came next. She had a thing about not making love in her place the first time.

"I've never seen your place so would it be okay if we go there? It's probably nice, right?" Izzy asked.

"Sure, we can go there if you want. But my place has no charm. Just neat and clean and super modern."

"That sounds kinky," Izzy said playfully.

They walked south several blocks to the tall modern apartment building in downtown Evanston and rode the elevator up to the 10th floor. Tom gave Izzy a quick tour of his apartment.

"Tom, your decorating is well-done. Post-modern, but it all works. Did someone help? Maybe an old girlfriend?" Izzy asked.

"No, the store had someone. She left Art School after two years. Like you, except she didn't switch to anything else. She just wanted to work in a store."

"A tall blonde named Dagmar?" Izzy asked.

"That was her. How'd you know?"

"Dagmar was one of the art students who modelled nude for the class."

"One of the exhibitionists who volunteered for the sake of art?"

"I'm not sure what her motivation was. One time she was posing nude, as instructed, with her hand held high in a patriotic fist salute. She had big phony boobs that didn't match the rest of her. The class painted her in the cubist style and we got in trouble for being anti-social. The most talented student drew her in a Picasso style. He disappeared from campus and social media the next day. There were rumors that he was hauled off to the Alaskan Reserve, but I heard he escaped and joined the underground."

Tom asked Izzy if she'd like him to play his guitar and serenade her. He explained that he took up the guitar after quitting music school. She said sure, so Tom went to his closet and brought out his Martin, sat down, tuned up the strings, strummed a few chords, did a few licks, and tried to calm down. He had been working on the Beatles' "Blackbird" for months. As it turned out, Tom's guitar playing was pretty good and so was his singing. He didn't have a professional voice but could hit every note in tune.

Izzy loved his performance, put her arms around his neck, and gave him a kiss. They broke so Tom could put away his guitar. When he came back, they sat on Tom's uncomfortable modern sofa and embraced and kissed for what seemed like a long time to both of them.

For the second time that evening, Tom was unprepared for what came next. Izzy asked, "Do you mind if we talk about some ground rules?"

"For making love? That might depend on what you have in mind."

"No rough stuff," Izzy said.

"No problem there."

"No male ego hang-ups about stuff," Izzy said.

"No problem there either."

"I like it to feel emotional and romantic … not just physical," Izzy said.

"Pretty old-fashioned, but that sounds good to me."

"Don't finish before me of course. Do math in your head or whatever."

"Okay."

"If you need help getting ready, I know some fun ways to cure that." Izzy spoke gently and was smiling.

"Okay. What happens if you're not ready?" Tom asked.

"When you're lying there all ready for me, I'll be ready. It's automatic. A medical student might say an autonomic response."

"Did you date a med student?"

"He was charming at first. Then I realized he was full of himself, which was especially uncool since he was only a first year med student. I mean, at least wait until you're a real doctor." She sounded upset and Tom wondered how long they had gone out.

Feeling deflated and out of the mood, Tom figured he had nothing to lose by keeping the conversation going, so he asked, "Was he tall like the London guy?"

"No, the med student was my same size."

They kissed and embraced some more, still on Tom's uncomfortable modern sofa.

Izzy said quietly, "You are also unique among my boyfriends because you are the perfect four inches taller than me, remember?"

"I thought that was about dancing."

"The four inch difference is about this too. It's a scientific fact that I heard about from Gina."

Izzy was silent for several moments while looking down. She stood up, walked to the window while crossing her arms as if holding herself, came back and sat at the other end of the sofa. Tom watched with concern but remained silent.

"Maybe this isn't the best time to explain, but I was raped when I was fifteen."

"Oh Izzy, I'm so sorry." Tom felt like he'd been punched in his chest with his heart pushed up to his throat as he imagined Izzy in a brutal scary situation at such a young age. He was angry at the guy without knowing any details.

Izzy was silent. "Do you want to talk about it?" Tom asked.

"I haven't talked about it since like forever," she said in a higher tone that sounded more like a scared teen as she began to cry. Tom cautiously offered a hug but she pushed him away.

Izzy pulled herself together and continued in a grown-up tone, "He suddenly showed up in my bedroom one night. Right after my parents went to a Party event. My brother was at college. I was on my phone looking at social media. He told me not to be afraid, and said he was a high school football quarterback. He said he was tired of cheerleaders and wanted to meet a young virgin who could be his buddy or something. I'd only been in this country a short time and my English with an American accent wasn't great, so I'm not sure. It seemed weird that he'd want to be my buddy. He looked like a normal person and tried to put on some charm while holding a hunting knife down at his side. He said I was so pretty I could turn lemons into lemonade."

Izzy closed her eyes and was picturing the scene. Tom didn't say anything. Izzy opened her eyes and looked away for a few moments. She closed her eyes again and continued, "He found me by chance on social media after impersonating someone and getting into my friend's account and saw posts of me in my bikini at the beach. He said I was really hot or something. I was confused because the beach was hot. I was scared and kept saying he should leave. He said his dad was a big shot in the Party and he could get away with anything since his dad could get him out of trouble. He said he could fly me on a private jet to a private island. I said no way and that he needed a psychiatrist. That's when he lost it and went from Dr. Jekyll to Mr. Hyde. He got super angry like a madman with bulging eyes and veins on his neck, grabbed my phone and threw it against the wall, put his knife to my neck, and said he'd kill me if I yelled or didn't cooperate." Izzy sounded like a scared teen again.

Izzy opened her eyes and looked up, took a deep breath and held it for a few moments. After exhaling, she was back to her grown-up voice and was looking down. "I don't want to talk about the rest. I was in shock and just sat there afterwards going over the scene and every word again and again. My dad called the police when my parents got home a few hours later. The police came but I wasn't taken to the hospital for an exam and they didn't collect evidence. They assigned a detective but he implied that it was my fault. He asked me about my boyfriends, how far I had gone with them, whether I wore bikinis to be a tease. My dad had enough connections to learn that the quarterback had called a really high Party official right after he left my room and someone had squashed the investigation. The final entry in the report said I had consensual sex with a boy in my class. We were both suspended for a week."

Tom said he felt really bad for her and that he'd like to beat up the creep with karate. Izzy said she could take care of herself now.

"My dad used his connections to get me a Smith & Wesson pocket pistol, registered with a concealed carry license, even though I was under-age, and taught me how to use it. I often sleep with it under my pillow. I have it in my purse right now."

"You seem so well-adjusted for someone who went through that," Tom said.

"I haven't told anyone since around the time it happened. But a faculty guy got fresh on the dance floor at that event where I helped the other evening. That made me think more about the rape again."

Izzy was silent for several moments. "I'm okay now. It felt good to talk about it. Want to see my gun?"

"Sure."

Izzy walked over and pulled her Smith & Wesson pocket pistol from her purse. She held it up quickly and aimed at the door, and then sat on the sofa next to Tom. She said it was loaded but checked that the safety was on, and let Tom hold the gun and aim at the door.

"I don't know if you want to say anything else, but I'm wondering if you got any counseling?" Tom asked.

"My mom got me to see a woman. We talked about what happened, my feelings of humiliation and lack of control. But talking wasn't enough. I didn't want to feel like a whiney victim. I felt better mainly because I had a gun. Then, I started working out really hard. I took judo and boxing, even kick-boxing like I mentioned. I wanted to be able to defend myself. Instead of a victim, I wanted to be a winner and come out on top." She smiled to herself and quickly looked down.

"All that stuff must have helped. Like I said, you seem so well adjusted," Tom said.

"I eventually dated guys and fooled around like everyone else. But it was never good until I worked out my guidelines for making love that we went over earlier."

They sat silently for several moments. Tom said maybe it wasn't the right night to make love. Izzy agreed and suggested they have another glass of wine. The music had stopped so Tom looked for another playlist.

By the time Izzy refilled the wine glasses and they sat together again on the sofa, Tom had set up some soft jazz and older romantic songs to lighten the mood. They drank their wine more quickly. They were smiling and kissing by the time they finished the wine.

When "Our Love is Here to Stay" came on, which they remembered from Stardust, they were in a close embrace, kissing deeply. Izzy said, while looking softly in Tom's eyes and smiling, "I still want to make love. How about you?"

"I was really in the mood before, but this thing that happened to you," Tom said.

"You'll be okay once we get started. You'll have a good time." She spoke quietly and gently with an encouraging smile.

"Okay," Tom said.

They rose and held hands and Izzy led Tom to his bedroom.

After they finished, Izzy rested with her face on Tom's shoulder and her lips gently kissing his neck.

Tom said quietly, "Isabella, that was awesome."

"Yeah," she replied dreamily before she took a deeper breath and slowly exhaled.

She rolled off, stretched and sighed, snuggled back close, then kissed him warmly on the lips.

"I love you, Tom."

"I love you, Izzy."

"Tom, I want to talk about something. We're really in love. I mean for real, right? I've never felt this way about anybody else. It doesn't matter that we haven't gone out very long. I don't ever want to be without you."

"I feel the same way," Tom said.

"Would it be crazy if we move in together?" Izzy asked.

"I was about to ask the same thing," Tom replied.

They smiled and kissed and eventually fell asleep.

Chapter Twelve

Tom and Izzy woke up early the next morning and Izzy decided to walk back to her place and then to the gym. It didn't make sense for Tom to bring over his uncomfortable modern furniture. He offered it all to his landlord who was glad to keep it for free. In exchange, the landlord agreed to give Tom his deposit back. Tom was so motivated about moving that he brought over the rest of his stuff in a few trips in his Subaru. Tom and Izzy had a late lunch of PB&J sandwiches to celebrate.

After Tom finished unpacking in the late afternoon, he decided to go for a walk along the lake while Izzy continued to work on her dad's project. As he reached the lake shore, he headed north toward the distant old lighthouse. He had mixed feelings about starting his new job. He liked the idea of working in downtown Chicago. He wondered if he'd like his manager and co-workers and whether they'd like him. He wondered what he'd work on, how much time he'd spend at Stalinsky's Bureau of Truth, and how much time working for Buddy Lemmon. He felt somewhat nervous about being a mole for Buddy.

Halfway to the lighthouse, Tom began to think about his early childhood. He had been an only child, yet his parents were always busy with their business activities and had little time for him. But the times they did spend together were good. He loved when his dad read books to him. His dad had wanted to be an actor and had started in Theatre at Northwestern. When his sensitive face skin couldn't handle the theatrical makeup, he switched to business school.

But Tom's dad had remained theatrical. He tried a Welsh accent when he read "A Child's Christmas in Wales" after hearing a recording of Dylan Thomas reading his work on the radio. Tom also remembered that his dad tried English dialects while reading Dickens' "A Christmas Carole." Tom thought about his dad's imitation of Scrooge, which was ironic because his dad was extraordinarily frugal. He studied ads and travelled from store to store to get the best deals. If he had to make a few stops in a shopping district, he'd put the lowest amount in a parking meter and jog around to make it back in time. Tom remembered waiting in the car and laughing when his dad returned as a patrol officer was writing a ticket. Now he wondered why that would be funny. Maybe he had laughed out of spite because he resented wearing bargain basement clothes that made him feel second rate around the rich kids.

Tom's memories included later squabbles between his parents over their business, what levels of beans and other supplies they should maintain, which employees and managers were good and what to do about the bad ones. They spent even less time with Tom and he increasingly felt neglected. At age ten, Tom was not a fan of the business world and all his parents' struggles, and thought he understood enough about the Soft Coup to believe that it was good. Tom's parents explained that they had to sell the coffee business and send the money to the government for taxes. They got late shift jobs as janitors in Chicago office buildings.

What Tom enjoyed were the afternoons when his parents were home and awake by the time he got back from school and they hung out together, unless he had extra-credit political classes or socialist marches. Tom's parents encouraged him to pursue those activities even though he sensed they had a private distain for the Party. When Tom asked about that, they said things about going along to get along and surviving by being clever and not drawing attention. Tom listened carefully but figured his parents were mainly sore about losing their business. Yet many times in the afternoons after Tom got home from school and before his parents had to leave for their janitor jobs, they explained about old-fashioned values and ideas. It was confusing, but Tom decided that he would work hard on Party-sponsored activities and not say anything controversial.

Everything changed after a couple of months when Tom was transported to the Party's middle school facility in Ann Arbor. He remained there for special accelerated fourth and fifth grade classes and then middle school. Students at the facility couldn't bring their own phones, laptops or other devices. The facility IT personnel provided phones and laptops with monitoring programs, blockers and firewall settings for incoming and outgoing communications and internet access. Communications with anyone outside the facility were limited to a one hour in-person family time visit once per month in a large room with rows of tables and chairs and facility personnel as monitors. Family members sat on one side of the tables and students sat on the other side, appropriately spaced apart. You could whisper briefly to your parents across the table before a monitor moved closer.

Tom took the Party's school curriculum seriously, joined and worked hard on projects in the Cadet Corps, and stayed away from bad kids who made jokes about the Party. He enjoyed the short monthly visits from his parents, except for a fateful visit when he was thirteen. His parents whispered that the Party was full of crap, socialism sucked compared to free enterprise, and they were planning to join the underground. Tom was shocked by their traitorous views and plans and also feared they'd be caught and executed. He denounced his parents to the school principal for their comments about the Party and socialism, but didn't reveal their plans to join the underground. Tom's reasons for denouncing his parents were partly patriotic but he also believed his parents would be safer and better served if they were put on probation and forced to take reeducation classes, the usual penalty for a first offence.

Unfortunately, Tom's parents had not told Tom that they were already on probation and had already taken mandatory reeducation classes for making negative posts on a social media site they thought was safe but was monitored by the Political Police. Tom didn't realize his denunciation would compound his parents' crimes and cause them to be rounded up for transport to the Alaskan Reserve.

Tom's mind returned to the present as he reached the Evanston lighthouse, which he liked to believe had been a favorite destination for his parents. He began to choke up as he grieved his lost relationship. He turned and began to walk back down the beach, but stopped to recall his favorite memory of the Youth Brigades, at the end of the summer when he was eighteen, when there were special events to celebrate another season of working for worthy causes and scoring a lot of social credits. He was at the place where the leaders had organized a giant bonfire on a Saturday night after hotdogs and hot chocolate.

The Youth Brigade bonfire had provided warmth as the night air became chilly. The Brigade kids had pulled blankets from the piles the leaders brought. Because the kids were between the ages of eighteen and twenty-two and were well-behaved, the leaders left after a few hours when the bonfire was settling down and some stars were visible. Two friendly old guys with beards and long hair had been playing their guitars and singing further down the beach, but they walked over and asked the kids if they'd like some music. The kids said yeah, so the old guys played and sang Bob Dylan's "Blowin' In the Wind" and "The Times They Are a-Changin." After a few more songs, they played and sang "Kumbaya," and the kids picked up enough to join in some of the singing. Tom had a feeling of peace whenever he thought back to being with the kids and old guys with folk music around the dwindling bonfire.

As the bonfire died down that night and more stars were visible, romance was in the chilly air. But Tom was no longer with Leah, and he had not yet met Jenny. So Tom was sitting that night by the bonfire on a blanket with his closest friend, Noah Greene. They had become friends when they met at age thirteen after Noah arrived at the Party's middle school facility in Ann Arbor.

Tom and Noah had grown close because they had similar personalities and shared a similar sense of humor. They had similar sensitivities, for example a sense of empathy and compassion for the underdog or anyone who was being picked on or teased. They actively defended ugly kids, runts, and awkward eggheads. Noah was sympathetic rather than judgmental when Tom disclosed that he had denounced his parents.

After they were taken to the Party's prestigious Petosky Academy for high school, Noah introduced Tom to several other Jewish teens. Noah had cautioned the group that Tom still talked like a Party believer, but that he had a good mind and heart and the potential to see things differently. Tom felt increasingly accepted as they met every evening at the end of the large dorm room near the bunk bed that Tom and Noah shared.

Tom's new circle of friends was respectful in raising thoughtful questions about Party doctrine, adding points about history, and discussing human nature in relation to economic and political systems. They didn't all agree on everything, but they made well-reasoned points and only escalated their discussions with mild rebukes. A favorite was ***"If a person is not a liberal at age twenty he lacks a heart, but if he is not a conservative by age thirty he lacks a brain."*** Tom was initially confused by that adage since his friends were only teenagers themselves, but they explained their interpretation - that they should accelerate the brain part and combine it with the heart part beginning at their current ages.

Tom's Jewish friends at Petosky Academy never spoke about subversive activities when he was with them. They talked about how they and their families might be able to go to the countries that would grant entrance visas if the Party implemented a Stalinsky proposal to reduce their social credits to promote equality of outcomes and put a Jewish "J" on their IDs and passports. They mainly focused on Israel as their safest destination. They also spoke about ideas for smuggling assets out.

Tom got a kick out of the way Noah secretly bucked the Boarding School System and stayed more closely in touch with his parents, beginning in Ann Arbor and continuing at Petosky. It was easier for Noah to get around the visit restrictions at the Ann Arbor facility since Noah's family lived in the area. His parents had identified a weekly midnight meeting time and four rotating meeting places. They didn't know if Noah would be able to get out and meet, but they drove to each meeting place and waited nervously at each scheduled time. They were disappointed for several weeks and were losing hope.

Then one night Noah came out of the shadows at midnight wearing dark clothes, dark shoes and a dark baseball cap. Noah was a short wiry guy and had been able to make his way out through a complex system of basement and sub-basement rooms, tunnels, passageways and crawlspaces that he discovered through a lot of perseverance and trial and error. The system had been created and expanded over time for utilities, janitor supplies, laundry service, and delivery of coal for furnaces a hundred years earlier. His parents would drive Noah back to their nearby home while talking quietly and being careful not to speed.

Tom was not very surprised to learn that Noah hadn't wanted to join the Party or Youth Brigades. His parents persuaded him that it would be best for his career and safety. His great grandfather, Peter, had told Noah about the Holocaust and was concerned about growing anti-Semitism in the Party. Peter Greene had been in the Intelligence Branch of the US Army in World War II when America and her western democracy allies fought back against the Nazis and fascists. He was a liaison with the British intelligence service and with the British 11th Armored Division when they liberated the Bergen-Belsen concentration camp. They discovered approximately 60,000 prisoners inside, most of them half-starved and seriously ill, and another 13,000 corpses lying around the camp unburied. Peter took photos as evidence for his job and kept copies which stayed in the family. Noah had explained this to Tom along with other information about the systematic oppression and extermination of European Jews under Nazi one-party totalitarian control.

Tom had lost touch with Noah and his circle of Jewish friends during the past couple of years and often wondered where they were and what they were doing.

A nearby barking dog suddenly brought Tom back to the present. He was still on the Evanston beach near the lighthouse. The runner with the dog ran further down the beach and the barking became distant. Tom was looking out at Lake Michigan. The wind had picked up more and the waves were bigger. The sail boats were gone. No one else was on the beach in either direction.

Tom checked the time on his phone and was surprised by how late it was. He didn't think he had agreed with Izzy on an exact time, but had a feeling that he had stayed out too late. He called her to say he was sorry that he lost track of the time and that he'd be there in about fifteen minutes. Izzy didn't say much.

Chapter Thirteen

By the time Tom got back to the apartment at 6:15 pm, Izzy had made an Italian salad and set the table, including candles and glasses of Chianti.

She had also made a spicy aromatic marinara sauce with Kalamata olives, Italian sausages, basil, oregano, rosemary, thyme, and garlic powder. She was stirring the simmering sauce while tapping her foot.

Tom came in and said "Hey." Izzy was cool. She tossed mostaccioli noodles in the boiling water and set a timer. She kept looking at the stove and tapping her foot.

"Izzy, I'm sorry again for not getting back sooner. But we didn't have any agreed time for me to get back here."

"So what if we didn't have an exact time? Anyone who cares about someone would know that 6:00 pm would be the latest that anyone would be thinking. Most people would be back by 5:00 or 5:30. I mean this is our first evening living together and you act like this? Like it's nothing special?"

Tom was not happy about being chastised for being late when there was no agreed time. But he guessed a debate might make it worse.

"Izzy, let's sit down so I can say this right. You'll like what I say."

They went over to the sofa and she slumped down in one corner while Tom sat at the other end. She was looking back toward the kitchen.

"Izzy, I'm really glad I moved in, and this evening is really special to me. I got lost in my own thoughts when I was walking by the lake. I didn't try to anticipate your time frame. I appreciate that you spent a lot of time making the perfect dinner to celebrate our living together."

Izzy was looking down and seemed to be thinking. Tom decided he should listen for the timer bell. After a long moment, she turned to face Tom and smiled warmly as their eyes met. "You said just the right stuff." Izzy came close, put her warm hands around Tom's neck, and drew him in for a kiss.

After a few moments, they heard the timer and Izzy jumped up to take the pasta off the burner. As they ate, Tom asked if he could meet Izzy's parents and brother sometime, and she said maybe in a few weeks. Izzy had told her parents about Tom, but not that he had moved in.

After they cleaned up, Tom gently asked Izzy if he could ask a question about the rape. She said he could ask but she might not answer. He asked how she'd feel and what she'd do if she found out who the rapist was and where he was living or ran into him. She was silent for several moments while looking down.

Izzy eventually said she'd like it if the guy had really changed. If she ran into him, she'd like it if he said he was really sorry and she felt he was sincere. If the guy hadn't changed and wouldn't say he was sorry, she doubted she'd be able to get him prosecuted, but she'd want to slap his face or maybe try to kick box him.

Tom had a theory about who the rapist was and asked if Izzy wanted to know more. She paused and then said okay.

"Okay, if I remember what you told me, the rapist told you that his dad was a big shot in the Party who could get him out of trouble.

He said he was a high school quarterback. He said he could fly you on a private jet to a private island. He said he wanted a buddy. He said you were so pretty you could turn lemons into lemonade. Did I get that right?" Tom asked.

"Yeah, that sounds right. It's so creepy to think about," Izzy said.

"Buddy Lemmon told me he had to get his son out of trouble. He said he got his son a position as a quarterback in high school. He said his son lives on the Party's private island. When the rapist said he wanted a buddy, maybe he was saying his name was Buddy, meaning Buddy Junior, and you didn't understand since your American English wasn't great yet. When he said you could turn lemons into lemonade, he may have been playing off his last name Lemmon."

"I can't believe this. You think it was Buddy Lemmon's son?" Izzy asked.

"His social media profile says he was a high school quarterback and he lives on the Party's island. I have a link on my laptop. You want to see the photo?"

Izzy nodded. Tom got his laptop and sat next to Izzy. She stared intently at the photo for several moments.

"He's several years older in this photo but this is the guy. Same eyes and face and overall look. The image was burned into my mind at the time and as I sat in bed afterwards going over what happened. And the things you said tie in. I have no doubt. This is him."

Izzy began to cry softly and Tom held her for a few minutes. He asked if he made a mistake by bringing up the rapist's identity. Izzy said no, she'd rather know since it gave partial closure by identifying the guy and knowing he was living on the island.

Izzy wanted a glass of wine and offered to get a glass for Tom. She went to the kitchen and Tom heard the fridge open and close and heard her pour the wine. Then there was silence for a few minutes.

Izzy was calm when she returned with two glasses of pinot noir. She didn't want to talk about the rapist any more. They sipped the wine for several minutes as some Italian opera music played quietly in the background. Tom hadn't noticed the music before.

"Do you want to know a Party secret?" Tom asked.

"Sure."

"The Party is nationalizing Mojo's. They will become Equality Cafes," Tom said.

"Oh crap! How come?"

"I didn't get a reason. I don't think they need one," Tom said.

"When will it happen?" Izzy asked.

"We need to stop going there beginning two weeks from yesterday. There will be agitator violence to drive down the acquisition price," Tom said.

Tom added, "Mojo's beans will still be at Equality Foods for a lot of money or social credits. I can get free bags if I go to Party headquarters."

After several moments to digest the news, Izzy said, "Let's get back to secrets. What else do you have?"

"The Party is probably going to change the status of Asians so they are no longer in the oppressed groups. They'll get the same lower social credits as Euros," Tom explained.

Izzy didn't say anything as she processed the information.

Tom added, "There was a worse proposal to give Asians even fewer social credits than Euros since Asians are more successful. You know how Asians sort of have a culture of focusing on education and hard work and close families? Buddy asked my view and I said why punish hard work and success. Buddy liked my input and there was a compromise. Asians won't get fewer credits than Euros, but they'll no longer get more credits either."

"I guess that's fair," Izzy said.

Izzy waited for a few moments. "Tom, I feel like you're holding back. Remember you said there was a personal thing you'd tell me sometime?"

Tom deflected. "I've been having even more cynical thoughts."

"Just cynical thoughts? Do you ever seriously think about doing something radical like joining the underground?" Izzy asked.

"I have ideas about working on changes from inside the Party based on my situation with Buddy Lemmon."

"Have you thought about staying in the Party and also joining the underground?"

"I suppose it's crossed my mind. But I already told you the Party secrets about Mojo's and the Asian re-class. You need to tell me a secret now."

Izzy stood up and walked over to look out the window before joining Tom back on the sofa. She finally spoke.

"I'm on the outskirts of the underground's political wing. I'm just a researcher, editor and courier. I mainly edit the newsletter. I fact-check things and make some changes to add clarity or impact. My research gets me all over the internet under a complex series of hacked computer connections, routers, and IP addresses around the world that no one could track back to me."

Tom was looking at Izzy intently. She continued, "In the courier role, we normally use thumb drives, but we also do handwritten messages with a variety of invisible inks that can only be read if you apply the right thing. You might apply heat with an iron, a chemical solution or UV rays in the dark. We write innocent phony messages over the invisible ink so it won't seem suspicious to have blank paper. This was my science project in school."

"Izzy, thanks for trusting me. I'm not too surprised. I was already starting to wonder. Are you ever afraid of the risks?

"Yeah. But I couldn't live with myself if I didn't help," Izzy said.

"I don't mind some risks but I don't want to mess up my ability to influence changes from inside. Buddy Lemmon just appointed me as his special assistant. That's how I get to talk to him about things like the Asian re-class," Tom said.

"This is so crazy! I'm living with the special assistant to the Chairman of the frigging Party? Is Comrade Lemmon open to changes or is it risky to say stuff to him?" Izzy asked.

"I don't think there's any risk. Buddy took an interest in me beginning back when I was in the Youth Brigades. His son was a disappointment and I'm sort of a substitute. Anyway, he's turning out to be open-minded. He actually wants new ideas and viewpoints. He's more likable than you'd think. He may even have hidden depths."

Izzy seemed to make a mental note. Tom had picked up on the idea that the term "hidden depths" could be a way of referring to someone with sympathies for freedom and the underground.

"By the way, I'm still supposed to go to my new job at Stalinsky's Bureau of Truth beginning on Monday, but that will be reduced to part-time. That way, I can work more with Buddy. But no one at the BOT is supposed to know about my relationship with Buddy."

"Will you be like a mole at BOT to find out Stalinsky stuff for Buddy Lemmon?" Izzy asked.

"I don't know for sure, but I'd guess that's it."

"Now I'm getting nervous," Izzy said.

"I'll be careful and Buddy knows what he's doing. He has other moles."

Tom asked Izzy if she wanted more wine. She didn't, but he did, so he went to the kitchen and came back with a half glass and sat in the corner of the sofa away from Izzy. She wondered what that meant.

"Okay, I'm going to tell you my deepest personal secret. I'm really ashamed about this. I denounced my parents when I was thirteen, about three years after I was taken to the Boarding School System in Ann Arbor."

Izzy replied slowly, "Lots of those kids did the same thing at that age. You were all brainwashed in those classrooms and dorms, at least until you got older."

"Thanks for saying that, Izzy." Tom was sobbing all of a sudden and covered his face with his hands. It was guilt and remorse, and sadness over not being able to do anything about it.

Izzy embraced Tom and said quietly, "It's not your fault, Tom. You were just a little brainwashed kid."

After Tom recovered, he said, "The other part of my secret is that I partly stay in the Party so I might find information about my parents. But Stalinsky controls the Alaskan Reserve data. It's super secure. I won't get any better access in an entry level job at BOT. It could me take years."

They were silent for several moments.

"Tom, if you join the underground, they may be able to track your parents. They recently hacked into Stalinsky's Alaskan Reserve data systems and finally have inmate data for Camps I and II."

"Okay, I want in." Tom felt more hopeful than he'd ever been.

"There will be a vetting process for you to join, but you can start by providing some information about your parents. I can write it down and get it to the underground in a safe way."

When Izzy was ready to write with invisible ink, Tom said, "They were in the last large round-up of stubborn capitalists in and were sent in a long train from Chicago to the Alaskan Reserve. My dad's name is John Hardy and he would be 54 now. My mom's name is Jane Hardy and she would be 53. Our last home was an apartment on Green Bay Road in Evanston. Before that we had a home on West Foster. They both graduated from Northwestern. They had a business called Paradise Coffee Cafe, but they had to sell it after the Soft Coup and then worked as janitors in Chicago office buildings."

Izzy wrote down the information and covered the invisible ink with a recipe for pesto using regular ink and put the sheet of paper in her purse.

Tom was jazzed about joining the underground and maybe finding his parents. They watched something on Planet Earth for distraction until Izzy said she really wanted to make love.

Afterwards, they put on their PJs and then Tom asked, "Have you ever thought about how people used to wait until they were married to make love?"

"I think there was a spiritual aspect. I mean, it was a formal religious rule, but it was also about marriage creating a spiritual bond and a deeper commitment."

"What do you think?" Tom asked.

"I can see that point of view, but I also like to "try before you buy." I mean, what if two virgins got married and weren't compatible about making love?"

"Do you think that happened a lot? I mean, maybe people didn't get it right at first but figured out what worked over time," Tom said.

"Most people had a lot of children so maybe they were having a good time. Wasn't sex a basic form of evening entertainment since they didn't have TV?" Izzy asked rhetorically.

Tom and Izzy watched TV for several minutes.

"So do you believe in God?" Tom asked.

Izzy thought for a few moments and said, "Most of the time I'm not sure what to think so maybe I'm agnostic. But when I'm out in nature or looking at the stars or watch nature documentaries that show so much diverse and complex stuff, I wonder if it's all sort of a revelation about something bigger than us. I mean the scientists agree on the origin of the universe billions of years ago in the "Big Bang," so I wonder how that could happen without some larger force that already existed and could cause it to happen.

"Even just on earth, I wonder how inorganic molecules could turn into a living cell with all the inner complexity and then grow and propagate and have complex DNA, without an outside designer. Darwin didn't have electron microscopes so he couldn't see the complexity in single cell organisms. I heard that a scientist figured the probability of getting a living cell from non-living molecules, by random chance even over hundreds of billions of years, would be like a tornado hitting a junkyard and creating a fully functional Boeing 747. There are banned books if you're interested." Izzy's books included "The Mystery of Life's Origin: The Continuing Controversy," published by various co-authors in 2020; Michael J. Behe's "Darwin Devolves: The New Science About DNA That Challenges Evolution" and "Darwin's Black Box: The Biochemical Challenge to Evolution;" and also Stephen C. Meyer's "Darwin's Doubt: The Explosive Origin of Animal Life and the Case for Intelligent Design."

"I sort of think the same way," Tom replied. "And there are times when something really good and amazing happens and it seems like a blessing rather than random chance. So, then I say, "Thanks God." Do you ever do that?"

"Sure, I've done that. I said that after I met you," Izzy said.

"Me too. After I met you."

"When something really bad happens, or seems like it's about to happen, I find comfort in saying a little prayer," Izzy said.

"I've done that, but I don't get why those prayers don't seem to work a lot of the time, or why there even has to be any bad stuff," Tom said.

"You are so full of tough questions tonight! You really want to talk more about this stuff?"

"Sure if you don't mind," Tom said.

"There are books with different explanations," Izzy said. "Ideas about having free will to choose good or evil, to accept or reject God. The idea that you can't really have good unless you have bad, and can't really have beauty unless you have a lack of beauty, for comparison. The idea about people wanting a personal relationship with God, a grounded moral compass or conscience, or being redeemed from the human sin of pride and other flaws like jealousy and greed that everyone has to some extent."

"Izzy, what about the Christian belief that says Jesus is the only way, the truth and the life? People say that's exclusive and intolerant of other beliefs. Like the Spanish Inquisition when they made Jews and Muslims convert or leave the country."

"The Catholic Church got a lot of stuff really wrong at various times. The Spanish Inquisition being an example. The Crusades involved a lot of bad things but they seemed more like a misguided response to Islamic expansion, which had taken over the Holy Lands, Middle East, North Africa, as well as Spain and Greece, and most of southeastern Europe. They even got to the gates of Vienna. Don't get me wrong, though. The Crusades were bad on so many levels. Maybe diplomacy could have worked."

Izzy continued, "But getting back to bad stuff, some clergy took a short passage from one of the Gospels out of context and blamed the Jewish people for killing Jesus. In context, the Bible says Jesus voluntarily gave his own life for the salvation of the world. But the wrong-headed preaching about Jews killing Jesus contributed to anti-Semitism. There were other stupid reasons for anti-Semitism but the role of the church in misinterpreting its own scriptures was significant. I mean, didn't they read the rest of the New Testament, the writings of Apostle Paul?"

There was a pause while Izzy brought up a note on her phone and quoted, "There is neither Jew nor Greek, slave nor free, male nor female, for you are all one in Christ Jesus. Galatians 3:28. Some of the issues with the Catholic Church gave rise to the Protestant Reformation. And, eventually, even the Church admitted they had messed up. It took a really long time, but they finally did it."

"But aren't Christians still into the exclusive stuff and isn't that intolerant?" Tom asked.

"They'd never go back to coercing anyone like in the Spanish Inquisition. That was so long ago and they admitted it was wrong."

"So, are you saying Christians aren't exclusive or intolerant anymore just because they no longer coerce people?"

"They were overly strict and judgmental for a long time. But they eventually focused more on core tenets of the Gospel, especially during the past 70 years or so. Even though they don't like sin as described in the Bible, they believe they should still love the sinner. They view themselves as sinners who were redeemed and saved by Jesus for an after-life. They feel sad about people who don't believe the same thing. They evangelize people who are open to their beliefs. But they don't press the issue anymore. It's up to each person to accept or reject what they believe. It's only a belief about who will be included or excluded in salvation, you know for heaven."

"I still find it confusing. What about someone in an isolated country who has never heard about their beliefs or had a chance to accept or reject them. Is that person doomed?" Tom asked.

"There are some different interpretations about the exclusive aspect of salvation. I think C. S. Lewis had a more inclusive view based on his interpretation. There's an interesting little book from around 1995 called something like, "What About Those Who Have Never heard?: Three Views on the Destiny of the Unevangelized."

"So there are these beliefs, but how do we know that Jesus even lived? What if someone made him up like a legend?" Tom asked.

Izzy paused for a moment. "You might like to read some of the books by skeptics who became believers. "The Case for Christ" by Lee Strobel is good. Or maybe start with an even shorter book, "More than a Carpenter," by Josh McDowell, then move on to his longer book, "Evidence That demands a Verdict: Life-Changing Truth for a Skeptical World," the 2017 revised version.

"But what good is any of it? I mean if people can misinterpret and misapply it?" Tom asked.

"Putting aside the redemption-salvation part, the core moral teachings which were drawn from the Jewish faith seem good. Maybe it comes down to whether religious belief systems do more good than harm. Some people would say more harm because of the Spanish Inquisition and incorrect anti-Semitic interpretations. But those things happened a long time ago. You'd also want to look at the bad stuff under atheist systems, like Stalinist Russia, China, North Korean, Cuba and Cambodia, with hundreds of millions of innocent people murdered, tortured, oppressed and imprisoned. Meantime, like I said, Christian beliefs have mellowed around the core teachings of Jesus and the apostles. You know, about loving God and everyone else. Christian beliefs also served as the moral force for abolishing slavery and later for the civil rights movement."

A new Planet Earth show began and they watched for several minutes.

"Wasn't Hitler a Catholic along with his fellow Nazi leaders?" Tom asked.

"Maybe as children. As Nazis, they despised Christians as weak and undesirable because of the Christian beliefs about loving everyone as yourself and helping the poor, the sick and disabled, and those in prison, with the belief that they were all born in the image of God. Christians also wanted to keep worshipping God instead of Hitler. Hitler used their beliefs opportunistically in some earlier speeches when he thought it would help him politically. There is good evidence that Hitler was a pantheist and his key associates were pantheists or atheists."

"How do you know so much about this?" Tom asked.

"We were Catholics when I was growing up. I lost interest when I started college. Mamma got to know some Protestants here in the Chicago area. She did a lot more reading and joined the Swedish Covenant Church. I also read a lot in the past couple of years, including some apologetic writings and watched some DVDs. I guess I pretty much believe in God most of the time, but I'm less sure about the details. I'm probably more of a theist than agnostic. I like to learn about things and keep an open mind," Izzy said.

Izzy added, "Tom, how would you feel if I ever became a serious Christian?"

"I'd be okay assuming you're talking about the modern enlightened interpretations and beliefs. Maybe I'd even get into it myself, but it's a free choice, right?"

"For sure. Maybe that's why you don't hear government people talk about God or say public prayers. They did that in the olden days, but some people thought it wasn't right for someone in political power to say religious things. I don't necessarily disagree with that at this point. I wish they had kept more latitude for private people to say religious things in public instead of making it a federal crime. Is it Hate Speech to talk with someone in public about "the peace that passes all understanding?""

Tom thought about that for several moments and then turned toward Izzy to ask a question but saw that she was asleep. She looked completely at peace. Tom looked up without focusing on anything and said softly, "Thanks for Izzy," then closed his eyes and was asleep several moments later.

Chapter Fourteen

The next day was Monday and Tom was excited about starting his new job in downtown Chicago. He gratefully took a bag lunch that Izzy made while he was getting ready. He had been told not to bring his own laptop.

He took the "L" down to the Chicago Loop and walked over to the Ministry Building. The security desk had him listed as a new employee in the Bureau of Truth. After Tom reached the 18th floor, he raised his head toward a camera for a facial recognition security scan and heard a system unlock the door. The BOT's reception area was nothing like Party headquarters, except for the patriotic socialist art on the walls. This reception area was a room without windows, the furnishings were starkly modern, the receptionist was cool and detached.

Tom's manager came out and introduced herself as Ms. Lilly Berman. She was in her early 50s with a surprisingly pleasant manner and warm eyes behind pink plastic frame glasses which matched the color of her spiky hair. She gave Tom a tour of the office layout, break rooms, restrooms, some private offices with closed doors, and several huge rooms filled with countless rows of desks. Tom's desk was at the end of a row in the back of the room.

Tom had a variety of orientation sessions. Some were in a group with other new employees. Others were self-paced webinars with pop-up questions to see if you were paying attention. There were several sessions on the lengthy employee code of conduct, with an emphasis on equality of outcomes, social justice, environmental justice, hate speech, micro-aggressions, toxic masculinity, and general political correctness.

There were some ways to volunteer for social credits and some ways you could get in trouble and receive demerits, sometimes for not volunteering.

After lunch, HR rounded up Tom and the few other new Euro employees for Diversity, Equity & Inclusion training exclusively designed for them. A long table was set up in front of the windowless class room. An HR person was sitting with several private consultant trainers from oppressed group categories. Tom noticed some Rolex watches and Gucci handbags. The consultants were polished but talked about stuff everyone already knew from school and college, like Euro privilege, unconscious bias, systematic institutional racism, critical race theory and intersectionality.

Tom could have provided the training himself with his degree in Equality Studies. The country was founded on slavery and the civil war wasn't redemptive because the other half of the country fought to keep slavery. It didn't matter if a Euro was descended from immigrants who lived in the north and never had slaves. It didn't matter if a Euro came from Europe after slavery was abolished and arrived with one dollar and no understanding of the English language. It didn't matter that many Euros had always been poor and worked in hard jobs. It didn't matter if not a single Euro was consciously racist anymore. Euro unconscious racist bias and Euro privilege were still systemic and institutional, having been coded into Euros' DNA over hundreds of years. Few people in the country believed it but feared being called a racist or Uncle Tom if they said anything.

During the final two hours, Tom and his fellow Euros had to kneel with chains around their necks attached to poles around the room. The trainers took light canes and beat the Euros from time to time for no reason at all. It didn't hurt very much but they were supposed to feel the humiliation of slaves. They had to chant in unison for twenty minutes: "We are racists, we are racists, we are racists." Before they could stand up and leave, they had to confess loudly and sincerely, one by one, that they were inherent racists with no way to redeem themselves, consciously or otherwise, due to Euro privilege and racist

DNA. They were warned that if anyone was judged not to be sincere, the person would be fired. They all chanted enthusiastically.

One of the Euros, a tall guy with red hair, didn't stay for the session in chains. He was apparently stubborn or not very bright. He stood up without permission and explained politely that his parents came from Ireland, no one in his ancestry owned any slaves or oppressed anyone, his parents were poor with only a small subsistence farm, they had scrimped and saved and worked their way over on a freighter, and had lowly jobs all their lives. Moments after the guy began talking, the HR monitor had pressed a security icon on her phone. Within minutes, two armed guys arrived and escorted the redheaded guy out.

The main practical thing Tom remembered from the training was that meritocracy was bad and mediocrity was good, and no one was supposed to work harder or better than anyone else because that created inequality of results. Tom didn't mind a policy against working hard in this job. He'd have more time for Izzy and to help on Buddy Lemmon's projects.

After Tom had left for his new job, Izzy drove down to Hyde Park faster than normal and didn't put on music. She had called ahead and her dad came out after she parked.

Izzy's brother showed up ten minutes later. His name in Italian was Giuseppe, but he was Joey in Chicago. Now 26, Joey worked as a car mechanic at an exclusive repair shop catering to Party leaders with luxury brands near the lake a few miles south of Evanston. He was a great mechanic but the owner also hired him for his Italian accent and good looks as a bonus for the fancy clientele. Joey knew everything about fixing Ferraris, Lamborghinis, Maseratis, Aston Martins, McLarens, Range Rovers, Jaguars, Mercedes, Porches, and the occasional Rolls Royce.

Some Party leaders liked Joey's work so much they took him under wing. They got him a Party membership card and he began joining their private parties. They flew him to an exotic island with many young women and teenage girls hanging around multiple swimming pools in bikinis. While Joey was talking to a woman with an Italian background, a facility director warned him that fraternizing with the females was limited to Party leaders and special guests and he wasn't on the list. He walked around the island, climbed the mountain, tried to keep his mind off the woman, and had some cynical and subversive thoughts. When Rocky told Joey about the underground, he was ready to join.

Professor Miller showed up shortly after Joey arrived. He looked completely different than when Izzy and Tom met him at Stardust. Now he looked the way he looked in the news and Wikipedia. Baseball cap on backwards. Short stubby beard growth. Faded loose fitting jeans, sandals, and a tie-dyed tee shirt with swirling multi-colors and the words "Grateful Dead."

Rocky said to the group, "Thanks for coming on short notice. Izzy can explain more."

Izzy took the cue and said, "My boyfriend wants to find his parents and the underground may be able to help. I also think he's ready to join us. He feels bad that he denounced his parents when he was thirteen in the Boarding School System. He thinks they're probably at the Alaskan Reserve. Professor Miller, you met him. He's the guy who was with me at Stardust the other night. We've been spending a lot of time together and I believe he's on the level. The fact is, we are in love and he just moved in with me. Sorry Mamma and Daddy if I should have told you first, but it happened pretty fast and there was no way you'd be able to talk me out of it anyhow." Izzy said this while glancing back and forth between her parents and looking down a few times.

The room was silent for several moments while everyone processed what Izzy had said. Her mom and dad were the first to react and said what Izzy knew they would say, that they were so glad she was in love with a nice boy, that they'd like to meet him, that they wished they could have met him before he had moved in with her.

"I don't get it. Why call us over instead of having our operatives do the usual background checks and vetting interviews?" the Professor asked.

Rocky explained. "Robert, here's the thing. Tom is viewed as a rising young star in the Party. He was not only in the Boarding School System, but also the Cadet Corps and Youth Brigades. He graduated with distinction in Equality Studies. Most significantly, he was recently promoted to work as a special assistant to Buddy Lemmon. Does anyone think this could be a sophisticated plan to use my daughter's affections to infiltrate us? Maybe we're supposed to think it's so audacious they couldn't possibly have made it up."

"It's odd that a young guy with a background like that would jeopardize his Party standing and benefits to join the underground. I don't know what to think," the Professor said.

Rocky waved his hand around like he wanted to make a key point. "That's why I wanted to go over this with you. I don't think our regular vetting process would reach any definite conclusions. Izzy only disclosed to this guy that she's in the underground, so he doesn't know about my involvement. It could be huge if he joins us while still working as Buddy's special assistant, and I basically trust my daughter's instincts. But what if he only cares about Izzy and plans to protect her as a confidential informant, while also trying to learn about other underground people or trying to get our full contact list. I can't feel 100% comfortable unless I meet this guy in person so I can read the metadata and get my own sense for him. But before even taking that step, I wanted to get your views."

"You're willing to take the risk of meeting him?" the Professor asked.

"Yeah, but I think it's a small risk given how my daughter feels. And I can manage the interview so it unfolds gradually. I'll say that I'll be in Evanston and would like to meet them for dinner like it's the next step in their relationship. I'll say I have private law clients that may have connections in the underground and see how the conversation goes. I don't really need to say much. I just need to get him to open up and then I can try to discern if he's real."

"Oh Daddy, Tom is so real," Izzy said.

"Is everyone agreed on this plan?" Rocky asked.

They confirmed their agreement, and Izzy asked her dad if he could come to dinner the next evening. Rocky nodded and Izzy texted Tom to say that her dad was going to be in Evanston the next evening and she'd like to have him over for dinner.

Within minutes, Izzy got a text back from Tom saying he looked forward to meeting her dad, but that he had to leave to go to Buddy's for dinner right away and he'd get home later that night. Izzy sent a reply to clarify that she was talking about dinner tomorrow.

Tom had recovered from the Euro-Only Diversity, Equity & Inclusion training at his new job a few minutes before 5:00 pm when he received a text asking if he could swing by Party headquarters and join Buddy for a drive to the North Shore where they could have dinner at Buddy's home. Tom thought this was odd, and then concluded that the oddness meant it was important. He texted back that he'd stop by Party headquarters about 5:15 pm.

When Tom reached the reception area, Buddy was waiting with a bag of Mojo's beans that he was taking home and gave another bag to Tom. Tom put his bag of beans into the crumpled paper bag that had contained his lunch. He was hoping Izzy could re-use the lunch bag since there was a bag shortage at Equality Foods.

Buddy led Tom to a different set of elevators down to a lower level parking garage where they found Buddy's Range Rover SUV. For an older guy, Buddy was pretty fast at pulling the SUV out of the garage and getting over to Lake Shore Drive. His security detail was barely able to keep up in their three Range Rovers. Once they were on LSD, one of the security vehicles pulled ahead, put its lights and siren on, and cleared the way for the group of SUVs to race north.

The caravan sped up Sheridan and through Evanston to reach Buddy's home along Lake Michigan in Wilmette. Buddy's home was surrounded by a high stone wall and they drove through a massive gate with an adjoining security building. The home was not enormous, but the grounds were unusually large, about five acres stretching along the lake. As they parked on the circular driveway near the entrance and got out of the vehicle, Tom appreciated the old world Tudor style charm and grace of the home. He hadn't really known what to expect, but Party leaders often favored a stark post-modern style.

A uniformed man with a holstered gun greeted them in a professional manner and offered to put Tom's crumpled bag in a closet. The man also asked for Tom's phone and did a security check to ensure that Tom had no weapons or any way of recording.

Buddy's wife, dressed in casual clothes, strode confidently into the large foyer where she and Buddy greeted each other with a warmer kiss than you might expect for people who have been married so long. Buddy introduced her as Beatriz and she shook hands with Tom. She was probably ten years younger than Buddy and projected energy. But the main thing for Tom was the intelligent look in her eyes and the genuineness of her smile. Tom wondered if she might be the power behind the throne.

They made small talk as Beatriz led them to the dining room.

After they sat down, Beatriz turned to Tom, smiled and said, "So my husband told me how he's taken an interest in you over the past four years, and about your new work as his special assistant. He says you have unusually good knowledge of political and economic systems. He says you're not afraid to give honest input and fresh views, under confidentiality of course. Buddy tells me you're his new brain trust."

"I've enjoyed helping out, but I don't think I've done much so far," Tom said.

The substance of the conversation increased with each course. The soup brought up a discussion of Tom's background with the Boarding School System, Cadet Corps and Youth Brigades.

Beatriz led most of the discussions and eventually got to comparisons of different political and economic systems in ways that suggested cynicism about socialism. Tom sensed that Beatriz was warming him up to feel safer in discussing controversial topics. He guessed that she shared Buddy's views about candid discussions and he began speaking more openly. Yet he also felt like he was being interviewed and his answers were being carefully assessed. He joined in expressing cynicism but stayed away from anything subversive.

When the main course arrived, Buddy dismissed the staff and said he didn't want to be disturbed. The staff carefully closed the dining room doors as they left.

Tom thought he had figured out the purpose for the meeting so he said, "Buddy, I contacted all current personnel and alumni of the Youth Brigades. I worked with your militia commander to organize everyone from the Youth Brigades into your local militia units. They have their weapons and are on high alert. Commander Laura Zena has been awesome at organizing and planning everything at warp speed."

"Tom, great work on doing that so fast. I already knew that, though, and it isn't the real purpose for having you over." Tom felt his face turn red.

Buddy looked like he wanted to say something but paused and then explained, "Tom, this is super confidential as always. I'd like to provide some very sensitive background information. Beatriz became a cynic and then a closet conservative over the past several years and has been working on me for the past few years. She did a lot of secure internet research, talked it over with me, and then I did my own research and liked what I read."

Tom was astonished that Buddy and Beatriz were basically admitting that they had gone to banned websites and had become secret conservatives. He wondered what was going on but decided he should say as little as possible.

Buddy added, "Tom, I mentioned the other day that I'm getting tired of trying to run the country in this centralized top down corrupt bureaucratic socialist fascist system. The economy keeps getting worse and most of the people are sinking into poverty. Then they try to dabble in the black market where they don't pay taxes. They are unhappy and deeply cynical. Marxist socialism has apparently been tried all over the world for over a hundred years and has failed every time. Boris and I share a concern that we're getting old and we want to make positive changes. The alternative is that I just retire and maybe someone like Stalinsky takes over."

"That would be a disaster," Tom said.

"Yeah, and Boris has a similar concern in Russia. So, we've both reached similar conclusions. I want to restore the US Constitution and Bill of Rights and the two party system so there's free speech and competition of ideas. Boris will go with the English Parliamentary system as a model. We both want personal liberty and less government control. I want a reasonable plan to wean the country away from socialism and the Social Credit Point System. We need free enterprise and lower taxes to grow the economy. But I also want a basic safety net of programs and I'd like to restore and fund Social Security. We also need to revamp our tax system to incentivize innovation, productivity, and competition, and get the budget under control. I want to assemble the best old constitutional scholars and economists and tax people."

Beatriz added, "I've put together a list of the top people we'd like to assemble. I have contact information for some who fled to other countries and I'm hoping we can persuade them to come back or participate remotely. But we suspect a lot of the top minds are in the Alaskan Reserve, and our own cyber people don't have access to any data about the inmates. We have some reason to believe the underground's cyber team may be able to track people there."

"Are you saying you think I have connections with the underground? And that you want me to ask the underground to help find people in Alaska?"

"Tom, that's accurate, but it's far more than that," Buddy said. "I want my militia to join forces with the underground as allies to get rid of Stalinsky and restore freedom and Constitutional government."

Tom was having a major adrenaline rush. After thinking for several moments while looking away at the far corner of the ceiling, he said, "I might be able to help, but to be clear, I'm not in the underground. I just may know people who know other people who may have a way of contacting the underground."

"Tom, we need to go really fast. Stalinsky has his militia on high alert. Beatriz and I have put our cards on the table. Either you trust us or you don't. We're hoping you do."

Tom's mind was racing. He took several moments to consider his response as he locked eyes with Buddy and then with Beatriz.

Tom finally said to himself "what the hell" and said to Buddy and Beatriz, "Are you available if I can schedule a meeting the day after tomorrow? Maybe a brain-storming and planning meeting starting that morning and going all day and into the evening? If so, where do you want the meeting, and how do you want to cover security for you and the underground?"

Buddy replied, "Tom, getting the meeting so fast would be terrific. We can't expect the underground to feel comfortable at Party headquarters or without security personnel. Let's say both groups can have six armed security people. But the security people will stay outside the meeting room. I'd be okay with another location, either here at our home or else at one of the underground's safe houses if they don't mind giving the location. But I'm not going to wear a hood and be driven around to some secret underground place."

Tom said he'd like some privacy to make a call. Beatriz pressed a button on the side of the dining table where she was sitting and the uniformed man who had opened the front door arrived several moments later with Tom's phone and his bag of coffee beans in his crumpled brown lunch bag. Buddy and Beatriz excused themselves from the dining room so Tom could make his call. Beatriz asked him to press her table call button when he finished.

Tom called Izzy and gave a five minute explanation, and then Izzy added Rocky and Professor Miller to the call over the next few minutes and switched the call to video. Izzy introduced them to Tom and then lied and told him that Rocky and Professor Miller weren't actually in the underground but had some contacts. Tom gave a full explanation of the extraordinary developments.

The Professor was cautious and said the underground would want to pick up Buddy without any of his security people, put a blindfold on him, and drive him in circles and then to a safe house. Tom spoke vigorously against that and explained that he had gotten to know Buddy and had a good feeling about him. Tom said those precautions would signal mistrust and delay everything and Buddy would never go for it anyway.

Rocky was leaning toward Tom's views. Rocky explained that he'd gotten to know Buddy while handling his legal work. He added that Buddy's home had a mortgage and that Buddy had only put aside enough overseas assets to be okay if he and his family ever had to flee from Stalinsky. Rocky contrasted that with the massive wealth that Stalinsky and his cronies had amassed. After ten minutes, the Professor said he was comfortable that the underground would accept the meeting proposal, and they discussed some details and a contingency.

As soon as they hung up, Tom pressed the button and Buddy and Beatriz came back. Tom said he'd spoken to someone who seemed to be able to speak on behalf of the underground and that they'd be okay with each group having six armed security personnel. They wanted the meeting at an underground safe house in Evanston, and they were willing to disclose the address. They could be ready in two days beginning at 9:00 am.

But there was one contingency. The underground had not yet officially cleared Tom, and they didn't want to rely so much on Tom's views before he was vetted. That was supposed to happen when Izzy's dad would be in Evanston to meet Tom the next evening. Buddy and Beatriz said that was fine and thanked Tom for moving so fast. Tom sent a brief text to Izzy confirming that the meeting was approved and she immediately forwarded the text to Rocky and Professor Miller.

As Buddy and Beatriz walked Tom back to the foyer, a guy came in the door who seemed to be in his mid or late twenties. Beatriz introduced him as Buddy Junior and said he was home for a week without mentioning where he had been. Junior offered to shake hands and Tom felt he had to go along.

Some people might consider Junior attractive, but Tom couldn't get past his knowledge that Junior had raped Izzy when she was fifteen. With Buddy and Beatriz standing there, Tom felt obligated to make some small talk so he asked Junior if he was having a nice visit and what he enjoyed doing with his time in the Chicago area.

Junior looked down and didn't have much to say and Tom got the sense that the visit wasn't Junior's idea of a good time. But Junior mentioned a sports bar and music lounge near the Evanston campus where he liked to hang out because there were college chicks.

Beatriz offered to have someone drive Tom to his place in Evanston. By the time he got there, Izzy had fallen asleep curled up on the sofa. Tom was concerned about startling her and concerned for himself if she made a defensive judo move. She had shown him some of her favorites. To wake her up, Tom began to speak to Izzy in a quiet voice from several feet away.

While Tom was dining and plotting with Buddy and Beatriz, Director Stalinsky was holding an emergency meeting of his Committee on Social Control. Ashley Bennington had joined the Committee to replace Professor Miller.

Stalinsky pounded his gavel and asked one of the sycophants for an update on plans to launch Saul Alinsky tactics against Buddy Lemmon and his supporters. Stalinsky believed the Soft Coup owed much of its success to the decades of work beginning in the late 1960s when the movement was a loose collaboration of grad students who idolized Saul Alinsky and his "Rules for Radicals." As the movement grew, Alinsky tactics became embedded as standard operating procedure. They especially liked Rule #5: *"Ridicule is man's most potent weapon (How do you defend?)"* But they were even more enamored of Rule #13: *"Pick the target, freeze it, personalize it, and polarize it. Cut off the support network and isolate the target from sympathy. Go after people and not institutions; people hurt faster than institutions."*

Stalinsky and others in the movement and the news media had done masterful work using Saul Alinsky tactics against the brash conservative President during his entire presidency leading to the Soft Coup. He was the perfect target. In fact, the Saul Alinsky tactics and smears against him were so pervasive and successful that a majority of people came to believe them, along with related phony narratives and investigations about Russian and Ukrainian collusion. As so many people came to believe that the brash conservative President was a racist and a fascist, maybe it seemed logical to assume that most of his supporters were also racists and fascists, even though they actually weren't either. In fact fascism and racism were anathema to him and his supporters. They all revered the Declaration of Independence, Constitution and Bill of Rights, and the two party system of representative government with a lot of checks and balances. They had no tolerance for racism or the variation called White Supremacy. Instead, they loved the Civil Rights Acts of the 1960s and all of the progress that society had made toward MLK's dream of a color blind society by the 1990s. The brash conservative President's supporters, which included many Black and Brown conservatives and free-thinkers, particularly liked his policies which helped Blacks and Browns more than most past politicians, for example with investment opportunity zones, better employment results, major prison reform, tighter immigration controls that helped the poor minority people who were already here, and better funding than the old liberal party ever gave to historically black colleges and universities (HBCUs). Of course, smaller fringe extremist groups may have included some racists or fascists, but they didn't represent the general conservative movement which was about freedom instead of fascism, tolerance instead of prejudice, and color blind equal opportunities instead of racism or discrimination.

Director Stalinsky's first sycophant reported that Cyber Command was ready with phony stories and phony evidence to ridicule and slander Chairman Buddy Lemmon and his supporters as secret corrupt capitalists and racist fascists. Stalinsky's team had no way of knowing whether that was true. They came up with their strategy based on what they knew about Stalinsky and assumed Buddy was the same. Accuracy was beside the point anyway.

The sycophant also reported that Cyber Command was ready to channel the fake news stories and slanders through their network of aligned news reporters, journalists and commentators, and would provide frequent updates until the stories and slanders were no longer doubted. If anyone tried to defend against the onslaught, Cyber Command was prepared to dox and destroy each person as a racist fascist capitalist or whatever seemed helpful.

Stalinsky only had one point to add. He wanted a simpler form of message that even the silly masses would understand if it became ubiquitous. The simpler message would be: ***"Buddy Bad. Stalinsky Good."*** He directed the Committee to assign maximum resources to the preparation and placement of posters and banners with that message everywhere possible, and for the message to pop up automatically in every email or text anyone opened and on every social media and internet site that anyone accessed. None of the sycophants dared to ask whether this might seriously annoy most people, though they were all thinking the same thing.

Stalinsky turned to Commander Ashley Bennington and asked for her update. Ashley explained that she had a series of video calls with the leaders of the far left vigilante militias, and they were all on-board and ready to rumble. They hated Buddy because he never actively endorsed their level of militant tactics, such as beating up people who publicly expressed or posted cynical views, for example when they tried to leave their homes or were discovered in a restaurant or at a gas station or in a department store or other public place. The far left militias viewed Buddy Lemmon as dangerously soft. Not only had Buddy remained silent instead of publicly endorsing their methods, but he even had the audacity to try to dissuade them in private.

Commander Bennington then summarized the battle plan she had worked out with the militia and Political Police leaders. The plan focused initially on occupying key government buildings in DC and each state capital and certain major cities. They had developed a list of the buildings and government officials who worked in each building. Then they divided the officials into categories. They'd put their supporters in charge and remove the other officials.

Stalinsky praised Ashley's work and the sycophants joined. But they were smart about it because they recognized that Ashley could emerge as a new power, maybe even Stalinsky's successor down the road. So each sycophant effused praise with somewhat different words. The last one to speak even personalized his statement by saying how much he looked forward to working with Ashley. Then the other sycophants said more or less the same thing.

Stalinsky directed that the Alinsky-style smear campaign should begin immediately. He said he'd probably launch the battle plan within a few days, as soon as the fake news and smears weakened support for Buddy. He asked the Committee to work on a speech he could give about taking control to save the Republic from the racist capitalist fascism of Chairman Buddy Lemmon.

Stalinsky pounded his gavel to close the meeting. He remained seated while everyone else stood and gave the fist salute before leaving the room. Then he leaned back in his chair and raised his feet and rested them on the marble conference table while he folded his hands behind his pointy head and indulged in a broad crooked smile.

Chapter Fifteen

Tom and Izzy began the next day the same as the day before, though it would end very differently. Tom took his new lunch in the same crumpled bag and caught the "L" down to the Chicago Loop for his second day at his new job. He was relieved to see a text from his manager excusing him from the additional two days of Euro D & I training and humiliation sessions.

Tom settled in at his desk and reviewed the Bureau's internal manuals and guides for social control. About 11:00 am, Tom's manager, Ms. Lilly Berman, stopped by and said she'd like to treat him to a cup of coffee to welcome him to the office. He was confused since he already had a half-empty cup of the office's free Equality Coffee at his desk and didn't think it was much of a treat.

Lilly sensed Tom's confusion and said she wanted to treat him to coffee at a good place. When they reached street level, Lilly led Tom to the basement of a nearby building. Lilly placed orders with the only employee while Tom sat in a booth at the back of the empty Mojo's.

Lilly sat down with the coffees and whispered, "I also work for Buddy. You need to go over right away and tell him that Stalinsky has a final battle plan to mobilize the far left militias and Political Police. They are on high alert and will implement the plan within two days, right after their smear campaign gets traction. I'll keep trying to get a copy of the battle plan."

Tom was nervous but quietly whispered the message back to Lilly to see if he got it right. When Tom reached the Party headquarters building, Buddy's admin was waiting in the ground floor lobby. He escorted Tom through security and up to an interior room where Buddy had set up a temporary command post. There was a "War Room" sign by the door.

Buddy and five senior staff members had been having video calls on large monitor screens but the screens were off now. Tom had already met Commander Laura Zena. Buddy introduced the others. Ben Shapiro worked on international relations. Naomi Brown worked on government relations. Jesse Owens was in charge of cyber security, and Lucy Valez worked on communications and social media.

Tom relayed Lilly's message about Stalinsky's smear campaign and battle plan timing. Lucy Valez spoke first. She said her communications team had received automated alerts about the Alinsky-style smear campaign as soon as it began to appear. She and her team had launched a counter campaign they had prepared proactively. They were also ready with a series of updates to try to take control of the narrative and news cycle. She said her team was jazzed and morale was high.

Tom said the person who gave him the message hadn't been able to get a copy of Stalinsky's battle plan, but would keep trying. Buddy asked Jesse Owens to put his best cyber people on hacking Stalinsky's data systems. Jesse said they'd keep trying but that Cyber Command had a strong firewall.

Buddy asked Tom for an update on the plans to meet with the underground leaders the next morning to discuss their proposed alliance against Stalinsky. Tom gave the address of the safe house in south Evanston, and reminded Buddy about the limit of six armed security personnel. Buddy asked about the underground's contingency of vetting Tom. Tom said it would happen when Izzy's dad came to meet him at dinner that same evening. Buddy told his staff to plan an all-day meeting with the underground beginning at 9:00 am the next morning.

Buddy told Tom not to go back to his job at BOT anymore and that he'd work full time on Buddy's staff for now. Buddy added that

Tom should take the rest of the day off because the next few days would be tough. Tom had left his bag lunch at BOT but didn't care because he was pumped about the political developments and about getting the rest of the day off. He texted Izzy that he'd be home by 3:00 pm.

Izzy greeted Tom with a long kiss and tight hug. She poured two glasses of chilled lemon water. They discussed the political developments and then tried to relax by watching a 1980s movie called "Crossing Delancey," a romantic comedy set in New York City with a good sound track by The Roches. Soon after the movie ended, Izzy got a call from her dad saying he would be at her place in twenty minutes. Izzy ordered pizzas from a local joint.

After Rocky arrived, small talk gradually changed to open ended questions that Rocky asked Tom, such as how he liked the Boarding School System, whether he had made some friends there and what they were like. He asked questions about the Youth Brigades, how Tom liked that service, whether he had made some friends there and what they were like. He asked Tom how he liked working as Buddy's special assistant and what he thought about Buddy and Stalinsky. He asked Tom about his views on political and economic systems. Tom knew he was being vetted for the underground and gave honest answers, though he was careful with his phrasing and avoided saying more than necessary. He also spoke quietly. You never knew who might be listening on some new technology.

"Tom, I need to get into a sensitive area involving your parents. I understand that you denounced them when you were thirteen. Can you tell me more about that?" Rocky asked.

Tom replied quietly, "I feel really embarrassed and bad about that. I was indoctrinated in the Boarding School System beginning at age ten. I was taken over 200 miles away and only saw my parents during limited visiting hours. With the indoctrination, I viewed my parents as selfish capitalists who harmed society with their coffee business and didn't understand socialism. I drank the Kool-Aid."

Rocky said, "Okay Tom. I listened to all of your answers this evening and sensed your sincerity. I'm also aware of what you've shared with Izzy. We are good here. I also have some good news. Our cyber team located your parents. They are in good health and run the coffee facility in Camp I at the Alaskan Reserve. They even have a private room with a double bed." He added with a droll smile in his charming Italian accent, "They must make excellent coffee."

Tom began to cry uncontrollably and Izzy embraced him and began to cry herself. Rocky didn't cry but looked empathetic. Izzy said she'd pour some wine so she went to the kitchen. Tom went over to adjust the music system.

Someone knocked loudly on the door three times. Rocky said he'd get the door since he was closest. Izzy's intuition kicked in and she stayed in the kitchen with her phone ready to text Gina.

Rocky opened the door and saw a short man pointing a gun at him while holding a Political Police badge in his other hand. Behind the short guy stood two bigger men in black Political Police uniforms and helmets. They were holding submachine guns pointing down and to the side.

"Are you Professor Fanella?" the short man said.

"Yes, that is true, but what is this about?" Rocky asked.

"Professor Fanella, you are under arrest. The charge is subversion. I have orders to take you to the Chicago Political Jail."

Izzy typed into the text box to Gina "dad tom me arrested Stalinsky chi pol jail," hit send, then turned her phone off and dropped it in her purse on the counter.

"There must be a mistake. I am a Professor of Law at the U of C in Hyde Park."

The short man said, "I listened through the keyhole to this unit. You were clever to ask open-ended questions, but I knew you were trying to recruit these kids. I couldn't hear the quieter statements. But, Professor Fanella, you made a serious mistake in disclosing information about the Alaskan Reserve. The only way you know that is through the underground."

"But that doesn't mean I'm in the underground. I have clients and I just handle interviews. I hereby assert attorney privilege on the conversation. Anyway, how could it be illegal to share some information I picked up about Tom's parents in the Alaskan Reserve? How does that prove I am in any underground?"

"Tell that to the interrogators," Iggy said. "Now, I need both of you to stand facing the wall to be handcuffed." He raised his voice and said, "Izzy, come out of the kitchen or wherever you are, and join the others facing the wall. You and your boyfriend are material witnesses."

"Iggy, can this be you?" Izzy asked pleasantly while smiling as she came into the room.

"The nerdy act was my cover. I'm not just a senior Block Minder. I'm in charge of Stalinsky's security team for Evanston. Now join your comrades facing the wall."

Iggy was talking and behaving like a street-wise person who was used to making decisions and taking charge. Izzy decided not to bother playing coy.

Iggy placed them in handcuffs behind their backs while the two big guys stood guard. He then directed them down the stairs and into the back seat of a black Chevy Suburban.

As soon as Gina got Izzy' text, she called Joey Fanella. They concluded that Rocky, Tom and Izzy had been arrested by Stalinsky's Political Police and were being taken to the Chicago Political Jail. Joey said he'd contact Professor Miller and they would contact the underground's military wing. Gina said she had her own plan and they hung up.

Gina changed into a short dress and checked her makeup. She went to her closet and found a small wood box. It was a collection of old coins she had inherited from her grandpa. She took a one ounce gold Krugerrand, probably worth $10,000, and slipped it into her bra.

Gina rushed down to her car and drove quickly south through Evanston and down further to get on Lake Shore Drive which she took to get near downtown Chicago where she made her way to an Equality Café near the building with the Justice Jail and Political Jail. The Café was closed at that time of night in that location. She parked in a nearby lot, walked over to the Equality Café, picked up a landscaping border brick, and heaved the brick through the plate glass window.

Gina stood there until a cop arrived. When the cop asked if she threw something through the window, she said that she threw a brick to protest the coffee. The cop cuffed her, walked her over to the jail building and booked her. Just before the attendant clicked a mug shot, Gina turned and tilted her head up slightly and smiled so it was more of a glamour shot and asked if she could get a copy for her mom. The dour attendant didn't react and turned Gina over to a female guard. The search did not require that Gina remove her underwear so the Krugerrand coin was safe.

Gina was relieved that no one else was in her cell or nearby cells, especially when a male guard in his mid-20s walked by and glanced over and seemed to admire her dress. Gina was ready with a friendly smile, so the guard came closer and they began to talk quietly. She introduced herself, and he said his name was Lars Swendson. As they began to flirt, Gina noticed his strong features, intelligent eyes, and an unusual sense of empathy for a jail guard. Lars liked Gina's friendly smile, amusing personality and short dress.

After a while, Gina explained to Lars what she was in for, and Lars whispered that he also thought the coffee at Equality Café was too weak and that he sometimes felt like throwing a brick. Gina said she had a clean record and was a good student at Northwestern and would be starting her senior year in the Fall. Lars said he had a degree in Criminal Justice from Loyola and wanted to become a detective. He said he really wanted to go on to grad school and become a professor, but the admission quota for Euros was so low it wasn't worthwhile. Gina asked if he was seeing anyone, and he said not currently, and asked her the same thing. She said she had been seeing a guy who was in Art School, but wasn't sure if he was right for her.

They also opened up enough to figure out that they both preferred Buddy Lemmon over Stalinsky. Gina decided a bribe wasn't necessary and might not go over well anyway, so she kept the gold coin in her bra. Instead, she told Lars that she got arrested on purpose. Gina disclosed that an armed conflict was imminent between Buddy's forces and Stalinsky's forces. Lars listened intently as Gina talked about Buddy's alliance with the underground and the shared vision of restoring Constitutional freedom. Then she said she needed a big favor and it was Lars' chance to be on the right side of history. After hearing Gina out, Lars helped form a quick plan. Lars let Gina out of the cell in the Justice Jail, cuffed her hands behind her back, and led her over to the Political Jail as though escorting an inmate for an official transfer.

When they reached the front desk of the Political Jail, Lars explained that he was supposed to transfer Gina to the holding cell where Professor Fanella was located. The desk sergeant took down Gina's name and gave Lars directions to the cell and a keycard. As they approached the cell, Lars held a finger to his lips to signal that Rocky, Tom and Izzy should remain quiet. Lars uncuffed Gina, opened the cell door, gestured for them to come out, then escorted them all down a service corridor that led to an indoor basketball court where the Guardian Team of Justice Jail guards often played against the Praetorian Team of Political Jail guards.

Lars rushed them across the empty indoor basketball court to a fire exit door at the far end. Lars didn't know if an alarm would sound when the door was opened. They quietly debated what to do. As Lars became comfortable that he was with the good guys and they were getting ready to fight for freedom, he asked if he could join. They welcomed him energetically while remaining quiet. On a count of three, they burst out through the door and a loud alarm siren began wailing and several lights lit up the alley where they found themselves.

They had decided to separate if an alarm rang, so Gina and Lars raced down the alley heading south. Rocky, Tom and Izzy raced up the alley north to Jackson and then turned east toward the Party headquarters building several blocks away. Within a block, they heard guards shouting and dogs barking and cop car sirens wailing from behind. They heard several quick three round automatic rifle blasts and the zing of bullets flying by and the sounds of the bullets hitting the nearby concrete building wall and ricocheting down the street. They got off Jackson by plunging into a dark alley and ran south down the alley as fast as they could go. A vehicle turned into the alley from the south end with its headlights pointing toward them. They heard the guards' shouts and dogs getting closer up Jackson nearing the entrance to the alley behind them. Tom shouted that they should look for an entrance to the building along the alley, so they frantically rushed over and tried a door but it was locked.

As they were trying the door, the vehicle flashed its lights quickly three times and the group froze. Someone got out and yelled the underground's password for the day. Rocky shouted the reply password. The guy got back in and raced the vehicle down the alley toward them and screeched to a hard stop a few feet from the group in a cloud of swirling alley dust visible in the head light beams. Rocky ran around to the left, while Tom and Izzy ran around to the right. They pulled open the back doors and piled into the back seat of the large black Jaguar XJ sedan.

The driver squealed the rubber and the engine roared as he raced the vehicle backwards until they emerged at the south end of the alley. He immediately pivoted and swung around so the vehicle faced east and then squealed the wheels in a cloud of street dust visible under a street lamp as he floored the accelerator. They headed fast down a one-way street the wrong way but it was late and no traffic was coming toward them. A cop car with swirling lights swerved in suddenly from a side street about ten yards ahead facing them, but the Jaguar driver veered sharply, smashed his side mirror against the cop car's side mirror, and raced east toward Lake Shore Drive.

Tom and Izzy were looking back out the rear window and yelled that they were being followed as soon as they saw two cop cars come out of an alley and accelerate to catch up with blaring sirens and flashing lights. The cops were good but the driver of the underground's Jaguar XJ was far better. He quickly got over to Lake Shore Drive, used his left hand to reach up and place a flashing light bubble with a magnetic base on the roof, floored the gas pedal, and maneuvered around every car in his way. He lost the cop cars after about five miles and turned off the light bubble. He got off LSD at Irving Park Road so they could continue on side streets in case the cops put a road block further up LSD.

Izzy told Tom the driver was her brother Joey, that he worked on fancy cars for a job, and that he raced as a serious hobby on a private course in the southwest suburbs. Izzy looked back and saw three helicopters shining spotlights down on LSD while heading north. Joey kept going west to Western Avenue which he took north all the way to Evanston where it became Asbury. He made his way through side streets to Ashland which he took north until he reached the safe house where the underground would meet Buddy and his staff the next morning. Joey dropped the others off and drove south to his condo where he parked in a garage in the back.

The safe house was a raised three-flat if you included the garden level half-basement unit. They entered the raised first level and Rocky gave a quick tour. It was well furnished and well-stocked. Rocky had used some of his own money to fix it up. They were all exhausted so they said goodnight, washed up and turned in.

Chapter Sixteen

By 8:00 am, Tom and Izzy were showered, dressed and eating some breakfast that Rocky had prepared in the kitchen of the underground's safe house. They heard a key turn in the front door. Rocky greeted his underground senior staff and brought them into the living room.

As Tom entered the living room, he recognized Noah Greene, his best friend from the Boarding School System. After a warm greeting, Noah explained that he was the Commander of the underground's military forces. Noah introduced the group to his key lieutenants, Sara Carter and Benny Goodman. Professor Miller, who had arrived with Noah, reminded Tom that they met at Stardust and explained that Stardust was an underground hang-out.

The group heard another key in the front door. Noah and his staff pulled their guns but relaxed as Izzy's brother Joey came in, followed by Gina and Lars. Gina introduced Lars as a new underground fighter and explained their role in the Political Jail rescue last night. Lars had traded his jail guard uniform for ill-fitting casual clothes that Izzy recalled seeing on Angelo before.

Buddy's security detail arrived shortly before 9:00 am wearing cargo pants and casual shirts. They had hand guns in their cargo pockets, but also brought submachine guns, AK-47s and extra ammunition in two violin cases, a viola case, and a cello case, as though they were musicians planning to practice string quartets. Tom found a playlist of early Hayden string quartets on his phone, put the speaker setting on, raised the volume, opened a window, and placed the phone on the sill facing out. The Hayden quartets were easy enough that semi-professionals or serious amateurs could be playing them.

Noah took Buddy's security detail upstairs to meet the underground's security team which had arrived at 6:00 am. The teams divided up surveillance and defensive positions on the upper floor and roof.

When Buddy and his senior staff arrived, Rocky disclosed that he was the national leader of the underground. Buddy said he wasn't surprised and they introduced their respective staffs. After they sat down, Buddy said he had an important question. "I need to know that the underground doesn't have any racists, White Supremacists, neo-Nazis, KKK, or anti-Semites, etc."

Noah said, "We don't have anything like that. We have a western civilization chauvinist group, but they just seem to value the development of western civilization political and economic systems, music, art and literature. They are especially fond of the Age of Enlightenment. We thoroughly vetted them to ensure they weren't White Supremacists."

"What's the name of that group?" Buddy asked.

"Friends of the Enlightenment."

Noah raised a concern. "Buddy, there have been unflattering news reports about you recently. Can you comment, including whether you are a wife beater?"

"That's Stalinsky's smear machine and Saul Alinsky tactics."

When the doorbell rang, Noah pulled his gun, opened the door, and was surprised to see an attractive middle aged woman, dressed to look younger. Few people would have recognized Buddy's wife, but she had worn a blonde wig under a baseball cap anyway.

Buddy introduced Beatriz to the group and explained that she had been working in the background, initially without Buddy's knowledge, for the past six years to get a majority of honorable talented people into seats in the Senate and House, and as governors, and in the state legislatures. Beatriz had also worked with the technical President and newer Senate leaders to fill Supreme Court vacancies with honorable talented people.

Buddy had indulged Beatriz's old-school ideas about getting good people in elected offices and as Justices, and routinely signed off on her choices in his role as Party Chairman. He didn't think it would make any difference one way or another. And he had been right so far. Beatriz had advised all the new officials to continue following the Party's directives until the time was ripe for freedom.

Director Stalinsky hadn't noticed the efforts to get good talented people in government positions because of his general arrogance and disdain for anyone below the level of himself. He was also confident in his ability to intimidate any official into saying and doing anything based on the successful results of his Ministry's earlier political and capitalist trials, his Political Police, Block Minders and Political Jails, his support from the far left vigilante groups, and the general fear of being sent to the Alaskan Reserve.

Rocky asked Buddy to provide some background about his views on freedom and Constitutional government. Buddy explained that he owed a debt of gratitude to Beatriz for getting him to read extensive materials she found on the dark web and foreign internet sites, and mentioned his favorite materials. Buddy then reported that he had been having excellent discussions with Ms. Georgia Washer, technically the President of the Republic, and summarized the vision for Georgia to emerge as a real President with a real cabinet, a real Congress, and a real Supreme Court.

Beatriz then explained how she came across Georgia Washer's impressive writings on politics and economics six years ago on the dark web. The postings were anonymous, but Beatriz was able to establish a rapport of trust in a series of secure communications and they eventually met at a small hotel in Montreal under false names, with sunglasses and wigs. Beatriz added for context that, before the Soft

Coup, Georgia grew up in urban poverty but had graduated at the top of her class from one of the leading historically black colleges and universities (HBCUs) on a full scholarship. After the Soft Coup, she had obtained a law degree and joint doctorate degrees in political science, economics, and finance at leading universities in England and Europe while working off the record for a low profile conservative think tank and policy group in London. She had then worked her way up to a very senior position of that group.

For more perspective, Beatriz forwarded a list of some of the people Georgia most admired: the Founding Fathers in the context of their times and for their constitutional vision and wisdom, as well as Abraham Lincoln, Fredrich Douglass, Booker T. Washington, Martin Luther King, and a number of prominent Black conservatives who disappeared after the Soft Coup, including Senator Tim Scott, Candace Owens, Leo Terrell, Larry Elder, David Webb, Ben Carson, Herman Cain, J.C. Watts, Clarence Thomas, Alveda King, Carol M. Swain, Michael E. Kerridge, Lt. Col Allen West, Thomas Sowell, Walter Williams, Ward Connerly, Vernon Jones, and John James who ran for Senator in Michigan and may have won if there hadn't been voting irregularities according to some views, and Shelby Steele, especially for his documentary "What Killed Michael Brown," about an event long ago in Ferguson Missouri. Beatriz noted that the list was not complete, but was a good representative sampling.

Rocky and Professor Miller had already read a lot of Georgia Washer's writings. After reviewing the list of people whom Georgia most admired, Rocky said a lot of them were already in the underground and others were either in safe countries or the Alaskan Reserve. They agreed that Georgia would be an excellent real President with Constitutional powers.

There was a pause while everyone processed what had been said. Professor Miller then announced that, when Stalinsky fired him from Cyber Command, he had kept a backdoor program that allowed the same computer access that he had as an inside mole. He now had Stalinsky's complete battle plan, which he summarized as follows:

"The Stalinsky plan focuses initially on occupying the White House, Capitol Hill and other key government buildings in DC and each state capital and certain major cities. They developed a list of the buildings and government officials who work in each building. Then they divided the officials into categories of Good, Bad, Unclear, and Blow With The Wind.

"The plan involves occupying and securing each key building, removing the Bad and Unclear officials and taking away their building access cards, phones, laptops and any other devices. Right after that step, the Stalinsky far left militia leaders in charge of each building will work out the details so the Good personnel in Stalinsky's plan will be in charge.

"The Stalinsky plan includes details such as the numbers of their militia forces overall and by location, and even the force assignments for each targeted building. So Stalinsky's plan has 50,000 troops in DC, 25,000 in Chicago, and 15,000 or less in each of the other key cities. This aligns with information obtained through our moles. We don't separately count Stalinsky's 50,000 Political Police because they are already included as active members of his far left vigilante militias.

"Antifa is an unknown. We haven't been able to infiltrate or recruit informers. Our best guess is that Antifa has 50,000 armed personnel, but that they will stay on the sidelines and then use the fog of war to infiltrate, attack and oust Stalinsky if he emerges as the winner.

"Now on our side, our underground forces are roughly equal to the Stalinsky forces in each location. So maybe we can deploy allied forces to each government building on Stalinsky's plan and get in position before the Stalinsky forces arrive. We'd have the element of surprise and the tactical advantage of defending the buildings instead of attacking."

Buddy said his own militia with the Youth Brigades had 250,000 troops, deployed in the same cities and the same proportions as the underground. So, combining the underground's military forces with Buddy's militia should significantly out-number the bad guys.

Everyone did high fives or knuckle knocks as they grasped the significance. Commander Zena commented that the fighting would be more like a really tough street brawl than a full-blown civil war.

But everyone agreed it was critical to move at warp speed before Stalinsky could gain a foothold and perhaps sway the regular military and the Blow With The Wind people. There was also a question about which way the FBI brass might go since they were part of Stalinsky's Ministry of Truth & Justice.

Buddy asked Commander Laura Zena, Commander Noah Greene, and Noah's Lieutenants Benny Goodman and Sarah Carter, to create a final battle plan that would essentially match the Stalinsky plan, but would have more freedom forces for each target building, with earlier deployment times, and with a change in the lists of government officials by simply reversing Stalinsky's designations of Good and Bad.

Tom asked whether there was a code name. Buddy suggested "Project F" for now and "Operation Freedom" when the operation became publicly known. Tom then suggested that they refer to their allied teams as "Freedom Forces" and the troops as "Freedom Fighters."

Professor Miller disclosed that he and his underground cyber team had been receiving volunteer assistance from the Israeli Intelligence Community through Noah's contacts. Noah added that he had arranged for 5,000 Israeli Defense Force commandos to help and they were deployed near DC.

Rocky added that he had arranged for the British to assist in DC through his father-in-law, Hans Huber, a senior consultant to the British Secret Intelligence Service (SIS/MI6). Hans was aboard a British battleship off the Delaware coast with 5,000 elite commandos in troop carriers.

Buddy asked if the Israelis or British expected anything in return for their support. Noah and Rocky affirmed that the Israelis and British were serving as volunteers because the Republic had helped them before the Soft Coup and they hoped for increased trade opportunities in the future.

Naomi Brown said she was working with Beatriz on a heads-up call that evening with President Washer and her cabinet, key leaders in the Senate and House, and the governors. Naomi added that she and Beatriz had held a confidential call with sympathetic officials in each state capital and the targeted major cities. Naomi offered to check her own list of sympathetic officials with the Good Officials on the battle plan, and walked over to join the military leaders who were reconvening in the dining room. As Naomi joined the military leaders, they were initiating a video call with Buddy's militia lieutenants and the underground's British and Israeli contacts.

Buddy switched topics to the proposed new foreign Alliance. He turned the floor over to Ben Shapiro, his senior international advisor, who reported that his team had finalized a proposed new international arrangement in which the Republic would abrogate its treaties with China and form a new Alliance with Russia and India, including details about Boris stepping aside in Russia and calling for a new constitutional form of government with guaranties for free speech, a free press, and free and fair elections.

Ben Shapiro then explained that, pursuant to a consensus among President Washer, Beatriz and Buddy, and key Senate leaders, the proposed Alliance was being expanded to include Great Britain, Israel, Japan, South Korea, and the remaining Western-style democracies for trade and defense. As the quiet applause and excited buzz in the room died down, Ben added that the expanded Alliance would be able to pay full value to buy Alaska to help the Republic pay down some of its massive debts.

Commander Noah Greene had taken a break from the military team in the dining room and asked if the Republic could still own Alaska and just get loans from the Alliance. Buddy explained that the country had gone too far with ruinous debt, and had no better option than to sell Alaska, but that the deal would be subject to public debate and Senate confirmation.

Buddy asked if the underground had a good command and control center. Miller said it was cramped and lacked redundant communication lines. Buddy made eye contact with Beatriz and asked Commander Noah Greene to bring Commander Laura Zena back from the dining room. As the two Commanders returned, Beatriz said she had worked with special contractors to build a large fully equipped, state of the art, command and control center about 100 feet below her home's basement in Wilmette, with elevator and stairway access.

Beatriz noted that her subterranean facility stretched far beyond the footprint of the Wilmette house and had special filtered air shafts, water supplies from Lake Michigan, sewerage disposal systems with pumps and pipes, backup generators powered by high capacity batteries with back-up power from solar installations and two diesel generators with storage tanks in camouflaged locations on the grounds.

She added that the Wilmette facility had full communications redundancy, secure encrypted VPN capabilities, heavy blast protection, internal back-up data systems with links to a back-up data center in Iowa. The facility included a cafeteria, showers, armory, and a large barracks room with bunkbeds.

Commander Greene wanted to discuss the risks of a surprise attack by Stalinsky forces on Buddy's house and command center. He asked whether Stalinsky operatives might have been watching the house through Google Earth or a military satellite. Buddy explained that three years ago he pressed Google and the military satellite commanders to put a permanent security freeze on images of his home and a one mile radius around the home to block all updates. Anyone looking now would see the home and one mile area as they looked three years ago.

But because Stalinsky had 25,000 Political Police and far left militia troops in the Chicago area, Commander Noah Greene was still concerned about a surprise attack in Wilmette, and asked if Stalinsky drones could have surveilled Buddy's house. Buddy said his team had an electronic jamming system that would have blocked any drone signals and that his team would shoot drones down anyway.

Commander Greene then asked if Stalinsky's local security personnel and Block Minders might be aware of the construction activities at Buddy's house. Commander Zena said that was doubtful because of the high wall and the security cameras around the estate. She noted that Stalinsky's local security leader, a short guy with a blonde buzz cut, was recently sighted rushing his team onto a train heading south toward the Chicago Loop.

Commander Zena added that she had arranged for extra defenses in Wilmette through sympathetic mid-level officers in the National Guard. They were providing a cargo ship with jeeps, trucks, armored personnel carriers, anti-aircraft systems, sandbags, shovels, uniforms and military belts, body armor and helmets, backpacks and canteens, food rations and water sterilization tablets, and other equipment and supplies, including extra weapons and ammunition. The ship was anchored outside Wilmette Harbor and support personnel were assembling pontoon docks. She said all assets would be on shore by the end of the afternoon and deployed to Buddy's home that night. The local mayor was in the underground and had agreed to block roads and put up signs announcing a military exercise.

Beatriz and Buddy urged the group to drive to Wilmette and convene at the command center. Commander Zena gave a password that would get them through their military checkpoints in Wilmette. Tom and Izzy got a ride with Joey, Gina and Lars in the Jaguar. They joined a group of military trucks and jeeps driving north on Sheridan. When they got through the checkpoints and headed up the driveway toward Buddy's home, they saw military vehicles, equipment and supplies, and bustling teams sorting, stacking, organizing and moving supplies into the house. Tom noticed an anti-aircraft system.

As they entered the home, Beatriz showed them how to access a secret elevator behind a movable bookcase and they took turns riding the elevator down to the command and control center 100 feet below ground. As they took seats around a large conference table in the main command room, they reviewed newly updated Project F battle plans. The roles of the Israelis and British special forces commandos were still undefined. Buddy asked that Noah work with the Israelis to deploy and help secure and protect the White House, President Georgia Washer and her Cabinet and the Supreme Court. Buddy asked Rocky to work with the British to deploy and help secure and protect Capitol Hill and the Senate and House members and staff.

Beatriz reported that she and Naomi had set up an urgent synch call later that evening with Buddy, President Georgia Washer and her cabinet, the key leaders in the Senate and House, and the governors. Naomi said they were working on tentative arrangements to broadcast a joint meeting of the Senate and House, with Buddy as a guest speaker followed by President Washer, contingent on sufficient battlefield success. Lucy Valez said she had been working on drafts of speeches with Beatriz and President Washer. Valez added that she was extraordinarily impressed by President Washer.

Professor Miller stood suddenly, waived his hands, and said he had urgent news. He had just received a text from his cyber team that Stalinsky forces would be deployed at their assigned government buildings at 7:00 am EST the next morning. The group agreed to implement their battle plan immediately so their forces could deploy overnight and be in place by 6:00 am EST.

As the military leaders continued to work, Beatriz said she'd send over sandwiches for dinner and led the rest of the group to a cafeteria in the underground facility. The food was military quality and no one had any complaints. After the meal break, everyone who had assignments went back to the main command center room.

Tom and Izzy didn't have any assignments and were tired, so they found the subterranean barracks room and chose a bunkbed in a far corner. While Izzy brushed her teeth and took a shower in the communal area, Tom read the latest news reports. He saw a pop-up cartoon of a huge cargo ship with solar panels and three gigantic wind turbines, apparently sitting still in the water with no waves on a moonlit night. The caption said, "Director Stalinsky, thanks for the turbines, now how about some wind?"

Chapter Seventeen

Tom and Izzy woke up about 6:30 am EST the next day and were disoriented until they remembered they were in subterranean barracks. They were surprised that nearly everyone else had apparently already gotten up in a hurry and left. They showered and pulled on their clothes from yesterday and the day before.

They went over to the command center and saw everyone working intensely. They didn't want to interrupt, so they walked over to the subterranean cafeteria for breakfast. The cafeteria was nearly empty but they saw Gina and Lars at a table, so they brought their trays and sat down. A monitor screen was reporting that the day was clear or partly cloudy across most of the country, and cooler than normal for June from Chicago to the east coast.

The four of them began to commiserate about not having assignments. Beatriz walked into the cafeteria and asked the staff to make two pots of coffee for the command center. Tom pulled a chair from another table and Beatriz sat down but said she only had a minute. Izzy said they wanted something to work on. Beatriz smiled quickly and said they could bring the coffee over to the command center when it was ready.

There was an awkward silence. Tom said they'd be glad to bring the coffee but wanted some real work too. Izzy explained that she and Gina had worked on the underground's communications and newsletters. Beatriz apologized that she hadn't stopped to consider their skills and said they could join the group working on communications.

Tom then said that he and Lars had weapons training and wanted to join the fighting. Beatriz said Buddy didn't want Tom in combat unless necessary to defend the command center. She suggested they join the lookouts on the roof.

The coffee was ready a few minutes after Beatriz left, so Tom and Lars grabbed the pots and the group walked briskly to the main command and control room. Izzy and Gina went excitedly over to join Beatriz with the communications team.

Tom asked Lars to follow him. They made their way over to Noah Greene. Noah was busy and haggard but brightened when he saw Tom and got off his call within a few minutes. The underground fighters didn't have uniforms but Noah had organized and delivered Kevlar bullet proof vests and helmets with communications systems. The vests and helmets not only provided protection, they also allowed Buddy's uniformed militia to avoid mistaking the underground fighters for Stalinsky's far left militia, most of whom would be wearing dark street clothes.

Tom told Noah that he and Lars were trained with weapons and wanted assignments. Noah told them to wait because he had to make calls and prepare to join Commander Laura Zena in a joint update. It was now 7:00 am EST and Stalinsky's forces were presumably arriving at their designated government buildings in DC, and might also be arriving in each state capital and the targeted major cities if they followed their battle plan.

The key question was whether the Freedom Forces had gotten into positions at the designated buildings before the Stalinsky forces had arrived. The communications from DC over the past hour had been intermittent and unclear. There were levels in the chains of command and there had been technical issues with disconnections and latency.

At 8:00 am EST, Commander Laura Zena and Commander Noah Greene made a joint announcement in the command center with a link to the British and Israeli commanders. Fierce fighting had broken out in DC and Fairfax County, Boston, Baltimore, Chicago and Springfield,

New York City and Albany, Minneapolis, Seattle, Portland, San Francisco, Los Angeles and the capitals of the three West Coast states. Buddy wondered if Stalinsky had a strategic vision of controlling the Pacific Coast perhaps in an alliance with China.

Commander Greene reported that the Freedom Fighters in DC had apparently reached most of their deployment positions by 6:45 am EST and were tenaciously defending against fierce attacks by Stalinsky forces. The Commanders went through the other cities. So far the results were mixed. The Freedom Forces had not reached all of their assigned positions in time at various cities, Stalinsky forces had taken control of some buildings, and fighting was raging back and forth in the streets around the buildings and from building entrances and windows.

After the joint announcement, Noah hurried back to Tom and Lars and said he could use them in downtown Chicago. There was heavy fighting within and around the State of Illinois Building, the combined Chicago City Hall and Cook County Building, Buddy's Equality Party building, and other government buildings, including the Chicago office of Stalinsky's Ministry of Truth & Justice. Tom said he was somewhat familiar with the Ministry's building since he had worked at BOT for two days.

Noah said Tom and Lars could either join a convoy of twenty armored personnel carriers or ten Chinook helicopters that would leave soon to provide reinforcements. Noah had scored the choppers by appealing to a senior officer in the Air National Guard through one of his contacts late the prior night. The personnel carriers would leave in ten minutes but would take longer to reach the action in downtown Chicago. The Chinooks would get there faster and would take off in twenty minutes from a staging area in Ryan Field, the Northwestern campus football stadium in Evanston.

Tom and Lars were both afraid to fly, mainly because they had never flown before. But they were more afraid to admit it, and they wanted to join the Freedom Fighters as soon as possible. They opted for the helicopters and Noah said he'd get a Range Rover to rush them to the staging area. Noah asked what kinds of weapons they could handle, so Tom said he'd like an AK-47 variant like the PSAK-47 GF3, a Smith & Wesson Model 29 .44 Magnum hand gun, and some hand grenades, since he had trained with those in the Youth Brigades. Lars said "ditto," except the grenades.

Noah scrambled Tom and Lars to a weapons depot in the subterranean command facility where they grabbed the assault rifles and hand guns. They were wearing their street clothes but put on military belts with holsters for the hand guns and pouches for ammo, grenades and a water canteen. Noah slid the hand guns and canteens onto their belts while Tom grabbed five grenades and stuffed them in his belt. Tom and Lars put on Kevlar helmets and fastened the chin straps and Noah turned on the communications devices. Noah handed body armor vests and said to put them on in the helicopter.

Tom and Lars put the assault rifle straps over their shoulders and raced to the subterranean elevator, rode it anxiously up to the main floor, pushed past the moveable bookcase as soon as the elevator door opened, and rushed through the open front door of Buddy's house to an idling Range Rover SUV. The Rover roared forward as soon as Tom and Lars dove into the back seat from each side. The driver raced like he was on amphetamines.

They reached the stadium staging area and saw the last troops entering the Chinooks in battle gear. Tom and Lars jumped out and ran toward the last helicopter with their assault rifles bouncing from their straps and the Kevlar vests swinging around as they struggled to hold them. A flight crew guy at the door helped pull them in and slammed the door shut. The craft took off abruptly and climbed steeply to a low cruising altitude heading south over Lake Shore Drive. The helicopter was crammed with equipment and personnel, including a medic unit.

Tom and Lars took some time to rest and catch their breath before trying to figure out the bullet-proof vests with extensions to protect the groin area and various adjustable Velcro straps. They had suppressed their fear of flying but were mildly air sick. Two young female militia fighters in full battle gear, their faces flushed, recognized Tom from college and the Youth Brigades and came over to help with his body armor. They reminded him of their names, but he couldn't hear above the engine noise so he shook his head and pointed at his ear. As the young women helped put on Tom's vest and adjusted the groin protector and Velcro straps, they leaned close so he could hear and reminded him that they were the Rosalia twins, Lucy and Carmen. He remembered they were good at gymnastics and tennis. They hovered close and said he looked good and asked if he still went to the gym a lot. He recalled that he had wanted to go out with one or the other, but could never tell them apart, so he had never asked.

Tom blushed and asked the Rosalia twins to help Lars with his body armor. After they returned to their seats, Tom saw the twins talking and wondered if they were talking about him. Then he wondered if he was becoming vain and decided he should keep that in check. Then he decided the twins were probably not talking about him anyway.

Tom remembered a kid at Petosky Academy who seemed vain because he tried to impress people by talking about his high grades and achievements. The kid had been raised in a family that defined themselves by their accomplishments. Nobody liked the kid and Tom tried to coach him not to say things like his family had climbed Mount Kilimanjaro, even if true, unless someone asked a direct question. It took a lot of coaching because the kid kept looking for direct enough questions for an excuse to boast. Tom made more progress after asking the kid why he wanted to boast, and the kid said he wanted people to like him. Tom explained that the kid was pursuing that goal backwards, that people were turned off by boasting and preferred self-deprecating humor. He coached the kid to get in touch with his own feelings and thoughts, and work on developing his inner personality rather than seeking self-esteem from what others might think. The kid became more popular but it took a few months.

Tom thought about Izzy and felt sad that they hadn't kissed before he left the command center. His eyes watered as he realized he might not see her again. He only had a basic knowledge of Judeo-Christian beliefs, but said a prayer anyway.

A senior guy came over and said Tom and Lars would be in his squad. Tom looked up and said, "Hi Professor Laska. I'm Tom Hardy from your class on Modern European History."

"Welcome to the freedom fight, Tom."

Professor Laska adjusted the communications devices in Tom's and Lars' helmets and turned up the volume. Tom heard him say some test words and answered in his microphone.

Izzy was thinking about Tom as she remained in the Wilmette subterranean command center. She wished they had kissed before he left and wondered if she'd see him again, and quietly cried. She still didn't consider herself a particularly religious person but said a prayer.

When Izzy finished her editing work, the center was still a beehive with multiple video calls on multiple screens with multiple parties on each screen. Buddy, Rocky, Laura and Noah sometimes moved between screens with on-going calls as their input and decisions were requested.

Beatriz was having calls with political contacts but glanced over and saw that Izzy was distressed. Beatriz took a quick break and came over and showed Izzy how to pull up the battle communications. Izzy plugged a pair of headphones into her laptop and filtered down to listen to the Chicago fighting. She thought she heard Tom's voice a few times.

Someone in the Chinook announced that heavy fighting was continuing in downtown Chicago. He said the choppers would unload in Equality Park where the troops would assemble and then move west to reinforce the Freedom Forces that were attacking Stalinsky's Chicago Ministry building.

After the Chinooks landed, the commanders quickly organized their squads of fifteen troops, which were each part of platoons of forty-five troops. They began moving west and crossed Michigan Avenue with medic teams following. The city was bereft of traffic and pedestrians, but the troops heard heavy fighting further west and closer as they approached their target building. The Freedom Force commanders conferred while checking a Google map and directed their units to spread out in a perimeter of three blocks around the Ministry building and then gradually move closer.

Tom and Lars were with Professor Laska's squad with the Rosalia twins heading west on Jackson. The commanders and squad leaders and teams were communicating through their helmet devices. They had been advised that, except for the Political Police, the Stalinsky forces were wearing black motorcycle helmets and a mix of street clothes, but mostly black jeans and black tee shirts. The Freedom Force squads stayed close to the building walls as they moved forward and rotated in various directions while pointing their automatic rifles and submachine guns to pick off targets and provide suppressive fire.

When they got within sight of the Ministry building, bullets began whistling by and ricocheting around and Tom's squad dove into a recessed building entrance. Over the next few minutes, they discerned that the other squads on their side of the Ministry building were pinned down in recessed entryways and alleys. The squads were taking quick pot shots to draw fire to see where it was coming from and were then trying to fire back.

The heaviest fire was coming from a dozen heavy caliber machine gun nests behind sandbags near the entrances to the building and from assault rifles and submachine guns poking through broken windows on the second, third and fourth floors. Tom guessed the Freedom Fighter squads on the other sides of the building were also pinned down. Without tanks or heavy artillery, the fight would be bloody or may devolve into a stand-off that could last for days, which would create a risk that the regular military brass might pick a side. Tom wondered if the fighting in DC was similarly stalled and whether the FBI might be supporting Stalinsky.

Tom and Lars and the other squad members took turns peering out and shooting rounds up at the broken windows but didn't want to waste ammo. Sometimes they'd get a bad guy but usually they didn't. Tom saw a bad guy leaning out a broken window, took a moment to aim, shot the guy through the neck, and saw him fall out the window and land with a thud and a bounce. Tom wanted to throw his grenades at the machine gun nests but they were too far way. He loaded a new ammo clip and sat back for a moment to take a drink of water from his canteen.

Tom looked up as he heard engine noise approaching from above. He saw a Chinook hovering over the roof of the Ministry building. The helicopter was having trouble staying steady due to heavy winds blowing in from Lake Michigan. Ropes came dangling down and troops came quickly down the ropes, twisting and turning in the wind to reach the roof. After the Chinook took off east, a second Chinook came into view from the west and took the same position and had the same challenges with the wind. More ropes came down and more the troops came down the twisting turning ropes.

Meantime, the first group on the roof had blasted through the roof door, gone down the access stairs and assembled on the top office floor near the entrance to the fire stairs in the northwest corner of the building. The second group came down the roof stairs and assembled on the top office floor near the other fire stairs in the southeast corner. The commanders of the two groups reviewed the attack plan though their helmet communications devices.

The squads that were pinned down at street level received messages about the plans for the troops from the choppers to clear the building from the top down, and ordering the street squads to defend their positions and capture or kill any Stalinsky forces who tried to flee the building.

The descending troops ran into stiff resistance and slowed their pace when they reached the fourth floor where they encountered bursts from submachine guns and explosions of hand grenades. After an hour, though, most of the remaining Stalinsky troops on the fourth floor retreated to the third floor. A dozen surrendered and were placed in handcuffs behind their backs and ordered to sit. Both sides had suffered dead and wounded. Medic teams from the choppers performed triage and first aid.

The Freedom Force commanders from the choppers assigned two squads with tear gas canisters and gas masks to lead the attack on the third floor. There were not enough gas masks for the other two chopper squads, so the commanders ordered them further down the fire stairs to attack the second floor. They met heavy machine gun fire when they approached the second floor door, which was propped part way open. As the troops went down and came within sight, the heavy machine gun sent bursts of rounds up the stairwell. After thirty seconds, the squad leader took two grenades off her belt, pulled the pin off one, counted off the time, and lobbed it down the stairwell toward the door. It bounced back off the door frame and exploded just after the commander and her troops covered their heads and crouched on the stairs. The commander and a few of the other Freedom Fighters, though protected by helmets and body armor, suffered some cuts and contusions on their arms and legs.

As the echoing noise from the grenade explosion receded, the squad leader took the second grenade, pulled the pin, waited a few moments, said a prayer, lobbed it down and took extra care with her aim. The squad members who could see what was going on held their breath as they saw the grenade bounce off the floor and rattle through the open door and explode on the other side. With a waving arm, the leader led her troops quickly down the stairs to the landing.

The squad leader stuck her helmeted head through the doorway to assess the situation. She saw five dead guys on the floor and several other guys running away down a hall. She shouted for them to stop or be shot but they kept running with their weapons. She came through the door with her Uzi submachine gun and blasted the running bad guys, trying to aim for the legs, and they all dropped, dead or wounded. She directed a few troops to handcuff the wounded and contact the medics. She synched with the leader of the squadron at the other stairwell who was about to follow a similar procedure. As they conferred about going down to the ground floor, they heard a series of blasts that sounded like rocket-launched grenade explosions.

The RPG blasts were from Freedom Fighter street forces that had circled around and approached the building from the west side. The RPG team had used Saab Dynamics Carl Gustaf M4s to destroy the bad guys' sandbagged heavy machine gun nests and the west entryway to the building. Another squad's light machine gunners had also sent a series of rounds at the bad guys, some of whom were now lying dead and some of whom were wounded and crying out in pain. A third squad with AK-47s rushed to the entrance, cuffed the wounded, and took defensive positions. The Freedom Fighters on other sides of the building had also suffered dozens of casualties.

The Freedom Fighters from the helicopters were moving methodically on the third and second floors and finding more bad guys who wanted to surrender. The street squad leader at the demolished west side entrance synched with the street squad leaders on the other sides who reported they were still receiving heavy fire from sandbagged machine gun nests at the other entrances. The squad leader on the west side asked for reinforcements to join his squad in entering the building and clearing the rest of the ground floor so they could come out the other entrances and make surprise attacks on the other machine gun nests from behind.

By the time the Freedom Force street squads had gone through and cleared the other entrances, the chopper squads were emerging through the east side ground floor entrance with dozens of body bags and cuffed prisoners, including many who were wounded. Stretcher-bearers were bringing other wounded fighters from both sides. The Freedom Fighters carefully checked the prisoners and dead guys against electronic photos of Stalinsky's top Chicago militia leaders. But they couldn't make any matches. They became concerned that Stalinsky's top Chicago leaders and some troops could be hiding in the basement or making their way through the subterranean pedestrian walkway system that helped commuters handle Chicago winters. They assigned two squads to clear the basement and any sub-basement.

The commanders then used their phones to bring up the Chicago Transit Authority website and found a downtown map with the subterranean Pedway system. They hadn't heard any trains through the sidewalk grates and figured the trains had been shut down. They ordered the other street squad leaders to bring up the map and ordered squads to spread out to create a wide perimeter at entrances to the Pedway system and then go down into the system to tighten the noose on any fleeing Stalinsky forces. The Rosalia twins said goodbye to Tom as they were reassigned to another squad that had suffered heavier casualties.

Tom and Lars went with Professor Laska and the rest of his squad to reach their deployment at the "L" stop at State and Lake several blocks north.   They worried when they heard sounds of vigorous fighting further west around other buildings but stayed on their assigned mission. The team was tired but mostly managed to jog. Tom's gym work paid off as he ran and got two blocks ahead of the others.

When Tom was about thirty feet from the subway entrance, a short guy emerged from the stairs and looked around like a lost tourist, wearing sunglasses, a baseball cap, jeans and a wind-breaker jacket. He paused and seemed frightened. Tom slowed to a casual walking pace and pointed his rifle down to the side to avoid scaring the guy. He was thinking about cuffing the guy to a nearby bike rack.

When they were about twenty feet away Tom said loudly, "Sir, I am with the Freedom Forces. Do not be afraid. Please raise your hands." The guy faked Tom out by suddenly looking up at the sky while yelling "What's that?" Tom glanced up briefly and then looked back down and saw the guy lift up his wind-breaker with his left hand, whip out a gun with his right hand, and fire three automatic rounds toward Tom.

When Tom saw the gun come up, he threw himself flat on the sidewalk and rolled over twice toward the adjacent building wall. He heard the rounds and felt impacts on his helmet and body armor and an impact and sharp sting in his upper right arm. He saw the guy trying to keep his balance as he reeled from his gun's recoil. Tom was lying on his stomach on the sidewalk and his right arm was hurting, but he managed to raise his AK-47 and pull the trigger to send three rounds at the guy. The guy fell and remained still and Tom said another prayer, this time a prayer of thanks.

Tom got up and noticed his upper right arm was bleeding through his sleeve. He carefully approached the guy on the ground with his rifle pointed at the guy's chest. When he got closer, Tom could see the guy was in bad shape and probably bleeding out. He looked south and saw the rest of his squad was still a block away so he called for a medic. Tom took out his canteen, kneeled down, took off the guy's baseball cap, and held up the guy's head while offering sips from the water canteen. Without the baseball cap, Tom recognized Iggy's buzz cut.

Iggy opened his eyes and looked at Tom and said in a weak halting voice, "They made me do it man ... my sister in Alaskan Reserve ... gonna die ... Izzy could have liked me."

Tom saw that Iggy was going fast and felt sorry for the guy so he said, "Izzy thought you had potential to be good, man. I mean, she thought that about everyone."

"Yeah, ...got in a bad crowd."

Iggy passed with that thought on his mind as the rest of the squad reached the scene. At the Wilmette command center, Izzy was continuing to monitor the Chicago battle channels and thought she heard Tom's voice say Izzy or Iggy. Then she heard a rapid burst of gunfire followed by another rapid burst and then she only heard shouts from commanders and other troops.

She ran over to Beatriz but had to wait several minutes for her to finish a call with Buddy about his upcoming speech. Izzy described what she heard and Beatriz suggested that Izzy contact the four hospitals that had been designated for battle casualties and morgue facilities: Rush University Medical Center and John H. Stroger Jr. Hospital of Cook County, both on the near west side of Chicago, Northwestern Memorial Hospital in the near north area of Chicago, and

Lake Shore Evanston Hospital. Izzy decided to start with the hospitals closest to the fighting.

Professor Laska had seen the action. He had then seen Tom stand up and check the bad guy and then saw Tom struggle to take his rifle off his shoulder and drop it on the street. He saw Tom become unsteady and lay down. By the time Laska reached Tom, he saw blood soaking through the sleeve around Tom's upper right arm and saw blood pooling on the sidewalk. Laska pulled a knife from his belt and cut Tom's sleeve to look at the wound. A medic arrived, cleaned the wound, and applied a military field pressure dressing.

After Laska conferred with the medic, he told Tom the battle was over for him. Laska led the rest of the team down into the subway / Pedway system while the medic gave Tom some morphine. Tom felt faint as he stood up. The medic asked if he needed help walking to the choppers and Tom nodded. The medic picked up Tom's AK-47 and walked him east a few blocks, across Michigan Avenue, and up into a Chinook idling in Equality Park. The medic took off Tom's helmet and Kevlar vest, helped him sit, strapped on his seatbelt and said good luck. Tom saw the medic toss Tom's helmet, vest and rifle in the back of the chopper and then move forward through the chopper checking on wounded troops sitting or lying on stretchers.

The engines roared and the helicopter lifted off. After triaging other cases, the medic came back and hooked Tom to an IV. The helicopter landed on the same college football stadium, several blocks west of Lake Shore Evanston Hospital. LSEH had been an excellent hospital, among the best in the country, but changed after the government took over following the Soft Coup. The government had rebranded and replaced administrators, staff, doctors and other health care workers with people who had higher social credit scores.

Some EMTs rushed up to the chopper and helped Tom and the others get down to a fleet of waiting ambulances. When Tom arrived at the hospital, someone wheeled him to the ER where they cut off his shirt and removed the rest of his clothes, put him under anesthesia, cleaned the wound after checking for more serious damage or bullet fragments, stitched him up and applied a clean dressing. Someone wheeled him to a recovery room and hooked him to monitoring machines and an IV.

Tom felt disoriented when he woke up from the anesthesia, but gradually remembered what happened and where he was. A senior nurse gave Tom a small cup of orange juice. She was wearing an old style starched white nurse's uniform, well-designed and smartly fitted, with a matching nurse's cap. Tom saw gray hair below her cap and figured she wore it in a bun. She sensed that Tom was surprised by her uniform and explained that the new administrator wanted a more traditional professional look. She explained that casual outfits and the resulting decrease in professionalism had contributed to a decline in hospital cleanliness and a rise in staph infections.

There was no phone in the room so Tom asked if he could get his phone and said it was probably in his pants. The nurse went out to track down Tom's pants but got tied up with other work. She came back about an hour later to check on Tom and he asked about his pants or phone. She apologized and went out to look for them and came back about twenty minutes later holding Tom's pants, socks, and shoes. He checked the pants but there was no phone.

Tom pleaded for a phone and she pulled out her own phone and said he could make one quick local call. Tom had to think for a moment because he always used his speed dial to call Izzy. When he remembered the number, his hands were shaking and he tapped in the number fast and made a mistake, so he said "son of a bitch" and started over. When he finally got through, Izzy's phone went to voice mail, so he left a message about where he was and said he loved her. He told the nurse in an urgent tone that his girlfriend's phone's battery may have run out of power. The nurse took her phone back and gave him a sedative.

Moments later a young doctor checked Tom's chart and vitals and told Tom he was a lucky guy because no bones were hit. Tom knew what he meant and said thanks, but thought he would have been luckier not to be shot. The doctor told the nurse to remove the IV after the remaining blood and fluids ran out so the IV equipment could be redeployed. He instructed the nurse to keep Tom in the hospital overnight for observation unless they ran out of beds.

The doctor and nurse were about to leave when a young nurse appeared. The doctor turned toward Tom and said, "enjoy your sponge bath" and gave Tom a wink.

Tom was starting to feel drowsy and didn't notice much about the new nurse except she was young and blonde and had the same type of white fitted uniform. She gave him some mouth wash and had him gargle.

Then she said, "Okay, time for your sponge bath."

Tom felt a little embarrassed and said, "Do you really need to do this?"

"Of course. Sanitation is really important. You smell bad, like sweat and grime and gun powder. Now I want you to turn on your side so I can come around and untie your gown."

Tom complied and the nurse untied the flimsy hospital gown and went to work with a warm wet sponge. She was very thorough and cleaned every part of him. She was nice and gentle and made small talk.

"So, you must go to the gym a lot?" she asked.

"Yeah, pretty much," Tom said.

"As a medical professional, I can say you have excellent muscle development."

"Thanks." Tom yawned.

"I just broke up with an intern I was seeing."

"Oh, that's too bad, I guess. I mean too bad for him if you wanted out, I guess. Sorry, I'm getting sleepy."

"There are a lot of nice interns, but mine turned out to be so full of himself."

"You'll find someone nice." Tom yawned again.

"By the way, I'm Lorna."

"Hi, I'm Tom."

"Okay Tom, I'm going to do a second washing of your underarms and front torso because they were the dirtiest areas. It's really important to avoid picking up a staph infection in a hospital."

Nurse Lorna wrung out the sponge and got it ready with fresh warm soapy water. She came back and performed the additional cleaning gently and thoroughly, lingering over Tom's chiseled pecs and six-pack abs.

Tom had been thinking about the battle and Izzy, but he looked up while Nurse Lorna performed the extra cleaning of his front torso. She looked down and smiled as their eyes met. Tom noticed that Lorna was rather pretty and quickly looked away.

As Nurse Lorna was leaving, she turned and made a point of saying she'd be back to make a special check on Tom after midnight, and winked and blew him a kiss.

Chapter Eighteen

Contrary to earlier optimistic reports, while the fighting was beginning in Chicago and several other major cities, about a quarter of the Freedom Fighters in DC were delayed in reaching their locations due to commuter traffic jams. The political class had more cars than ever and were exempt from car-pooling laws. As a result, Stalinsky's forces already controlled several of the assigned DC buildings and were putting up a strong defense.

Stalinsky's first goal in DC had been the FBI Building where he and Commander Ashley Bennington set up a command and control center. While Ashley took operational command of the militia units, Stalinsky entered into intense discussions to persuade the FBI leaders to join Stalinsky's forces because, after all, the FBI was part of Stalinsky's Ministry of Truth & Justice. But most of the FBI leaders and other personnel privately liked Buddy Lemmon better.

At the Supreme Court building, Stalinsky's forces had arrived first and were putting up a vigorous defense against attacks by the underground and allied British commandos. At the White House, though, the Freedom Forces had gotten to their positions on time and were defending against Stalinsky's militia attacks. Israeli snipers on the White House roof were targeting Stalinsky militia leaders as they came into view. At the Capitol Building, the Freedom Forces and Stalinsky forces had arrived about the same time and were engaged in heavy street fighting. Elsewhere in DC, the fighting ebbed and flowed on various streets and around the buildings as Commander Ashley Bennington pulled Stalinsky forces from some locations and consolidated to reinforce or attack other locations. Surveillance drones for both sides were hovering and swooping above the streets and buildings. Some drones were armed and their operators were taking opportunistic shots.

The Stalinsky forces were brutally aggressive at first, but the Freedom Forces were larger, smarter, and better trained and organized. In DC the Stalinsky forces were somewhat lightly armed because Stalinsky feared that a well-armed militia, even his own, might turn him out of power. As a result, the DC battle mainly involved thousands of automatic assault weapons and machine guns and intermittent explosions of hand grenades. That changed somewhat when Buddy's militia brought up dozens of M252 81 mm mortars to fire on Stalinsky positions.

The Freedom Fighters' morale around the country was high because Buddy's militia liked him and despised Stalinsky, and the underground fighters had been dedicated for many years to the goal of freedom. The Stalinsky forces began to lose steam quickly. They had not expected the underground to join Buddy Lemmon. They were outnumbered in nearly every location and were running low on ammo. Few had liked Stalinsky much anyway and their morale began to collapse. As their morale collapsed and they began to surrender or disband, the Freedom Forces' morale rose even higher.

By 2:00 pm EST, most Stalinsky forces around the country were retreating, or had surrendered or disbanded, or had been killed or wounded, except a division of 3,000 heavily armed troops that had consolidated at the FBI Building in DC. No one had told them about the collapse of their comrades around the country and the news media was issuing conflicting reports.

To help with the heavy fighting at the FBI Building, five fresh platoons of Commander Greene's underground reserves arrived along with several old M551 Sheridan tanks. Noah got the tanks through another last minute connection in the National Guard, which had dropped them out of the huge opening at the back of a C-130 Hercules cargo plane while it flew 150 mph only a few feet above the ground at Reagan Washington National Airport.

As the Sheridan tanks and the underground's reinforcements approached the FBI Building, Stalinsky and Commander Ashley Bennington directed a fierce surprise counter-attack by several helicopters which had been circling at a high altitude. The attack helicopters swooped down and destroyed three tanks in fiery explosions with Hellfire guided anti-tank missiles, and then targeted the street squads and platoons of Freedom Fighters with the choppers' heavy caliber machine guns.

Commander Greene saw the helicopter attack from the Wilmette command center through Professor Miller's surveillance drones in DC and yelled into his microphone to the DC commanders that they needed Stingers. A fourth tank was destroyed in another fiery explosion by a Hellfire missile launched from an attack helicopter just before the Stinger teams blasted five helicopters out of the sky almost simultaneously.

The two remaining attack helicopters gave up and sped off. One of the retreating helicopters lost communications and headed west toward Camp David, which the crew mistakenly believed was a Stalinsky stronghold. The personnel on the other fleeing helicopter were the only people who knew Stalinsky was on board. That helicopter headed northeast toward Baltimore, which was a bastion of Stalinsky support. They planned to land at Baltimore-Washington International Airport, where a private jet would fly Stalinsky to the Party's private island. He planned to check into the island's private hospital under a different name and get cosmetic surgery to disguise his identity.

The island hospital specialized mostly in breast implants, butt tucks and implants, and liposuction, but Stalinsky knew the chief cosmetic surgeon also did face lifts, nose jobs, chin implants, eye lifts, nips and tucks, and other enhancements. He smiled as he thought about becoming more attractive than he already thought he was. He then planned, while still wearing the cosmetic surgery bandages, to be medically transported to Cuba with two of his closest supporters. His team would make the arrangements and explain the changes in his appearance and he'd be welcomed by the small Cuban political ruling class. Stalinsky felt good about Cuba, despite the poverty of the masses, and planned to live the rest of his life as a hero of revolutionary struggle among the elites.

By 2:30 pm EST, the rank and file FBI agents and personnel, who had been following developments on various dark web citizen news sites, began speaking openly with the FBI leaders and they all decided to support the Freedom Forces. At that point, the FBI Building had huge blast holes and crumbling walls and collapsing parts of roofs, and the Stalinsky militia forces that had consolidated at the FBI Building were shell-shocked. They lost their remaining morale as they realized that Stalinsky had disappeared. That left Commander Ashley Bennington in charge of the Stalinsky forces. Then she disappeared and the next person in command of the Stalinsky forces surrendered to the Freedom Forces and the allied FBI personnel.

Commander Noah Greene dispatched his remaining underground reserve force to race from Fairfax County crammed into 25 large troop transport trucks to consolidate and protect the DC victory, help control the defeated forces, and help suppress any opportunistic Antifa activity. For the same reasons, Commander Laura Zena had dispatched Buddy's DC militia reserves on 20 Chinooks and they were approaching the National Mall west of the Capitol Building.

By 3:00 pm EST, Buddy announced in the Wilmette command and control center that the Freedom Fighters had mostly defeated the Stalinsky forces in every city and were engaging in pursuit and mop-up activities. Buddy said that he and Rocky, their senior staffs, and a security detail would leave in fifteen minutes for Chicago's O'Hare airport where they planned to take the Party's Gulfstream G700 to DC. Almost as an after-thought, Buddy looked over at Commander Noah Greene and Commander Laura Zena, and said he wanted Laura to stay in Wilmette and control the central command, while Noah could join the team heading to DC and command any further operations in the DC area. Noah and Laura would synch up periodically.

The team leaving Wilmette grabbed their phones, laptops and chargers and took turns using the elevator to get up to ground level where they pushed past the movable bookcase and rushed to a caravan of idling Range Rovers, which included heavily armed security personnel in the first and last vehicles. The Range Rovers took off urgently as soon as the teams climbed in. Light bars were flashing and sirens were screaming and horns were honking as they sped and maneuvered around sparse traffic toward O'Hare.

As the Range Rovers approached the private flight area, the passengers broke out in cheers. A crew had painted "Operation Freedom" on the jet. The team piled out and ran to the movable stairs which they clambered up vigorously to board the plane. The jet was fueled and ready to go so they took the closest seats they could find and fastened their seatbelts. At 4:00 pm EST, the engines roared and the jet screamed down the runway, took off and climbed quickly, and banked a sharp turn toward DC.

On the way to DC a small flight crew served sandwiches and beverages. Some people began to relax while watching news reports on their phones between official briefings from Buddy as he received updates. Buddy and Commander Noah Greene were continuously connecting with Freedom Force commanders in DC and the other cities and touching base with Commander Zena in the Wilmette command center. They also brought up screens with views from Professor Miller's surveillance drones circling over Chicago and DC.

Many news organizations had the story wrong and were reporting that Stalinsky was winning, probably influenced by his communications and cyber teams and supporters in the news media and tech company controllers. Buddy got on a call with Beatriz and the communications team in the Wilmette command center, and they patched together a video call with their network of sympathetic news media contacts. Buddy gave an accurate update and asked that they send camera crews and reporters to the Capitol Building where they would be given new press credentials and allowed to broadcast a special joint session of the House and Senate at 8:00 pm EST. Beatriz and the communications team then prepared and issued a formal announcement about the joint session to the national, local and foreign news services.

Some people had fallen asleep by the time the Gulfstream roughly touched down at DC National Airport at 6:30 pm EST where a convoy of Range Rovers was ready on the tarmac apron. Everyone got up and hurried off the plane and into the Rovers, and the convoy raced toward the Capitol Building. Noah's underground forces had cleared and blocked off US 1 and other connecting roads. Buddy spent time in the vehicle reviewing his speech and made a few edits.

The convoy screeched to a jolting stop in front of the Capitol Building about 7:15 pm EST. As they got out of the vehicles, the group saw troop transport trucks, tanks, anti-aircraft and mortar positions, and thousands of troops dug into trenches and fox holes or behind sandbagged heavy caliber machine guns in defensive positions, and dozens of snipers on the balcony around the Capitol dome.

Buddy and the rest of the tired group trudged up the long flight of steps of the Capitol Building accompanied by their nervous security detail. Several battle-weary DC squads of Buddy's militia and Commander Noah Greene's underground forces emerged from behind the columns on the portico to wave and cheer.

Moments later a smaller convoy pulled up fast with President Georgia Washer and her key staff and a security detail. They walked briskly up the long steps to the portico where Buddy and his team were standing. The President and Buddy greeted each other warmly and hugged for several moments. President Washer led the way into the Capitol Building and over to a meeting room adjacent to the House Chamber.

It was now 7:45 pm EST and all Senators and Representatives had made their way through the security checks and were sitting in the Chamber talking or looking at their phones. The Supreme Court Justices were sitting near the front, along with President Washer's Cabinet members and the top brass of the regular military and the FBI leaders. Several foreign ambassadors had been cleared and seated in the gallery above the main floor, including those from England and Israel. Numerous news media personnel were waiting eagerly in line outside the Chamber to be admitted to the gallery.

Tom had awakened in the hospital about thirty minutes earlier, around 7:15 pm EST. He had moved his head around since his neck was stiff. He had stretched out his left arm, but didn't move his right arm which had a wound dressing. He noticed someone on a chair in the darkened room. The chair looked like a living room reclining chair and was mostly reclined.

When Izzy had arrived an hour earlier, an intern had been chatting up the nurses at the nursing station and had taken a break to talk to Izzy. He said Tom had a two hole puncture wound. He explained that a bullet, probably a 9 mm with a full metal jacket, had entered Tom's upper right arm in the front and exited in the back. He said the bullet did not hit any bones and that Tom was hooked up to monitors and an IV. The intern was interested in Izzy and asked if she'd done any modelling. Izzy said Tom was her boyfriend, and the intern then remembered that he should only talk to a family member about Tom anyway. He pleaded that she not report a privacy breach under HIPAA. She said okay since she didn't understand his problem.

"Tom, are you okay?" It was Izzy's voice.

"I think so. How about you?"

"I'm okay." Izzy came over and kissed him.

"Izzy, I thought I might get killed and not see you again. I felt bad that we didn't kiss before I rushed out."

"I felt the same way. Does your arm hurt a lot?"

"Not much. A dull pain. It's only a flesh wound. I'm probably still on morphine."

It was 7:50 pm EST so Izzy tuned in a news station on the screen hanging from the ceiling. They were watching a scene in the House Chambers and the camera was panning around as the reporters and commentators described what they saw and who was present. The screen zoomed in on some people in the gallery balcony.

Izzy suddenly said that she saw her grandad, Hans Huber. He was sitting next to Noah Greene. She jumped up and ran to the screen to point them out. Izzy looked back and saw a confused look on Tom's face. She reminded him that Hans was her mom's dad, the East Berliner who had emigrated to London. Tom looked more confused when Izzy said Hans did some consulting for the British Secret Service and had developed a bond with Rocky. Tom still looked confused so Izzy reminded him that her mom, Audrey, was Hans' daughter, which meant Rocky was Hans' son-in-law. Tom said "okay," but still didn't follow and figured it was the morphine.

At 8:03 pm EST, President Georgia Washer and Buddy Lemmon emerged from a door to the right behind the podium in the House Chamber. They had dressed in old style formal clothes as a sign of renewed respect for the office of the President and the other branches of government, and to help restore a calming sense of tradition and professionalism.

President Washer looked like a middle aged presidential version of Diana Ross. Buddy looked like a senior statesman and even bore a resemblance to Ronald Reagan. Coincidentally, he had read a lot about Reagan and knew they shared a common background in the old liberal party earlier in their lives. Based partly on Reagan's experiences with strong arm tactics of communist operatives when he led the screen actor's union, he was eventually quoted as saying, *"If fascism ever comes to America, it will come in the name of liberalism."*

Buddy stepped to the microphone and delivered the following speech:

"Madame President, members of your Cabinet, members of the Senate and House, Justices of the Supreme Court, other distinguished guests, and the people of the Republic who may be watching this broadcast.

"I'm stepping down and supporting freedom and Constitutional representative government. I have obtained agreement from the Central Committee to dissolve the Party and turn over the Party's assets to the Republic, in exchange for pardons by the President. There are two exceptions to the pardons, which the President will address in her remarks.

"You've all heard the reports on the fighting. To summarize, I learned that Director Stalinsky was organizing his far left militias to take over. So, I formed an alliance between my militia and the underground. We called our alliance the Freedom Force and our troops Freedom Fighters. I am very grateful to the underground. I won't identify their leaders because they want privacy for now.

"I am grateful to my wife, Beatriz, who opened my eyes over time based on her family's experience with socialism in Cuba and her grad school education in England and Europe. She also learned a lot on banned websites and then I read a lot.

"I read the truth about the American Revolution and its founders and their documents. They thought a lot about human nature. They figured that any person or group that got too powerful would do self-serving things and also make poor decisions without opposition groups who could dissent and debate, contribute other ideas, and serve as a watchdog and a check and balance.

"The founders liked the idea that people have some basic natural rights, like life, liberty and the pursuit of property and happiness, freedom of expression, assembly and religion, free enterprise and competition, the right to bear arms to defend against criminals as well as kings, dictators or totalitarian governments, whether from the left or the right. They said the government doesn't give you these rights because you already have these inalienable rights. And a key purpose of government is to defend and protect these rights."

"The founders didn't rush into it. They studied government systems around the world and through history back to ancient Greece. They had a lot of experience with town hall meetings and legislative assemblies in the original thirteen colonies before they joined together. Washington, Jefferson, Adams, Madison, Hamilton and the other founders put their own lives at risk by signing a Declaration of Independence from England and fought a long tough war to win and establish a system of representative self-government.

"After they won freedom from England, they wrote and debated and finalized the Constitution with checks and balances and the Bill of Rights to preserve their rights and freedoms from any tyrant or mob group taking over. They included provisions making it hard to change the Constitution unless there was widespread agreement. The whole thing was brilliant.

"In contrast, the French Revolution a few years later was a nightmare because it was mob rule without a comprehensive constitutional framework of protections. Same with the Russian revolution and the other socialist take-overs.

"Even with all the protections set up for our country, the founders worried that freedom could be lost if the people were not honorable and vigilant in respecting and protecting everyone's rights and freedoms. That's what happened in the Soft Coup with one party socialist control.

"Now your future belongs to you again. I have high expectations that President Georgia Washer and the elected representatives will carry forward with honor, intelligence, and respectful exchanges of views to reach good decisions."

The Chamber was completely silent during Buddy's speech. Not a single clap or shout of acclamation. When he finished, the silence continued for about forty-five seconds while everyone looked around to assess the mood, and many considered how their reactions might affect their careers and personal safety. Someone in the back row began clapping. The people near her joined and then loud applause and cheers broke out all across the Chamber and lasted for ten minutes. Buddy stood tall and smiled and waved, but eventually quieted the Chamber with hand gestures. He introduced President Georgia Washer and then stepped away so she could step up to the mic.

"Thanks Buddy. Members of the Cabinet and the Senate and House, Justices of the Supreme Court, other distinguished guests, and the people of the Republic who may be watching this broadcast.

"First, I'd like to extend my heart-felt thanks to Buddy Lemmon for his vision of freedom and his hard work in this voluntary turn-over of power back to the people. I'd also like to thank Buddy's spouse, Beatriz, and Buddy's staff, including Commander Laura Zena, for all of their help and hard work. I'm offering to incorporate Buddy's militia personnel into the National Guard if they are interested.

"I'd also like to thank all of the brave people in the underground who worked to keep the freedom dream alive, and for joining forces with Buddy to stand up against Director Stalinsky and his brutal forces. The House and Senate have passed a bill to end Stalinsky's Political Police, Political Jails and Block Minders. Later tonight I will sign that bill and pardon and release everyone in the Political Jails.

"I'd like to recognize Great Britain's Ambassador, Mr. Mark English, for the support of his country. And I'd like to recognize Israel's Ambassador, Ms. Rachel Kaplan, for the support of her country. Great Britain and Israel each provided 5,000 highly trained and skilled commandos to help secure DC. The camera zoomed in on the ambassadors.

"About the pardons for the Party leaders. First, they will forfeit all excess wealth they derived from their positions. Second, we will prosecute Director Stalinsky and others for violations of the Bill of Rights relating to the Political Jails and Alaskan Reserve.

"We're still trying to get more information and access to the Alaskan Reserve. But it's clear that all prisoners were innocent. To avoid any misunderstanding of their status, I'm issuing pardons for all Alaskan prisoners tonight.

"I'm asking my staff to organize "Freedom Trains" to bring those people back to their families. The Freedom Trains may include actual trains, busses and other vehicles. We'll also have arrangements to let family and friends travel to Alaska to pick up their loved ones by car. We'll have a public data base so people don't duplicate efforts.

"With the dissolution of the Equality Party, I will be free to work with my Cabinet and the House and Senate to rescind the laws and rules the Party put in place. Based on discussions during the past few weeks, we'll reinstate the US Constitution, including the Bill of Rights and amendments that were in effect before the Soft Coup.

"Let me address international relations for a moment. Buddy has worked out a proposed pivot away from China and a new alliance with Russia, India, Israel, England and the other western style democracies. While I'm giving this address, Boris Goodinsky is speaking to the Russian people about his plan to transform Russia into a representative parliamentary government with freedom similar to England. For our country to join the alliance, there will be a process of public debate and a vote on the details in the Senate. There is a controversial component that involves selling Alaska to the new alliance to help pay down our massive debts.

"I regret that it's too late to get Hawaii back. We may also need to sell California or New York, or else sell Oregon and the State of Washington as a package deal. Someone has also proposed to move the federal capital to Wyoming and sell Washington DC to Disneyworld as a political theme park and tourist attraction to help pay our debts.

"In discussions with key leaders in the Senate and House, there's a lot of support for ending the Social Credit Point System. We have huge budget issues paying the credits. In my opinion, the social credit system is a creepy form of social control and there's a negative racist aspect. Congress will look at providing a transition period.

"The House and Senate are going to debate various proposals to reduce regulations, restore and encourage free enterprise, and revise the tax system to provide appropriate incentives. We'd like to be a country where anyone with a good idea may have a shot at opening a business and creating employment opportunities for others.

"There is a lot of interest in restoring and funding Social Security, at least for people who are over 75 years old. There will also be debates about the best ways to provide health care, and the best ways of having a welfare safety net for people in need. Because we're going back to free speech and representative government, you will be able to share your views with your elected representatives.

"We've got to do something better about lobbyists and crony capitalism this time, while also maintaining free speech. At a minimum, it will involve full transparency so there aren't secret backroom deals.

"In restoring Social Security for old people, we won't be able to continue providing free four year college for everyone. A lot of kids might be happiest and best served skipping college or getting two years of community college to learn a skill or professional trade. Naturally, if someone does well during the two years and wants to complete a four year degree, there should be opportunities.

"At the same time, there's plenty of support for funding personal college scholarships based on merit, at least for engineering, math, and the hard sciences. There's less support for funding scholarships for kids who want four years of easy courses and fun majors.

"But to help provide equal opportunities for personal college merit scholarships, we must ensure that the grammar school systems provide equal opportunities with fair funding in lower income areas. We need to look at the role of the teachers' unions. Let's also provide tutor programs, remedial education classes, and summer school programs, for kids who aren't getting strong enough educational opportunities in local schools. Families can also have a strong role in their kids' education and opportunities through encouragement and support for the kids, being involved with parent teacher organizations, pressing for school choice and charter schools.

"Timing-wise, once the Constitutional framework is back in place next week, we will schedule free and fair elections for about nine months from now with a two party system and plenty of checks and balances. Two political parties are already in the process of being formed. One of the parties plans to call itself the "Common Sense Liberals" and the other party plans to call itself the "Common Sense Conservatives." Over time, I expect the names will be shortened to Liberals and Conservatives, but I hope the idea of common sense remains.

"I've met the proposed initial senior leaders of the two new political parties. They are committed to working together in an honorable, professional manner. The new parties will launch their websites tomorrow so everyone can see who is involved and read their current ideas and policies. Everyone will be free to join either party on their websites. Anyone can form other parties, though I personally don't believe that's advisable unless we switch to a parliamentary system.

"I have high hopes for the future of the Republic. Hope for respectful free thinkers. Enlightenment and reason informed by real history. Common sense, robust public debates, tolerance for anyone who is willing to speak truth to power. Unrelenting support for the value of free speech, including speech that is unpopular or controversial in the moment.

"I can't emphasize how strongly I believe that the right of free speech is extraordinary and paramount. Without free speech rights, you eventually have no other rights. To protect free speech, you must allow the expression of views you don't like. After all, other people may not like your views, and you wouldn't want to be censored or harassed. Let's remember the quote attributed to the French philosopher and Enlightenment writer, Voltaire: *"I may disapprove of what you say, but I will defend to the death your right to say it."*

"We must never censor an unpopular speaker under the excuse of protecting the speaker from violence or harassment by other people. That rewards the group that threatens violence or harassment.

"Let me be more specific. If you believe someone is expressing wrongful or offensive views, the remedy is not less free speech, but even more free speech. Give your own speech or write something in which you present better views in a persuasive respectful way, with logic and reason, common sense and references to history or science or whatever is involved. As an aside, we need to end the college campus limited speech zones and general intolerance of unpopular speech, and end the broader cancel culture of suppressing, bullying and harassing anyone who doesn't agree with the prevailing group-think.

"So you might wonder what I think about the Party's Crimes of Disinformation or Hate Speech Laws. The remedy for disinformation is more information by other people, not the unilateral suppression of so-called disinformation by minders in the government or technology platform companies. Those laws were written far too broadly and lack insight and historical context about the paramount importance of free speech. The Senate and House will pass a bill repealing those laws and I will sign the bill. Meantime, my understanding of the Bill of Rights prevents me from enforcing those laws. We have the same views on the overly-broad aspects of the Soft Coup's Crimes Against Domestic Terrorism. Let us never again hear that it should be a crime for anyone to speak or write, or peacefully march, to question or challenge the integrity of an election or to exercise any and all lawful rights to appeal the results for further lawful review.

"Does my emphasis on the paramount importance of free speech mean that I like hateful or offensive speech? No, of course not. But, the most effective counter-protest could be a lot of people standing quietly and holding signs that say "SHAME" and offering leaflets and website addresses for information explaining their views. But don't dox anyone, don't get in anyone's face, play loud music, beat on drums, yell, spit or throw stuff like an obnoxious child with a temperature tantrum.

"Let history be a guide. Peaceful protests, passive resistance, and civil disobedience were the ways we won the Civil Rights movement in the 1960s. And that's how Ghandi and his supporters won India's independence from England. But these methods must be quiet, peaceful and respectful. People would sit down and let themselves be arrested instead of fighting the cops. It created sympathy among the masses and changed hearts and minds. You can win hearts and minds with free speech and reason, maturity and respect, kindness and love. Don't let us ever again hear the words "mostly peaceful protest" when there's nightly rioting, arson, looting, beating people up, loud angry harassment of people, or anarchists taking over city blocks and police stations.

"As your second Black President, I also have a vision of a more color blind society like the goal of the 1960s civil rights movement, and like the result we largely achieved by the 1990s. By the 1990s kids had been raised for over two decades to understand that racism was unfair and uncool. We should now focus on dealing with the few bad apples instead of saying the whole system is bad, especially since we've had people of color as mayors and police chiefs and well-represented on the police forces in a lot of places for decades. And don't tell me that Black and Brown cops are Uncle Toms. That's nuts and also racist.

"Now I don't mean a totally color blind society because that's not realistic and maybe not even good in some ways. I just mean the most important thing about a person shouldn't be race. Race can be part and we can celebrate our heritage, but let's not make race the main thing. There are so many unique differences about each individual. It doesn't make sense to lump everyone in a race together. People are individuals first."

"On a personal note, I'd like to say that I get annoyed and creeped out when white people, sorry I mean Euro people, journalists and commentators, gush and fawn over my being Black. I know they mean well, but it feels racist to me. I'm a person and a human being, and I don't want to be used in racial identity politics or to make naïve bleeding heart liberals feel better about themselves. And what really annoys me even more is when they criticize the idea of being a Black or Brown conservative. We Black and Brown conservatives are intelligent free thinkers with our own minds.

"My next point involves journalism. Having a robust inquisitive free press is vital for maintaining freedom as another check and balance on government power. But a strange thing happened in the 2000s. Journalism faculties taught college kids that reporting should be selectively narrated and driven by left wing political and cultural views, as an idealistic way to change society through agenda-driven spinning and subtle advocacy.

"So the younger journalists mostly joined the old liberal party and believed they should accept the talking points and narratives of the movement without digging or challenging, and felt they should only dig and challenge the old conservative party. That party-biased role of the journalists seriously harmed our freedoms and contributed to the Soft Coup.

"As we restore the two party system, journalists need to learn more about our Constitutional history, our founders and their beliefs and concerns, and our systems of government and economics compared to one-party control and socialist totalitarianism. Then they need to fulfill their professional obligation to dig deeply and challenge all politicians and their policies, without bias based on nonsense they picked up in college.

"I'd like you to think about something else. If our worst global foes wanted to weaken and destroy our country, they could not have done anything more than what we did to ourselves by casting so much hate and disdain on our history and traditional values, our founders and founding documents. How many young people would fight in our military against our global foes if our young people believe this country is racist and horrible and not worth defending? That self-loathing way of thinking was driven by narratives focusing only on bad things and ignoring good things and all the progress. I'm serious when I say our foes could not have done a better job in weakening or destroying us, and I sometimes wonder if a few of our foes were behind it. If that happened, shame on our liberal academics, intelligentsia and journalists for being so incredibly naïve.

"Finally, there's going to be a debate about whether to change the name of the country back to the United States of America and change our flag back to the prior design. I favor that, as do most of members of the Senate and House. The public will have a chance to voice its views before any vote.

"Okay, that concludes my remarks this evening. I have high hopes for this country. It won't be easy because we still have massive debts. But we can get through this and come out with a robust economy and a lot of good jobs fueled by freedom. Thanks and God Bless all of you and our Republic."

Everyone in the Chamber remained silent during President Georgia Washer's speech. But there was not a single moment of silence after President Washer concluded her remarks. There was an immediate thunder of cheers and applause, perhaps the longest and loudest that had ever occurred in the Chamber. President Washer stood tall and confident, smiled and waved, and held up her right hand, not as a fist salute, but with her index and middle fingers held up to form a "V" for victory while curling her thumb the other fingers down to get out of the way.

President Georgia Washer gestured for Buddy to join her while the applause and cheers continued, so he stepped forward and they shook hands and embraced for several moments. Buddy turned and waved to the crowd and then stepped back from the limelight to affirm his message that he was done. Interestingly, there was a crescendo in the cheers and applause as Buddy stepped back. He wondered at first if they were expressing enthusiasm for his departure. Then he realized they appreciated his freedom vision and voluntary turn-over of power. Buddy stepped up toward the mic, leaned in and said they really should be thanking his wife, Beatriz. Someone in the control room was on the ball and brought up a photo of Beatriz on the video screens and there was another crescendo of cheers and applause.

President Washer and Buddy walked down the aisle to the front entrance of the Chamber surrounded by on-going cheers and applause. Tom and Izzy loved the speeches as much as anyone else, but they nodded off and feel asleep in the hospital bed during the post speech news summaries, analysis and commentaries.

Tom woke up suddenly in a cold sweat at about 11:30 pm CST. He had been having a nightmare about the helicopter ride, street fighting, and an awkward hospital scene in which a pretty blonde nurse returned at midnight for another sponge bath while Izzy was in the room.

Tom gently rocked Izzy awake and said, "Izzy I had a bad dream. Do you mind if we go home?"

"Sounds good to me. Should I get an Uber or Lyft?"

"We're only several blocks away. Do you mind if we walk? I feel okay and I'd like some fresh night air. "

"That sounds good if you're up to it."

Izzy pulled on her dirty clothes, helped Tom with his dirty pants, socks and shoes, and asked where his shirt was. He said they cut it off, so Izzy went out and came back several minutes later with a green scrub shirt, size XL, that she obtained from a young blonde nurse who was willing to take a short break from a major project of re-doing her makeup at the nurse's station.

When Izzy got back to the room, she put the scrub shirt on Tom while carefully avoiding any movement that might hurt his wound. Izzy thought they needed to check out in some formal way, but Tom said he didn't think so and they had his information to send a bill. So they rode down the elevator, walked out the main entrance, walked east to Sherman, then south to their place.

It was after midnight when they got upstairs, and Tom had a quick image of the blonde nurse looking surprised when she found the empty hospital room.

Chapter Nineteen

Tom woke up gradually the next morning. He got out of bed and grabbed a night stand table to steady himself. He felt better after a few moments and managed to put on his robe and slippers.

When he got to the kitchen, Izzy was making breakfast. They kissed and sat down to eat. When they finished the food, Izzy got the coffee pot and topped off their mugs. They sat and sipped in comfortable silence.

As they finished the coffee, Izzy asked, "Do you remember last night when I had to go find a shirt for you?"

"Sure, thanks."

"I got the scrub shirt from a blonde nurse, maybe in her mid-twenties, in an old-fashioned white fitted nurse's uniform."

"That's nice."

"She was at the nurses' station. I startled her. She was fixing herself up. She smelled nice too. Cologne probably."

Tom didn't say anything.

"It was cute. You know, a pretty nurse and probably an intern, working a late shift. Maybe going to a club to de-stress."

Izzy had been looking at Tom as she spoke, and he had been mostly looking down at his coffee mug.

Izzy was now looking at Tom skeptically and he glanced up and saw the look. He knew Izzy was perceptive and he wanted to be honest, especially before she pressed the point.

"Okay, I remember the nurse. She gave me a sponge bath."

"All over you?"

"Yeah, she took her job seriously. She said people get staph infections."

"Was she getting fixed up for you? I mean, did she flirt and say she'd come back later?"

"She said she'd come back to check on me after midnight. She winked and blew a kiss. But I never gave any encouragement."

There was an awkward silence while Izzy looked at Tom, and he looked at his coffee mug.

"So when were you going to tell me?"

"I thought I just did."

"Only after I pried it out of you."

"Okay Izzy. Here's the thing. There was no way I was going to do anything wrong. I had already decided I'd tell her to go away. When I saw you in the room, I forgot about her. When I woke up before midnight, I wanted to go home to avoid a scene."

There was silence for several moments.

"I believe you, Tom. I'm not sure how I feel about it though."

"I passed that test you set up with Gina."

"Oh yeah, I totally forgot the Gina love test!"

Izzy went to the bedroom to call her parents, Gina and Joey. Gina told Izzy excitedly that Lars was her new boyfriend.

Beatriz called Tom a half hour later and asked if he had heard the latest news about the Alaskan Reserve.

"No. What's going on?"

"Tom, it's a mess. It could affect your parents, so you're welcome to join a call in fifteen minutes, if you'd like."

"Sure, just send me the invite. Thanks."

Tom relayed the information to Izzy, and they hurried to dress.

When Tom and Izzy were admitted to the video call, they saw Beatriz and Buddy sharing a screen in Wilmette, Professor Miller on a screen in Hyde Park, President Washer and two staff people sharing a screen in DC, and Noah and an Israeli commander sharing a screen in DC.

Professor Miller spoke urgently. His cyber team had checked the Alaskan Reserve data base to update the liberation plans. But someone had destroyed the Camp III records. Someone had also moved and blended the Camp I records into the Camp II records and was making more edits.

Professor Miller said he accessed the records himself and found a series of work orders issued during the past two weeks. The inmates of Camps I and II had been organized into work details to dig a massive system of long deep trenches and pits in open fields at Camp III.

Miller believed this work was the preparation of mass graves. He reminded the group that Google Earth and other satellites had been blocked from viewing the Alaskan Reserve and no aircraft or drones had ever been able to fly over and take surveillance photos due to the massive electronic jamming system and laser defenses.

The President's young staffers, feeling wise beyond their years, cautioned about over-reacting and speculated that the President's full pardon for the inmates last night would have ended any bad activities.

But Professor Miller was concerned that the President's pardon may have infuriated Stalinsky into a final act of vengeance. He also questioned whether the Alaskan Reserve administration and guards had even heard about the pardons or speeches.

President Washer turned toward one of her staffers and asked, "So have you or anyone else been able to make direct contact with the Alaskan Reserve administration?"

"Stalinsky's people claim they don't know how to communicate with the administration in Alaska. We've had problems finding the security codes and decryption programs. We've been putting more resources into tracking down Stalinsky and Bennington. We assumed the Alaskan Reserve would be run like any other prison in the meantime."

Noah Greene, Professor Miller, Tom and the Israeli commander argued for immediate action. President Washer asked Professor Miller how many guards and armed administrators were at the Alaskan Reserve. Miller said the personnel records indicated a fluctuating number between 10,000 to 20,000, most of whom had submachine guns and hand grenades. He said he would circulate a map of the camps, which were about 50 miles from Anchorage.

President Washer directed her staffers to set up an emergency call with the Governor of Alaska for immediate mobilization of all Alaskan National Guard assets to converge on the Alaskan Reserve with a goal of liberation. One of the President's staffers had just checked the size of the National Guard assets in Anchorage and reported that the entire force was about 10,000 troops. The staffer excused herself to set up the call with the Governor.

President Washer asked if anyone had concerns about the Alaskan National Guard force level. Everyone agreed that a supplemental force was required. Beatriz said to forget about the Governors of Washington and Oregon. Noah Greene turned to the Israeli commander on their shared screen and asked if his team could move fast. Noah offered to go along and bring 3,000 underground fighters who were still in DC. The Israeli commander said he could probably get the British to join an emergency mission and that their combined air assets could move 7,000 troops and equipment as soon as they could get to Langley Air Force Base.

Noah asked President Washer if that plan was okay. She turned to her other staff person and said she wanted him to prepare an executive order establishing a temporary "Freedom Brigade" of the underground's troops with Noah Greene commissioned as its commander with a special mission of assisting with the liberation of the Alaskan Reserve. Noah excused himself and the Israeli commander so they could proceed.

After the others disconnected, Buddy, Beatriz, Tom and Izzy stayed on the video call to catch up. Buddy and Beatriz ended the call by saying they felt a great weight was lifted in turning over power, and that they were going to spend more time with Buddy Junior for the next few days.

Tom had been sure he'd be reunited with his parents after Professor Miller located their Alaskan records the other day. Now his mind raced with concern as he lingered in his morning shower. When Izzy helped Tom get dressed, she noticed his wound dressing was soaking wet. She called the hospital and reached a senior nurse on the fifth floor.

"I'm calling about a patient named Tom Hardy. He was in Room 505. We left last night about 11:30. Should I bring him back to get his dressing changed?"

"What is your name?"

"Isabella Fanella."

"That's your real name? This isn't a prank right?"

"No, that's my name. I go by Izzy."

"Please spell your first and last names."

"ISABELLA. FANELLA."

"Are you a family member?"

"I'm his fiancé. He doesn't have any other family around."

"I guess that's okay. I'm pulling up his chart on my screen."

"His full first name is Thomas, I think."

"You aren't sure about his first name?"

"Sorry. It never came up. I always call him Tom."

"Okay, I have the chart for Thomas Hardy on my screen. Did you help Tom leave last night?"

"Yes, is there a problem? I'm calling about bringing him back there."

"No patient should leave the hospital without checking out," the nurse said in a scolding tone. "You need to get him back right away so we can change his dressing and clean the wound."

The nurse was in some sort of a mood after a double shift of triage and treating battle wounds. She added, again in a scolding tone, "Are you aware that some infections morph into the flesh eating disease - necrotizing fasciitis - which can lead to amputation or death?"

"Oh wow! I'll bring him right away."

Tom had heard Izzy's side of the call. He stood up and walked over to the door while Izzy pulled her keys from her purse. She held his hand while they walked down the three flights and over to her Mazda Miata.

Izzy offered to help Tom get into the sporty little car. He said he was fine but winced as he got in the passenger side. She drove fast and pulled into the emergency drive up area where she came to an abrupt stop and Tom winced again. An attendant came out with a wheel chair.

Tom didn't want the wheel chair, so the attendant asked them to park in the garage. By the time they parked and found their way to the nursing station on the fifth floor, the nurse on duty said she was not the nurse who had taken Izzy's call. She sent them back down to the first floor to check in officially.

It took over an hour to check in because Tom had not checked out the prior night. The admissions person had to check him out and then in again. Tom also had to use a lot of social credits to pay his hospital bill from the prior night before he could check back in. At the end of the process, an attendant came by with a wheel chair and said Tom had to sit in it. Tom and Izzy looked at each other and shrugged as if to say, "why not?" As it turned out, Tom enjoyed being pushed around in the wheel chair.

When they reached the fifth floor, the attendant wheeled Tom past the nursing station and back into Room 505. The attendant insisted that Tom put on a hospital gown and get into bed. Tom tried to debate the point but the attendant had instructions from the senior nurse who had taken Izzy's earlier call. The nurse's notes also said Tom was a "flight risk" so the attendant gave a short lecture on the need to check out properly.

After Tom and Izzy had waited in Room 505 for nearly an hour, the blonde nurse from the prior night entered the room looking sleepy and hung over. She wasn't focusing but managed to say she needed to do a sponge bath. She was holding a sponge and bucket of warm disinfecting water.

"Are you kidding me?" Izzy asked.

"Yeah, are you kidding us?" Tom added.

"Oh my gosh, it's you!" the blonde nurse said while looking at Tom.

The blonde nurse added, "Where did you go last night and how did you show up here again? I feel like I'm in the Twilight Zone."

The blonde nurse then looked at Izzy and said, "Are you the girl who asked me for a scrub shirt?" She paused and added, "Are you, like, his sister?"

"I'm Izzy, Tom's fiancé. I helped him last night. I thought we should probably check out, but you know how men can be." She didn't offer to shake hands.

"Sure, I know how men can be," said the blonde nurse. She suddenly blushed and looked up at the ceiling.

"Hey, I know about your sexy sponge bath thing, by the way. And Tom said you winked and blew him a kiss and said you'd come back after midnight," Izzy said.

The blonde nurse paused to collect her thoughts. "So Izzy, I'm really sorry about that. I wouldn't want to cause a problem in a relationship. I didn't see a ring. I don't come back very often, but he's like, you know, so nice looking."

"Okay, thanks, I guess," Izzy said.

"You know, I did end up going out last night since I was all fixed up and met a guy at a sports bar. But I think he's full of himself. My friend Tawny, another nurse, was with me and she thought so too," the blonde nurse said.

Izzy didn't respond but the nurse continued anyway.

"Yeah, we all talked for a while and he seemed sort of charming so I asked him over for a night cap when Tawny had to go home. She's my roommate too. So we get home, Tawny goes to bed, I'm sitting with this guy and we start making out. One thing leads to another, you know, and we're in bed, and he gets kind of rough and aggressive and insists on being on top. Then he finished way too soon."

"Yeah, I hate when guys are like that," Izzy said.

"He lay there for a while afterwards and said he had been a high school quarterback, and his dad was a big shot who was on the news last night, and he could fly me to a private island for a party. I was glad when he left," the blonde nurse said.

"So what sports bar?" Izzy asked in a cooler tone.

"Harry's Sports Bar near the campus. They also call it a Music Lounge. He said it's his favorite hang-out when he's not on the island. Isn't that pretentious? The island?" the blonde nurse asked rhetorically.

"I might know who that is. What was his name?" Izzy asked.

"Buddy. Then he said Buddy Junior when he mentioned his big shot dad."

"Well, it's been nice chatting, I guess. But are you going to change Tom's dressing and clean the wound or do you just do sponge baths?" Izzy asked.

"I do both."

"Okay, we're skipping the sponge bath," Izzy said. "I'll help him at home. So can you please do the other stuff?"

"Okay. By the way, I'm Lorna. No hard feelings?" the blonde nurse asked.

"Okay, no hard feelings." Izzy made a perfunctory smile.

Lorna was surprisingly professional and careful, especially considering she was sleepy and hung-over, in removing the old dressing, cleaning out the entrance and exit holes and surrounding area, and applying a new dressing. She gave Izzy a seven day supply of dressings, antibiotics and pain pills.

"Okay, all set," Lorna said. "You'll need to make an out-patient appointment for a check-up in seven days. Of course, come in right away if there is any bleeding or sign of infection. And, please remember to check out this time."

Izzy smiled at Lorna and said, "Thanks. You're probably okay. Just stay away from my boyfriend."

"I thought you said fiancé before. He's just a boyfriend?" Nurse Lorna asked.

"Fiancé," said Tom. "We just got engaged."

Izzy came over to Tom and said she loved him, and he said he loved her, and they got into a long kiss. Lorna smiled, slipped out and shut the door.

"So, Tom, you really want to be engaged?"

"The sooner the better. Maybe getting shot makes me want to go faster," Tom said.

Tom and Izzy found their way down to the first floor check out booth. Tom got a credit of $5.00 because of the large amount he prepaid when he checked in. They found Izzy's car after wandering around in the hospital garage. Tom got in the passenger side and managed to use his left hand to fasten his seatbelt shortly before they got home.

They ordered pizza and Izzy turned on a news station. A Presidential address was scheduled for 9:00 pm EST. They made a mental note to watch at 8:00 pm CST and turned the news off.

To lift their spirits, Izzy put on the eclectic "Bach's Greatest Hits" album from 1963 by the Swingle Singers, a Paris-based vocal group that had applied jazz stylings to Bach's classical music with a double bass and drums as accompaniment.

Tom said, "I'm still distracted about my parents."

"Well, there's nothing we can do about it. How about if we work on wedding plans to distract you," Izzy said.

"Okay. So who do you want to invite?" Tom asked.

Izzy pulled out her phone and brought up a notes app.

"My parents," Izzy said.

"Yeah, mine too, assuming they get back and are okay."

"I'd love if we can get my grandparents from London and Italy," Izzy said.

Izzy added, "Joey, and if Joey wants to bring someone. I'm thinking about fixing him up with Nurse Lorna."

"Fast cars and a fast girl."

Izzy thought for a few moments and added, "Gina and Lars. He's moving in with her."

"That was quick. How about Buddy and Beatriz?" Tom asked.

"Sounds good," Izzy said.

After a few moments, Izzy asked, "How about Professor Miller and a guest?"

"Sure. How about Noah Greene and a date?" Tom asked. "Oh, and Noah's parents. I got to know them when I was in the Boarding School System."

"Okay. How long do you want the list to be?" Izzy asked.

"I'd like to keep it short. I was mainly friends with fascist socialists for cover. The kids I liked have left and I wouldn't want to ask them to travel. Do you want to add some more of your friends?"

"Sure. How about a venue?" Izzy asked.

"You mean like a church?"

"I'm open to the idea."

"I heard about a nice old church for weddings in Park Ridge," Tom said.

"Sounds better than City Hall."

"What about the reception? Do you want a DJ and dancing?"

"Hey Tom, how about Stardust? Do they do that?"

"I can ask."

Izzy came closer to Tom on the sofa and gave him a sweet lingering kiss, and they said they loved each other. Izzy then went to the bedroom to call her parents, Gina, and Joey.

Chapter Twenty

Izzy turned on the news at 7:30 pm CST and they watched emotional interviews of people whose loved ones had been taken to the Alaskan Reserve. The interviewees didn't know anything beyond the names and dates when their loved ones were taken. None of them understood why their loved ones were rounded up. They all thought it was a bunch of crap.

The screen switched to President Georgia Washer sitting at the Resolute Desk in the Oval House. She was wearing reading glasses and looked serious. As the President spoke, she periodically looked down at her notes and then back up at the camera.

"Today, units of our military forces, supported by Israeli and British commandos, liberated the Alaskan Reserve. Most guards and administrators surrendered peacefully.

"However, our troops ran into resistance by some senior administrators and guards who were trying to destroy records and had planned to escape. Several of them are dead. A dozen more were wounded and are being detained and treated. Nineteen of our troops suffered gunshot wounds. They are stable and expected to recover.

We took this action under emergency circumstances. We discovered plans to murder all of the prisoners beginning with Camp III. The prisoners of Camps I and II were forced to work on a massive system of long deep trenches and pits in Camp III to serve as mass graves. That work was completed during the past two weeks.

"The plan called for guards to put handcuffs and blindfolds on successive groups of prisoners. Heavily armed guard units with attack dogs would then march the prisoners out to line up along the trenches and pits. In a long series of such actions, the guards would machine-gun, in cold blood, all of these innocent people so they'd fall into the trenches and pits. The trenches and pits were far enough away from the barracks that the remaining prisoners probably wouldn't hear. If anyone did hear, the guards were supposed to say that it was target practice.

"Remember, none of the prisoners had ever been tried or convicted in a real court of any crimes. This should be a wake-up call for anyone who still believes that one-party socialism differs from fascism in leading to an oppressive police state with cruel results. We need to do a better job teaching our young people about the horrors of socialism in places like the Soviet Union, China, Cuba, Cambodia, North Korea, and Venezuela.

"So, on the one hand, we prevented the final step in the mass murder plan. But, on the other hand, the plan itself was horrifying, along with the whole camp system, and the mind-boggling number of deaths from slow starvation, disease, brutally hard work and exposure to the elements. We will investigate thoroughly and hold people accountable for conspiracy to commit crimes against humanity. Preliminary interviews with a dozen guards indicate that a few incorrectly felt they would be justified in following orders. Others planned to aim their guns over the heads of the prisoners. Some planned to shoot whoever gave the orders.

"Now, turning to the prisoner population, Camp III has about 100,000 surviving prisoners and they are in bad condition. Camp III was mainly for people who were considered irredeemable deplorables. It was also used as a punishment camp and disincentive for prisoners in the other camps to complain. The Camp III prisoners did hard labor in coal mines and lived in horrid conditions. The coal was used for a power plant for the camp system in violation of environmental laws.

"The Camp III survivors – again all innocent people - are suffering from injuries, malnutrition, harsh cold primitive conditions, exhausting forced labor work, lice and bedbugs, and outbreaks of typhoid and typhus. We are hearing reports of verbal and physical abuse by guards, including frequent random beatings and vicious guard dog attacks. We have some medical units at Camp III and we are bringing in more units.

"Based on early interviews, it appears that about 2,300,000 innocent people perished in Camp III since the Soft Coup. Most of the deaths appear to have involved gradual starvation, malnutrition and wasting away, often combined with various diseases, extreme exhaustion, and exposure to horrific weather and living conditions. Again, we will investigate this matter thoroughly and hold people accountable.

"Camp II has about 250,000 surviving prisoners – again all innocent people. Camp II was another unpaid forced labor camp. Much of the labor was hard forestry work in harsh conditions, though it wasn't as brutal as the coal mining operations in Camp III.

"Based on early interviews, it appears that about 1,250,000 innocent people perished in Camp II from diseases, injuries and malnutrition during the past several years. Many of the Camp II surviving prisoners are in poor health. We have one medical unit at Camp II and we are bringing in more medical units.

"Camp I has about 35,000 surviving prisoners. It does not appear that Camp I resulted in very many excess deaths. Camp I prisoners had lighter agricultural work with decent vehicles and equipment, decent food and medical care, and they are generally in good health. Camp I was a reward-incentive camp. Prisoners in the other camps strived for transfers to Camp I by obeying all rules enthusiastically and not complaining. Some transfers apparently occurred, but only from Camp II.

"Regarding the administrators and guards, we are holding them under detention in the Camp III barracks that are vacant due to the past deaths of so many prisoners. We cleaned and disinfected the barracks first. We are providing food and water, and we are protecting them from retribution by the surviving prisoners.

"Now I have an update on the Freedom Trains that I announced last night. I have directed that the Freedom Train project be accelerated to warp speed and that medical transports be added as soon as possible.

"We will produce records and photographic evidence, including videos of camp conditions, prisoners, and the crematoria for disposal of those who perished, and the open trenches and pits that were prepared for the mass murders. We will also allow the news media into the camps as soon as we develop some protocols.

"I am going to form a commission to develop a plan to compensate the prisoners for their unpaid labor and any other issues the commission believes to be appropriate. The plan will be submitted to Congress for authorization.

"That is the end of my formal update, but not the end of our need to focus on this horrendous episode in our nation's history. I also plan to form a commission of the best free thinkers and historians in the country, and from other countries, to study how the Alaskan Reserve came about, digging into underlying causes, and developing recommendations so we will never forget nor repeat this shameful blot on our history.

"That commission will need time to reach its conclusions, but I'd like to make some personal observations. When one political group or movement denigrates and de-humanizes another group as deplorables or any other negative label, the first group and its supporters invariably feel entitled, or even obligated, to oppress the second group. This can lead to verbal and physical harassment, denial of rights and opportunities, political trials and imprisonment, even mass murder and genocide. This happened when the Nazis systematically denigrated and dehumanized the Jewish people. The Holocaust was even worse, of course, and I weep when I read about those horrors. But we must avoid ever going down the path of dehumanizing any group of people because that could lead to similar results.

"The Alaskan Reserve shows this evil process began to happen in our country after the left wing movement, and then the Equality Party, characterized Euros, conservatives and business owners as inherent racists, fascists and capitalist deplorables who didn't care about other people. That smear was never true as a generalization, but people believed the lie because it was repeated incessantly. We need to remember that the "Big Lie" was a standard Nazi propaganda tactic. The left wing movement in this country shamefully adopted the same Big Lie fascist tactic. The news media and big tech companies shamefully collaborated to advance the Big Lies, whether intentionally or because they themselves naïvely drank the Kool-Aid. Among the left's worst Big Lies were accusations that the old conservatives themselves were using Big Lie tactics. That would have been completely out of character for the old conservative party and the vast majority of its members, and did not happen, unless you count the old conservative brash President's tendency to exaggerate in his rally speeches. His supporters and anyone else who watched the full speeches objectively saw the exaggerations as amusing showmanship and obvious hyperbole rather than to be taken literally.

"I sincerely believe the vast majority of Euros, conservatives and business owners at the time of the Soft Coup had good hearts and minds and wanted to help people of all races and classes, but just had different ideas about how to do it. You may not agree with their ideas, but that doesn't make them bad people.

"We former minorities didn't like it when we were denigrated and picked on as a group. Now that we are the majority, let's not do the same thing to Euros, conservatives or business owners. It's not fair and not even smart because it will only perpetuate divisiveness and racism going both directions.

"Thank you and goodnight, and may God have mercy on this country, and turn us from our wicked ways, and heal our land through saving grace."

The news channel switched to a panel of talking heads who remained silent for a few moments and seemed deep in thought, perhaps thinking about their own past roles and how they could be better informed about history and political and economic systems, and more analytical and objective, in the future.

Tom's phone vibrated. Noah Green was calling on a video app. Tom opened the app and turned on the speaker.

"Hey Noah, how are you and where are you?"

"Hey Tom, I'm tired but okay up here in Alaska. And I have two people who want to talk to you."

Noah appeared to hand his phone to someone and Tom saw his mom and dad on the screen weeping and talking to him at the same time, saying how much they loved him and missed him, how he looked very handsome and so much older, that they had never given up on him, and that they couldn't wait to get back to see him.

Tom was overwhelmed and had a hard time vocalizing anything because he was weeping too, excited and glad to see them, and concerned that they looked so much older and haggard, wondering how soon they'd get back, and trying to ask about the timing while they were still saying they couldn't wait to get back.

Someone took the phone and Noah reappeared on the screen.

Noah said, "Tom, there's so much in-bound air traffic that it's tough getting out. But I have arranged for your parents to join me on a military flight that will arrive at O'Hare the day after tomorrow. I can't provide details yet. Can you hang tight until then?"

"Sure thing. Noah, I can't begin to tell you how grateful I am."

"Okay, Tom. Take care." Noah hung up but Tom kept staring at the screen for a few moments.

After Tom put his phone away, Izzy hugged him tightly for several moments. He was still in a daze. They went over and sat on the sofa.

Izzy set her music device to play Nat King Cole singing "Smoke Gets In Your Eyes" followed by the "Charlie Brown Christmas" album. She knew it was a bizarre segue, but playing tunes she liked, in any order she wanted, had been part of her way of protesting a system in which so many millions had been ruled and controlled by so few, the leftist ideologue mastermind politicians and academics, the allied news media and tech companies that had suppressed conservative views and real history. She shuddered as the "1619 Project" came to her mind.

Izzy curled up by Tom as they listened to the music and they were both soon asleep. Tom woke up around midnight in a cold sweat from a dream in which he was denouncing his parents when he was thirteen in the Party's Boarding School System facility in Ann Arbor.

Chapter Twenty-One

When Tom and Izzy got up the next morning, they noticed a new sense of openness on the news. The journalists and commentators no longer seemed concerned about staying within any particular talking points or groupthink, or violating Party doctrines or unwritten speech codes, or unknowingly committing micro-aggressions that no one had ever really defined.

Tom didn't want to go to the gym with his wounded arm, so Izzy went by herself to work on her boxing, kick-boxing and judo. After Izzy got back and showered and dressed, they sat on the sofa with mugs of coffee.

"So, let's talk about Buddy Junior," Izzy said.

"Okay."

"Nurse Lorna apparently went out with him the other night," Izzy said.

"I picked up on that."

"Beatriz said something earlier that tipped me off that he's visiting," Izzy said.

"Buddy also said something a few days ago. I was wondering if I should tell you, but then the battle came up."

"It sounds like Junior hangs out at Harry's Sports Bar and Music Lounge. I found it on the internet in south Evanston," Izzy said.

"You want me to beat him up? My right arm is out of commission."

"I did at first. But now I want to handle it myself," Izzy said.

"You're going to kick-box him or something?" Tom asked.

"Remember, I said I'd like to have a dialogue. Maybe he's changed. Maybe he'll feel some empathy if I explain my feelings. Maybe he'll view me as a person and say he's sorry," Izzy said.

"I guess that might happen. But it doesn't sound like he's changed based on what Nurse Lorna said."

"Lorna wasn't the one who was raped and she may not be the best person for picking up on feelings and empathy," Izzy said.

"True," Tom said. "You want me to come along, right?"

"No, he might just say something he doesn't mean," Izzy said.

"But will you feel safe?"

"Yeah, there'll be bartenders and probably other customers," Izzy said.

Izzy made sandwiches for lunch and Tom turned on a news channel. There were fly-over videos of the massive Alaskan Reserve. The views of Camps I and II showed masses of inmates spread over the large grounds moving around or standing in lines for medical checks, food, showers or latrines. For privacy, the cameras were too high to see individual faces.

Body language told some of the story, though. Camp I inmates were better dressed, generally buoyant, and waved enthusiastically at the drones and helicopters. Camp II inmates looked more tired and haggard, some were visibly joyful, some were too worn out to express their joy, and many were too numb to feel it yet.

Camp III was very different. Medical and military personnel were moving around. The few inmates who were able to drag themselves outside the barracks were emaciated, stooped over and standing in small groups or slowly shuffling about. Some Camp III inmates were helping their friends stand or shuffle. Some inmates tried to look up at the helicopters but raising their heads was an effort.

There was an extraordinarily disturbing fly-over video of the huge system of long deep trenches and pits in Camp III that were intended to serve as mass graves in a final action of horror. The screen then focused on a large building with ten smokestacks which the news reporter described as a crematorium for the bodies of people who previously perished in the camp system. Dozens of emaciated bodies were stacked like cordwood outside.

Tom and Izzy were deeply moved and kept asking each other how this could happen in a so-called civilized society and how it could be avoided again. Tom said the adage that kept coming to his mind, **"power corrupts and absolute power corrupts absolutely."**

Izzy turned off the news and they were silent for several minutes. They said they weren't sure about praying but it couldn't hurt, so Izzy said a prayer for the survivors and their families and friends and the future of the country, and Tom prayed along silently.

Tom put on a recording of the solemnly graceful "Bach Air on the G String," arranged for string orchestra, which was played when musicians in the Chicago Symphony passed away.

After the music ended, they spent more time talking about what had happened and more time in silent reflection.

Eventually, after a lengthy silence, Izzy gently asked Tom if it would be okay if she called Stardust to ask about the wedding reception.

"Good idea. Should I call the church in Park Ridge?"

"Sure. I want to call Gina too."

Izzy kissed Tom and headed to the bedroom to make her calls. She eventually came back and sat on the sofa.

"What do you want to do for a honeymoon?" Tom asked.

"Can you get a passport yet? You know, as a Euro?"

"I don't know, but I have friends in high places who might help," Tom said.

"How about a week in London and then a week in Italy?"

"How about one week in London and two weeks in Italy?" Tom asked.

They were silent for a long moment.

"Tom, what about your parents? You'll want to spend time with them."

"If they get back tomorrow and we have the wedding in about two weeks, they might be okay if we then go on a honeymoon."

"Then would you want the honeymoon to be two weeks?"

"I really like three weeks," Tom said.

"Me too."

Izzy said she wanted some water and offered to get Tom a glass. After she came back, she said, "So I wonder if Buddy Junior is at Harry's."

"Maybe. Are you going to wear what you have on?" Tom asked.

"Yeah, I picked these looser slacks and these shoes with low heels," Izzy said as she turned her foot to model her low pointy shoe.

"Are you sure you want to wear that makeup and lipstick?"

"I want it to be real," Izzy said.

"You'd take your pocket pistol, right?"

"Yeah. But I wonder if I should put it in my waist band in back instead of my purse. Like in the movies. In case someone snatches my purse."

"Why don't I just go with you? My left arm is good," Tom said.

"I need to do this myself. I don't think it will get into a gun fight anyway."

"Probably not," Tom said.

"So should I put my gun in my waist band in back?"

"That might be okay if the safety is on and you're well-trained in how to pull out the gun. You need to be careful not to release the safety by accident when you pull out the gun."

"How about if you train me."

Izzy went to the bedroom and returned wearing an untucked oxford style top. Tom helped adjust her belt and showed her how to secure the gun, after checking the safety, in the back of her waistband under her blouse.

By late afternoon, they felt good about Izzy's speed and dexterity in pulling the gun out quickly and then releasing the safety. She kissed Tom and said she'd be back within an hour if Junior was at the bar. Otherwise she'd call or text to let Tom know when Junior showed up.

As Izzy got in her Miata, Tom was debating what to do. He wanted to honor Izzy's desire to handle Junior her own way but wanted her to be safe. He decided to drive his car to the bar, wait in the lot, and maybe look through the door or window. He didn't need to check the address for Harry's Sports Bar and Music Lounge since he had looked it up after he first met Junior at Buddy's home and Junior had mentioned hanging out at a sports and music bar near campus.

After Tom had left Buddy's home that prior evening, he had found Harry's on his phone and had driven down to check it out. He had stood in the entryway to see the layout and get a sense for the place. After his eyes adjusted, he had seen a guy halfway down the bar swiveling on a stool and staring at his phone. The guy looked like he could be Junior but Tom hadn't seen a side view before. A woman in her 30s had come out of the restroom area in back, and walked along the bar toward the front, but hesitated and paused as she passed the guy on the swiveling stool. She had turned back toward the guy, leaned close and said something, and the guy turned and looked up and said something back. As the guy's face was turned, Tom had seen that the guy was Junior.

The website for Harry's Sports Bar and Music Lounge was interesting and Tom had found Harry's even more interesting when he had stopped by. Harry was tall and had a pony tail and a Fibonacci spiral tattoo on his right arm that looked like a large snail shell. Harry had never played sports in any serious way beyond high school basketball. Instead, he had eked out an existence as a semi-professional drummer in various bands in the Chicago area for decades while working various day jobs. Harry must have saved or inherited some money, or recruited some investors, in order to fix up and open Harry's. It was way nicer than a neighborhood sports bar.

The décor was a throw-back to the 1950s. A long polished oak wood bar counter with a brass rail and foot rest and floor-mounted swivel stools with burgundy leather seats. A central area with dark wood tables and chairs, and large comfortable booths along the wall across from the long bar. Modest size monitor screens were hanging to view sports or music videos without overwhelming the room. There was a low stage at the far end where a DJ or small band could set up. A studio piano was on the left side of the stage and a set of Ludwig drums and Zildjian cymbals was on the right side. There was a small dance floor area in front of the stage.

Harry limited the screens to live national sports games and any live college sports games that involved Northwestern teams. He didn't play sports re-runs or sports news or commentary. When he didn't have sports on the screens, Harry's was all about music. Harry was an expert in most genres except classical. But he never let the volume get too loud because he wanted customers to be able to talk. Some of the time he played music videos on the screens, which were connected to a high end sound system. At other times he ran custom music playlists. To pull in customers on off nights, he served as a DJ on the stage or jammed on the drums with musical friends. Sometimes he paid local soloists or small bands to perform or held talent contests.

After Izzy pulled into Harry's parking lot, she sat and gathered her thoughts. She said a silent prayer, got out of her car, reached back to touch her gun, walked casually through the entrance, and glanced around as she let her eyes adjust to the lower lighting.

    She saw one guy on a stool at the far end of the bar counter and another guy in about the middle. She saw a couple at the close end of the counter who were laughing loudly. She saw some other couples in booths. The Beatles' "Let It Be" had just begun to play.

    Izzy began to walk casually toward the restrooms in the back as though going to freshen up. She hoped to glance at the mirror behind the bar to check the faces of the guys sitting on stools, but bottles of booze mostly blocked the mirror.

    As she approached the guy midway down the bar, she could only see him from the side but knew he wasn't Buddy Junior. As she neared the guy at the far end of the bar, she wasn't sure so she looked again at the mirror and no bottles blocked the view. Even in the dim light she realized she was looking at a reflection of her rapist. He was on the last stool talking on his phone.

    Junior wasn't big and tall like his dad. He was about average in size, in his mid to late twenties, and was sort of good looking. He was wearing blue jeans and a colorful long sleeve shirt with the cuffs rolled partly up his forearms which were resting on the bar.

Izzy entered the restroom and ran the water in a sink for no particular reason while her mind raced. Izzy turned the water off, went back and took a stool between Junior and the other guy midway up the bar. Izzy reached back to touch her gun through her untucked blouse.

Junior glanced over as Izzy was glancing over and they made eye contact. Izzy stayed cool on the surface but felt nervous and flustered. She didn't smile and instead looked away. She put her purse on the bar counter and pulled out her phone and went into her text app as if to check for a message from someone she was going to meet. She saw a message from Gina saying something funny about Lars, and she hesitated over a message from Tom about staying safe and that he loved her.

Izzy noticed when someone sat on the stool to her left and quickly glanced up. Junior was smiling and said he was Buddy. His shirt had buttons all the way down, but the top three were unbuttoned. Izzy was thankful that no chest hair was showing, but then guessed that he might shave or wax it off. She was grateful that most people disliked the toxic masculinity of chest hair now. She'd heard her dad complain about people with domineering personalities in board meetings, but they seemed fairly evenly represented between senior males and senior females, all of whom had climbed the corporate ladder rung by rung. Still, Izzy never liked chest hair and was glad not to see it.

Izzy said "hey" but didn't smile or give her name, and turned back to look at her phone.

"Don't you want to be friendly to a stranger in a stranger land?"

Izzy rolled her eyes. While still looking at her phone, she said, "What strange land?"

"I live on our private island. I'm just here visiting my parents. They have a place on the lake in Wilmette."

"That's nice," Izzy said, still looking at her phone.

"You look like you're in great shape, if you don't mind a compliment. Do you go to the gym a lot?"

Izzy turned toward Junior and said, "Are you Buddy Junior, the son of Buddy Lemmon?"

"That's me. It's great being the son of a big shot." He added with a laugh, "He gets me out of all the trouble I get in."

"Can he still do that? You know, with the political changes?" Izzy asked.

"I just say that stuff to be cute. You know. Some girls like bad boys."

"Do these lines ever work?" Izzy asked.

"Sure, just last night. I met a pretty blonde nurse who got off her late shift. She was all fixed up and ready for action."

"You raped me when I was fifteen years old," Izzy said, while looking Junior straight in the eyes."

"You gotta be kidding me. Is this for reality TV?" Junior asked in a testy tone.

"It was about six years ago. I was in my home in Hyde Park. You said you were a high school quarterback and your dad was a big shot. You said I was so pretty I could turn a lemon into lemonade. You tried to charm me but you had a knife. You raped me, dude." Izzy wasn't yelling and hadn't even raised her voice.

"I'm not admitting anything, but for the sake of debate, the statute of limitations expired by now, so what's the point?" Junior asked.

Izzy paused to calm down and collect her thoughts. "Okay, here's where I'm coming from. I believe everyone has the potential to be good, with maybe a few exceptions like Hitler. I was hoping you'd say you're sorry and mean it. I was hoping for closure on a positive note. You know, so I can feel better and move on."

"Oh man, I'm not like Hitler at all. I may have done some stuff back then, but not now. No way. By the way, you're really beautiful," Junior said.

"Thanks, but that's not a good enough answer. I remember you, dude. You did this. I'm looking for a sincere apology with an explanation about how you've changed. Okay, think of it this way. Put yourself in the situation of a fifteen year old girl who is minding her own business, and then a guy shows up with a knife, makes her undress, and rapes her? Or think how you'd feel if that happened to your sister or daughter if you had one. How would you feel?" Izzy asked.

Junior looked down at his beer mug and was silent for several moments. He made eye contact and said, "You've given me a lot to think about. It's sort of weird since I'm a guy, so maybe I don't identify with girls so well. But, wow, I really do feel bad. I never wanted to hurt anyone. Okay, I did some bad things when I was young, but that's not who I am now. I remember you and what happened, and I've felt bad about that for a long time. I am just really, really, really sorry."

Junior looked down again and seemed emotionally moved as he took his beer mug napkin and dabbed the corners of his eyes and sniffed. He was still looking down.

Junior continued, "I was so messed up. My parents were way too busy for me and I felt really neglected growing up. I had no sisters or brothers so I felt really alone. I was awkward with girls and they teased me. Even when I was a quarterback. I sucked at football and they knew my dad got me on the team. Growing up was just brutal." Junior continued to look down and sniffed and dabbed his eyes again.

Izzy said sympathetically, "Oh, gee, I'm sorry. That must have been rough."

"Thanks, I'll be okay. But what about you. I really hope you were able to get past it somehow," Junior said.

"I developed some ways to cope. But hearing you say you're sorry and that you changed is a really important part of closure for me. I mean, I feel so much better than when I came in here. I really didn't know how you'd react. Thanks," Izzy said.

Junior raised his head and they smiled at each other. Then he said, "You know, how 'bout if I buy you a drink? It's the least I can do. What do you like?"

"Oh, I don't know. I should probably go," Izzy said.

"Not just one drink to celebrate my redemption and closure for you?"

Izzy was silent for several moments as she considered the situation and looked at the colorful bottles behind the bar.

"Oh, why not, maybe a glass of white wine," Izzy said.

"How about a Champagne cocktail? For more of a celebration."

Izzy noticed that "Bridge Over Troubles Waters" by Simon & Garfunkel was playing. She thought for a several more moments while she listened to the music.

"Okay, why not."

Junior snapped his fingers at Harry who was helping at the bar and ordered two Atomic Champagne Cocktails and then said to make them doubles.

"So what is an Atomic Champagne Cocktail?" Izzy asked.

"A chilled mix of vodka, brandy, sherry, and brut Champagne. You'll like it."

They listened to Simon & Garfunkel until Harry came back with two colorful cocktails. He said he used tall glasses since they were doubles. Harry then made an announcement in his head microphone that he was going to play some music by the Beach Boys beginning with "Californian Girls.""

Junior and Izzy chatted and listened to the music as they sipped the cocktails. Junior asked Izzy how she liked college and what her major was. He was a good conversationalist with a surprising knowledge of modern European history in the 1930s and 1940s.

"Fun Fun Fun" began playing and Izzy said, "This one has cute lyrics. About a teenage chick driving around in her dad's T-Bird car."

Junior asked, with interest, about Izzy's family, her parents, whether she had siblings, and took an interest in her earlier childhood growing up in Italy. He asked if she ever had pets, and she said she had a tabby kitten named Muffin. He said that was sweet. She said she had to give Muffin away because her brother had allergies and she had cried for hours. He said he was really sorry about that.

Izzy said, "This music brings back good memories. I went through a rebellious phase in the summer when I was thirteen and listened to the Beatles and Beach Boys all the time. Also the Carpenters."

"That was your rebellion?"

"Yeah, I was a good kid. My parents were more into classical music."

"I never got into classical music, but I have a lot of respect for anyone who does. I bet you're really smart and cultured."

Junior had turned his stool toward Izzy and occasionally glanced at the entrance doors in the distance as people entered. When a guy in his 30s came in, Buddy asked if Izzy recognized the guy from TV.

As Izzy turned to look, Junior slipped a carefully calibrated new date rape drug in her cocktail and saw it dissolve. The drug was designed to place a person in a dreamy state of mind, feeling love for everyone and aggressively amorous toward the closest person regardless of gender or anything else.

Izzy didn't recognize the guy who came in. She was enjoying the buzz from the Atomic Champagne Cocktail. Junior seemed charming as he continued to take an interest in her as a person and asked what kinds of movies she liked, and then told stories with a playful smile about celebrities he'd partied with. She relaxed with the cocktail and flowing Beach Boys music, feeling happy that everything had worked out.

"That's Not Me" came on. Junior said with a friendly smile, "I love this song. It speaks to me." Izzy nodded and smiled and said she understood. The next song was "Sloop John B." They listened and sipped their drinks.

By the end of "Don't Worry Baby," Izzy felt a soft warm aura wrapping around her with peace and love for everyone everywhere. She didn't think she should finish the drink but finished it anyway. She wondered if she had missed out on any sort of rite of passage now that she was twenty-one and all grown up.

The music picked up as "Kokomo" began. Junior said, "This is perfect for a friendly dance. Freestyle. How 'bout it?"

Izzy was seeing Junior through the soft dreamy warmth of the cocktail and date rape drug. She had an impulse to kiss him but thought it was the cocktail, enhanced by the idea of his redemption from bad to good, and an amorous feeling that she tried to re-classify as agape love.

"I guess maybe. Final closure on a good note."

They slid off their bar stools. Izzy was surprised that she didn't feel unsteady or physically impaired. They walked a few yards over to the dimly lit dance floor area which had no other couples.

They danced free style, not touching, but gently swaying and moving their arms and feet to the music, as Izzy recalled her fun summer when she was thirteen.

When "All I Wanna Do" came on, Junior held his hands up to offer a standard box step position with a respectful six to eight inches between them. Izzy was surprised that Junior knew how to dance this way and remembered what she learned from Stardust. Junior led well and they glided around the small dance floor and he spun her in a series of twirls. After dancing somewhat closer, Junior led her gently through a series of underarm turns, each time bringing her back closer to him.

The next song was "Little Surfer Girl" with its slow rich unfolding harmonies rolling over them. As they danced under the influence of cocktails and music, and Izzy felt even more amorous warmth from the date rape drug, she closed her eyes and, in her dreamy mind, she was with Tom at Stardust.

Junior was holding her closer and affectionately, so they were lightly touching. She placed her left wrist around and behind Junior's neck and rested her head against his shoulder with her eyes still closed. He gently slowed and stopped dancing and held Izzy tighter and began moving his hands slowly down her back while telling her she was beautiful. Junior sounded like Tom and she liked that Tom was being so affectionate.

Junior kept holding Izzy close and continued to move his hands slowly down her back, but didn't get down to the gun in her waist band. Izzy opened her eyes and was surprised to see Junior and said he was getting fresh and tried to push him away. Junior held her even tighter and said he was glad she found him, and then whispered that he'd like to take her home for sex.

Izzy shook her head to clear her mind and recalled more clearly where she was and realized what was happening in the dim light. She tried to push Junior away again, but he grabbed her butt with both hands, pulled her even tighter, kissed and licked her neck, moved his right hand up to her left breast, and said something about flying her to a private island.

Izzy had heard that line before and had a visceral reaction with a rush of adrenaline and a contraction of her stomach muscles, and went into a fast automatic heavily practiced defensive movement. Instead of pushing Junior away, she grabbed the bottoms of his shirt sleeves with both hands and very quickly took a few quick steps backwards while pulling him toward her to get him off balance and create momentum, then spun quickly on her left heel while bending her knees, then quickly used the continuing momentum from pulling him forward to pull him all the way over her back so he landed on the floor as she straightened her knees. He landed on his back with his head at her feet. "Seoi Nage" was one of her favorite judo throws.

Izzy took a step back and then kicked Junior hard in the head with her pointed shoe, as her gun clattered to the floor and landed near Junior's right hand. He raised his head enough to look up at Izzy with shock and anger. He turned his head, grabbed the gun, pointed it at Izzy and screamed, "No girl throws me on the floor! I'm gonna kill you, bitch!"

Junior pulled the trigger but nothing happened because the safety was on. Izzy kicked the gun out of his hand and then kicked him hard in the head again and his head fell back down to the floor. Izzy rushed over to pick up her gun and clicked off the safety. Junior raised his head but seemed dazed and confused when he saw Izzy pointing her gun. Izzy yelled at Harry to call 911. Harry yelled back that he had already called and the cops were on their way.

All of this had happened in a matter of moments. Izzy tried to calm down as she tried to hold her gun steady. She looked down at Junior and yelled, "You're the exception like Hitler! You're gonna rot in prison for attempted murder, asshole."

By that point, Junior was trying to focus on what she said and didn't like the sound of prison. He got up unsteadily and shook his head, gave Izzy a venomous evil look, and ran as fast as he could go through the bar and out the door. He guessed she wouldn't shoot and he was right. She was concerned about hitting the guy halfway up the bar and the couple at the end.

Izzy was feeling an adrenaline rush and post-trauma stress response more than the booze and date rape drug at the moment. She grabbed her purse from the counter and started to walk through the bar, grabbing a few vacant stools with her left hand along the way. She was thinking she could get a description of Junior's car and maybe shoot the tires.

Harry stopped the music and Izzy was surprised to see Fred and Ginger from Stardust hurry over from a booth where they had been having cocktails. They asked if Izzy was okay and offered to let her join them in their booth while she waited for the cops. She kept walking and said she wanted to get a description of the car, so Fred and Ginger went with her.

As they opened the door they looked to the right where they heard a powerful car engine roar and the screech of rubber spinning on pavement as Junior sped away from the far end of the lot. Izzy thought it looked like a Lamborghini based on the fancy cars Joey had shown her at the repair shop. It was candy apple red but too far to read the license plate.

Izzy put her gun in her purse and looked up, and was surprised to see Tom to her left. He was pressing his left hand over a bleeding wound on his right arm.

As Junior sped off, he began to form a plan to drive north a few miles past his parents' home, get out and push the car down a ravine, walk over to nearby Lake Michigan and then down the shore line to his parents' home, avoid his parents, get the groundskeeper to drive him to the private airport and get the pilot of his dad's jet to fly him to the island. He knew the groundskeeper and pilot, and also knew a cosmetic surgeon on the island who could probably change his appearance. He figured on getting to Cuba. He hated that his dad no longer had the political clout to keep him out of trouble.

After speeding past the Evanston campus heading north on Sheridan and maneuvering the turns to reach Wilmette still heading north, Junior wondered if the chicks were hotter in Venezuela than

Cuba. Junior then wondered if he was thinking about Latinas because his mother, Beatriz the Latina, hadn't been around enough when he was growing up. Then he realized that he was thinking about places like Cuba and Venezuela out of habit because they were far left socialist regimes. Then he wondered if they'd not want him because his dad had turned from socialism to freedom. He raced the car even faster and flew through Winnetka as he became furious with the jerk who sold him the date rape drug that hadn't worked well enough on the bitch at Harry's.

Junior clenched the steering wheel with white knuckles and floored the accelerator as he became full of rage at the image of the chick throwing him on the floor and realized he'd never come back to the country to rape her again. He raced and veered around cars in his lane, and swerved to avoid the honking on-coming cars in the passing lane, and felt in the moment that he didn't care if he lived or died.

Tom had watched the scene unfold at Harry's. He had parked and found a place to stand outside a window in front with a decent view of the interior. He had seen Junior get up and sit next to Izzy. He had been puzzled when he saw cocktails arrive. He hadn't known what to think when he saw them start to dance. Yet, they were dancing freestyle at first, and then switched to a box step with a decent distance between them.

When Tom had seen Junior holding Izzy closer so they were touching, he felt something might be wrong. He had been torn between honoring Izzy's request to handle it herself and going in to break it up. But breaking it up might not work with his right arm out of commission. He had pulled out his phone and pressed 911. When he was connected, he said a young woman was going to be accosted at Harry's Sports Bar in Evanston. The 911 operator said she couldn't do anything unless there was an actual assault or imminent threat.

While Tom had been speaking with the operator, he was peering through the window. He had seen Junior grab Izzy's butt and pull her tight and had seen Izzy trying hard to push him away. Tom had yelled into the phone that the girl was being assaulted right then on the dance floor. The operator said she was dispatching a patrol car immediately, but asked Tom to stay on the line so she could ask more questions, whether he knew their names and could provide descriptions and whether domestic violence was involved. He then saw Izzy's judo move and saw Junior land on the floor on his back.

As Tom was asking the 911 operator how soon the police would arrive, he had seen Junior grab and point the gun at Izzy. Tom's heart almost stopped when he saw Junior pull the trigger, but was ecstatic when the gun didn't fire and Izzy kicked it away. He had said "yeah!" to himself when he saw Izzy grab the gun and point it at Junior. Then he had seen Junior get up and run through the bar toward the entrance.

Tom had put his phone in his pocket, stepped closer to the entrance and used his left hand to grab Junior's shirt as he came running out. Tom wanted to hold Junior for the police and not get in trouble for using karate on a fleeing perp rather than in self-defense. He also doubted he could be very effective with left handed karate. But with his left hand, Tom got a tight grip on Junior's shirt and they struggled as Junior tried to break away.

Junior pulled a switch blade from his pocket, clicked the release, and slashed a deep gash across Tom's right forearm. Tom felt searing pain and let Junior go so Tom could press his left hand over the cut as the blood began to flow. He saw Junior run toward the far end of the lot where he took off in a sports car. He saw Izzy push through the door followed by Fred and Ginger and saw them look at the car as it sped off. They then saw Tom and his bleeding arm and rushed over. Ginger called 911 for an ambulance.

Izzy ran back inside and yelled at Harry that she needed something to stop the bleeding from a bad knife wound. Harry pulled a trap door in the floor behind the bar, hurried down narrow stairs to the supply room and found cloth napkins. He clambered back up and handed them to Izzy while trying to control his wheezing. Izzy raced back outside and wrapped the napkins around Tom's arm and applied pressure.

They heard a siren as a police car came around a corner and screeched to a hard stop close to where they were standing. One officer went inside with his gun drawn while the other officer came over to the group. They heard another siren and a second police car came from a different direction and jolted to a stop. Again, one cop went inside while the other cop came over to the group.

The outside cops checked Tom's arm and saw blood seeping through and around the cloth napkins. They helped Tom lay down on the pavement. The senior cop asked if they had called for an ambulance, and Ginger said she did that. Izzy was feeling a combination of anxiety, adrenaline, cocktails and the dreamy effects of the date rape drug. She kneeled down, leaned over, and began to give Tom a slow French kiss. The senior cop squatted down and said to knock it off and that her husband would be okay.

The other cop had been talking to Fred and Ginger. He asked them whether Tom was the perpetrator of an assault on a young female based on a 911 call. Izzy had stood up by then, overheard the question, and began to laugh hysterically.

After Izzy calmed down, she explained that Tom was her fiancé and the bad guy had taken off in a fancy sports car heading north. The cop asked for details and Izzy said it was candy apple red and might be a Lamborghini.

Izzy added, "Oh, sir, the guy's name is Buddy Lemmon Junior and he might be going to his dad's house in Wilmette. His dad is Buddy Lemmon."

The cops conferred for several moments and then spoke into their shoulder mics to their partners inside the bar and asked them to interview witnesses. Then they said they were going after the perp. They chose one of the cop cars, jumped in, slammed the doors and took off fast heading north.

An ambulance pulled up and emergency medical technicians jumped out and rushed over to Tom who was still lying on the pavement. After a quick check, they got Tom on a gurney and rolled the gurney into the back of the ambulance.

Izzy got in back with Tom and the ambulance raced toward Lake Shore Evanston Hospital with the siren blaring and the lights flashing. The technician in back removed Harry's cloth napkins, cleaned the wound and applied a pressure dressing. He asked why there was already a military dressing higher up Tom's arm and Izzy said it was a long story.

Chapter Twenty-Two

When the ambulance reached the hospital, the EMT went off to check Tom in. He never came back but a different attendant showed up pushing a hospital bed, and helped Tom get off the ambulance gurney and onto the bed. The attendant said Tom was still checked into the hospital from the prior day. Izzy tried to explain what had happened and that there must have been a mix up. The explanation was too complicated, so Izzy apologized and said they'd never do that again. The attendant brought up a different screen and said Tom didn't owe a balance so it didn't really matter.

Tom and Izzy were tired and stressed. Tom was light-headed from the blood loss, while Izzy was light-headed from stress and the after-effects of the cocktails and the date rape drug. Izzy followed Tom in the hospital bed wherever it went while her mind tried to focus. Somewhere on the ground floor, the attendant gave custody of Tom and the bed to another attendant who explained that the ER was no longer in triage mode from the battle. Izzy tried to process that but then decided it was small talk. The new attendant pushed the bed to the elevator which they rode up to the ER. Izzy sat anxiously in the waiting area.

After about two hours, a young doctor entered the waiting area, asked who was waiting for Tom Hardy, and saw Izzy raise her hand. He introduced himself as Doctor Cutler. He said Tom would be fine, and explained that he had put Tom under anesthesia, cleaned and stitched up the knife wound, applied a new dressing, and gave two blood units. He explained that Tom would get one more blood unit and an IV in a recovery room.

Doctor Cutler was professional, calm, respectful, patient, caring and kind. He was also nice looking, trim and about Izzy's height and she noticed that he had no wedding ring. Izzy sometimes looked for that in case Gina wanted to be fixed up, but then she remembered that Gina was now with Lars. Unlike the interns Izzy had encountered, Doctor Cutler didn't engage in flirtatious banter with questions about whether she had done any modelling or wanted to be an actress. She felt a sense of hope that the interns she had previously met would become more mature and felt better about the male gender overall.

Doctor Cutler left before Izzy thought about asking where she should go next, and she wasn't sure if a recovery room differed from a regular hospital room. She went through a door to look for a station where someone would tell her where to go. But she was in a hallway which she walked along unsteadily until she reached the elevators. She went down to the ground floor and wandered around until she found the main admission center. The admissions person thought she wanted to be admitted and asked what her symptoms were. She carefully explained that she was only tipsy and wanted to know about Tom Hardy and said he was already admitted.

The admissions person said Izzy needed to pre-pay $10,500 for Tom's new ER procedure and an overnight stay for observation. Izzy asked if she could pay extra for a single premium room with a reclining chair. The admissions person said that would be a total of $15,000.

It took a series of attempts for the amount to go through on Izzy's card over a thirty minute period and she fell asleep for brief moments while sitting in the chair. After her card cleared, the admissions person told Izzy to take the elevator to the fifth floor and go to Room 505.

When Izzy got up to the fifth floor, she crept past the nurses' station, where they were busy with other visitors, and found her way to Room 505.

But Tom was not in Room 505, so Izzy went back to the nurses' station, cleared her throat and said, "Hi Lorna."

"Hi, uh, Izzy right? How are you and what are you doing here again?"

"Tom was wounded in a knife fight so we took an ambulance here. He was in the ER and the doctor said he'd be in a recovery room, but then someone told me to come to 505."

"Was that the admissions center on the ground floor?" Nurse Lorna asked.

"Yeah," Izzy said.

"There's a glitch in the computer system. It should be fixed soon."

"I was beginning to wonder about this place," Izzy said.

"We're normally good for patient care and administrative stuff too. I heard we were excellent before the government took us over. I can say that now, right?"

Izzy didn't respond.

Nurse Lorna added, "So, the doctor mentioned the recovery room? That's where patients come out of anesthesia."

"So he's in a recovery room, and then he'll show up here?" Izzy asked.

Lorna checked some screens and said "Yeah, Room 505. In about an hour."

"Okay, Lorna, I'm going out to pick up my car and drive back here. No sponge bath, okay?"

Nurse Lorna said okay, so Izzy walked all the way down to Harry's Sports Bar and Music Lounge. She needed a long walk and enjoyed the mild June evening with a light breeze and bluish sky turning dusky. Her mind became clearer the farther she walked.

Izzy found her Mazda Miata but walked further and checked that Tom's car was still there. Then she wondered why she had bothered since it was 30 years old. Then she remembered it was a Subaru.

When she got in her 15 year old car, it didn't start and she gave a hard whack of pent-up frustration on the steering wheel with both fists while saying "Scheisse!" Her grandad Hans used that word a lot. Her fists hurt and it seemed unlikely that the whack or German cuss word made a difference, but the car started when she tried again.

Izzy drove back to the hospital, parked and spent twenty minutes wandering back and forth, here and there, from wing to wing, before finding Room 505. When she peered into the darkened room, she saw Tom sleeping in the hospital bed with monitor wires and an IV. She smiled as she saw a reclining arm chair.

Izzy was playing solitaire on her phone when Tom woke up. They greeted each other and Izzy kissed and hugged Tom as well as could be expected with the wires and tubes. They talked for a while. At 6:00 pm a local news program began on the screen hanging from the ceiling.

The lead story was a breaking report which began with a scene of a bad car crash. The camera crew was apparently filming from a higher elevation to show a road descending steeply, then crossing a small bridge, then turning sharply right and ascending again. There was a deep ravine that began at the higher elevation on the side of the road closer to the camera team. The ravine descended down under the small bridge and continued to descend steeply on the other side of the bridge. The camera zoomed closer to the wrecked car on fire further down the ravine where it had crashed into a stand of trees, apparently after turning over.

A news reporter appeared with the scene behind her. She speculated that the driver was speeding and slammed the brakes when the quick descent to the small bridge came into view. The camera zoomed in to show skid marks indicating the driver lost control and spun out before plunging into the ravine. The reporter speculated that the gas tank may have exploded when the car turned over on the way down.

Tom said he knew where the ravine was on Sheridan Road about a half mile north of Tower. The camera panned over to show a police car and an ambulance with flashing lights. The camera zoomed in on two EMTs standing away from the smoldering wrecked car.

The news reporter came back on the screen and explained that there had been a high speed police chase of a man who had been accused of assaulting a young woman. The reporter listened to her ear bud for a moment and then said the driver had been pronounced dead. His name was being withheld pending notification of next of kin. The news camera switched back to the scene in the ravine and showed the EMTs drag a limp body out of the car, place it on a stretcher, strap it down, and cover it with a blanket.

Izzy began crying and reached for a tissue. Tom wasn't sure if she was crying as a release of tension and relief that Junior wouldn't assault her again, or from sadness over the way some people mess up their lives. He guessed it was both reasons. Tom tried to comfort Izzy but it was awkward since he couldn't get up and hug her with the monitor wires and IV tubes. The pain medication was making Tom drowsy. Izzy was exhausted and turned off the news. Nurse Lorna checked a few times and then left a note in Tom's chart to let them sleep through the night.

When they woke up late the next morning, Lorna had just started a new shift. She removed both wound dressings, cleaned Tom's bullet holes and knife wound and put on new dressings. She explained that the doctor had released Tom but he had to return in seven days for a checkup. She gave Izzy a new seven day supply of dressings, antibiotics and pain pills. An attendant arrived with a mandatory wheel chair.

Izzy went to get her car so she could pull up at the exit area. By the time she pulled up, Tom was sitting in the wheel chair and the attendant was standing by to assist. But Tom said he was tired of being treated like a baby, stood up all by himself, opened the passenger door and got in the car. Then he asked Izzy to buckle his seat belt since he couldn't use his right arm. She went around, buckled his seat belt, French kissed him, and said she doesn't kiss babies like that.

As Izzy drove to their apartment, she wondered why she had recently developed a desire to French kiss Tom even more than before. She guessed it was a latent gene expression based on her dad's mom having been French. She had no way of knowing that Junior's date rape drug was developed by a French chemist in a secret lab outside Paris and had a long-term side effect involving a heightened desire to kiss.

Tom and Izzy had checked out of the hospital by early afternoon and were back at the apartment when Tom got a call from Noah. He was at O'Hare airport with Tom's parents, John and Jane Hardy. They were tired from the flight, but energized about seeing Tom. They were waiting in line for a cab.

Tom felt an agitated range of emotions, buoyant excitement, nervous anticipation and fear. He hoped for a joyful reunion and wondered if his parents would like the way he turned out. He dreaded the idea that they might ask why he denounced them. Izzy was concerned about Tom's emotional state as he rotated between sitting, standing up, walking around the living room, and glancing out the window, often with his arms folded. She came over by the window and put her arm around his waist.

Tom was looking out the window when the cab pulled up. He felt better when he saw his parents and Noah get out, look up at the building, and point and wave enthusiastically at him. Izzy went over to press the button to unlock the building door. Tom leaned over the stairwell and saw his parents having some difficulty climbing up the three flights.

Tom shouted down, "Hello, do you want to take the freight elevator?"

"No, we'll make it," his dad said while breathing heavily as they reached the second floor landing.

After all the emotions and tears of the initial greetings and hugs, there was tension in the room as they sat and struggled to find comfortable topics and questions. Tom's parents commented a lot on how handsome and grown-up Tom looked, and asked about his bandages and how he was wounded, but he didn't want to talk much about that. His parents were happy to hear that he graduated from Northwestern but seemed puzzled and concerned when he told them about his major. They asked about his job and career prospects, but there was not much he could say since he didn't know himself. Tom asked about the Alaskan Reserve but his parents didn't want to say much. Tom told his parents about working for Buddy Lemmon and they said they enjoyed the speeches, but lowered their voices like they were afraid of being overheard.

After Izzy brought out some wine, John and Jane began to open up more. They talked about their good fortune to be reassigned to Camp I, the benefits of operating the coffee service, the pilfered coffee beans and illicit bartering system. They talked about several people they had become friends with and who had helped each other, and about a person who had been a snitch and was eventually tossed in the stinky open latrine ditch in the middle of the night. They didn't want to talk about the bad aspects of the camp system and weren't sure if anyone would even believe how bad it was in Camp II.

Though sitting, Tom and John and Jane were leaning in toward each other with their forearms resting on their knees and making steady eye contact. Izzy and Noah were smiling and sitting back in their chairs as they listened and observed the reunion, including body language and other metadata. Izzy shifted her gaze frequently, trying to sense the feelings and discern the dynamics. John and Jane had talked with Noah on the flight and knew that Tom and Noah had been close friends. They brought Noah into the conversation, asking questions that led to animated dialogues between Noah and Tom about the Party's Boarding School System, their circle of Jewish friends at Petosky Academy, stories about how Noah would sneak out to meet his parents, and how the circle of friends would sneak out to dance and sing songs.

After a lull, Tom asked his parents, "So where's your luggage?"

Noah replied, "They didn't have much. Mostly coffee beans. We dropped their stuff at the underground's safe house. They can stay there until the end of July."

Noah's phone rang with a distinctive tone. He said he needed to take the call and went to the kitchen. He came back a few minutes later and said they should turn on the news for a special Presidential announcement about the Alaskan Reserve.

When they turned on the news, some commentators were speculating about the upcoming announcement but didn't know anything. The scene switched to the Oval Office where President Georgia Washer was sitting at the Resolute Desk with a solemn look and folded hands. She made the following announcement:

"Good evening. Our investigation into the Alaskan Reserve has taken an unexpected turn and I want to let you know what we learned so far. At this time, we believe Director Stalinsky had no knowledge of the final mass murder plans. Instead, we believe Stalinsky's Commander, Ashley Bennington, gave the orders.

"Evidently, Bennington was a long-time member of a radical environmental group called "Humans Are Terrible Evil" or "HATE." Based on the manifesto we discovered, this group views humans as a scourge on the earth, a source of widespread dreadful affliction and devastation. HATE rejects the idea that humans have any unique qualities among the species, such as self-awareness, will, reason, knowledge, complex emotions, morality, spirituality, or the ability to talk and think at complex levels.

"HATE also rejects any idea that humans provide redeeming contributions, such as their ability to create art, music, literature, to record and analyze historical events and learn from them, to develop cures for diseases and treatments for broken bones and broken hearts, to develop political systems for self-government with laws and courts to limit the power of their rulers, or to develop concerns about the environment and create reasonable programs to mitigate either natural or human impacts in a balanced manner.

"HATE similarly rejects the idea that human ingenuity could play a role in solving environmental problems in any creative way other than by simply returning the environment to its natural state. For example, HATE utterly rejects the idea that advanced logging and forestry management practices could reduce forest fires compared with ignoring the forests and letting them fend for themselves. HATE completely refused to engage in the forest management debate because debate was beside the point in their twisted view.

"For many years HATE supported typical environmental causes such as diverting millions of gallons of fresh water annually away from California agriculture and into the Pacific Ocean for debatable scientific reasons and a general environmentalist goal of curtailing human expansion by impairing agricultural production. But HATE's ultimate solution was to reduce the human population by two thirds by any means necessary. We found video of the leaders drinking Champagne to celebrate news about mass starvation in Africa.

"Ashley Bennington was planning a major new depopulation initiative. She wanted to start by liquidating all prisoners at the Alaskan Reserve. Future plans included poisoning the water supplies in one country after another beginning in Africa. It turned out that she was also a racist.

"The FBI has issued a warrant for Bennington's arrest and will team with agencies in other countries to locate this person and bring her to justice, along with her supporters. The FBI believes she may currently be in Cuba. She is a trust fund baby, the daughter of Billy Bennington, the well-known billionaire. We do not have any reason to believe he ever read the HATE policies, but the records show he was a major donor.

"My last comment is that I care deeply about the environment. But we need transparent accurate fully vetted scientific studies and respectful policy debates. We can seek a reasonable balance without going nuts. That's it. Good evening."

The screen switched from President Washer to the talking heads and Izzy turned off the news.

"Wow. That is so horrible! I can't believe I went out with her," Tom said.

"You didn't see any symptoms back then?" Izzy asked.

"Not really, except she said humans were less worthy than plants and animals. I thought she was being facetious about moral relativism."

"Don't take it personally. We already learned about the mass graves at the Alaskan Reserve. Someone was behind it. So it was your old girlfriend. No one can blame you," Izzy said.

Everyone was tired so Noah called a Lyft and said he'd drop off Tom's parents at the underground's safe house.

There were more hugs and tears as John and Jane were leaving. They made plans to get together the next day and Tom said he'd like to introduce his parents to Buddy and Beatriz.

The wedding ceremony took place three weeks later at 6:00 pm in an old stone church in Park Ridge. A remarkable thing about the ceremony was that it took place at all. Few people bothered anymore and, if they did, they usually got married at city hall. Tom and Izzy had researched how weddings were handled in the 1950s. The organist played the Wedding March from Wagner's "Lohengrin" for Izzy's entrance, and the standard selection from Mendelssohn's "A Midsummer Night's Dream" for the couple's exit.

Izzy and Tom arrived in traditional 1950s outfits they borrowed for moderate fees from the Northwestern Theatre Department. Izzy wore a full length white gown. Tom had a white shirt and black tuxedo suit. He was glad the bow tie was a clip-on. He didn't want to spend an extra fee to rent shiny black shoes and figured his dark brown loafers would be okay. Izzy was horrified about the brown loafers but calmed down as she realized she could use Tom's poor aesthetic judgment and undue frugality as a future debating point. Maybe the frugal part wouldn't be a problem anyway. She had a three carat sparkling clear square diamond set in a wide platinum band on her ring finger. Tom had used most of his remaining social credits.

Gina had blabbed about the traditional ceremony to her friend, Doreen Rivers, a nationally syndicated cultural columnist. Doreen didn't have an invitation but showed up with press credentials. Izzy welcomed Doreen graciously and she wrote a story with photos and a headline about the return of 1950s wedding ceremonies. The column went viral and old-fashioned weddings became trendy for people of all races and backgrounds, even in other countries like Japan.

The reception at Stardust seemed larger because most of Stardust was open and festive strangers were sitting and talking at other tables or out on the dance floor. The mood of the whole country was buoyant with freedom. At Izzy's request, the DJ was playing Rod Stewart performances of songs from the 1930s through the 1950s.

By the time the wedding guests were mingling and chatting and drinking cocktails amid peels and roars of laughter rising periodically above the music and general din, Izzy and Tom were standing with several of Izzy's college friends near the back of the room. As her friends howled about another political joke that would have been highly imprudent only a few weeks earlier, Izzy took Tom's hand and nodded toward a hallway with a small sign, *"To The Veranda."*

They quietly left the group, walked down the hallway, through a set of French doors, and onto an unlit terrace balcony where no one else was present. They remained silent as they walked over to the edge in the moonlight and leaned on an ornate railing. They looked out at the cityscape of buildings and views of Lake Michigan in the distance with moonlight dancing playfully on dark water waves.

Izzy turned toward Tom and, as he turned toward her, she pulled him close. They kissed warmly and embraced tightly.

"So Tom, I know you like old movies and music, but real life isn't going to be like living in a Norman Rockwell painting," Izzy said quietly as they held the embrace.

"I know. Not everything was so great in the past anyway. The Depression, World War II, the bad stuff people of color dealt with."

"Yeah, every generation has problems. Probably every couple too," Izzy said.

"We'll be fine. I love you, Izzy."

"I love you, Tom."

They continued to hold each other for a few minutes while listening to the big band music wafting down the hallway above the party sounds.

Buddy and Beatriz had brought Tom's parents to the reception. The two couples had taken an interest in each other and Tom's parents were now staying with Buddy and Beatriz. Having company also helped distract from their sorrow over Junior.

Tom's parents had decided to open a new coffee shop and develop a small chain in the Chicago area. Buddy and Beatriz agreed to invest in the business and Rocky handled the legal work to acquire options for the Mojo's in Evanston and a few other locations. John and

Jane planned to rebrand the business with their old name, Paradise Coffee Café.

Tom and Izzy returned from the veranda holding hands. Buddy and Beatriz, along with Tom's parents, came over to talk.

"So, I understand you're going on a three week honeymoon in England and Italy?" Beatriz asked.

"Yeah," said Izzy and Tom almost simultaneously.

Izzy added, "We'll take an overnight train to Boston and then go down to New York City to sail on the Queen Mary 3."

"That sounds very romantic," Beatriz said with a smile.

"Yeah," said Izzy and Tom. Izzy placed her left hand behind Tom's neck, raised her face up and pulled him down for a kiss.

"So, Tom, we just worked out a plan for you to receive a six month severance package as we eliminate your position in connection with dissolving the Party. You'll still be paid to the end of July and then the severance will start."

"Buddy, that's awesome! I had no idea!" Tom said.

"You deserve it. Have you made up your mind about President Washer's offer to work for her in DC?" Buddy asked.

"I thought about it and talked with Izzy and my parents. I called Georgia yesterday and she took the call, but I declined the job. I explained our attachment to the Chicago area, with Izzy's parents in Hyde Park and my parents back now."

"It takes guts to turn down the President. But where does that leave you? I mean what will you do?" Beatriz asked.

"Tom's joining us in the coffee business," Tom's mom and dad answered almost simultaneously.

"I'm going to work there too," Izzy added.

Tom and Izzy kissed and embraced. The DJ returned from a break and dimmed the lights to begin a new set with Andy Williams singing his hauntingly romantic version of "Moon River."

Tom asked if Izzy would like to dance. She smiled and came close and raised her right hand to meet Tom's left hand and rested her head on Tom's shoulder. She placed her left arm around so the back of her left wrist rested behind Tom's neck. Izzy's hair was fresh with the fragrance of rosemary and mint. She closed her eyes as they held each other and moved to the music and shifting patterns of light and shadows from the slowly turning cut glass ball above.

THE END

Thank you for reading and I hope you enjoyed my book.

As an independently published author, I rely on happy readers to spread the word. If you enjoyed my book, please tell your friends, family and others.

If it wouldn't be much trouble, I'd appreciate a brief review on Amazon and ideally Goodreads. If you ordered the book via Amazon, just click into your Order, scroll down to find your Order for my book, then click the button to the right that says "Write a product review."

If you received a complimentary book, please search the Amazon book section with the full book title and my name to find my book page. Click to open the book page, scroll down to the customer reviews where it says "Top Reviews from the United States." To the left, you can click the "Write a customer review" field.

Many thanks and best wishes.

David Hejna

Made in the USA
Middletown, DE
22 August 2021